Also by Joe Joyce

WITHDRAWN

Fiction

Echowave

Echobeat

The Trigger Man

Off the Record

Non-Fiction

*The Guinnesses: The Untold Story of
Ireland's Most Successful Family*

Blind Justice (with Peter Murtagh)

The Boss: Charles J Haughey in Government
(with Peter Murtagh)

Plays

The Tower

www.joejoyce.ie

First published in 2013 by
Liberties Press
140 Terenure Road North | Terenure | Dublin 6W
T: +353 (1) 905-6072 | W: libertiespress.com | E: info@libertiespress.com

Trade enquiries to Gill & Macmillan Distribution
Hume Avenue | Park West | Dublin 12
T: +353 (1) 500 9534 | F: +353 (1) 500 9595 | E: sales@gillmacmillan.ie

Distributed in the United Kingdom by
Turnaround Publisher Services
Unit 3 | Olympia Trading Estate | Coburg Road | London N22 6TZ
T: +44 (0) 20 8829 3000 | E: orders@turnaround-uk.com

Distributed in the United States by
Casemate-IPM | 1950 Lawrence Road, Havertown, PA 19083
T: +1 (610) 853-9131 | E: casemate@casematepublishers.com

A CIP record for this title is available from the British Library.

Cover design by Anna Morrison
Internal design by Liberties Press

The publishers gratefully acknowledge
financial assistance from the Arts Council.

*All characters in this book are fictitious, and any resemblance to
actual persons, living or dead, is purely coincidental.*

ECHOLAND

Joe Joyce

LIB ERT IES

In memory of
Meta Glennon 1916–2011
and
Martin Joyce 1909–1991

One

He read down to the end of the letter, turned it over to the beginning, and looked up. Captain Charles McClure was giving him a quizzical eye across the large table they used as a desk, an unlit cigarette hanging from his mouth.

'Well,' Duggan said, 'it's certainly suspicious.'

McClure nodded, flicked his lighter, and blew smoke out around the cigarette.

'I mean,' Duggan glanced down the handwritten page again, 'where he says, "Our friends in Belfast are waiting for a shipment of tools and spares", it's obviously a code. Weapons for the IRA?'

'Could be,' McClure conceded.

'And the bit about Harland and Wolff requiring a visit before they finish their latest project at the end of July. Is he telling them to attack before then?'

McClure blinked smoke from his left eye and took the cigarette from his mouth. The phone rang on the table between them and he picked up the receiver. 'G2,' he said. 'McClure.' He listened a moment and then stretched it across the desk, 'For you.'

He took the phone and said, 'Duggan.'

'Wouldn't that be First Lieutenant Paul Duggan now?' a hearty voice said.

'Yes. Oh, Uncle Timmy,' he blurted out, biting his tongue as soon as he said it and resisting the urge to look up and see if McClure had reacted. Fuck, he thought.

'A meteoric rise up the ranks,' his uncle said.

'Hardly that.'

'Only in there a wet week and you'll be running the place by Christmas. Head of intelligence.'

'Ah, I doubt that.'

'Listen,' Timmy got down to business. 'There's something I want to talk to you about.'

'I can't really at the moment. It's very busy here.'

'In person.'

'I'll drop around to the house at the weekend.'

'Can't wait till then. Come down to Leinster House for your tea.'

Duggan shook his head at the phone. There was no way he was going down there to have Timmy parade him around his political friends. 'I don't know what time I'll get away. It could be late.'

'Come out to the house then,' Timmy said. 'Whenever you're finished. It's important.'

'I'll try my best.'

McClure was reading a report and looked up as Duggan put down the receiver. 'You were saying?' he prompted.

'Yeah,' Duggan reined in the various thoughts that Timmy's cryptic conversation had created. What was he up to now? Whatever it was, Duggan knew it was going to be trouble. Timmy hadn't become a successful politician without knowing how to get people to do his bidding. 'Yeah,' he repeated, getting back to the letter, 'is he telling them to bomb the Belfast shipyards before the end of June?'

'Could be,' McClure nodded, an encouraging teacher with a promising pupil. He was a decade or so older than Duggan, in his early thirties, and had a natural air of authority, helped by his experience and knowledge of intelligence work. He had been in G2 a few years before the Munich crisis.

'Is that a deadline for something they're building? The end of June? A warship or something?'

McClure nodded his approval again as if Duggan had passed some kind of test. 'I've asked our friends across the corridor but haven't heard back yet,' he sighed as if competence and the section of army intelligence dealing with the British and the North were strangers. 'All in due course no doubt. Meanwhile . . .' He shifted some files from one pile to another, stubbed out his cigarette. 'I want you to go down to Harbusch's place in Merrion Square. The Special Branch is keeping an eye on him. A detective called Peter Gifford. Find out everything you can from him about Harbusch and don't tell him anything. Okay?'

Duggan nodded. He put the letter back in its envelope and looked at the address as he stood up. It said Danske something and had a street number and name in Copenhagen.

'Are we going to post it?' he asked.

'Up to them,' McClure pointed at the ceiling. 'Probably.'

'There've been others?'

'Oh, yes. Hans spends a lot of time writing letters.'

'Like this one?'

'More or less. There's usually a respectful request for commissions on sales or expenses in there too. We really want to know if he does anything other than write letters.'

'Are they all to the same address?'

McClure nodded. 'It's an Abwehr post box.'

'Really,' Duggan sounded surprised. 'So he is a German spy then?'

McClure leaned back in his chair and gave Duggan his thoughtful look. 'Yes. We need to find out what he's up to.'

'What else should I know about him?' Duggan dared to ask. He found McClure a little disconcerting, especially his habit of freezing for a moment while he looked without seeing into the distance. As if he was thinking great thoughts.

'Hans Harbusch, aged forty-six, German national, came to Ireland from England last year, a couple of months before the war started. Accompanied by an English woman who they say is his wife and may or may not be. Operates an import/export business from his flat in Merrion Square. Sends letters to a long-standing Abwehr post box in Copenhagen and gets occasional letters from a woman in Amsterdam who may or may not be a post box too.'

'The same kind of letters?'

'No, very amorous letters. But could be code too.' McClure leaned forward and tapped another file. 'You can read them later. They're a bit more imaginative than the business ones. If they're a code. Imaginative too if they're just love letters.'

Duggan tried not to blush and McClure gave him a faint smile. 'You're one of us now. You need to know all this stuff. But no one else needs to know any of it. It is not to be shared with anyone, especially not this' – he looked for the name on his pad – 'Gifford fellow or any Special Branch men or guard.' He paused. 'Or family for that matter.'

Duggan nodded. Fucking Timmy, he thought. Why did he have to ring here?

McClure opened another file. 'Get out of uniform and go and see what a German spy looks like.'

There was a languorous air to the afternoon as he cycled down the quays, crossed over O'Connell Bridge and rounded the front of Trinity College. The sun was hot, one of the first days of summer, promising more. Men were out in their shirtsleeves, women in short sleeves, awnings over the pavements to protect shop windows, all overreacting to the unaccustomed sunshine. He swung into Merrion Square, careful to cross the tramlines at a right angle; he still hadn't got used to city traffic. He went past the National Gallery and Leinster Lawn and turned left into the southern side of the square and a whiff of new-cut grass from the park brought a sudden wave of homesickness.

They'd be saving the hay today, he thought. The sweet smell of mown meadow. The raking and turning and making into cocks. The chat of his father and the other men about characters, epic card games, ghost stories, practical jokes. And his mother bringing bottles of strong tea, already milked, and sandwiches in a biscuit tin into the field. But there wouldn't be much of that this year. The big meadow was mostly tilled now. Government orders. And he wouldn't be there for any of it. For the first time.

Near the end of the street he swung his left leg over the saddle and coasted on one pedal into the railings of the park. He clicked the padlock shut on his chain, hearing the sound of men digging and talking inside the park. Through a gap in the bushes he caught a glimpse of a mound of earth. Another air-raid shelter, he thought. Their voices mixed with the sound of their shovels sloughing into the earth and then an angry voice shouted 'Fuck the lot of ye' and there was a chorus of raucous laughter and catcalls.

Duggan walked across the road to a building with a polished plaque on the door and pushed it open. There was a reception desk in the room on the left and a young woman behind it.

'I'm looking for . . .' he began.

'Top floor,' she smiled. 'Keep going up till you can't go any further and it's the door straight ahead of you.'

The wide staircase narrowed as it went up. The last flight was steep and wide enough for only one person and led onto a corridor with a low ceiling. He went to the door facing him and knocked. A voice inside said something and he went in.

Peter Gifford was sitting on a kitchen chair tipped back against the side of the window, the *Evening Herald* in his hands, his feet against the other side of the window. 'Ah,' he looked up. 'The cavalry's here. I'm saved.'

He dropped his feet and the chair's front legs to the floor and let the newspaper fall down as he stood up. He was about the same age as Duggan, a stockier build, and an inch or so shorter, maybe five ten. His black hair was combed straight back and set solid with Brylcreem, the comb marks as clear as the ridges of a ploughed field. He held out his hand. 'Detective Superintendent Peter Gifford.'

'Superintendent?' Duggan said, shaking his hand.

'In my head. I should be one in reality too, of course.'

Duggan laughed and introduced himself.

'Only a lieutenant,' Gifford shook his head. 'But what are you in your head? Commandant? Colonel? General?'

'Probably a private.'

'A modest man. You're a culchie.' It wasn't a question.

Duggan nodded. 'And you're a Dublin jackeen?'

'One of the originals. Here since before the Vikings. Welcome to my humble abode.' He waved his hand as if it was anything but humble. The chair in the window was the only furniture. The white paint on the walls was beginning to peel in places and there were no curtains on the window. There was a tray on the floor beside the chair with a used cup and a plate with biscuit crumbs.

'How long have you been here?'

'Since the bloody Vikings. A month or so. On and off.'

'On your own?'

Gifford nodded. 'There were two of us to begin with. But your man rarely goes out. Doesn't seem to do anything. So they decided he could be left to the young lads. Us.'

Duggan went over to the window. Over the treetops he could see the edge of the hole they were digging for the shelter in the park and the first few houses on the next side of the square. 'Which one is it?'

Gifford moved the chair out of the way and joined him at the window. 'Fourth house down. Second floor. Windows on the left.'

The sun was glancing off the windows and he could see nothing inside. 'Can you ever see anything?'

'No. The most exciting part of the day is when they put on a light at night and pull the curtains. That's the only way we know there's anyone there most of the time.'

'Maybe he's going out the back.'

'If he's dug a tunnel. The back garden's a jungle. The door hasn't been opened in years. And I can't see Hans climbing the wall.'

'Why not?'

'He's not exactly the athletic type.'

'Does he have any visitors?'

'No. Only people going in or out live there. All checked out at the start of the stakeout.'

'All cleared?'

Gifford nodded.

'So what's he doing?'

'I don't know, Herr Oberst,' Gifford clicked his heels. 'Is this an interrogation?'

'No,' Duggan shook his head. 'Sorry. It just doesn't seem to make any sense.'

'That's why you're here. Bring the superior deviousness of G2 to it. Make sense of it.'

Duggan grimaced.

'So why'd they put you in the German section?' Gifford asked.

'Because I know some German, I think. But who knows why the army does things? I was in an infantry battalion, western command.

Transferred a couple of weeks ago out of the blue.'

'They must have detected a twisted mind in you.'

Duggan laughed and shook his head.

'How do you like it?'

'Not a lot, to tell you the truth. I haven't a clue what's going on.'

'Ah,' Gifford said with satisfaction. 'That's why you're in military intelligence.'

'I'm here right now,' Duggan smiled back, 'so the experts can tell me what's going on.'

'Haven't you read the letters?'

'What letters?'

'The only thing Hans does regularly is post letters. What do they say?'

Duggan shrugged. 'I don't know anything about any letters.'

'Bullshit,' Gifford nodded to himself.

'Are you interrogating me now?' Duggan smiled. 'Do you have electrodes and things here?'

Gifford laughed in turn. 'Okay. Ceasefire.' He looked at his watch. 'Nearly afternoon tea time. Did you order a cup and a biscuit with Sinéad on your way in? Mariettas, no choice.'

'The girl at the desk? How did she know I was looking for you before I even mentioned your name?'

'Because you're in uniform.'

'I'm not in uniform.'

'You might as well be in uniform.' Gifford looked him up and down. 'D'you want me to start at the top, with the hair? Or the bottom, with the shiny brown shoes? You might as well be on the parade ground down in Renmore. And what're you wearing a suit for on a day like this anyway?'

Duggan scratched his head and picked the newspaper off the floor. 'Germans Seize Channel Ports', a headline said. 'British Claim

Successful Evacuation from Dunkirk', another said. He read the first few paragraphs and dropped the paper on the chair. 'I've got to find out something about Harbusch. Have you talked to the neighbours? Had a look . . .'

'Fuck me!' Gifford interrupted, looking out the window behind him. 'Beginner's luck. They're moving.'

Duggan turned to the window but Gifford was already out the door and taking the stairs three at a time. Duggan turned without looking out and chased after him. Gifford hit the ground floor and blew a kiss to Sinéad at the reception desk. She was still smiling a wistful smile when Duggan went by a few moments later and crashed through the front door. Gifford was strolling calmly up the street when he joined him.

'Well, hello,' Gifford said as Duggan came alongside as if they were meeting by accident. 'Fancy meeting you here. Slow down.'

They crossed the road and turned into the other side of the square alongside the park railings. There was no one on the footpath but Hans Harbusch and a woman. He was short and fat and was wearing a navy suit and a navy hat. The woman linking him was half a head taller than his hat, her golden hair curled up at her collar. She had on a brown two-piece suit with a short jacket that showed off her hourglass figure.

'Ah, Eliza,' Gifford sighed. 'The beacon in the darkness of my life. My only consolation. Walking behind Eliza.'

'Eliza who?'

'Eliza Godfrey, aka Eliza Harbusch. Born London 1913. A pearl beyond compare.'

'What was Hans doing in London?'

'Shacking up with Eliza.'

'Apart from that.'

'I don't know. Your fellows know but they haven't told me.'

'How would they know?'

'Because they're like that' – Gifford held up the two first fingers of his right hand together – 'with MI5.'

Duggan gave a disbelieving laugh. 'I doubt that.'

Gifford glanced sideways at him, realized he was serious, and shook his head.

Hans and Eliza rounded the corner opposite Holles Street hospital and they hurried after them. The couple were walking alongside the park railings, heading towards the city centre.

'Aw, Eliza,' Gifford said, slowing down to a dawdle to lengthen the gap between them. 'Will you look at that.'

'What's she doing with him?' Duggan asked.

'That's Hansi's big secret. His biggest one as far as I'm concerned. When I find the answer I'll bottle it and take a spoonful three times a day.'

Duggan laughed. 'Can I have a spoonful or two?'

'We'll go into business together. Mass produce it. PG's tips. Send the whole country sex mad. Nobody'll ever leave home.'

A number 8 tram went wobbling by towards Dalkey as they crossed the junction into Clare Street. Duggan stopped to let two cyclists go past and then was held up by a car while Gifford skipped ahead.

'Aren't you the smart boyo?' Gifford said when Duggan caught up with him.

'What? Crossing the road without getting knocked down?'

'Getting my theory about Hans out of me. He and Eliza are breeding storm troopers in that flat. They'll all emerge some day while you fellows are looking out to sea and up in the air.' Gifford stopped and leaned his head back and looked skywards, then turned round with his hand shading his eye, scanning the horizon. A man coming out of Greene's bookshop gave him a sour look and walked around him.

'They'll just saunter across Merrion Square there and take over Government Buildings and Leinster House. Invasion over.'

'I should put that in my report. They might send me back to western command.'

'Back to crawling around the bogs on your belly. The fellow behind you prodding you in the arse with his bayonet. You're a strange lad.'

Gifford was the smart boyo, Duggan thought. Keeping up his constant patter: anyone seeing them would think they were two friends out for the afternoon. One a soldier, but the country was becoming full of soldiers now, more every day as the government upped its appeals for recruits. Nobody would think they were following anybody.

The Harbusches walked on at a steady pace, not talking, looking neither left nor right, he waddling slightly with the gait of an overweight man, she swaying seductively on her high heel shoes. They continued down South Leinster Street and into Nassau Street. From behind the wall of Trinity College came the smack of a hard ball on a cricket bat followed by a sprinkling of applause. A light stream of traffic went by in both directions, the growl of car engines interspersed by the clip-clop of an occasional dray. They went past a succession of bookshops.

'You read it?' Gifford pointed to a copy of *Mein Kampf* by Adolf Hitler in the window of Fred Hanna's. It was alongside *The Whiteoak Chronicles* by Mazo de la Roche, the biggest selling non-fiction and fiction books of the week.

'I don't have time. Maybe after the war.'

'You might be reciting it by then. The new catechism.'

'Seven hundred pages,' Duggan said. 'I'm supposed to be reading it. Father Murphy's translation.'

'Heap of shit.'

'You've read it?'

'No,' Gifford said. 'That's what I heard in a pub. Mind you, the fellow that said it found himself in the centre of an argument. He has a point, the others said. Hitler.'

'They'd all read it?' Duggan said in surprise.

'Probably not. Did you ever know actual knowledge to get in the way of a pub argument?'

'You think they're going to win?'

'Looking good for Adolf,' Gifford shrugged. 'France is tottering.'

'But they still have a big army, mostly intact,' Duggan said, relaying mess chat he had overheard.

'All the same to me. Whoever wins will need policemen. They'll shoot everybody in military intelligence, of course. First thing the victor always does. Can't trust you lads with your warped minds.'

'Thanks,' Duggan said. 'I'm sure they'll shoot the secret police too.'

'Interesting. You think that's what we are? Secret police?' Gifford turned to him. 'You a republican?'

'I'm a member of Óglaigh na hÉireann. Like it says on my cap that I'm not wearing but you can still see.'

'Not the Óglaigh na hÉireann that's causing a lot of trouble at the moment? Bombed our headquarters in the castle last month and wants Hansi's friends to win the war.'

'No. The Óglaigh na hÉireann that'll defend Ireland against all comers.'

'Right,' Gifford said, as if that explained everything.

The Harbusches turned into Grafton Street and stopped on the pavement, waiting to cross the road. He and Duggan also stopped, waiting to cross near them, and then followed them up the street on the other side.

'Ah,' Gifford said. 'Going to the bank.'

But they stopped just short of the junction with Wicklow Street, outside Weir's jewellery shop, and Eliza bent down to kiss Hans on the cheek and went into the jewellers. 'Stick with her,' Gifford said. 'Meet back in my hideout.'

Duggan went into the shop and tried to adjust from the brightness outside to the dark, wood-lined interior. She had stopped at the first display case inside the door and he almost bumped into her, catching her scent, something musky, as he went around her. There were no other customers. A salesman was saying 'Good day, madam' to her as Duggan wandered down the counter, looking in glass cases at rings, gold watches, silver watches, brooches. He retraced his steps slowly, feigning interest, trying to hear what she was saying, looking her way while pretending to look sideways at the contents of a case. The salesman was laying out a selection of gold necklaces for her. She picked up one, draped it over her fingers and held her hand out in front of her, letting it swing from side to side.

'If you'd like to try it on,' the salesman said, producing a handheld mirror from under the counter.

'How much is this one?' she pointed at another one. Her accent was diamond-sharp English.

Duggan didn't hear the reply as another salesman appeared in front on him and said, 'May I help you, sir?' There was a barely noticeable pause before the 'sir'.

'No, I'm, ah, just looking,' Duggan stammered. 'Thanks.'

'An engagement ring, is it?' the salesman opened his hands over the display case between them.

Duggan nodded.

'Do you have any idea of the young lady's preferences?' The salesman was cadaverous, in his late thirties and balding prematurely.

'Not really, I'm afraid.'

'Single diamond? Cluster? Type? Shape? Cut? Number of carats?'

Duggan shrugged, helpless. He glanced towards Eliza Harbusch who was looking at herself in a mirror, moving her head from side to side and smiling at something her salesman was saying.

'Colour? Grade? Clarity? Facets?'

Duggan pointed at a single diamond at random. 'How much is that one?'

The salesman hesitated, then opened the case, and looked at the coded tag tied to the ring. 'Four hundred pounds,' he said. 'Well, three hundred and ninety nine and nineteen and eleven pence actually.'

'Oh,' Duggan blanched, beginning to blush and wish he was out of there.

'These start at about two hundred,' the salesman waved his hand over the case like a blessing. 'I would suggest that you try and determine the young lady's preference. And finger size.'

Duggan nodded, grateful for the out.

'Perhaps you might consider the Happy Ring House. They have a, er, wider price range there.'

'Where's that?'

'Beside the Pillar.'

Duggan headed for the door. As he passed, the salesman was telling Eliza that that necklace matched her colouring perfectly and was ninety-nine pounds. 'I'll take it,' she said.

Duggan breasted the bridge over the canal at Portobello and Rathmines Road stretched before him, the wires above its tram tracks undulating like the long troughs of waves leading to the dull green humps of the Dublin mountains in the distance. The evening was cooling, the sun still above the horizon to the west. Its light lay along the canal, turning the murky water golden. A family of ducks circled by the reeds.

He free-wheeled down the hill, hearing the smooth whirr of the wheels and the rub of the tyres on the tarmac as he went past the church of Mary Immaculate, its new dome top-heavy and seeming to push it into the ground. A truckload of soldiers pulled out of the army barracks in front of him, the soldiers at the back glaring at him impassively, their Lee Enfield rifles upright between their knees, as they accelerated away from him.

He turned left at the Stella Cinema and threaded his way through suburban streets up to Palmerston Road. The road was empty between its heavy trees, the large houses silent, the air still. The only sounds were of some children shrieking somewhere distant and a dog barking. He pulled into Timmy's gate and the gravel slowed him to halt. He walked the bike around a shiny new Ford and left it beside the granite steps.

Light footsteps came along the hall in response to his knock and the door was opened by a young girl wearing a white apron.

'Hello,' Duggan said. 'I'm Paul.'

She looked at him, unknowing.

'Mr Monaghan's nephew,' he added.

A door banged inside and Timmy Monaghan came bustling down the hall.

'The man himself,' he boomed as Duggan came in and Timmy pumped his hand. 'This is Cait,' he added. 'She's just come to us from Aran.'

'Ah,' Duggan turned to her. '*Conas ata tú?*'

'*Go maith*,' she said, taking his hand and giving him an uncertain curtsey.

'This is First Lieutenant Paul Duggan,' Timmy told her. 'A very important man these days. And one of the family.'

Duggan shook his head and she looked from one to the other. She was about fifteen and uncertain in English.

'You'll have something to eat,' Timmy said, putting his arm around Duggan's shoulder. 'Cait'll get you something, won't you, Cait?' he said over his shoulder to her as he guided Duggan into a high-ceilinged room overlooking the back garden. The walls were a washed green and there were large leather armchairs on either side of the marble fireplace. A fire was set in the grate but unlit. A large mahogany table took up the centre of the room with an uneven scattering of dining chairs around it. It was covered with newspapers, green Dáil order papers, parliamentary bills and volumes of debates. On one side there was a blotter pad surrounded by a neat stack of headed Dáil notepaper and prepaid envelopes, a pen and ink set, and a full ashtray. A silver cigarette case lay open beside it.

Duggan walked around the table to the window. A large hole had been dug in the lawn, mounds of earth on both sides of it. Grass and weeds were beginning to sprout in the hole and on the mounds.

'A shelter,' Monaghan said when he saw Duggan looking at it. 'A couple of fellows started digging it for me last year when the Emergency started. Then they fecked off to England to join the British army, leaving it like that. There wasn't much happening at the time so I didn't bother having it finished. I don't know. What d'you think? Should I get someone to finish it?'

'I don't know,' Duggan said.

'You're in the nerve centre. The fellows who know what's going on.'

'They haven't told me, I'm afraid.'

'You enjoyed the intelligence course?'

'It was interesting,' Duggan said, noncommittal, keeping any surprise out of his voice. So it's true, he thought, as I suspected. Timmy's the reason I'm in G2. Pulled some strings to get me in there. As he had feared.

'And weren't you right to take my advice about the German?'

Duggan said nothing, not knowing what he was talking about.

'Didn't I tell you to learn German when you went to college? Not to bother with that French. German's the coming language.'

Duggan nodded though he had no memory of that. He'd learned long ago not to bother arguing facts with Timmy.

'And look at you now,' Timmy gave him a knowing smile, knowing that a message had been delivered. It was what he loved about politics, the mind games, the subtle messages and manipulations, outwitting the other guys. He knew it was unlikely that he'd rise above the backbenches but he still hadn't abandoned all ambitions. Age was coming against him now, forty-five last birthday, heading for fifty, but anything was possible in politics. He had done his bit in the War of Independence and the Civil War. Nobody could challenge his national record, the foundation of his electoral success and impenetrable protection against some of his internal opponents in Fianna Fáil.

'A hard language, they say. A bit like Irish.'

'I like it. It's a nice language.'

'Good, good,' Timmy rubbed his hands. 'The language of the future.'

Great, Duggan though. Gifford has me up against a wall facing a firing squad. Timmy has me marked out as some kind of *gauleiter*.

'The English are fucked,' Timmy said, gesticulating towards the table. He sat down in front of the blotter. Duggan took the chair across the table.

'The lion has had its day,' Timmy went on, pacing every word as if he was coming to the climax of a public speech. 'Going to find out now what it's like to be an occupied country. But' – he raised a finger – 'the lion can be dangerous when wounded. Lash out. You know what I mean? Last desperate twitch of the tail.' He paused. 'Don't be surprised if they come over the border. Try to take back what they lost. Churchill has never forgiven us for beating them the last time, you know. Nothing he'd like better than revenge. Play the game again. Hitler's right about him, he's a war monger. They made a bad choice there. And he'll use any excuse to invade. The ports. Pretend to be protecting us from the Germans.'

Timmy paused and shook his head as though he couldn't believe what he was saying. 'Bastards,' he muttered under his breath. He put his elbows on the blotting pad and leaned forward. 'This is only between us. To be kept in the family. Just marking your cards for you.'

He paused until Duggan nodded.

'The powers that be know the score. They can see the writing on the wall. The Chief made a speech in Galway a week or two back, criticising the Germans for breaching the neutrality of Denmark and Holland. You remember that?'

Duggan nodded although he didn't really remember anything more than a headline about the Taoiseach criticising Germany for ignoring the neutral status of some countries.

'Big mistake. God knows, the Chief is very good at seeing five steps ahead of everybody else but I think he fucked up this time. We have no argument with Germany and they have none with us.'

'Wasn't he just defending neutrals?' Duggan ventured. 'Like us.'

'Yeah, well. Look at what the British thought of Norway's neutrality,' Timmy waved away his opinion. 'Anyway, it's no time to be making new enemies. The German legation was very angry about Dev's speech. Herr Hempel demanded an explanation. And word was sent back that it wouldn't happen again.'

Timmy sat back in his chair and joined his hands over his stomach with satisfaction. Duggan didn't know what to say. He was saved by a knock on the door and Cait entered with a tray. Duggan cleared a pile of letters from Timmy's constituents to one side and she put down the tray and began taking the plates from the tray and putting them on the table.

'Don't bother with that,' Timmy interrupted. 'We don't stand on ceremony here. He can eat off the tray.'

Duggan thanked her in Irish and re-arranged the plates and cup and saucer on the tray. The main plate had two cuts of cold chicken, two of ham, a few leaves of lettuce and half a tomato. A side plate had three cuts of buttered brown bread. He poured himself a cup of tea.

'Whatever happens,' Timmy said, 'we won't go hungry. We can always feed ourselves, thank God. Unlike the English. They'll find out now what a bit of starvation's like as well.'

He watched Duggan eat for a few moments. 'Anyway, that was all bye the bye. For your own information. To be kept to yourself,' he repeated. 'The reason I wanted to talk to you was about a family matter.'

Duggan looked up in surprise. He assumed he had already got the messages. I got you transferred to G2. Be nice to the Germans. Beware of perfidious Albion. He went on eating, realizing that he was starving. He hadn't had anything to eat after getting back to the Red House and writing a report on the Harbusches' visit to Grafton Street. Timmy watched him in silence for a minute and reached for a cigarette and lit it with a heavy desk lighter.

'Nuala,' he said eventually. Nuala was his eldest daughter, a year or two older than Duggan. A change in his tone caught Duggan's attention and he stopped eating. 'Nuala,' Timmy said again and sighed. 'She's gone . . . We don't know where she is.'

'She's missing?'

'No, no, not missing.' Timmy didn't seem to want to use the word. 'We don't know where she is.'

'How long? When did she . . . go?'

Timmy took a deep breath. 'Two weeks ago. Maybe a bit more. About two weeks ago we realized she wasn't where we thought she was.'

'She didn't come home?'

Timmy looked at him in surprise and then realized Duggan knew nothing about Nuala's movements. 'She's been living in a flat in town for the last few months. Since the new year, actually. But she usually comes home for the Sunday dinner. And she didn't turn up last Sunday fortnight. Her mother went to the flat. No sign of her, then or since. Mona's going up the walls. You can imagine.'

Duggan could imagine. His aunt Mona was known in the family for suffering from nerves, which Duggan had never found surprising. Timmy would turn anyone into a nervous wreck, as Duggan's father pointed out from time to time when Timmy had over-tried his patience. It was one of the few bones of contention between Duggan's parents. His father had no time for Timmy; his mother felt a need to defend her sister's choice of husband.

Duggan put a dab of strawberry jam on the last slice of bread and poured himself another cup of tea.

'Have you told the guards?'

'Ah, no, no,' Timmy tipped the ash from his cigarette. 'It's not like that.'

'If she's been missing for two weeks . . .' Duggan let the thought hang in the air.

'Not . . . missing.' Timmy, never short of words, seemed to be finding them elusive now.

'I don't understand.'

'It's her mother, you know. She's very upset. Wants me to do something about it. But I keep telling her Nuala's just gone away for a bit. She's all right. She'll be back.'

Timmy suddenly held out the cigarette case to him. 'You smoke Players, don't you?'

'Afton, usually.'

'Well, try one of these.'

Duggan took the cigarette and Timmy pushed the lighter over to him.

'Aye, she'll be back,' Timmy said, staring at his cigarette. 'She's just trying to . . . trying to . . . teach me a lesson.' He paused and then looked up at Duggan. 'You know we don't see eye to eye a lot of the time. Too alike, Mona says. Knock sparks off each other. But it does- n't mean anything. Still the best of friends behind it all.'

Duggan didn't know that. He and Nuala were more or less the same age and had been thrown together as children at family events; they had ignored each other as far as possible. As they grew up, they hadn't much more to say to each other, beyond an occasional effort at politeness. Duggan found her bossy and had no idea what she thought of him, probably found him boring. He couldn't remember ever having had a real conversation with her.

Timmy straightened himself up in the chair like a man facing up to his fate. 'We had an argument. Over the Christmas. Terrible time to be having an argument in a family but God knows it happens. She wanted to move into a flat in the town. I couldn't see any sense to it. She's not working, you know. No money. She gave up that job I got her in Clery's. Wanted to do a secretarial course. Fine, I said. But what'd you be wasting money for on a flat when we have the house here? Plenty of room. But nothing would do her. Mona sided with her, of course. Said she'd pay for the flat out of the housekeeping. So she, Nuala, moved into this little place. And I ended up paying for it anyway. Couldn't have it said that I wasn't giving the wife enough to keep the house.'

He stubbed out his cigarette and got up suddenly and walked to the window. 'Jesus. Women.' He stared at the hole in the garden. 'It's so hard to get anything done in this country sometimes,' he said to himself. 'Anyway,' he turned back to Duggan, 'it all blew up again the last Sunday she was here. I was under orders not to mention the fucking flat but you know how it is. One thing led to another and it got a bit hot and heavy and she stamped out.'

He sat down and lit another cigarette. 'That's it,' he said.

'I see,' Duggan said. 'Sorry to hear . . .'

Timmy waved his sympathy away with his cigarette, leaving a faint trail of smoke in the air.

'Two weeks,' Duggan began and paused, 'is a long time. And she hasn't been in touch with auntie Mona or her sisters?'

'No. That's the thing. I could understand her cutting me off. I could handle that. I've had my share of knocks. I could take it. But she knows that too. So she's staying away from everyone, knowing that'll put the pressure on me. Dropped out of her course as well. Hasn't been seen there for two weeks either.' He paused. 'Anyway. You see why I don't want the guards? Apart from anything else, it's not a headline you want in the papers. "TD's Daughter Missing".'

'You could keep it out of the papers.'

'Oh, aye, Aiken. He loves being the censor in chief. Telling all those fuckers what to put in their papers now,' he laughed. 'Getting our own back for all the shite they wrote about us. No, the papers wouldn't be the problem. But everyone'd know about it if the guards got involved. Still a lot of Free Staters and Blueshirts among them, keeping their heads down and talking out of the sides of their mouths. Only too happy to spread any dirt about the party.

'No,' Timmy went on. 'What we need is some discreet inquiries to be made. Find out where Nuala is. Reassure your auntie Mona and the other girls. Put their minds at rest that she's all right.'

Oh fuck, Duggan thought. This was worse than he had feared, worse than some political manoeuvre involving G2 information. 'I don't know how I could help,' he said. 'I've no idea how to find some-body.'

'You're moving in those general areas. Investigations, and the like.'

'I'm not, you know. I'm in an office, just moving files around. Today was the first day I was actually out of the office. In the field, so to speak.'

'There you go,' Timmy said, as if that proved his point. 'Just make some discreet inquiries.'

'I . . .'

'I always say that there are times when you can only rely on family. When you can't trust anybody. And Christ knows, you can never trust anybody in my business. Family's all you've got.'

Timmy eased a sheet of paper from under the blotter on the table and handed it to Duggan.

'That's the address of the flat. You know Mount Street? The one with the Pepper Canister church in the middle of it?'

'I think so.'

'The secretarial place she's supposed to be in is just around the corner. Gillespie's Metropolitan College. That's the name of one of her friends,' he pointed at the sheet. 'Stella Maloney. A nurse in Sir Patrick Dun's. They have a nurses' home around there too. That's why she moved there. To be near Stella.'

'And she hasn't seen Nuala either?'

'Not hide nor hair of her,' Timmy said. 'She says.'

Now that he had done what he wanted, Timmy snapped back to his jovial self. Duggan had a passing thought that his earlier look of anguish was a façade, part of an act. As if to kill the thought Timmy added: 'Your auntie Mona will be so grateful if you can reassure her that Nuala's all right. You don't have to persuade her to come home. Just find her and talk to her and tell Mona she's all right. It'll ease her mind. Be the answer to her prayers.' He looked at his watch and pressed a bell on the wall beside the fireplace. 'These things still work you know,' he said as if it was a surprise.

There was a tap at the door a few moments later and Cait

returned. 'Has the missus come back yet?' Timmy asked her.

'No, sir,' she said.

'Okay. You can take that tray away now.'

'*Go raibh maith agat. Bhí sé sin go an-bhlasta*,' Duggan said to her as she left with the tray. That was lovely.

'She should be back any minute. She went off to the sodality, doing a novena for Nuala's safe return. Pity she's not here and she could tell you herself, what a weight it'll be off her mind if you can find Nuala.'

Mother of God, Duggan sighed to himself.

'Right,' Timmy rubbed his hands together, making clear that he was finished. Duggan got up and went ahead of him into the hall.

'Great things are happening in our times,' Timmy said as he opened the hall door. 'I've a fiver bet on with that Free State fecker Connolly that we'll have a united Ireland by the end of all this.' Connolly was a rival Fine Gael TD in his constituency.

'You think so?'

'A certainty. As long as we can hold off the British if they invade. Don't want them creating a united Ireland.' He laughed. 'Though I'd still be able to collect off Connolly, wouldn't I?'

'Why are you so sure?'

'Because the Germans have no interest in partition. Why would they? That fellow Hempel is sound on the national question. A dry old stick, bit stuck up, distant. Could be English actually. But he makes no secret of it, Germany will reunite Ireland.'

'Do you think they'll invade?'

'Germany? No. Why would they? We're not their enemy. Look to the Border, I tell you. That's where the fight will be. Are you ready for it?'

'I don't know,' I seem to be saying that a lot today, Duggan thought. But he really didn't know the answer to this one. The big question. How would he shape up if the shooting started?

Timmy clapped him on the back. 'You'll be grand. Your father and I beat them in our day. And we hadn't half the men and guns you have now.'

'Different kind of war now, though.'

'Have you met that fellow Petersen? The press fellow in the legation?'

Duggan shook his head.

'He has a saying, *krieg ist krieg, schnapps ist schnapps*. What does that mean?'

'War is war and schnapps is schnapps. It must be a proverb or something.'

'That's it,' Timmy said and clapped him on the back again. 'War is war. We beat them once and you'll beat them again. You'll be fine when the fighting starts. You'll do your duty. Like we did in our day. And you'll run them out of the country. Like we did.'

'I hope you're right.'

Timmy went down the steps and ran a hand along the sloping side of the Ford in the driveway. 'What d'you think of the car? The new V8. Eight cylinders. Twenty-seven miles to the gallon. Sixty miles an hour no problem. Two hundred and fifty pounds all in.'

'It's lovely.'

'Your father'll be green with envy. I might drive over to see them when I'm down at the weekend for the constituency clinics.'

More likely puce with anger, Duggan thought. As Timmy seemed to go from strength to strength, getting richer and richer, he became more and more insufferable in his father's view. He got his bicycle, turned it towards the gate and mounted it.

'They're all well? At home?'

'I haven't been down since I came to Dublin.'

'Come down with me any weekend you want,' Timmy said,

running his hand along the slope of the car's bonnet. 'I'll let you drive a bit of the way. Feel the power of her.'

'Thanks.'

Timmy clapped him on the back and Duggan pushed hard on the pedals to get him through the gravel and onto the road.

Two

The sentry on the gate saluted Duggan as he walked out of the barracks and headed down to the Liffey, stretching the distance to the Red House to give himself a longer walk. It was another lovely morning, the air still and cool with a sharp tang of hops from the brewery across the river. He paused at the river wall to light a cigarette with his mother of pearl lighter, a commissioning present from his parents, and inhaled the first sweet smoke of the day. The sky was a soft blue, cloudless, and the river was full, the tide covering the stench of its bed. A barge, already loaded with wooden barrels, was getting up steam on the brewery's quay and he could see a plume of smoke from a train pulling into Kingsbridge Station as he set off up river.

He took his time and tossed the butt away as he went up the hill to Infirmary Road and through the checkpoint into army headquarters. A group of dispatch riders were firing up their motorbike engines and Captain McClure came out the door of the Red House with two bulky envelopes, handed one each to two dispatch riders. He stepped back and pointed both index fingers at the gate and shouted 'Go!' over the clatter of their engines, as if he was starting a race. Duggan stepped out of their way as they took off at speed.

McClure caught sight of him and called him over with an impatient wave of his hand. 'Can you drive a car?'

'Yes, sir.'

'Get the keys of one of those from the duty office.' He pointed to two dark green saloons parked nearby. Ford V8s, just like Timmy's new car.

Duggan followed him inside and realized at once that something had happened. The normally sedate corridors were filled with officers and orderlies, all looking grim, nobody talking, everybody busy. He got the car key and went up to his office. McClure was selecting files from various piles and handing an occasional one to an orderly who held open a large canvas sack with one hand. On the side of the sack was painted in capital letters in red the word 'BURN'.

'Okay,' he said to the orderly when he saw Duggan arrive. 'That'll do for the moment. And remember, don't do it yet, until you get a direct order. But be ready to destroy everything when you get the order.'

'Yes, sir,' the orderly saluted and went out.

Duggan felt his stomach turn and his breath caught in his throat for a moment. It's happening, he thought as McClure turned to him and said, 'Come on.' Duggan followed him down the corridor and out to the car. He sat in and started the engine.

'What's going on?' he asked finally.

'Invasion,' McClure said, sounding preoccupied. 'We're going to Dublin Castle. D'you know the way?'

'Where?'

'Dublin Castle.'

'Sorry. I meant where's the invasion.'

'It's imminent. Hasn't happened yet, as far as I know.'

The sentry at the gate raised the barrier for the car and Duggan drove through and stopped. 'Left,' McClure said. 'And left again.'

'The British or the Germans?'

The question seemed to break through McClure's preoccupation and he looked sideways at Duggan. 'Germans. Why'd you think it was the British?'

'I didn't,' Duggan said, aware of Timmy's warning to look towards the border. 'Just thought it could be either.'

'Or both,' McClure said, almost to himself. 'We'll end up a battleground for both of them. Just a matter of who comes first.'

Duggan felt his stomach turn again and glanced at McClure. A phrase from the nights of family rosaries ran through his mind: pray for us now and at the hour of our death. They were driving past the Four Courts, the sun shining brightly, the sky still blue. The pavements were empty down here away from the city centre, few pedestrians about. It was hard to think they could be at war. Were already, for all he knew.

McClure rubbed his eyes and took his cigarette case from his tunic. He rolled down his window, lit a cigarette and breathed the smoke deeply. 'What a night,' he said. 'Take the next right. Over the bridge.'

'What happened?' Duggan asked eventually, his need to find out what was happening overcoming his uncertainty about questioning a superior. 'Last night?'

'Special Branch raided a house out in Templeogue. Looking for a German parachutist who we think landed here a week or so ago. They fucked it up as usual. Should've waited till they were sure he was there. Only the owner's mother was there.'

'The German got away.'

'He wasn't there. And I don't think he'll be coming back. But they found a lot of interesting stuff in a locked room. Transmitter. Code books. Picked up the owner of the house when he eventually turned up in the early hours. Stephen Held, businessman, half-German.'

'He's working for them?'

'We have to assume so,' McClure sighed and indicated with his hand that Duggan should turn left at the junction facing the city hall. 'And, to make it worse, he's friendly with our local lads.'

'The IRA.'

'The self-styled IRA,' McClure corrected him. 'Go right here.'

Duggan stopped opposite the Olympia Theatre and waited for a strung out line of cyclists to go past before pulling across the road into the narrow laneway that led to the lower yard of Dublin Castle. A uniformed guard stopped the car and Duggan could see two plain-clothes men with submachine guns behind him. McClure waved an identity card at the guard, who insisted on reading it before letting them through. The men with the submachine guns watched them closely as they drove in.

'Typical,' McClure snorted as he stared back at them. 'Locking the stable door after the horse has bolted.'

McClure directed him around the back and told him to park when they neared the Ship Street gate. Duggan stayed in the car as the captain got out and then turned back to him and said, 'Come with me. You may as well see this, too.'

Duggan followed him down a laneway, both slowing as they passed the building which had been badly damaged by an early morn-ing IRA bomb that had injured five detectives and a caretaker a month earlier. A retaliation for the deaths in jail of two IRA hunger strikers, it was said. Rubble had been pushed to the side of the passageway and thick timbers propped against the sides of the blackened holes and the sagging roof. They went on and entered another building where McClure asked for a superintendent whose name Duggan couldn't catch. A detective brought them to another room where he knocked, spoke to someone inside, and ushered them in.

The Superintendent took off his reading glasses, stood up and came around his desk as they went in. 'Morning, men,' he said. He was tall, in his fifties, balding and beginning to sag a little. 'This is what you want to see.'

He brought them over to a table beside a window looking out on a lawn, the early summer grass almost luminous in the sunshine. One end of the table was covered with neat rows of American dollars of different depths, each bound with an elastic band. 'Each pile's a thousand dollars,' the Superintendent said. 'Twenty thousand altogether.'

'Were they like that when you found them?' McClure asked. 'In thousand dollar packs?'

'No. They were in a box. All mixed up. Ten dollar bills, twenties, so on. We had to count them.'

'Twenty thousand exactly?'

The Superintendent nodded. 'About five thousand pounds' worth, I'm told.'

'So he hadn't got to spend any of it yet,' McClure said.

At the other end of the table was a folded white silk parachute. It reminded Duggan for some reason of vestments. Between the money and the parachute were the wireless set, a pad of letters and numbers, several maps, crude drawings of what looked like ports and airports, and a small sheaf of papers clipped together with 'Plan Kathleen' typed on the cover. A Luftwaffe breast patch of blue-grey wool depicting an eagle with a swastika hanging from its claws, a German army officer's cap, and some old military medals were also among the collection.

'He wasn't a pilot shot down anyway,' the Superintendent said drily. 'I'm sure the Germans don't give all their pilots twenty thousand dollars to buy their way out of trouble.'

'Or invasion plans for other countries.' McClure pointed to the document that said Plan Kathleen. 'Have you read it?'

The Superintendent nodded and gave a succinct summary. 'Germans to drop by parachute in the west of the Six Counties. The

IRA to move across the border from Leitrim to Fermanagh. They combine and throw the British out.'

'When?' Duggan asked and was sorry when they both looked at him.

'It doesn't say,' the Superintendent said.

'Have you had copies made?' McClure asked him.

'Done. One was sent over to you. Probably crossed paths when you were on your way here.'

McClure bent over some of the hand-drawn maps and turned his head sideways to get their orientation right. He didn't touch anything. Duggan looked at the wireless. It didn't look that different from the one his father had built years ago to listen to 2RN, a collection of valves, tuning coils, knobs and a dial. Except for the Morse keypad connected to it by a rubber-covered wire. He went on to the Luftwaffe badge and bent down to peer more closely at the inscriptions on one of the medals. It was a bronze cross, all the arms equal in size and the same shape, with swords crossed behind it and the figures 1914 above 1918 in a wreath at its centre.

'Hindenburg Cross,' McClure tapped his finger on the table beside it and Duggan straightened up. 'The swords mean he served in the front line. Bit old to be a fly boy now if he was in the trenches. Bit old to be jumping out of planes too.'

'Maybe it was his father's,' Duggan suggested.

McClure rested his chin on his thumb and forefinger and looked at it again. 'That'd make sense. Father's or some other close relative's. Something of sentimental value. Why else pack that in your rucksack with all this other stuff?'

He stared at the table for a moment, scanning one item after the other, and then turned to the Superintendent. 'What's Held saying?'

'Usual cock and bull story. Doesn't know your man from a hole in the road. He turned up at his house the other day, asking to rent a room. Said his name was Heinrich Brandy. Held and his mother talked it over and agreed. Sheet metal business isn't doing too well at the moment, he says. The war and everything. They could do with the bit of extra money.'

'And he has no idea where Herr Brandy is now?'

'Of course not. Last he saw of him was the evening before when they went for a walk and Brandy invited him into a local pub for a drink. Held declined because he had to be up early yesterday for a business meeting. And hasn't seen him since.'

'And what was Brandy's reason for picking his house of all the houses in Dublin to look for digs?'

The Superintendent rolled his eyes. 'He's a bit evasive on that. Something about a friend of a friend in the German community recommending him. But he doesn't know what friend. Or what friend of a friend.'

'Okay.' McClure said, glancing at Duggan. 'I think we're finished here.'

'I'll let you know if he says anything else of interest,' the Superintendent walked to the door and opened it for them. 'You'd think they might all leave us alone,' he said in a tired voice, shaking his head. 'We haven't even had twenty years yet of being in control of our own destiny after all those centuries.'

McClure nodded and shook hands with him.

Back in the car McClure said, 'Get on to Dr Hayes when we get back to the office and tell him about those codes. He should see them as soon as possible.'

'Dr Hayes?'

'In the National Library or the film censor's office. Our cryptographer.' He noticed Duggan's surprised look. 'He's very good at it.

That code pad could be a gold mine.'

'Okay.'

McClure took out his cigarette case and lit a Players. 'I'm smoking so many of these things I'm beginning to hate them,' he said.

The Castle's gate was blocked by a car coming in, the guard talking to its driver. The plainclothes men with the submachine guns were watching it intently. One of them turned back and put out a hand, waving their car back. Duggan stopped about twenty yards short of the gate, held down the clutch and put it into first gear. He and McClure watched the tableau in front of them in silence. Eventually the guard stepped back from the car at the gate and it began to move slowly backwards, reversed into a side lane and turned and drove away. One of the plainclothes detectives went to talk to the guard and the other waved them through.

There were more people about now on Dame Street, tempted out for early lunches by the growing heat of the day. Duggan retraced the journey they had taken earlier. McClure sat in a pensive mode, staring out his side window at the passing wall of the river and beyond it at the undistinguished skyline on its southern bank, broken only by church spires and dowdy buildings seemingly heaped up behind each other.

'Don't be afraid to ask questions,' he said suddenly. 'It's the best way for you to learn. And it's also a help to me.'

'Okay.' Duggan took a deep breath and plunged on with the only question in his mind. 'Is the invasion really imminent?'

McClure sighed. 'There are a lot of straws in the wind right now. All pointing in the same direction.'

'So it's not just this German, Brandy?'

'No, it's not just him. But he's one of the stronger straws. Sent some people into a tizzy last night. Taking precautions.' He rolled down the window and flicked out the cigarette, still a generous butt. 'He obviously came on a serious mission. The transmitter. All that money. The sketch maps. Possible landing sites and so on. All point to him being here to prepare the ground. It's clear what he's up to. Unlike Harbusch.'

'And the plan, Plan Kathleen.'

'I'm not sure about that,' McClure said. 'It doesn't really fit with all the other stuff. If they already had a plan, why would he be scouting other locations? Why would he be carrying a copy? Too risky, if he got caught.'

'So what is it then? If it's not a real plan?'

'A deliberate plant to try and fool us. Make us think they were going to attack the North.'

'All that stuff was put there just to fool us?'

McClure shook his head. 'No, no. Just Plan Kathleen. Brandy might've been going to plant that through some channel or other. I don't think he planned to lose the transmitter and the dollars.' He paused. 'Or the medals, for that matter.'

'If he's only been here a few days, scouting locations, how could an invasion be imminent?' Duggan sought reassurance that their fears were unfounded.

'We don't know how long he's been here. He could've been here for months.'

'But he only landed a week or two ago?'

'We don't know that for sure. There was a parachute found in a ditch in County Meath last week. But that could've been somebody else. He had a used parachute.'

'But he hadn't got to spend any of the money yet.'

'Looks that way. But it could be my wishful thinking. I don't know how much he had to start with.'

Jesus, Duggan thought. This was like trying to stop a burst pipe with your finger. Water spraying everywhere. Move your finger one way and it went another.

'Brandy confirms without doubt that the Germans are serious about us. But he's not the only straw,' McClure said. 'The IRA's upped their activities dramatically in recent weeks.'

'I thought that was just a response to the hunger strikers' deaths,' Duggan said, realizing as he said it that he was clutching at a straw himself.

McClure shook his head. 'They've been in contact with the Germans since before the war, looking for arms and so on. They're their fifth columnists here. Think they're going to get a united Ireland out of it. And that they'll be running it. For the Germans.'

They aren't the only ones, Duggan thought, thinking of Timmy.

'And the British have warned us that an invasion could be imminent.'

Duggan gave an involuntary snort. 'Can we believe them?'

'Not necessarily,' McClure said. He took out another cigarette. 'Want one?'

'Yes, please.'

McClure tapped the end of another cigarette on his case and put it between Duggan's lips. 'You watch the road,' he said, putting the flame of his lighter to the tip of Duggan's cigarette. Duggan inhaled deeply, got stronger smoke than he was used to, and began to cough. He took the cigarette from his mouth and held it with the steering wheel as he caught his breath.

'Scepticism is good in this business,' McClure said. 'Paranoia isn't.'

'Yes, sir,' Duggan blushed, the 'sir' slipping out without thinking.

'Yes,' McClure continued. 'The British want Berehaven to protect their Atlantic convoys. They want us in on their side. Last thing they want, I imagine, is another front right now. If they force their way, we'll fight them. Have to. And our German friends would come to our aid.' He gave a short laugh. 'Like they rescued Denmark from an imminent Allied invasion.'

Duggan turned into Infirmary Road and into the entrance to headquarters and stopped at the barrier. A soldier came out of the sandbagged sentry post, raised the barrier and saluted as they went in. He parked the car where it had been previously.

'That's the real danger,' McClure said, making no move to get out. 'That one or other will make a pre-emptive move. Because they think the other is going to. And that's why we need to know what's going on. And not let our hopes or fears get in the way of careful analysis.'

Duggan knew he was being given a lesson, but he didn't resent it this time. Something had changed in his relationship with McClure this morning; he was now treating him more seriously.

'Just to finish the straws,' McClure said. 'MI5 passed on some documents that Dutch intelligence had found on a captured German before they were overrun. They included references to the invasion of England and Ireland, *Unternehmen Seelöwe* and *Unternehmen Grün*.'

He looked at him to see if he understood.

'Not very imaginative names.' McClure went on, 'And the biggest straw of all of course is the war itself. France is defeated.'

'But most of its army's still intact,' Duggan said.

'The size of an army doesn't necessarily matter. Its effectiveness as a fighting force is what matters. The French army is finished. Italy's shaping up to declare war and will probably invade the south of France any day now. Spain might do the same. France is now a mopping up operation. So the Germans are looking at their next objective.'

England, Duggan thought. And us. Opening another front on England's western flank. Especially before the English had time to regroup after Dunkirk. It was imminent, he thought. Oh, God.

McClure stepped out of the car and ground his cigarette under his foot. Inside, the corridors had calmed down. Duggan dropped back the car key to the duty office and made his way upstairs to his own office. When he got there, McClure was standing by the table, scanning a copy of Plan Kathleen, its pages held together by a metal clip. He shook his head when he had finished. 'I don't believe it,' he said. 'I don't think it adds up. If they're going to invade, the south is best for beaches and strategically for parachutists. They only have to deal with us and we don't have the heavy stuff to stop them getting a secure foothold. So they'd get a bigger foothold much quicker. Why take on the British directly in the North? Even if they could get there.'

He looked at Duggan who was trying to form a defence of the Irish army in his mind. But McClure was thinking out loud.

'It'd cause us no end of trouble, of course. Politically. The Germans and IRA fighting the British in the North. Nationalist uprising there. Usual unionist reaction. Massacres of Catholics. Outrage and uproar down here. What're we supposed to do?' McClure looked at him again but Duggan had no response, knew none was required. 'Have to join in. Fucking nightmare.' He thought about it for a moment. 'That's it,' he concluded. 'Militarily, it's ridiculous. Politically, it's a nightmare.'

McClure dropped the document on the table, selected some other papers, put them on top of it, and picked them all up in one hand. 'Got a meeting about this,' he said. 'See what the experts think. After you call Dr Hayes, go back down to the Harbusch stakeout and see if you can pick up anything else down there.'

He was turning to the door when he caught the disappointed look on Duggan's face. Balding and waddling Hans Harbusch seemed a long way from what was really going on. 'That was useful stuff you got yesterday,' McClure said. 'Ninety-nine pounds for a necklace. We've got to pay more attention to the money. Remember,' he added as he went out, 'straws in the wind. And what might bind them together. That's what we're looking for.'

*

The workmen digging the air-raid shelter in Merrion Square were still there but must have been on a break as he chained his bicycle to the railings. There was no sound of shovelling soil, only of men's voices in a confusion of conversations. He crossed the road to the building where Gifford had his perch and waved to the receptionist as he went by the open door of her office. He stopped and went back.

'Ah,' he said to her, 'd'you think I could get a cup of tea too? If someone is bringing it upstairs?'

She turned and looked at the clock on the wall behind her. 'Certainly,' she said. 'Just in time. Would you like a biscuit, too?'

'If that's not too much trouble.'

'Less trouble than trying to steal one of Petey's,' she smiled.

He thanked her and went on up to Gifford's room.

'Ah,' Gifford was sitting in the window, reading the *Evening Herald*. 'Herr Oberst.'

'Sinéad downstairs calls you Petey,' Duggan said.

'Sinéad's a dote. She can call me anything she likes.' He pointed a finger at Duggan. 'Don't you be trying anything there.'

'I was just asking for a cup of tea.'

'Fucking culchies,' Gifford stood up and stretched himself. 'Walk into your house and next thing you know they're drinking your tea, eating your biscuits. Sleeping in your bed.'

Duggan took off his jacket and looked for somewhere to put it. There was nowhere, so he hung it on the knob of the door.

'There you are,' Gifford said, as if that proved his point. 'Would you like to take my chair?'

'No, thanks.' Duggan went to the window and looked out. There was no sign of life in the Harbusches' flat. The sun was still shining but the blue of the sky was now spotted with small white clouds that looked as high as they were wide. The weather's going to break, he thought, the small clouds an advance party ahead of the main force. He couldn't shake the thought of an invasion. The image of the sky full of parachutists and screaming Stukas and lumbering Heinkels. Which town would they make an example of? Like they had of Rotterdam. It was a different kind of warfare, no matter what Timmy said, fast and fierce, brutal and inhuman, soft bodies against hard machines. Not like the last war, not like Timmy's and his father's guerrilla days. Denmark had lasted six hours, Holland five days. How long will we last?

'No news?' he asked Gifford.

'Not a word,' Gifford gestured to the newspaper, 'about Herr Brandy.'

'Were you out there?'

'No, I'm here. On the punishment detail.'

'What are they punishing you for?'

'If I knew that I could get them to stop. Instead, they're torturing me day after day. Forcing me to sit here and drive myself mad thinking of what Hansi's doing in there.'

There was a knock on the door and Sinéad came in, balancing a tray on one hand as she opened the door.

'The saviour of my sanity,' Gifford said as he went to help her.

She blushed slightly as he took the tray from her. There were two cups of tea on it, a sugar bowl, and a plate with four plain biscuits. 'I didn't know if you took sugar,' she said to Duggan.

'Two spoons,' he said.

'And you made her carry all that extra weight up those flights of stairs,' Gifford said to him. 'You couldn't have told her that downstairs?' He turned to her. 'Typical of the bloody army. Trample all over us poor civilians.'

'Don't fight over the biscuits,' she said. 'Two each.' She waved her fingers above her shoulder as she went out.

'Nice girl,' Duggan said, taking a cup of tea and stirring two spoons of sugar into it. 'And a culchie too.'

'Different rules for culchie women,' Gifford took the other cup and bit on a biscuit. 'They can come into my house and sleep in my bed anytime.' Gifford took a noisy slurp of tea. 'The money came from Switzerland,' he said. 'Five hundred pounds.'

'Five hundred?' Duggan gave a low whistle – that was a good year's salary. Gifford had followed Harbusch into the Royal Bank on Grafton Street the previous day while Duggan was with Eliza in the jewellers. He had got into a queue behind Harbusch and heard him ask the teller if a deposit had arrived for his account. The teller went away and came back and said it had. He wrote the amount on a slip of paper and handed it to Harbusch. Hans looked pleased, thanked him and clicked his heels.

'No wonder Eliza was blowing it,' Gifford said. 'Hansi was obviously expecting it.'

'How'd you find out?'

'One of our Kerrymen talked to the manager this morning. The kind that like their meat raw with blood dripping from it. The manager hummed and hawed about the sanctity of bank secrecy and customer confidentiality. Our man ground his molars and the manager caved in. Hansi's been getting regular irregular lumps of money from this Swiss bank since he got here.'

'How much?'

'I don't know the total but the five hundred is the biggest single one yet,' Gifford said. 'Somebody must be pleased with Hansi.' He looked out the window and drained the cup. 'And to think of the pleasure he gets from his work.'

'Some fellows have all the luck.'

'That's the main thing I've learned from this job,' Gifford sighed. 'Everybody we watch is having a better time than we're having watching them.'

'Which bank is it? In Switzerland?'

'I don't know that. But your lads will get the answer now that they know the right question to ask.' Gifford gave him a conspiratorial look.

Duggan nodded. This was perfect. Pay more attention to the money, McClure had suggested. 'Thanks,' he said.

Gifford looked surprised. 'Couldn't have you sent back to the bogs. Now that you've seen the city lights.'

Duggan finished his tea and sat down on the chair and picked the *Evening Herald* off the floor. Gifford stretched out on the linoleum, put his hands behind his head and closed his eyes with a sigh of pleasure. The news was all about the war, rival communiqués interspersed with smudgy hand-drawn maps covered in arrows. The British were saying their escape from Dunkirk was a great victory. The Germans were saying they'd taken a hundred thousand Allied prisoners. The French were on the run everywhere. Italy was hinting at a big announcement very soon. Poland had disappeared between the claws of the Wehrmacht and the Red Army.

He was too restless to concentrate on all the details but the big picture was clear. The Germans were going through everything before them, like a hot knife through butter. He looked out on the afternoon calm, the sun still shining, a gentle breeze barely stirring the leaves on the top of the trees, a lone seagull up from the sea at Ringsend floating on outstretched wings. It was hard to imagine the newspaper world of arrows and maps, broken-up buildings, bodies lying on streets coming here. But it was hard to see how we could avoid it. Unless the British did a deal. But everyone said Churchill wouldn't do a deal. If they'd picked someone else . . .

At best I'll probably end up a prisoner of war, he thought. At worst, dead. Or somewhere in between, wounded or on the run, fighting a doomed guerrilla campaign. Like the War of Independence, but against impossible odds this time. And how would he stand up? He had no idea.

Duggan got up and dropped the paper on the chair. He had to be doing something. Sitting around thinking bleak thoughts about the future wasn't doing him any good. 'I'm going out for a walk,' he said.

'A walk?' Gifford kept his eyes closed.

'Just going up to Mount Street. To see someone.'

'Ah,' Gifford sighed with satisfaction. 'To see how the other side's doing?'

'What?'

Gifford opened one eye. 'What the British are up to.' He saw Duggan's confusion. 'Their representative's office's up there. You didn't know that?'

Duggan shook his head, embarrassed.

'I won't tell anyone.' Gifford closed his eyes again. 'And to think that some people believe you fellows know what you're doing. Our first line of defence. Jaysus.'

'I'll be back in a little while,' Duggan muttered as he gathered his jacket and left. Going down the stairs, he got the piece of paper Timmy had given him out of his pocket and looked at the number on it. Twenty-eight.

He crossed the street into Upper Mount Street, which looked like a continuation of Merrion Square, four-storeyed, redbrick Georgian houses, a couple of steps up to the front doors, half-moon fanlights above them. He checked the numbers on the nearest houses: 28 had to be down the other end, near the Pepper Canister church which stood in the middle of the street, forcing the road to embrace it with two arms. He passed by the British pensions office. Two red-faced men were coming out, looking like they were off to a pub to spend their ex-servicemen's money. Farther on, a uniformed guard stood outside the office of the British representative. He resisted an urge to look up at the windows on the opposite side of the road. The Special Branch had to be up there somewhere, keeping an eye on visitors, the comings and goings.

Number 28 had a line of bell pushes beside the door, the few names on tabs unreadable. He tried the door but it was locked and he pressed a bell at random. Nothing happened and he tried another one, lower down. After a few moments he heard footsteps clicking down the hall and the door opened. A woman in her thirties eyed him with some suspicion.

'Sorry for troubling you,' Duggan said. 'I'm looking for Nuala Monaghan.'

'Second bell from the top,' she said and shut the door and he heard its lock click into place.

He pressed the second bell from the top. Nothing happened. He should've asked Timmy if they had a key, he thought. But his aunt Mona must have had a look inside already.

He walked on, round the side of the church, and asked a man passing by where Gillespie's Metropolitan College was. 'The other Mount Street,' he said. 'Turn left over there at the canal. Just up from the next bridge.' Duggan followed his directions. People were stretched out on the grass along the banks of the canal, soaking up the sun. Shouts and splashes came from a lock down towards the sea where a group of boys were jumping off the gates, trying to outdo each others' splashes.

The college was near the bridge, on Lower Mount Street, another

Georgian house turned into a commercial building. A no-nonsense looking woman sat in an office inside the door and looked up at him over her glasses as he came in.

'I'm looking for Nuala Monaghan,' he said. She stared at him and he added quickly. 'I'm her cousin. Up from the country for the day. I was hoping I could meet her for a cup of tea.'

She said nothing and opened a ledger book and ran her name down several lists until she stopped. 'Mr Devlin's class. On the next floor. First door.' She looked at her watch. 'They're just finished now so you can go up.'

Duggan thanked her and climbed the stairs, keeping to the wall as a stream of young women came down. The classroom was almost empty, one young woman waiting for a friend to put her books away. Mr Devlin, a small, balding old man, was at a table in front of the unused fireplace, putting his papers into a leather briefcase. A blackboard stood on an easel on the window side of the desk, covered in shorthand symbols.

'Miss Monaghan,' he said after Duggan gave him his story, 'has not been here for some time.' He took a hard-backed notebook from his briefcase and consulted it. 'Not for two weeks. Since last Friday fortnight.' He looked up at Duggan as though it was his fault.

'Oh,' Duggan said. 'I'll call around to her home.'

'You should inform her that she ought to come back immediately,' Mr Devlin said. 'Or she'll have fallen so far behind that she won't be able to catch up. She may have to repeat the term in the autumn.'

Why would she stop going to the classes? Duggan wondered as he went downstairs. If she'd wanted to do them, as Timmy said. Though Timmy wasn't necessarily a reliable judge of what Nuala wanted. Still, it pointed to a sudden disappearance. Maybe, he thought, something had really happened to her. He'd been inclined to accept Timmy's view that she was simply lying low, paying him back. But what if something had really happened to make her disappear suddenly? He should report her missing.

Across the street was the nurses' home for Sir Patrick Dun's hospital. Her friend, Stella Maloney, was a nurse there. On the off-chance that she might be there he crossed the road and went into the building. A doorman barred his way.

'I'm looking for my cousin, Stella Maloney,' Duggan told him. 'I'm just up from the country for the day and I was hoping she might be off duty and have time for a cup of tea. Before I get my train back to the barracks.'

'Wait there,' the doorman said and disappeared through a door.

The wait stretched into minutes and Duggan lit a Sweet Afton and stared out the window beside the door. Nurses came and went, most of them in uniform. He sensed suddenly that someone was staring at him and he turned around. A young woman with dark eyes and black hair in tight curls was giving him a quizzical look, her arms folded over her uniform.

'Stella?' The doorman re-emerged behind her and was watching him. 'I'm just up for the day,' he stuttered. 'Nuala told me you might be free. For a cup of tea.'

Understanding dawned in her eyes. 'We'll go down to Morelli's,' she said, leading the way out the door.

'Thanks,' Duggan said to the doorman as he passed him.

'I'm Paul Duggan,' he said outside. 'Nuala's cousin.'

'Right,' she said. Something in her inflection made him wonder for a fleeting moment if she had thought he was somebody else. 'I've heard of you,' she went. 'You're in the army. Your uncle's very proud of you.'

That makes my heart leap with joy, Duggan thought. 'I've been trying to find Nuala,' he said.

'Why're you trying to find her?' They went by a line of small shops, a grocer's, butcher's and a newsagent's. A newspaper board outside said in big black letters, 'French Govt Flees Paris'. She guided him across the road to Morelli's fish and ice cream shop and they took a table inside the door.

'I'm getting worried about her. She seems to have disappeared.'

Stella looked at the handwritten menu. 'I'll have ice cream and tea,' she said. 'Ice cream for breakfast.'

'You're just getting up?'

She nodded. 'Night duty this month. Turns everything upside down. So I can have ice cream for breakfast.'

Duggan ordered the same when a waitress came to them.

'Is it you that's worried,' Stella stared at him. 'Or her father?'

'He told me they haven't seen her for a few weeks. And she hasn't been to her secretarial classes.'

'So you're here on his behalf.'

Duggan shook his head. 'Well, yes and no. He asked me to try and find her. But I'm worried too. If you can tell me she's fine, that's it. I'll be happy.'

'And you'll go back and tell him?'

'Not if you don't want me to.' She gave him a sceptical look. 'But you might let her mother and sisters know. It's not fair on them if she's just trying to give her father a hard time.'

The waitress brought them a tin pot of weak tea and two tin bowls of vanilla ice cream with strawberry cordial dribbling down the sides. 'Would you like your tea now?' Stella asked him. He nodded and she poured it for both of them.

'I don't know where she is,' she said.

Duggan gave a worried sigh. 'So she really is missing?'

'I haven't seen her for a couple of weeks. Like I told you, I've been on nights. It turns your life upside down. You don't see anybody. Miss all this lovely weather.'

She's avoiding the question, Duggan thought. She obviously knows something. But she's not going to tell me. He waited until he caught her eye and asked, 'Is she in trouble?'

'I don't know,' she said, breaking eye contact to take a spoonful of the smooth ice cream.

'I promise I won't tell Timmy,' he tried again. 'I just want to know for my own sake if she's all right. If you can tell me she is, that's the end of it as far as I'm concerned. I'll tell Timmy I couldn't find out anything.'

She continued to eat her ice cream slowly, savouring each mouthful. He had finished his and drank his tea. It tasted flat after the ice cream. Neither said anything until they had both finished.

'Is there anyone else who might know?' he asked. 'Any other friends? Does she have a boyfriend?'

Stella smiled as if at a private joke. 'Nuala's never short of boyfriends. You know her.'

I don't actually, Duggan thought. He wouldn't have thought that the impatient girl he remembered would have been very attractive to men. But, then, he hadn't the faintest idea what attracted women to men. 'Is there a particular one at the moment?'

She shrugged her shoulders and said, 'Sorry. I don't know.'

'Okay,' he nodded, letting her know that he was giving up. She could keep her secrets. She wasn't going to share them with him.

'Where are you based?' She sounded more friendly, aware that the questioning was over.

'Collins Barracks,' he said. 'I've only been up in Dublin a couple of weeks.'

'You're an officer, aren't you?'

'Only a lieutenant. The bottom of the pole.'

'How do you like it?'

'Dublin or the army?'

'Both?'

He shrugged. 'They're interesting. It's an interesting time.'

He called the waitress and got the bill. Stella took it from his hand after he had looked at it, and said they would split it. She took a purse from her pocket and left a shilling and a threepenny bit on the table. He put down two sixpenny pieces and three copper pennies.

'Do you have a key to Nuala's flat?' he asked her, out of the blue.

She looked at him for a moment and then said, 'Wait here.'

Three

She opened the door and he followed her up the stairs. A strip of yellow linoleum ran up the centre of the steps, the black paint on either side greyed by ingrained dust. Small flakes of once white paint were beginning to droop from the ceiling here and there and the faded green walls were scuffed in places. She led him up to the top landing where two electricity meters with coin slots stood between two doors. She turned the key in the lock of the door on the right and they went in.

The room was stuffy, heavy with the stagnant air of the last few days' heat. There was a single bed against one wall, made up neatly with a maroon coloured eiderdown on top. A wardrobe with a door ajar stood against the wall at the end of the bed, a small cardboard suitcase on top of it. On the opposite wall there was a sink with a gas geyser above it and two gas rings alongside. Beside the sink there was a press of the same height; a cup sat on a plate on top of it. There was a small square table in front of the window with a single chair facing the glass. Everything was old and mismatched, castoffs.

Stella went to one side of the table and leant sideways to unlatch the window. She tried to pull down the top but it wouldn't move. Duggan went to the other side of the table and pulled at the other

side of the window. It gave way with a lurch and came down a couple
of inches.

Duggan stood back and looked around. Now that he was here he
had no idea what it was he hoped to find. 'How does it seem to you?'
he asked Stella, going over to look at the cup and plate beside the
sink. The bottom of the cup was a congealed green and there were
some toasted crumbs on the plate. 'Have you been here before?'

'The same as usual,' she shrugged. 'Nuala's very neat.'

'It looks like she left in a hurry,' he pointed to the cup and plate.
She went over and looked at them but said nothing.

'Went out after breakfast,' he suggested. 'But not to the college.'
On the table there was a copy of *Pitman's Shorthand Instructor*, a
worn copy of *Pitman's Shorthand Dictionary*, and some copybooks.
He flicked through them. They were filled with what looked like
shorthand exercises, the same symbols repeated over and over again.
Near the end of one there appeared to be a passage of text in shorthand. 'Can you read shorthand?' he asked her. She shook her head.

He pulled open the table's shallow drawer. There were a couple of
pencils, a sharpener, a rubber; a memorial card for his and Nuala's
grandmother with the date of her death, 24 September 1923; an
envelope with small square, box camera photographs, and some newspaper cuttings. He took out the photographs and glanced through
them. There were some of his aunt Mona and his own mother as
young women, Mona with a young Nuala, Nuala and her younger
sisters, some people he didn't recognise, and one of a young man. It
wasn't as faded as the others. He was wearing a short-sleeved pullover
over an open-necked shirt, his head tilted in a slightly forced smile.

He handed it to Stella. 'That's Jim,' she said, 'Jim Bradley.'

'Her boyfriend?'

Stella made a noncommittal gesture. 'I wouldn't say that. One of
her admirers.'

He fished out the newspaper cuttings. The main one was a page from the *Irish Times*, folded in four. He opened it out on the table. It was dated 30 November 1920 and the first two lines of the four-deck headline in the centre of the page said 'Auxiliary Police Ambushed in County Cork/ Fifteen Killed, One Wounded, and One Missing.' He read down a little and realized that it was an account of the famous Kilmichael ambush when Tom Barry's Flying Column had wiped out a patrol of Auxiliaries in the War of Independence. Why would Nuala keep that?

The other main report on the page was of an official inquiry into the shooting of three Republicans in Dublin Castle while said to be trying to escape. Duggan knew their names well, everybody did, but he couldn't imagine why Nuala would be particularly interested in them or the attempted cover-up of their murders. The rest of the page was short pieces about various attacks, arrests, deaths from wounds, all minor compared to Kilmichael. Nothing caught his attention and he turned the page over: Irish questions in the British parliament, a review of a show in the Gaiety Theatre, the American stock market report, an ad for White's Wafer Oatmeal.

Another cutting from the *Irish Independent* made more sense. It was a photograph of two couples taken at a dinner dance in the Metropole the previous winter and identified Nuala and the others.

'Richie Cummins,' Stella said. 'And friends of his.'

'Not a boyfriend?'

'You know Nuala,' she said. 'Very independent minded. Won't let herself be tied down by being too attached to any one man. Not yet anyway.'

He put everything back into the drawer.

'Listen,' she said, 'I've got to be getting back.'

He opened the wardrobe and stepped back, inviting her to look at the row of dresses and blouses on hangers and two pairs of shoes on the floor. 'Would you know if there's anything missing?' He felt uneasy looking into her clothes, as if it was a step too far.

She shrugged an apology. 'Impossible to know. She still kept some of her clothes at home.'

He closed the door. 'Okay,' he said. 'Thanks for bringing me in.'

'Did you find what you wanted?' she asked as she locked the door behind them.

'I don't know what I wanted,' he said. 'She seems to have left intending to come back.'

'That's the bathroom,' Stella said as they passed the return. He opened the frosted glass door and looked in. A bath with a green stain under a tap had a gas geyser above it, the toilet had a cistern up near the ceiling, a long chain hanging down.

'Why did she leave Clery's?' Duggan asked as he followed her down the stairs.

'Boss was a bitch,' Stella said over her shoulder. 'Gave Nuala a terrible time because she was forced to take her into her section by someone on high. Her father had pulled strings.'

Duggan nodded. He could understand Nuala's decision. Timmy couldn't resist trying to run everyone's life. Even my own, he thought.

On the street, Stella held out her hand formally. 'Nice to meet you,' she said as he shook it.

'Will you let me know if you hear anything?' he asked. 'Just for my own information. I won't tell anyone if that's the way Nuala wants it.'

'How do I contact you?'

'If you leave a message at Collins Barracks I should get it,' he said.

Sinéad was just leaving the building when he got back to Merrion Square.

'Is he still up there?' he asked her.

'Does he have a home to go to at all?' she said. 'I think he sleeps on the floor up there. Poor lamb.'

Duggan laughed, assuming she was joking, and went on up.

'So, how was the Swedish massage?' Gifford greeted him.

'What?'

'I've always wondered about that place in Mount Street. The Swedish institute of gymnastics and massage. You couldn't go wrong with that combination.'

'I didn't notice it.'

Gifford shook his head, like he was a hopeless case.

'Sinéad's worried you're sleeping here.'

'The secret police never sleep,' Gifford sniggered. 'Hope you didn't tell her that.'

Duggan took a perfunctory look out the window at the Harbusches' flat. 'Nothing moving over there?'

'Not a sausage.'

'Seriously,' Duggan said. 'What d'you think he's up to?'

'Apart from the obvious?'

'Nobody's paying him from a Swiss bank for that.'

'You're right,' Gifford clicked his fingers, as if that hadn't occurred to him. 'Even Hansi couldn't be that lucky.'

They stood in silence, side by side, looking out the window for a few moments. Gifford shrugged and turned back into the room. 'Fucked if I know,' he said, serious for once. 'I presume our masters know more than they're telling us.'

'I suppose so,' Duggan said. He looked down at the street, busier now as the offices around the square emptied for the day and bicycles and a few cars headed for the suburbs. He was still thinking about Nuala. What was she up to? There was no doubt her friend Stella knew more than she was saying. And she didn't seem to be really worried about Nuala? Why had she let him look at Nuala's flat? She didn't have to. Had she been trying to tell him something without saying anything? What? Fucked if I know, he thought, echoing Gifford.

'Could I ask your advice about something?' Duggan turned from the window.

Gifford was pacing up and down the room like it was a cage, swinging his arms. 'Sure,' he said.

'Not official. A . . . a personal matter.' Gifford stopped pacing and nodded. Duggan went on, 'How hard would it be to find out if someone's gone to England?'

Gifford shrugged. 'Not hard. Not since the British introduced the permit requirements. Their office is just up the road. They'd have a record of everybody travelling.'

Duggan nodded. 'Would it be possible to check someone out? To see if someone had gone to England in the last fortnight?'

'Last fortnight shouldn't be a great problem,' Gifford said. 'Short period to check.'

'This is totally unofficial. A family matter.'

'I'll see what I can do. I know one of the lads who liaises with the British permit guys. They're always checking out who's coming and going.' Gifford took a pen from his shirt pocket and tore a strip off a page of the *Evening Herald*. 'What's the name and address?'

'Nuala Monaghan,' Duggan said and gave her Mount Street address.

Gifford wrote down the details and folded the slip of paper and put it in his shirt pocket. 'No problemo,' he said. 'Take a day or two, I suppose.'

'Thanks.'

'Tut, tut,' Gifford shook his head at him. 'She up the pole?'

'She's my cousin.'

'Oh,' Gifford laughed. 'Sorry. I thought you were about to surprise me. Reveal more hidden depths.'

'She could be in trouble,' Duggan agreed. 'Or she could've just gone there to work. Either way, she's gone somewhere without telling anybody. Her mother's doing her nut. You can imagine.'

Gifford nodded in sympathy. 'Family's usually the last to know in those situations. Sudden disappearance of young woman is either a love child or pursuit of a man. It's all in the secret policeman's handbook. Chapter seven, Affairs of the Heart.'

Back in the Red House Duggan found a thick buff file marked Hans Harbusch dob 11/7/1897 on the table in front of his chair with a note from McClure saying, 'For your information'.

Lieutenant Bill Sullivan, another member of the German section of G2 with whom he shared an office, was huddled over a type written document, underlining phrases with red ink. 'Something I wanted to ask you,' he said, raising a finger to signal to Duggan to wait as he looked around the desk for another piece of paper. He found it, a list of names in Irish, and pointed to one which had a question mark in pencil after it.

Duggan took the page – it was the latest list he had compiled of people mentioned in Professor Ludwig Mühlhausen's weekly broadcast in Irish from Germany. He had had the job of listening to the professor's broadcast the previous Sunday night. It was the usual stuff, a recitation of Black and Tan atrocities in Ireland, the burnings of Balbriggan, Cork and Mallow this time, and greetings to friends in the Gaeltacht where Mühlhausen had studied Irish. G2's interest was in the people he named.

'Are you sure about that name?' Sullivan asked him. 'The guards don't know anyone of that name in Gweedore.'

Duggan cast his mind back to Mühlhausen's slightly accented Irish, a more structured and precise intonation than the native speaker. He closed his eyes and could hear him talking about the man and the lovely day, *lá breá álainn*, they had once spent on his boat off the Donegal coast.

'I'm nearly certain that was the name,' Duggan said. 'That's what it sounded like.'

'Okay,' Sullivan said, 'I'll tell them. The reference to a boat got them all excited.'

'I can imagine,' Duggan said. There was a lot of activity off the Donegal coast, regular rumbles of torpedo explosions coming ashore, followed by bodies and debris from the daily attacks and counterattacks on the British convoys and their U-boat hunters just over the horizon.

'By the way, the admin officer was looking for you,' Sullivan said.

'What?'

'You haven't filled in your AF90. Your bicycle allowance.'

'Right,' Duggan nodded absently. 'Where's the boss?'

'Around somewhere,' Sullivan went back to his reading.

Duggan found McClure coming out of another office and told him that the Special Branch had found where Harbusch's money had come from. 'Good work,' McClure said. 'Get onto the Superintendent's office in the Castle and get the details. I've left the complete Harbusch file on your desk. I want you to take charge of him from now on.'

'Oh, okay,' Duggan said, pleased to be given responsibility.

'He's more important than ever with this Brandy fellow on the loose,' McClure added. 'Possible he's a sleeper waiting for something like Brandy's arrival. So any changes in his pattern of activity could be important.'

Duggan nodded his understanding.

'How're you getting on with that Branch man watching Harbusch?'

'Well,' Duggan said. 'He seems helpful.'

'Good. But don't tell him more than he needs to know.' He paused at a door. 'A lot of people are playing their own games these days.' He knocked at the door and waited for an answer before entering.

Back in his room, Duggan settled himself at his table, lit a cigarette and opened the Harbusch file. Much of the information in it had come from the British, from MI5, who had tracked Harbusch from his arrival in London in 1936. They had tried without a lot of success to fill in his background in Germany but there were no indications of military activity or intelligence involvement. It was all a bit sketchy. In London he had had an import/export company too, but never seemed to do anything other than send vague business letters to a couple of addresses on the Continent, including the one in Copenhagen to which he had sent his latest. Surveillance on him had never tied him to any other suspected spies or places in which they might be interested. Indeed, he didn't seem to go out much at all. He had arrived in London with a woman called Inge who was presumed to be his wife and about whom even less was known. She seemed to have gone back to Germany late in 1938. Shortly afterwards he met Eliza.

The file was much more detailed about Eliza. She was born in 1909, parents a small shopkeeper and a seamstress in the east end of London, minimal schooling, and a variety of jobs. She had come to MI5's notice as a hanger-on at some of the British Union of Fascists' marches and meetings. 'Her interest is less in politics than in her apparent attraction to men in black uniforms, straight arm salutes, and the so-called charisma of Oswald Mosley,' one sour British Special Branch man had written about her. Interesting, Duggan thought, that may explain what she's doing with Hans, a political connection. Though Hans would not look good in a black or brown shirt. In fact, he thought, he'd look stupid giving straight-arm salutes. But Hitler was no film star either.

The telephone rang and he picked it up. 'G2. Duggan.'

'The hard man,' Timmy said.

'Uncle Timmy,' Duggan said, his body slumping back in the chair.

'We need to talk.' Timmy was unusually businesslike.

'I'm still at work.'

'Like myself, like myself,' Timmy said. 'It wouldn't be a good idea for you to come in here' – Duggan assumed he meant Leinster House – 'but I'll see you in Buswell's Hotel in an hour.'

'I don't know if I can get—'

'There've been developments,' Timmy cut him short. 'A lot of things you need to know.'

He hung up as Duggan was about to protest that he was in the army and couldn't just go off about family business at the drop of a hat. Not that that argument would have cut any ice with Timmy. Family business was national business to him. Why, he wondered, didn't Timmy want him to come into Leinster House today when he wanted to parade him around there yesterday?

He sighed and went back to the Harbusch file. The British thought Harbusch moved to Ireland in July 1939 because he saw the war coming and didn't want to be executed as a spy. Even though they seemed to have no hard evidence that he was spying. At the very least, they would have interned him as an enemy alien. So was his, and Eliza's, move to Dublin just to save their own skins? Duggan wondered. She could've been interned too in England for her fascist sympathies, whether they were political or sexual; Mosley himself had just been locked up. Or was Hans acting under Abwehr orders?

He flicked quickly through the surveillance reports on the couple since their arrival in Ireland. They were mainly a collection of negatives; they didn't go near the German legation, didn't go to any of the depleted German community's functions in the Gresham Hotel, didn't mix with the Irish German Friendship Society in the Red Bank restaurant. A report of a surreptitious search of their flat caught his attention. The Special Branch had broken in when the couple were on one of their rare outings but had found nothing incriminating. No transmitters, no code books, only some German novels and English romantic ones. Duggan wondered if Gifford had been on the search.

He flicked forward to copies of letters from a woman in Holland, addressed to Hans care of a shop in Westland Row. A Special Branch report noted that the shopkeeper had been questioned and was co-operating, tipping them off when letters arrived, delaying their delivery to Hans. 'I remember with passion our last night of love,' Duggan read at random from one, its English slightly off key. 'God willing it will not be long before we do it again and I can still your trembling body with the caress of mine.' Jesus, Duggan thought, I don't understand any of this. Why was Hans getting love letters from another woman? In English from a non-English speaker? Using a different address meant he didn't want Eliza to know about her. Or was it all some kind of elaborate setup? For what?

He put a slip of paper in the file to mark where he had finished reading, left the office half expecting someone to ask him where he was going but nobody did. He got on his bicycle and sped down the hill to the quays and headed for the city centre. There was hardly any traffic and he kept up the initial momentum, cycling fast and enjoying the exercise, letting it clear his head of all the mysteries it was accumulating. The setting sun was just above a bank of cloud rising from the western horizon and cast a long shadow ahead of him. Beside him, the Liffey was now running faster to the sea as the tide ebbed, hurrying under the bridges as their pillars narrowed its path.

Over the sounds of the still evening he became aware of a droning noise, growing steadily. He looked up but couldn't see the aircraft anywhere; it sounded like a couple of them. It stopped growing louder and began to fade. Probably out over the sea, he thought.

He left his bicycle at the railings in front of Buswell's Hotel, a couple of Georgian houses knocked into one inside. He climbed the steps and glanced over at Leinster House. There were a handful of cars parked inside the railings, on either side of the incongruous statue of a lugubrious Queen Victoria. 'Should've been blown up years ago,' Timmy would shake his head regularly. But blowing it up would've broken every window in Leinster House, the National Library and the National Museum. At the very least.

Timmy was in the bar, holding court with a circle of cronies, all laughing too loudly at some banter. 'I must talk to this man here,' Timmy slapped one of them on the back when he saw Duggan. 'Man of the future. Not like you fucking has-beens.'

Timmy had recovered his hail-fellow-well-met demeanour and led Duggan to a quiet corner of the bar. 'What'll you have?' he asked. 'Brandy seems to be the order of the day.'

'Glass of Guinness will be fine,' Duggan said, pretending to ignore Timmy's broad wink. His heart sank, hoping Timmy hadn't dragged him here just to pump him for information about the latest German spy. Timmy called to the barman and raised his almost empty glass for another whiskey.

'Somebody's happy with his day's work today,' Timmy said in a disapproving tone. 'Must've been laughing their heads off when they saw the black smoke coming out of the departments' chimneys this morning. On a boiling hot summer's day.'

The barman gave Timmy another glass of Paddy and put a half-pint glass of water beside it. Duggan waited for him to explain what he was talking about, knowing he didn't need to ask, he'd be told.

'Caused a right old panic,' Timmy tipped the remnants of his old glass into the new one and topped it up with a splash of water. 'Herr Brandy's arrival. Had them burning files all over the place. Until wiser heads prevailed. Realized what it was all about.'

Duggan said nothing, remembering the bags of documents marked 'BURN' in the Red House. Timmy tasted the whiskey and nodded and put it down on a coaster. 'Brandy,' he said slowly, 'is a plant.'

'A plant?'

'Fucking Brits,' Timmy said. 'You can't be up to them. Just the sort of trick they love to pull.'

'Brandy is a British agent?' Duggan looked at him.

Timmy gave him a solemn nod. 'Some of us are too long in the tooth to be fooled by this kind of trickery. Might have worked once upon a time. Not anymore.'

'I don't know.' Duggan thought of the array of material seized from Held's house. The money, the military insignia, the transmitter, the code book, Plan Kathleen.

'Take a step back,' Timmy took an unconscious step backwards. 'Think about it. Who benefited from all the panic this morning? Sensitive files being burned in some places. The Germans coming, moryah. Parachutists raining down on us any minute.' Timmy gave a snort, dismissing the idea as ludicrous. 'Whose interest was all that in?' He nodded at Duggan as if he had answered him. 'Right. The Brits.'

The barman put the glass of Guinness in front of Duggan and Timmy dug some coins out of his trouser pocket and put the price of the drinks on the counter. Duggan took a sip of the stout.

'Result was a right old panic,' Timmy continued. 'Everyone on high alert. A step away from falling on our knees and begging the British to come over the border and save us.'

Timmy put down his drink and took out his cigarette case, finished. He offered Duggan a cigarette but he said he'd have one of his own. Timmy lit both of them and inhaled a lungful of smoke with satisfaction.

'Do you think Held is a British agent too?' Duggan asked.

'Who knows what Held is?' Timmy gave an expansive wave with the hand holding the cigarette.

'He's half German.'

Timmy conceded that with a nod. 'But do you know who's living with him?'

'Who?'

'A woman who's not his wife,' Timmy said. 'A woman who's the wife of an RAF officer.'

'Really?'

'Really.' Timmy said with satisfaction, resting his case.

They sipped at their drinks, pulled on their cigarettes, thinking their own thoughts. If Timmy only knew about G2's contacts with MI5, Duggan thought. And that MI5 had added to the overnight panic with a warning of an imminent German invasion. *Unternehmen Seelöwe* and *Unternehmen Grün*. Straws in the wind? And the ties that bind them together? The code book, he thought. That'd prove who Brandy worked for. If it deciphered other encrypted German messages.

Timmy looked around the bar. It wasn't full but it was getting to the stage where voices were too loud, laughter was too hearty, and stories were being repeated and seemed even funnier than the first time round. Two of his earlier drinking companions came over to him.

'Can we get a lift up to Lamb Doyle's later?' one of them asked while the other swayed in front of Timmy and Duggan.

'If I'm going,' Timmy said.

'Why wouldn't you be going?' the drunker of the two demanded.

'Later, men, later,' Timmy shooed them away. He turned his back to the room and took a typed document from his inside pocket, unfolded it slowly, keeping it shielded by his body. 'Take a quick look at that.'

The first sentences grabbed Duggan's attention: 'England is beaten. Neither time nor gold can save her now.' His eyes ran down the page, absorbing, rather than reading, the content. Now was not the time, it argued, to do anything to alienate the Germans. Every other remaining neutral was trying to come to terms with them, getting off the fence, getting on the winning side, looking to the post-war world, Germany ruling all of Europe. Joining the Allies now would be disastrous, no matter what they offered on the North; we'd be on the losing side and pay the penalty. We'd be occupied, maybe lumped together with Britain in one colonised unit. At the very least a pro-German neutrality would leave us in an advantageous position in relation to the national question when the post-war situation was being negotiated. There was even a case to be made for joining . . . Timmy took it from his hand before he could read any more, folded it and put it back in his pocket.

Duggan gave him a questioning look. There had been no heading on the document, no name at the end of it.

'Top secret.' Timmy put his finger to his lips. 'Top. Top. Secret.'

Duggan wondered if he was drunk. He had seen Timmy down copious glasses of whiskey at family gatherings and never appear as drunk as others who had matched him. His speech sometimes became just a little disjointed, that was all.

'That's from the top,' he began again, suddenly fixated with the word top. 'From the very top. The top. And secret. Very secret.'

'The Taoiseach?' Duggan dropped his voice.

Timmy nodded. 'Men around him. Good men. Good advisers.'

He glanced around him. 'I've been a bit worried about the Chief, you know. Told you that the other night. I know he sees things the rest of us can't see. But I've a theory. I'm worried he spent too long negotiating with the Brits about the ports and the annuities. Big mistake to spend too long talking to them. Big mistake to talk to them at all. Look what happened Collins. Just tell them to fuck off and leave us alone. Only way to deal with them. But,' he tapped his jacket where he had put the document, 'he's getting the right advice now. On the right track at last.' He raised his glass, as if proposing a toast. 'A nation once again.'

Duggan raised his glass too and took a drink.

'What does your father think?' Timmy asked.

'About all this? I don't know. I haven't been home in over a month.' Anyway, his father never talked about politics.

'He'd see through all the old British tricks,' Timmy said. 'From the old days.'

Duggan's father had been in the IRA during the War of Independence as well as Timmy but had taken no part in the Civil War afterwards. He never spoke to Duggan, or, as far as he knew, to anyone about those days. Timmy was always curious about his father's political opinions, confirming that his father never spoke to him about them either.

Timmy signalled to the barman for another round. Duggan protested that he had to get back to the barracks.

'There's one other thing,' Timmy said with a heavy breath. He seemed totally sober again. 'Nuala.'

'I talked to her friend Stella today,' Duggan said. 'She said she doesn't know where she is. She's been on night duty and out of touch with everyone.'

Timmy gave no indication that he had heard. He reached into his other inside pocket and took out a brown envelope and handed it to Duggan. He took out the single sheet of paper and unfolded it.

'Jesus Christ,' Duggan said and looked at Timmy with horror.

'It's a joke,' Timmy said.

'You've got to call in the guards now.' Duggan dropped the sheet onto the bar, realizing that they shouldn't be touching it at all. There could be fingerprints on it.

Timmy snatched if off the bar and shook his head. 'It's ridiculous.'

Duggan took it back from him; whatever prints had been there had probably been destroyed by now. Letters and words had been cut from newspapers and stuck to the page in a crude message. *We have your daughter*, they said. *£5,000 to get her back. Ad in* Herald *before weekend to signal his agreement: Thanks to Our Lady of Perpetual Succour for prayers answered – TM.*

'Even if it is a joke,' Duggan said. 'You should tell the guards. It's not funny.'

'It's ridiculous,' Timmy shook his head. 'Where would anyone get five thousand pounds?'

Duggan folded the sheet of paper as the barman came with their drinks. He looked at the envelope it came in. It was addressed to Mr Timothy Monaghan TD PC, Dáil Éireann. Nothing else. The postmark appeared to be Dublin but he couldn't make out the date. Somebody who knew Timmy well, Duggan thought. The PC on the envelope. Peace Commissioner. Timmy always signed his letters with that as well as TD. Some kind of private joke. Former gunman now a peace commissioner, Duggan had always thought.

'When did you get it?'

'Last week,' Timmy said.

'Last week,' Duggan raised his voice and Timmy signalled to him to quieten down. 'For fuck's sake. Call the guards.'

Timmy shook his head again. 'Some Blueshirt fucker. Playing games,' he said. 'You should see some of the stuff I get in the post.'

'Doesn't matter who it is. How funny they think it is,' Duggan said. 'Let the guards deal with it.'

'And be a laughing stock,' Timmy said. 'That's what they want.'

'They won't be laughing if they end up in jail for blackmail. Extortion. Whatever.'

'And I'll lose my seat.'

Duggan was about to ask how he could lose his seat over it but held back. Something to do with loss of face, he thought, not being in control. Not the man to make things happen, a victim. Nuala, he thought. She's probably behind it. And Timmy knows that. Stella, too. She's probably in on it. That'd explain her lack of concern about her friend.

'Another one today,' Timmy sighed and took another envelope from his pocket. No ad this weekend next message to her mother, this one said. Ransom now £10,000.

'Shit,' Duggan said.

Timmy looked defeated. 'Mona'd go berserk. There'd be no talking to her.'

Would Nuala really do that to her mother? Duggan wondered. He doubted it. But he really had no idea what she would or wouldn't do. And it could be a bluff. Probably was. But it was an effective turn of the screw. Mona would go berserk all right, force him to pay up.

'You talk to her,' Timmy said.

'To aunt Mona?'

'Jesus, no. Nuala.'

'I don't know where she is.'

'To that friend of hers.'

'Okay,' Duggan agreed.

'Put a stop to this before it gets out of hand.' Timmy drained half his glass of Paddy in one go.

'You think she's behind it? Nuala?'

'If she wants money all she has to do is ask. I've never refused her anything.' Timmy put the glass on the bar, a full stop. 'Not that kind of money, of course. Where would I get that kind of money?'

Four

Duggan was on the phone waiting to be put through to the Superintendent's office in Dublin Castle when Lieutenant Bill Sullivan came in, carrying an armful of files. Duggan put his hand over the mouthpiece. 'What's happening?' he asked as Sullivan dumped the files on the other end of the table and drew up a chair for himself.

'They've taken over the other office for the Brandy operation,' Sullivan said as he sat down. 'Co-ordinating the results of this morning's raids on IRA members.'

'Anything yet?'

'Lot of fellows for Tintown,' he said.

'Tintown?' Duggan shook his head.

'Internment camp in the Curragh,' Sullivan looked at him curiously. 'Where've you been? The government's introduced internment. Republicans being rounded up.'

Jesus, Duggan thought, how did I not hear that? He had heard something about raids on IRA members. 'I thought the raids were part of the search for Brandy,' he said.

'That, too,' Sullivan said. 'That's our interest. No sign of him, though. They're going through all the stuff picked up and the interrogations. See if there's any leads.'

'Is Captain McClure up there?'

'Running it,' Sullivan said but Duggan didn't hear him. A gruff and bored voice had said 'Superintendent's office' in his ear at the same time.

'Lieutenant Duggan, G2,' Duggan said into the phone. 'We're looking for the information about the deposits in the Royal Bank in Grafton Street in Hans Harbusch's account.'

There was a pause at the other end, then the voice, sounding even more bored, said, 'What?'

Duggan began to repeat himself but the voice cut him off. 'I wouldn't know anything about that.'

Fucking Special Branch, Duggan thought. Not all charmers like Gifford. 'You've got some information about where the money came from,' Duggan said, 'that we need to see as soon as possible.'

'Why?'

'It's okay,' Duggan said with sudden impatience. 'I'll get the Colonel to call the Superintendent.'

He thought for a moment that the Special Branch man had hung up on him. Then the voice said, still bored, 'Hold on.'

Duggan put his hand over the mouthpiece and let out a deep breath. He'd never have had the nerve to say that in person. Especially to someone who sounded like he'd been there since the Civil War and knew where the bodies were buried. Probably buried a few himself. The telephone was a great thing.

Sullivan was looking at him with sudden admiration. 'I'll have my Colonel talk to your superiors,' he mimicked. 'I'll remember that line.'

Duggan shook a Sweet Afton out of its golden packet with one hand and lit it.

'You're the Harbusch case officer now?' Sullivan said, half question, half complaint. Why hadn't it been given to him? He was more experienced and not someone who was only there because he spoke

German. 'I'd heard that. How'd you manage that?'

'I don't know,' Duggan shrugged, aware of what he was thinking. 'Probably because everybody's bored with Harbusch. A dead end. Never seems to do anything.'

The Special Branch man came back on the line. 'That information was sent to you. Through the usual channels.'

'I haven't got it,' Duggan said. 'And I'm the case officer in this case.'

'Somebody probably lost it over there.'

'I need it as soon as possible. Can you send it again? Please?' Duggan held his breath.

There was a strangled snort on the phone. 'We've more to be doing than covering up for the army's incompetence. Especially today.' Then the voice muttered, 'All right', and the line went dead.

Duggan put down the phone with a smile. Case officer, he thought. That sounded good. Even if it was a case that nobody else could be bothered about. He re-opened the Harbusch file at the spot where he had left it the night before.

'That the Harbusch file?' Sullivan asked. 'The one with the dirty letters?'

Duggan nodded and read aloud from the one in front of him. 'I wriggle my toes and think of you sucking them and the sleep goes far away like you. When will you come back and suck my toes? All ten, my ten little piggy wiggys. Ah, I cannot sleep.'

'Fuck me,' Sullivan said and burst out laughing.

Duggan joined in and raised his hands in a helpless gesture. 'Is that a code?' he laughed.

'Sucking her toes,' Sullivan said, giving the idea some thought. 'I don't remember anything about sucking toes in the Catholic Truth Society booklet on sex.'

'I hope you are a big boy now, thinking of me and my little piggy wiggy,' Duggan went on reading. 'I am too heated to sleep but will go with dreams.'

'Oh, Jesus,' Sullivan's face was red with laughter. 'I get that code all right. Big boy. Piggy wiggy.' He went into another paroxysm of laughter. Duggan couldn't help joining in, thinking this little pig went to the market. What was the rest of that? This little piggy cried all the way home. Was there a message in there somewhere?

An orderly came in, a long brown, government-issue envelope in his hand, and looked from one to the other. He saluted Duggan who stopped laughing. 'Captain McClure said this was for you, sir.'

'Thanks, corporal.' Duggan took the envelope, thinking that was quick, the Special Branch report on Harbusch's money. Its flap was already open and he tipped its contents onto the table. It wasn't the branch report: it was another letter from Harbusch to the Copenhagen address. It had been posted the previous day and been opened by the postal censors. He shook out the single page and opened it out on the table.

The letter sounded positively enthusiastic compared to the earlier ones Duggan had seen. 'We have a very important buyer for the surplus equipment,' Hans had written. 'The customer's senior staff are enthusiastic about it and the difference it will make to their production. All that is awaited is the formal approval of the managing director. Please advise soonest on delivery arrangements and final price.'

Duggan read through the central paragraph several times. A deal had been done, he thought. Arms for the IRA. Whatever had been blocking a deal had been unblocked. Something had happened to turn the tone positive. Was that why internment had been introduced? Could that be linked to Brandy? he wondered, conscious of McClure's instruction to look out for changes in Harbusch's activities. This looked like a change of activity. Certainly a change of tone. McClure had already seen it, he realized, he had sent the orderly around with it.

'Any more piggy wiggy stuff?' Sullivan broke into his thoughts.

'Pages of it,' he pointed at the file. 'Gets a bit boring after a while though. Doesn't go into any real detail.'

'Not as boring as this,' Sullivan indicated his pile of files.

'What is it?'

'Trawling through old files looking for references to Stephen Held. See if we can track down any of his other associates. Who might be hiding Brandy.'

'I'll tell you if I see anything else interesting.'

'Them continentals,' Sullivan shook his head. 'All sex mad.'

Sex mad, all right, Duggan thought. Held was half a continental and living with an English woman who was someone else's wife. If Timmy was right. Hans had been with Inge in London, was now shacked up with Eliza, getting lovelorn letters through a secret box office from this woman in Holland who only signed herself P and sometimes didn't sign them at all. He went back to the Harbusch file but flicked through the rest of the love letters at speed. They were repetitive. And if there was a hidden meaning in them he couldn't see it.

The only other thing in the file was a report on the other residents of the house where the Harbusches had their flat. There were six flats there altogether, two of them unoccupied when the report was done two months earlier. The ground floor had a newly married couple, he a junior doctor, she a civil servant until her marriage, and an elderly man who taught piano at the Royal Irish Academy of Music. On the first floor was a spinster who had retired home to Dublin after a lifetime working for an insurance company in London and, in the other flat, two girls from Cork who worked in the Land Commission on the other side of Merrion Square. The Harbusches were on the second floor and the empty flats on the top floor. Discreet checks on all of them had shown no connections with

Germans or subversives or raised any suspicions.

He closed the file and got up. 'I'm off to see Hans,' he said.

'Mind your piggy wiggy.' Sullivan set himself off giggling again.

'You're only coming here for the biscuits,' Sinéad said to him as he passed her desk.

'It's the tea,' he said. 'The way you make it.'

'Just like your mammy, I suppose,' she gave him a sideways look, as if to say she knew his type. 'You're just in time. As usual.'

'I'll bring it up,' he offered. 'Save you the trouble.'

'Okay,' she said and went down the hall to the return where there was a small kitchen with an electric kettle, a bottle of milk, a packet of Marietta biscuits, and a scattering of cups on a small table. The kettle was already boiled and he waited while she made a fresh pot of tea, took a tray from behind the door and poured out two cups. She put four biscuits on a plate, then took an extra one from the packet. 'For you,' she said. 'For saving me a journey.'

'I'll give it to Petey,' he said. 'He's so lonely up there.'

She gave him an odd look and he climbed the stairs too quickly with the tray in both hands and was breathing heavily when he got to the top.

Gifford shook his head at him when he arrived. 'No,' he said. 'Doesn't work. You still look like a soldier. Maybe if you put on a little white apron, a black dress. And got some new shoes . . .'

'I was going to give you the extra biscuit,' Duggan said. 'But you can fuck off now.'

'An extra biscuit?' Gifford narrowed his eyes and pointed a finger at him. 'You keep away from her.'

'Are you, ah, going out with her?'

'Fucking culchies,' Gifford took a cup of tea and three biscuits.

'Arrive in the big city with mouths hanging open. Looking like gob-daws. Then start getting uppity. Eating your biscuits, moving into your house, stealing the love of your life. Trying to.'

'Afraid you can't compete with a real uniform?' Duggan laughed.

'Uppity or what,' Gifford bit into the three biscuits together and they broke up and bits fell to the floor. 'Fuck,' he muttered through a mouthful of biscuit.

Duggan laughed and went to the window. The spell of good weather was over, the day was dull and the heat lay heavy on the city, trapped under an off-white eiderdown of cloud. 'Are they still digging the shelter down there?' he asked. He couldn't see any activity over the curtain of trees.

'They've stopped,' Gifford said. 'Must've finished. Or else found themselves in Australia. Could be a useful bolthole. Run over there, dive in and find yourself in Australia.'

'Could be,' Duggan said. 'Things are looking dangerous.'

Gifford nodded to himself behind his back. 'Busy morning in the Red House?'

'Busier in the Castle, I'd say.'

'Yeah,' Gifford kicked a copy of the *Irish Press* that was lying on the floor. 'I read all about it in the paper.'

Duggan turned to look at him, surprised at the bitter edge in his voice. He had thought Gifford never took anything seriously, could make a joke out of everything.

'We're the ugly ducklings,' Gifford sighed. 'But we'll have our day. Right, General?'

'If you say so, Commissioner.'

Gifford laughed and said to the window, 'Come on, Hansi, show us your hand.'

'Nothing moving there?'

Gifford waved a hand at the view in answer. The leaves on the trees were a still life against the matt canvas of the sky.

'Did they go out at all yesterday?' Duggan asked.

Gifford shook his head. But they must have, Duggan thought. One or other or both of them. To post the letter. Gifford must've missed it. Reading the paper, chatting up Sinéad, lying on the floor. Or else they had another way out.

Gifford gave him a questioning look but Duggan pretended not to see it. 'Were you in their flat for the search?' he asked.

'Ah, you've read the file,' Gifford said.

'At last. They gave it to me.'

'I'm sure it didn't say what really happened.'

'It said nothing suspicious was found.'

'That's one way of putting it,' Gifford laughed. 'It was a right fuck-up.'

'You were there?'

'No. I was the runner.' Gifford saw the question coming and explained. 'Hansi and Eliza were on one of their shopping and banking sprees. And my job was to run back ahead of them when they were coming home. To alert the lads who were breaking and entering.'

'Breaking and entering?' Duggan said. 'Wasn't there a search warrant?'

Gifford looked at him like he was a bit slow. 'Anyway,' he continued, 'the genius who was supposed to pick the lock couldn't get it open. The other fellows with him were all gathered around the door, cursing and swearing. Making such a racket that this old fellow who lives downstairs put his head up the stairwell and threatened to call the guards. One of them had to go down and explain they were the forces of law and order. Scared the bejaysus out of him. They were only in the place about five minutes when I got there, telling them to get the hell out.'

'Jesus,' Duggan shook his head.

'Then the genius with the locks couldn't lock the door. I don't know if he ever got it locked properly. We were out just before the lovely couple waltzed around the corner. Went scurrying into Mount Street. Looking as guilty as sin.'

'So it wasn't much of a search?'

'They wouldn't have found anything incriminating unless there'd been a big signed picture of Adolf on the wall saying, Hansi, I love you, you are my number one best spy.'

'Shit.'

'And don't start getting all superior,' Gifford warned. 'There are stories I could tell you about your fellows.'

'I know, I know,' Duggan said without conviction. 'But it means that the place hasn't been searched. And Hansi knows someone was there.'

'Probably. I doubt our man got the door locked. He said he did, nobody believed him.'

'I suppose he knows he's being watched anyway,' Duggan suggested.

'An exhibitionist if you ask me. The way he parades Eliza around.' Gifford gave him a sly look. 'And writes dirty letters.'

The thought struck Duggan, why were there no love letters from Hans to the woman in Amsterdam? Did he not write to her? Then why would she keep writing to him? There weren't any references in her letters to any from him, he realized. They were just a one-sided lovelorn yearning. 'Does everybody know about these letters?' he asked.

Gifford nodded. 'We lead such unexciting lives. A file with sex in it is gold dust.'

'You haven't read them?'

'We don't get to see such things. Too busy with the local patriots. And trying to do your dirty work, of course.'

'They're not very exciting,' Duggan said. 'Funny rather than dirty.'

'Do tell.'

Duggan tried to remember some of the phrases but couldn't get their strange phrasing. 'They're just romantic stuff but the English is a bit odd. Makes them funny. I'll bring you a sample.'

'Something to look forward to,' Gifford rubbed his hands and changed tack. 'What happened yesterday that makes you think Hansi went out?'

Duggan looked at him, unable to dodge the direct question. 'He posted a letter,' he said. Maybe somebody else was writing the letter in Hans's name, he thought. No. That's getting too complicated.

'Ah,' Gifford nodded. 'You think he slipped out while I was having a piss. Or something.'

'No,' Duggan lied.

'He could've gone out while I was otherwise engaged,' Gifford conceded. 'But I didn't see him come back either. Chances of me not looking when he was going and coming are a bit less, I think.'

'Maybe we should have another look. See if there's some other way out of there.'

'Have a look around the back,' Gifford suggested. 'He could be crossing into a neighbour's garden and coming out their back gate.'

'We should really have somebody around there all the time.'

'Hansi's not a priority. Unless that's changed.'

'No,' Duggan said. 'Only if some link with Brandy emerges.'

'Hmm,' Gifford said. 'The pace of things has speeded up. Always a bad sign. For us in the lazy brigade. Not you, of course.'

'I'll have a look around the back,' Duggan said. 'I've got to go up to Mount Street anyway.'

'You could sit on your bike there for a while,' Gifford suggested. 'Pretend to mend a puncture. A slow puncture.'

'Great idea,' Duggan tried to give him a sarcastic look. 'Thanks.'

'By the way,' Gifford said, 'I should have some information about your cousin later.'

Duggan cycled through the archway on Mount Street that lead behind the Merrion Square houses and braked on the incline to slow himself to a minimum. He counted the backs of the houses to Hans's and looked at the second floor windows: they were as bland as the milky sky, whether with blinds or reflection wasn't clear. The back wall was overgrown with greenery which drooped over into the lane. A weathered door, its paint peeling, looked as if it hadn't opened for years. He freewheeled by and stood on the pedals to see if he could see anything inside but the walls were too high.

He went on through the archway onto Lower Mount Street and sped up down the road to the nurses' home. The doorman gave him a look that said you're not fooling me when he asked for Stella Maloney. 'Up for the day again,' he sneered. 'Cycled all the way this time.'

'Please,' Duggan said. 'It's important. Family business.'

The doorman went away with a snort of scepticism that said he knew what kind of family business Duggan had in mind.

Stella appeared in uniform a few minutes later, nodded to Duggan and walked by him. He followed her and they turned towards the canal and crossed the road to its bank. Two boys were fishing a little farther up, their corks still on the surface, broken here and there with tiny ripples from some underwater activity. Stella stopped and turned to him, folding her arms in a defensive gesture. 'I've told you all I know,' she said.

'I've seen the ransom note,' he said.

She stared at him, looking from one eye to the other.

'We need to put a stop to this before it goes any further. Gets out of hand.'

She shook her head from side to side, still staring at him. 'What?'

'I've seen the ransom note,' he repeated. 'And the second one threatening to tell her mother.'

'What ransom note?' Her face twisted into a squint-eyed question. 'What are you talking about?'

'Her father got a note saying she was being held hostage. Demanding five thousand pounds,' he said, watching her reactions.

'She's been kidnapped?' Her astonishment seemed genuine. 'Nuala?'

'Well,' Duggan began, trying to phrase this the best way, 'she appears to have been kidnapped. But I don't think she has been.'

'She,' Stella began, 'she's been kidnapped but she hasn't been?'

Duggan took out his packet of Sweet Afton and offered her one. She shook her head and kept her eyes on him while he lit a cigarette.

'She's pretending to have been kidnapped,' he turned a little to one side to blow a stream of smoke away from her face. 'To give her father a hard time.'

'You're mad,' she finally broke her stare. 'Raving mad.'

'I understand her wanting to give her father a hard time,' he said. 'And I can certainly sympathise with that. I really can. But we've got to call it off before it goes any further.'

She turned a full circle and fixed her eyes on his again. 'What d'you mean? Goes further?'

'Sends a ransom note to her mother. Upsets her. And,' he added, 'Timmy calls in the guards.'

'My God.' She put a hand to her neck and dropped her chin on it. 'I don't believe it.'

'You didn't know about this?'

She looked up at him and shook her head and he believed her. He took a deep drag on the cigarette and said in an even tone, 'You didn't tell me everything yesterday.'

She dropped her head and rubbed her eyes. 'Nuala's gone to England,' she said after a moment.

'Is she in trouble?'

'Why does everyone assume she's pregnant?' she shot back, her tone full of sudden anger.

'I'm sorry . . .'

'She's not,' Stella snapped. She took a few steps away and stared at the canal. Up the bank one of the boys had started to jerk his fishing line, bored with the unmoving cork. If Nuala's in England someone else is sending the letters, Duggan thought. Either another accomplice, or someone else altogether. Someone who knew about her movements. Or someone who had really kidnapped her. He dropped his cigarette butt into the reeds at the water's edge.

'I'm sorry,' he said. 'I didn't mean to upset you. But now you understand why I'm worried.'

'What do you do?' she asked, not looking at him. 'In the army?'

'Me? I'm attached to headquarters. Just a messenger boy really. Carrying files around.'

She gave no sign that she had heard. He waited.

'Nuala's been very restless for a while. All year, really. Decided she wanted a change. Try her luck in London. There's lots of jobs there.'

'Any particular reason?' he asked, thinking of the photo of Nuala with that guy at a dinner dance in the Metropole. Richie something.

'Just bored. Restless. You know.' She shrugged.

'When did she go?'

'About three weeks ago. I was supposed to go out to Dun Laoghaire to see her off on the boat. But I was called back into work. Fill in for someone who was sick.'

'Did she go on her own?'

Stella nodded.

'Have you heard from her since?'

'No. She was to write to me when she got settled in.'

Shit, Duggan thought. Maybe she really has been kidnapped. 'Anybody else heard from her?'

'I don't know. I don't know anyone else who would've heard from her.'

'What about that guy she was with at the Metropole?'

'That wasn't serious. Over a long time ago.'

'What about the other guy? Jim?'

'Jim Bradley?' She paused. 'I'm not sure. She wouldn't talk about him.'

'Why not?'

'I don't mean she wouldn't talk about him. I mean she didn't encourage any chat about him.'

What does that mean? Duggan wondered. 'Was he her boyfriend?' He corrected himself, realizing he was talking about her in the past tense. 'Is he?'

Stella sighed like it was a deep philosophical question. 'They're good friends. I don't know beyond that.'

'Where would I find him?'

'He's a student in Trinity College. Doing law.'

'Where does he live?'

'In there. In the college. The place they call Botany Bay.'

'Do you know the number or . . . ?'

She shook her head. 'I've never been there.'

'Did she tell anyone else she was going?'

'I don't know. She made me promise not to tell anyone.'

'Why?'

She shrugged. 'She didn't want a fuss. Just wanted to go off for a few months. See how it worked out.'

'And she didn't tell her mother? Her sisters?'

'I assumed she did.' She looked at him. 'She didn't?'

'I don't know,' Duggan said, wondering if it was possible and they hadn't told Timmy. 'Her father doesn't know.'

'Don't tell him,' she said. 'You said yesterday you wouldn't tell him if I told you.'

'Oh, God,' he sighed. 'I didn't know yesterday that he'd got a ransom demand.'

'When did he get it?'

'Last week. And another one this week.'

'Posted here?'

He nodded. 'I saw the envelopes.'

They stood in silence for a moment. 'I don't know what to do,' he said.

'Do you think she's in danger?'

'I don't know,' he said. 'Maybe. Maybe it's a confidence trick. Someone who knows she's gone away secretly.'

'Who would do that?'

'Somebody she fell out with. Is there anybody like that?'

'Not that I know.'

'Any old boyfriend? Someone who might turn nasty?'

They fell silent again for a moment and then she began walking back to the nurses' home. 'Can I ask you something?' he said as he fell into step beside her. She nodded. 'Why did you show me her flat yesterday?'

'Because you asked me to,' she said in surprise.

'Was there something there I was supposed to see?'

'What do you mean?'

Duggan wasn't too sure what he meant, just a suspicion that now seemed unfair. 'Why didn't you tell me then that she'd gone to London?'

'Because she swore me to secrecy.'

They reached his bicycle before the door of the nurses' home and he stopped.

'Let me know if you find out anything,' she said. 'Please.'

He nodded. 'Is it still a secret? London?'

'Oh God, I don't know,' she said. 'Do what you think is best. In Nuala's interest. Not anybody else's.'

Back in Merrion Square he left his bicycle in its usual spot. There was no sound of any activity from inside the park; the work seemed to have finished. He wondered idly who the shelter was for, just the residents of the square or anyone. He crossed the road and went into the building and asked Sinéad if there was a telephone he could use.

'The boardroom is empty at the moment,' she said, pointing to a door off her office. It was dominated by a large rectangular table, polished to a reflective brown, lined by ten chairs with padded brown leather. The telephone was on a side table beside a door into the hallway. He had to go back and borrow Sinéad's phonebook to get the number for Leinster House.

'What's the news?' Timmy greeted him.

'Nothing much, I'm afraid,' Duggan said. 'I haven't got anywhere yet. But I was thinking it might be a good idea to put that ad in the paper.'

There was a pause at Timmy's end. 'Might it now?' he said at last.

'Just in case. To give us more time.'

'More time,' Timmy repeated.

'Yeah,' Duggan said. 'To try and find out what's going on.'

There was another long pause.

'It can be hard to get a job done properly,' Timmy said with a sigh.

Then he came to life suddenly. 'Thought that fucker'd never leave the room. You haven't found her?'

'No.'

'And you think we should put the ad in the paper?'

'Yeah.'

'To give us more time?'

'Yeah.'

'And then what?'

'We'll see. Maybe nothing'll happen.'

'Putting the ad in means I'll pay the money.'

Jesus, Duggan thought, he's only concerned about the money. 'Not necessarily. If this keeps going on you'll have to call in the guards anyway.'

'Yeah, we'll call her bluff with the ad,' Timmy told himself. 'Good idea.'

That wasn't what Duggan had had in mind, but he said nothing.

'Good man,' Timmy went on. 'You'll do it for me.'

'What?'

'Put in the ad. You can't have me going into a newspaper office asking to put an ad in the paper thanking Our Lady of Perpetual Succour,' Timmy laughed. 'Jaysus. If anyone saw me, I'd be ruined.'

'I don't think I'll have time,' Duggan said. 'Things are very busy . . .'

'This fucking country,' Timmy interrupted him, 'jailing good patriots and letting fellows who should be shot walk the streets.'

'That's why . . .'

'And not just walking the streets. In the guards and army too.' Timmy took a deep breath, as if he was addressing a public meeting. 'I said it at the time. We should've abolished both of them when we got in. Started from scratch again. With the right people.'

'Okay,' Duggan said. 'What's the wording again?'

'I'll put it in an envelope. Leave it at the front gate of Leinster House for you.'

'I'll be there in five minutes,' Duggan said angrily, expecting Timmy to ask for more time.

'Good man yourself,' Timmy said. 'I knew I could rely on you.'

Duggan slammed down the phone and left the room, muttering curses. Being treated like a dogsbody by Timmy. As if he had nothing else to do. He was going to end up in trouble with all this running around over Nuala. Sinéad looked up from her desk and sat back at the look on his face. 'If you see him,' Duggan pointed upstairs, 'tell him I'll be back.' He was out the door before she could tell him Gifford had gone out too. He crossed the road, jumped on his bicycle and pedalled with venom towards Leinster House. If Timmy's message isn't there when I get around to Kildare Street, he can fuck off and do it himself, he thought.

To his surprise, there was an envelope waiting for him when he got to the Dáil. He thanked the usher who gave it to him, got back on his bicycle, and tore it open. A pound note almost fell out as he unfolded the paper. The surprisingly childlike handwriting said, 'Thanks to Our Lady of Perpetual Succour for prayers answered – You're a great lad altogether'. Timmy had dropped his initials from the text of the ad; there was nothing in the envelope to identify him.

He put it in his pocket and cycled down Kildare Street and was about to swing into Nassau Street when Hans and Eliza Harbusch crossed the road in front of him, hand in hand, ignoring the little traffic there was. He braked to let them by and looked back towards Merrion Square. Gifford was walking towards him, waving.

'Howya,' Gifford said in a loud voice from ten yards away. 'Pity you didn't have a car and keep going,' he dropped his voice when he reached him. 'Saved the world a lot of trouble if you'd run them down.'

Duggan dismounted and walked alongside him with his bicycle on the pavement. 'Where're they going?'

'Grafton Street, I suppose,' Gifford sighed. 'I have news for you.'

Duggan had to wheel his bicycle onto the road to avoid two young women who were not going to make way for him.

'First,' Gifford said when he was back beside him. 'They haven't posted anything. And second, your cousin hasn't gone to England.'

'What?' Duggan said, making no attempt to hide his surprise.

'Definitely not,' Gifford looked at him. 'Forced my eyes away from the lovely Eliza every time we came near a pillar box. They didn't go within a foot of one.'

'Okay,' Duggan said. 'Nuala?'

Gifford shook his head. 'She didn't get a permit. Didn't ask for one.'

'You're sure?'

'That's what my man says.'

'Her friend says she went on the Holyhead boat.' Was Stella spinning me another story? he wondered. No. He'd have put money on her telling the truth. She was too surprised, too taken aback by the ransom stuff.

'Did he see her go?' Gifford asked.

'She,' Duggan corrected him. 'No, she didn't. She was supposed to go out to Dun Laoghaire with her. But couldn't at the last minute.'

They crossed the bottom of Dawson Street, Hans and Eliza still striding along ahead of them, not paying attention to anything to the left or right of them.

'Maybe there are ways around the permits,' Gifford offered. 'But my man says it's strict enough. Applies in the North as well, so there's no use getting a train to Belfast and trying to go from there.'

'It doesn't make any sense,' Duggan said, repeating a growing refrain in his own head. 'She told her friend she was going. Wanted her to come to the boat with her. But had no entry permit.'

'And didn't apply for one either.'

'And she couldn't have known her friend wouldn't go to the boat with her,' Duggan said. 'It couldn't have been a pretence.' Shit, he thought, Stella has to be lying. But he would have sworn she wasn't.

They followed the Harbusches across Grafton Street and went up the opposite footpath behind them, Duggan stepping into the gutter with his bicycle to avoid the pedestrians on the narrow footpath. He had to step back onto the footpath and stop to let a bus go by. He was so busy manoeuvring the bicycle through both kinds of traffic that he lost sight of the couple until Gifford said, 'Go with him this time.'

Hans and Eliza had stopped outside Switzers. She bent down to kiss him on the cheek and he went into the department store while she continued up the street. Duggan looked for somewhere to leave the bicycle which wasn't against a shop window, found a narrow stretch of wall, and hurried in after him.

Hans was wandering slowly through the make-up department, pausing to look at displays of lipsticks and powder-compacts. A saleswoman offered to help him but he declined with a smile and a little bow, doffing his hat. Duggan meandered around behind him, keeping what he thought was a discreet distance. The shop was not busy, a scattering of women wandering around, browsing. Hans wandered into the lingerie department, studied some mannequin displays at his leisure, picked up a flesh-coloured silk slip and held it out in front of him on its hanger. A young saleswoman gave him a filthy look as she went by, not offering any assistance. Hans bowed slightly, doffed his hat, and said in a soft voice, '*Fraulein*.' She passed by Duggan giving him a look that also said 'pervert'. He blushed a bright red, cursed to himself, and retreated to the staircase in the centre of the floor and took refuge behind it.

He could still see Hans's hat wandering about, in no hurry. What was he doing? Trying to meet somebody? Shake off anyone following him? If he was meeting someone it had to be a woman: there were no men at all on the floor apart from the two of them. If he was trying to spot a follower, he'd probably succeeded. Duggan felt himself stick out like a red warning signal.

Hans eventually drifted towards a door onto Wicklow Street and Duggan waited until he went through it before he made a dash for it. He looked left and right as he exited. Hans was going back towards Grafton Street. He followed him up the street past Bewley's Café. Hans stopped outside the Royal Bank on the corner of Harry Street and seemed to be trying to make up his mind about something. Duggan halted a few doors down outside the Grafton Cinema and pretended to look at the poster for *The Stars Look Down*. It showed Michael Redgrave bending down to kiss Margaret Lockwood's forehead as she looked towards the future with satisfaction. Hans seemed to change his mind about going into the bank and waited instead for a gap in the traffic to cross the street. Duggan crossed too and followed him.

Hans turned into the Monument Creamery Café and Duggan saw Gifford sitting inside the window, pouring himself a cup of tea. Hans went into the back of the room where Eliza was waiting. Duggan sat down opposite Gifford, facing the street.

'You been running?' Gifford asked. 'You're looking a little flushed.'

Duggan reddened again as he told Gifford what had happened.

'Oh, Hansi,' Gifford laughed. 'Imagine if he's our *gauleiter* in waiting. What the country'll be like if he ends up in charge of it.'

Duggan looked at the *Evening Herald* folded on the table. A half-page ad shouted in big type 'Ireland Wants Men! She wants them at once! – She wants you ALL!' The recruiting campaign had gone into overdrive with the imminent collapse of France. And the discovery of Brandy, Duggan thought. He's more likely to be the *gauleiter* in waiting.

'Listen,' he said as Gifford detached the paper from a queen cake with a glob of cream on top. 'I've got to go and do something.'

'The cousin?'

Duggan nodded. 'I'm sorry. It's a mess. But I've got to do it.' If he didn't get the ad in the *Herald* today it mightn't appear before the weekend.

'Not to worry.' Gifford turned the cake around to see how best to attack it without getting cream all over his face. 'We'll just be saunter-ing home after this little outing.'

'Thanks,' Duggan said.

'And I'll keep an eye on the pillar boxes.' Gifford took a large bite.

Duggan walked back to his bicycle which he was half surprised to find where he left it. He cycled down Grafton Street and over O'Connell Bridge and into Middle Abbey Street where he climbed the granite steps into the newspaper office. Its public office had a long counter on one side and a couple of lectern-like stands on the other with bound copies of its recent newspapers. A few old men were thumbing through past copies. He told a grey man at the counter what he wanted and got a form to fill in. Duggan copied the text from Timmy's note and put his TM initials at the end of it.

'Thanksgiving section,' the man said when he returned it to him. 'Name and address. You have to put it there. For anything in the Thanksgiving section.'

Fucking Timmy, Duggan thought. He must've known that. Didn't want to be recognised and have to put in his real name and address or risk putting in a false name. He wrote in his own name and put down his home address.

'One insertion?'

'In tomorrow's *Herald*, please.'

The man turned to the clock on the wall behind him; it was just after 4.30. 'Bit late for tomorrow,' he said. 'Might have to wait till Saturday now.'

'Oh,' Duggan said. 'It'd be a great help if it could go in tomorrow's paper.'

The man pursed his lips, wondering what difference a day would make to Our Lady of Perpetual Succour. 'Very well,' he said and counted the words. 'That'll be one shilling.'

'Thanks very much,' Duggan said. The man rooted in a drawer for the change for Timmy's pound, counted out a half crown, a shilling and a sixpenny bit on the counter and smoothed out a ten shilling note beside them.

Five

'Orders from the captain,' Bill Sullivan told Duggan when he got back to his office. 'We're to go out to Monkstown at half seven. Keep an eye on a party at the German envoy's house.'

'Where's that?' Duggan asked.

'I know where it is,' Sullivan told him.

'And what're we supposed to do about them?'

'Observe and report.'

Duggan saw the envelope with Hans Harbusch's latest letter still on his desk. 'He didn't say anything about this?' he waved the envelope.

Sullivan shook his head. 'More piggy wiggy stuff?'

'No. Boring.'

He took the envelope and went in search of Captain McClure and found him in the other office. He and another officer were looking at a map of south Dublin pinned on a blackboard and easel. Duggan waited until McClure saw him.

'This letter. Should we send it on?'

McClure looked at it briefly. 'What do you think?'

'I think we should. Something seems to have happened. The whole tone of it is much more enthusiastic than his usual letters.'

McClure tapped it against his fingernails. 'Brandy?'

'Could be.'

'Okay. I'll pass on your recommendation.'

'If I could make another suggestion?' McClure nodded at him and Duggan continued. 'It might be a good idea to increase the surveillance on Harbusch.'

'Because of this letter?'

'Yes. And he managed to put it in the post without the surveillance seeing him do it.'

'Damn Special Branch,' McClure sighed.

'I don't think it's his fault,' Duggan said, feeling a twinge of guilt over Gifford. 'He's all alone. Only one man. And we need a closer eye on Harbusch in case Brandy links up with him.'

'Any other changes in his routine?'

Duggan shook his head and told him about Hans's visit to Switzers lingerie department, trying and failing to stop himself from blushing.

'We don't have the manpower to put more men on Harbusch at the moment,' McClure ignored his blushes. 'The Branch is stretched to the limit with the IRA. Did Sullivan tell you I want the two of you to go out to Herr Hempel's house this evening?'

'Yes.'

'He's having a garden party. At short notice. A victory party, apparently. Though they're not calling it that.' McClure saw the look of surprise on Duggan's face. 'The Wehrmacht marched into Paris today. Unopposed.'

'Oh,' Duggan said, not knowing what else to say. 'Has France surrendered?'

'It will, as soon as they can find someone in charge to do it,' McClure said. 'Not a surprise after the last few weeks. Still, changes everything.'

'Plan Kathleen?'

McClure made a noncommittal gesture with one hand. 'The experts think it's a non-runner. Flying paratroopers across England to get to Fermanagh is too risky. The RAF'd be all over them. But if they have airfields in Normandy and Brittany that changes the situation. The improbable becomes possible. A possible invasion becomes probable.'

Jesus, Duggan thought. Concentrating on Nuala and Harbusch had pushed the prospect of an invasion to the back of his mind.

'So,' McClure continued, 'we've got to keep on top of all possibilities. See who's going to celebrate this historic day with Herr Hempel.'

Duggan was about to suggest that he was not the person to do this as he wouldn't recognise anyone, but McClure added: 'I've arranged for a local sergeant to go along with you and Sullivan. Not a Branch man, a good local guard. He knows everyone out there.'

On the way back to his office Duggan diverted to the toilet and pushed in the door. It banged against someone coming out, a tall man of military bearing wearing a well-cut civilian suit. 'Sorry, sir,' Duggan saluted automatically.

'I do beg your pardon,' the man said in an unmistakable upper-class English accent.

Duggan watched him go. At least a colonel, he thought, going by his age and demeanour. But not in this army.

Sullivan drove, jerking the car as they set off and cursing each time he crashed the gears as they went down the quays and through the city centre. 'This thing's like a tank,' he said.

'Have you driven much?' Duggan asked, offering him a cigarette. He refused and Duggan lit one for himself.

'Not a lot,' Sullivan swore again as he mangled the move into second gear turning onto O'Connell Bridge. The guard on point duty made a face as they went by. The neon signs overlooking the bridge were all unlit, their tubes like faint ghosts of the pre-war era saying 'Players Please' and 'Smoke Bendico'. 'Obvious, I suppose.'

The sun had broken through again and the streets were bathed in its light. There were few people about, the evening rush hour over, too early for the evening cinemagoers and entertainment seekers. They went along Westmoreland Street, past Trinity College, along Nassau Street, and into Merrion Square. 'Harbusch's hideout's up there,' Duggan indicated as they went by. 'I wonder if he'll be out for the celebration.'

They went on down Lower Mount Street where a group of young women were coming out of the nurses' home, laughing. Stella was not among them, Duggan noted as they went by. Stella. He found it difficult to believe that she was lying about Nuala going to London. That she was that good a liar. But how else could he square the circle between her story and the fact that Nuala never sought a travel permit?

'You heard the news from France?' Sullivan asked as they went over Ball's bridge. 'You know Italy's about to invade them too?'

'I hadn't heard that bit. What about Spain?'

'They haven't moved. So far.'

'You think we're next?'

'Looks that way.' Sullivan swung by a slow-moving tram on the Merrion Road.

'Jesus,' Duggan wound down his window and tossed out his cigarette end. 'How long'll we last against them?'

Sullivan shrugged. 'Not long. Not in a formal sense anyway. We'll be in flying columns pretty quickly, I think. Hit and run stuff.'

'You're probably right.'

'Was your family involved in the War of Independence?'

'Yeah,' Duggan said. 'My father.'

'Mine too. He stuck with de Valera afterwards.' It was a subtle question, to see where Duggan's father had stood during the Civil War.

'Mine didn't take sides. He kept out of it all afterwards.'

'Wise man.'

'Never talks about it.'

'Jaysus, you're lucky,' Sullivan gave a short laugh. 'My old fellow never shuts up about it. Politics morning, noon and night in our house. That's why I had to join the army. Get some peace.'

Duggan laughed. 'That mightn't last too long.'

'Every time I go home I get lectures on strategies. How to fight the Germans on the beaches and the British on the border. One or other or both at the same time.'

'Was he in a Flying Column?'

'Flying Column my arse. He was never out of the city in his life. That's not to say he didn't do his bit. He certainly did. If even half his stories are true. Or even half true.'

It was hard to imagine, Duggan thought. A beautiful summer's evening like this. And somebody somewhere might be unrolling their plan to invade. Bring all that death and destruction here. Just as part of a bigger game. Not even the main objective. A sideshow. But there wouldn't be much time for imagining once it began.

'Where d'you think they'll land? The Germans?'

'Waterford. That's what the old fellow says. Just like the Normans, he says. And if we'd stopped the fucking Normans in Waterford in eleven whatever it was we'd have saved ourselves a load of trouble.'

'As good a guess as anywhere else.'

'Yeah, he has it all worked out. If we don't stop them on the beaches we fall back to the line of the Suir.'

'I doubt there'd be only one front,' Duggan offered, wondering if Sullivan knew about Plan Kathleen. 'They'll bomb the hell out of some place. Dublin probably. Land paratroopers somewhere else. And invade from the sea.'

'Jesus,' Sullivan glanced at him. 'Is that what the captain thinks?'

'I don't know what he thinks. That's the way they've done it with the other neutrals. Once they get the numbers and the armour on the ground they'll go like the clappers.'

And we don't have the men or equipment to stop them, he thought. They'd go for the North, engage the British there, defeat them, and take over the whole island as another base for invading Britain. Or, at the very least, tie up a lot of British troops there, keep open the option of invading England or Wales from the west as well as the south and east. And where would we be in the middle of it? Just pawns. With the IRA backing the Germans. Others backing the British. Another civil war in the middle of a world war. Jesus.

'I saw a stranger in the corridor today,' Duggan said.

'Oh,' Sullivan said. 'You met the top secret?'

'I ran into him as I was going into the jacks. Who is he?'

'A British Army colonel. Don't know his name.'

'And what's he doing here?'

'That's the question,' Sullivan said. 'You know Murphy?' – another young officer whom Duggan knew slightly – 'He asked one of the lads in the British section about him and got a lecture about the Official Secrets Act and the Treason Act.'

'Treason?'

'Yeah. It's obviously very sensitive. And very secret,' Sullivan said. 'I suppose it's about contingency planning. About asking the Brits for help if the Germans invade.'

'I thought we were neutral,' Duggan said. 'Are we doing any contingency planning with the Germans? In case the British invade?'

'Don't ask me. Haven't seen any goose-steppers around. Have you?'

'No.'

They drove down into Blackrock village and stopped outside the Garda station. Sullivan went inside and returned after a moment with a middle-aged guard with a sergeant's stripes on his uniform. Duggan got out of the front passenger seat and climbed into the back seat.

'Well, boys,' the sergeant said as they drove off, up Temple Road, 'a grand evening for a garden party. Do you know this neck of the woods at all?'

'A little,' Sullivan said. 'I'm from Dundrum.' He indicated back to Duggan. 'He's up from the country.'

'What part?' the sergeant asked over his shoulder. He had a ruddy round face and his hair was receding, beginning to grey.

'Galway.'

'I'm a Mayo man myself. Been here a long time now. Was on my way to the mail boat in 1918 but events got in the way.' He didn't elaborate and neither of them asked him for an explanation.

They went up Temple Hill and rounded a tram stopped in its tracks as the conductor tried to re-connect the trolley to the overhead wire. The sergeant waved at him and shook his head as they passed by. 'Always the same spot,' he said.

They veered into Monkstown Road, to the left of the church, and then the sergeant said, 'Look out for a sharp turn to the right around the bend here now.' Sullivan slowed and they turned into a twisty stretch of road leading uphill to De Vesci Terrace. 'Down at the end,' the sergeant said. 'And park it on this side.' They went by the terrace of large houses and stopped before a T-junction. A large house opposite them with two entrances and a circular driveway had a flagstaff in front, the German swastika hanging from it barely moving in the gentle evening breeze. There were a number of cars already in the driveway.

'Are you boys looking for someone in particular?'

'No,' Sullivan said, taking a notebook and a pen from his pockets. 'Just note down everyone who attends.'

'Everyone,' the sergeant repeated, taking out his pipe and smoker's knife. 'That could be quite a job. I expect we'll have a good turnout this evening. Given the day that's in it. But we'll do our best.'

He scraped loose the ash in the pipe, lowered his window, and tipped the ash out of the bowl. 'There's the Count,' he said as a black car swept into the driveway.

'The Count?'

'Count Berardis. The Italian envoy.' The sergeant took out a tobacco pouch and began to fill his pipe. Sullivan made a note. 'Good friend of Herr Hempel these days. Following their leaders.'

'Do you know him? Herr Hempel?' Sullivan asked.

'Oh, yes. Very old school. Prim and proper. A straight dealer, the Herr Doktor.' The sergeant put a match to his pipe, blew out a cloud of smoke and tamped the burning tobacco with the flat end of his knife. Sullivan had a fit of coughing. Duggan opened his window and lit a Sweet Afton.

Four men came walking up the path, looking serious. The sergeant rattled off their names, two of them in Irish. Members of the Irish Friends of Germany, he said. They all glowered across at the car. A few minutes later a young man in a dark suit marched down the driveway to the nearest entrance gate, looked at them, and came across the road. Sullivan slipped his notebook under his thigh.

'Good evening, Herr Thomsen,' the sergeant said through his open window.

'Good evening, sergeant,' Thomsen said in accented English. 'Is there a problem?'

'Not at all. Just here to make sure that nobody bothers you.'

Thomsen did not look convinced, glanced at Duggan and Sullivan. 'You have a great evening for it,' the sergeant offered.

'It is a great day.' Thomsen gave them the Hitler salute, turned and walked back into the grounds of Gortleitragh.

'A great day for them all right,' the sergeant said calmly. 'Certainly got their own back on the French now. Herr Thomsen is number two at the legation. And Herr Hempel's minder. They say he's the Gestapo man there. But I wouldn't know anything about that.'

'He had the Nazi party badge in his lapel,' Duggan said.

'They all wear that now,' the sergeant said. 'Like the *fáinne*, I suppose.'

Another black car came up the road with two men in it and turned into the driveway.

'The general and his factotum,' the sergeant puffed on his pipe and continued in a reminiscing tone. 'General Eoin O'Duffy. A man who thinks that his time might be coming again. Only have to swap his blue shirt for a brown one any day now. A good man in his day. Gone off the rails. And his second in command, Liam Walsh. He had a nice little number with the Italian legation but I hear they dispensed with his services recently. Probably dipping his hand in the till again.'

Sullivan wrote down the names. Duggan had barely caught a glimpse of O'Duffy, a round face, balding, as the car turned in. Their position gave them only a moment to spot occupants but it didn't seem to cause the sergeant any difficulty. Duggan doubted if he'd recognise General O'Duffy again. He hadn't seen Walsh, the driver, at all.

'Some of the neighbours,' the sergeant continued his running commentary as two middle-aged couples came down the road from behind them and crossed into Gortleitragh. 'Him I don't recognise,' he added about a tall middle-aged man who appeared behind the neighbours and followed them in.

'Hah,' he said as another car drew up outside the gates and a gaunt-looking man got out of the passenger seat. 'Sean MacBride.

Not so long since we were chasing him around the streets. Big lawyer now. Wonder if he'll be representing his sister, his half-sister, when she's up in court next week for helping Herr Brandy.' He paused. 'You've heard about Mr Brandy, I take it?'

Sullivan nodded and Duggan said, 'Yes. But not about this.'

'He left a suit behind him in Held's house. It was traced back to Switzers. Bought there by MacBride's sister, Mrs Stuart, who has some questions to answer. About why she was buying a man's suit in Switzers when her husband's in Berlin. Why it ended up in Held's house. And why someone disappeared out her back door when our lads called to her house in Laragh.' The pipe appeared to have gone out and he put another match to the bowl and puffed out a cloud of smoke. 'The bed was still warm.'

Mrs Stuart. Switzers. Hans. Duggan wondered was there a connection. Mrs Stuart could have been in the shop when Hans was there. He had no idea what she looked like. Should I mention it to McClure? he wondered. But he probably knew about the Switzers suit and all that already. Could ask him anyway.

'Timmy Monaghan,' the sergeant was saying, and Duggan looked up to see his uncle driving in the gate as two other cars slowed behind him and their indicators popped out to signal right turns as well. 'Fianna Fáil TD. Followed by his colleague, Dan Breen. The hard man himself, still dying to have another crack at the British. And,' he paused for effect as the third car turned in, 'one of your own.'

Duggan glanced at Sullivan who looked up from his notebook at the back of the car disappearing through the gateway and said, 'Who?'

'Your assistant chief of staff,' the sergeant said. 'Major General Hugo MacNeill.'

Sullivan turned around to give Duggan an interrogative look. Duggan shrugged. Maybe MacNeill is the liaison with the Germans, he thought. The equivalent of the British colonel in headquarters.

'Ours not to reason why,' the sergeant smiled at their surprise. 'When you've been at this business as long as me you'll learn not to be surprised by anything. One day you're arresting people. Next day you're protecting the same people. The day after, who knows? They're shooting you, or you're saluting them.'

The number of arrivals dwindled to an occasional latecomer and they settled down to silence. The sergeant puffed at his pipe, Duggan stretched himself out along the back seat, his head resting beside the open window. The evening was cool in the shade of the trees and the hum of conversation rose occasionally from the grounds of the house along with the strings of some classical music from an open window. After a period of silence there was a scattering of applause. Shortly afterwards a few people began to leave.

The man they had seen enter earlier whom the sergeant didn't know emerged along with a woman, middle-aged like himself. They had not seen her go in. 'Interesting,' the sergeant said, clicking his fingers with impatience. 'That's ... Her name escapes me at the moment. One of the republican women. Not one of the really frightening ones. But a true believer all the same.' He shook his head with irritation. 'It'll come to me in a minute. Might be no harm to see where they're going.'

'I'll go,' Duggan offered. He got out of the car, glad to get some exercise, and walked down Sloperton hill after the couple. They were going around the bend and he sped up and then slowed again as he followed them across the road at Longford Place and turned down the short hill towards the sea. They stopped at Dunleary Road and Duggan caught a glimpse of the man's side face as he turned to the right to check the traffic before crossing. A boxer's face, Duggan thought. They crossed the road and walked alongside the railway line towards the town. Duggan kept to the other side of the road, following the high wall of the gasworks. A couple of boats, their sails bulging to the right, headed into the old harbour from the main harbour with the help of the westerly breeze. Beyond, in the distance, lay the smudge of Howth Head. A train went by towards the city, its smoke blown back inland, stinking the sea air with its acrid taste of coal.

The woman seemed to be talking most of the time, the man nodding occasionally. They went on, like an old married couple out for an evening stroll, up the gradual incline to the Coal Quay Bridge and onto Crofton Road. Duggan kept his distance, confident that they weren't aware of his presence. The main harbour opened out to their left, above the railway lines and beyond the coastguard station and the cranes at the Irish Lights depot. A line of dinghies was making its way in towards the Royal Irish Yacht Club after their evening's racing. Duggan was just passing the Anglesey Hotel when a car came to a sudden stop, heading in the same direction. 'Well, well,' Timmy said across the road at him. 'Out for a breath of sea air?'

'Hello,' Duggan said, stopping and eyeing the couple on the other side of the road ahead of him. They weren't paying any attention to Timmy or him.

'Hop in here,' Timmy said, leaning across to open the passenger door.

Duggan hesitated. The road was empty and quiet and he didn't want to have a conversation across it. He went and sat in the car. 'Just pull in for a minute,' he said. 'Ah, I'm working.'

'Working,' Timmy hooted at him. 'What're you doing?'

Up ahead, the man and the woman had stopped for a moment at the edge of the road to check the traffic and then crossed in front of them. Timmy saw Duggan watch them.

'You're not following your man, are you?' Timmy laughed. 'Robinson?'

'Who is he?' Duggan asked as the couple crossed and went up Charlemont Avenue.

'Fellow called Robinson. A commercial traveller.'

'You know him?'

'Just met him a while ago.' The penny dropped with Timmy. 'Jaysus, were you spying on Hempel's house?'

Duggan said nothing, thinking he should get out and follow the couple up the avenue. He couldn't see them anymore.

'For fuck's sake,' Timmy said.

'Who's the woman?'

'Jaysus,' Timmy said and let the clutch out and drove on.

'Stop,' Duggan pleaded as they went by the bottom of Charlemont Avenue. There was nobody on it, no sign of the man and woman. Fuck, he thought. 'I've got to get out,' he said.

'You didn't join the army for this,' Timmy said. 'I didn't risk my life for this either. To have you fellows fucking up the greatest opportunity this country might ever have.'

Duggan was in no mood to listen to one of Timmy's lectures but there wasn't much he could do about it. He could jump from the car but there was no point in being dramatic. He had lost the couple anyway. He sat back and lit a cigarette. Timmy drove on past the railway station and the Carlisle Pier where the mail boat was waiting, a thin wisp of smoke rising from a funnel. He pulled in to the side of the road and parked just beyond the East Pier. The evening was full of strollers here.

'I was going to go for a breath of air myself,' he said. 'D'you want a walk.'

'I'm working,' Duggan said.

'Spying on decent people. Who have nothing against this country. While the real enemy is scheming away. Up to his usual tricks.'

'Who is Robinson?' Duggan asked, more out of anger than an

expectation of getting information. It was no wonder Nuala took the mail boat. If he was her, he'd have taken it too. If she had taken it.

'I don't know,' Timmy said. 'A commercial traveller. Somebody introduced me. We just said hello and that was it.'

'Where's he live?'

'Jaysus, I don't know. I didn't know I was going to get the fucking third degree over him either,' Timmy said. 'What's so interesting about him?'

'Nobody knows who he is.'

'Really,' Timmy's interest was piqued by the fact that he might have some information no one else had. 'I'd say he's spent time in the States. Touch of a Yankee accent there.'

'And the woman?'

'The one with him just now? Oh, that's just Miss Coffey. A decent old skin.'

'What was he doing at the party?'

'How would I know? Probably the same as the rest of us. There because we were invited.'

'Were you talking to General O'Duffy?' Duggan asked vindictively. He had heard Timmy's rants before about O'Duffy and his Blueshirts and what he'd do to him if he came across him on a lonely road on a dark night.

'That fucker,' Timmy said. 'I've marked Herr Hempel's cards about him. Put him right about him. Fucking opportunist. Told him not to take my word for it either. To talk to General Franco about having O'Duffy on your side. You know what happened when O'Duffy's brigade arrived outside Madrid to help out Franco?'

'I know,' Duggan said quickly. Timmy had been chortling about it for years. How O'Duffy's men marched up behind some of Franco's Moors who thought they were being attacked from the rear and turned on them with devastating effect. 'You told me before.'

Timmy laughed at the memory of the fiasco that O'Duffy's Spanish adventure had been. 'Since you're looking for information,' he said, 'I'll give you some information. Straight from the horse's mouth.' He paused. Duggan tossed his cigarette butt out of the window. 'There are no German spies in Ireland.'

'Herr Hempel told you that?'

Timmy put his finger to his lips. 'My lips are sealed. But I can guarantee you that there are no Germans here to spy on Ireland.' Timmy nodded his head at Duggan. 'That's gospel. And you can tell your lads that. As a fact. But not where it came from.'

'Not from you?'

'Leave me out of it. Not from you-know-who.'

Duggan doubted that McClure would be impressed if he turned up with information like that from a confidential source that he wouldn't name. 'So Brandy is not a spy?'

Timmy nodded. 'Now you're getting the picture.'

'You told me he was a British agent. A plant.'

'That's what we thought at first. It was all a bit too convenient. The timing. Creating a scare. Rounding up the lads.'

'So he is a German?'

Timmy nodded again.

'But not a spy?'

Timmy shook his head.

'So what is he?'

Timmy looked around him for dramatic effect and dropped his voice. 'An intelligence officer.'

Duggan stared at him.

'You're not a spy, are you?' Timmy said and answered his own question. 'No. You're an intelligence officer. And what's the job of an intelligence officer?' Timmy didn't wait for an answer. 'To get information about the enemy. His forces. Strengths. Weaknesses. All that.

Right?' It was another rhetorical question. 'And who's his enemy? Not us. The British, of course. They're at war with them, for fuck's sake. They declared war on them. And it's no crime for an intelligence officer to be in Ireland to get information about a foreign army.'

Timmy shifted in his seat, offered Duggan a cigarette from his case, and lit one for himself. There was still a steady stream of people strolling by. Scotsman's Bay was calm, the sea darkening as the day was coming to a slow end. A couple of sailing boats were beating their way slowly across the bay from the Forty Foot, making slow headway against the ebb tide.

'Why is he here?' Duggan asked at last. 'We're neutral.'

'Because his enemy is here. Still occupying part of our country.'

'So he's gone to the North, has he?'

'I don't know where he is. But he's not spying on us.'

'Why did he have maps of our harbours?' Duggan demanded and regretted it when he saw the flicker of surprise cross Timmy's face. Curb your irritation, he told himself. Don't give him any information.

'I don't know about that,' Timmy said. 'Are you sure they were his?'

Duggan took out the copy of the ad he had put in the *Evening Herald*, with Timmy's change rolled up inside. 'Your change,' he said.

'No, no,' Timmy protested. 'You keep it.'

'It was only a shilling.'

'You got it into tomorrow's paper?'

Duggan nodded.

'Have a few pints on me,' Timmy pushed back the money Duggan was still proffering. 'For your trouble.'

Duggan put the money back in his pocket and opened the door and put one foot out.

'Hold on,' Timmy said. 'I'll give you a lift back.'

'It's all right,' Duggan stepped out. 'I'll walk.'

'I knew it,' Timmy smiled up at him. 'You're the man to find out things. You'll find her all right.'

Duggan stepped out and banged the door harder than he needed to.

Sullivan parked the car outside the Red House and they went inside. 'What's new?' he asked another captain who was hurrying down a corridor.

'The usual,' the captain said. 'Someone thinks they saw parachutists land in Tipperary. Strange lights off the coast in Mayo.'

'Nothing confirmed?' Sullivan asked.

'Nothing confirmed.'

'Jaysus,' Sullivan said, 'the whole country'll be a nervous wreck if this goes on much longer. Waiting's always the worst.'

'Don't say that,' Duggan suggested. 'Invasion will be a whole lot worse.'

'At least you'll know where you stand then,' Sullivan said as he lifted a heavy typewriter onto his end of the table in their office.

Or where you're lying, Duggan thought. In a ditch. Dead.

A handwritten note on top of the Harbusch file caught his attention. 'Call your cousin Peter when you get back,' it said and gave a phone number. He didn't have a cousin called Peter and was about to ask Sullivan if the message was for him when he turned it over and saw his own name on it. He thought about it for a moment, watching Sullivan put carbon papers between three sheets of typing paper, straighten them out, and feed them into the platen of the typewriter. He picked up the phone and asked the switchboard for the number.

'Swastika Imports,' a voice answered almost immediately. Gifford.

'Cousin Peter,' Duggan said, adding for the benefit of the operator if he was still listening. 'Still acting the maggot.'

Gifford laughed. 'You got my message.'

'Just in now.'

'We should have that drink tonight.'

'It can't wait? Been a long day.'

'No time like the present.'

'Okay,' Duggan said.

'Usual place.'

'It'll take me about half an hour to finish up.'

'See you then.'

Duggan wondered why Gifford wanted to see him so urgently. It couldn't be anything to do with Harbusch or he'd have said so. Hinted at it, at least. It had to be Nuala. As he had hinted with his 'cousin'.

'Can you include a line about Robinson in your report?' he asked Sullivan.

'Sure. And that woman,' Sullivan flipped through his notebook. 'The sergeant remembered her name. Mabel Coffey.' He looked up from the notebook. 'How'll I say you identified Robinson?'

Duggan thought for a moment: he didn't want any mention of Timmy in any report. 'Just say I did. And they were last seen turning into Charlemont Avenue.' Sullivan gave him a quizzical look. 'I've got to go out.'

'Busy man.'

'Family,' Duggan shrugged.

There was still a lingering light in the western sky as he cycled fast towards the city centre. The street lights on the corners, the compromise blackout, were beginning to come on with little effect. There were few cars out, moving with their sidelights only. He cycled past a horse-drawn cab, moving slowly. A tram crossing O'Connell Bridge threw out sparks from the overhead wires as it crossed the junction of the lines at Bachelors Walk. Talk flowed from the opening doors of pubs.

On Merrion Square he coasted up towards Gifford's lookout building, unsure if he would find him there. But he knew of no other usual place for them to meet. Between the tall houses and the park, the area was gloomy, sinking into the night before the quays. As he neared Gifford's building, a figure stepped from the doorway of a neighbouring house and raised an arm in greeting.

'Is there someone up there?' Duggan indicated. 'Watching Hans?'

'The night shift. He must've done something even worse than me. Although we might be swapping places now.'

'What do you mean?'

'We'll go around to Murphy's,' Gifford said.

Duggan left his bicycle and they walked around the corner and up Lower Fitzwilliam Street towards Baggot Street.

'I've suggested that they put more people on Hans,' Duggan said. 'Increase the surveillance.'

'That won't go down too well with my people. They've got their hands full with the IRA. Another of our lads wounded in a shootout in Cork today.'

They turned into Murphy's, went past the grocery counter and into the pub. It was half full with men, the cigarette smoke and the talk building up as closing time approached. They stood at a free space at the bar and ordered two pints of Guinness. Duggan took out the shilling from Timmy's change and left it on the counter.

'I got the third degree this evening,' Gifford settled on a stool, 'about your cousin Nuala.'

Duggan sat up too and stared at him.

'Called in by an inspector and interrogated.' Gifford paused. 'Yeah, no other word for it, interrogated about my interest in Nuala. Why was I making inquiries about her? How did I know her? Why was she of interest? What did I know about her? So on and so forth.'

'Fuck,' Duggan said. 'What's going on?'

'You tell me,' Gifford said, watching the Guinness settle in their half poured pints.

'I'm sorry,' Duggan shook his head. 'It's like I told you. She's been missing for a couple of weeks. And her father . . .'

'A famous Fianna Fáil TD,' Gifford interjected.

'Yeah. I should've told you. But I don't like to mention that. He's not my favourite uncle.'

'Go on.'

'He got a ransom note.'

'Fuck,' Gifford said in surprise. 'She's been kidnapped?'

Duggan sighed. 'I don't know. Timmy thinks she's just pretending. That she's behind it. She doesn't get on with him. And she's trying to get him back for something. Her best friend now says she's gone to London. And your man says she never got a travel permit. I don't know what the fuck's going on. But I'm sorry for involving you in it. For getting you into trouble.'

They fell silent while the barman came back and topped off their pints.

'I had to tell them about you.'

Fuck, Duggan thought. 'I understand.'

'Who's James Bradley?'

'A friend of hers. Boyfriend maybe. Probably. I'm not sure. Student in Trinity College. What's he got to do with it?'

Gifford lifted his pint and took a slow sip. 'Fucked if I know.'

'They know about the ransom,' Duggan said, half a statement, half a question.

'Nobody said anything about a ransom. Or kidnapping.'

'I've been at him to report it. But he won't. Thinks it'll damage him politically if it gets out. But they know about it anyway.'

'I wouldn't assume that,' Gifford took a longer drink. 'Do you have any idea what you're involved in?'

'No.' Duggan sighed. Fuck Timmy anyway, he thought. He was never anything but trouble.

'I was hauled in,' Gifford said slowly, 'because someone else has been making inquiries about your cousin and Bradley. Someone with IRA connections. Why would they be interested in her and her boyfriend?'

'No idea. I've no idea.'

'Has she been involved?'

'With the IRA? I've no idea,' he repeated. 'I hardly know her, for fuck's sake. She's a cousin. We didn't get on particularly well. Or badly, for that matter. Just had nothing to do with each other. Meeting at family things. With nothing to say to each other. I haven't a clue what she thinks about anything.'

Gifford took another drink. Duggan lit a cigarette. Behind them an old man started to sing 'Kevin Barry' and the barman asked him to stop. He didn't.

'So, it's possible.'

'It's possible,' Duggan conceded. 'I don't know. One way or the other.'

'You could ask your uncle,' Gifford suggested.

Duggan nodded. He's been told to get information from me, he thought. Fair enough. He could hardly object to Gifford trying to use him, like he had used Gifford. 'Why would the IRA be looking for her?'

'Who knows? They're in a nervy state at the moment. Ready to shoot at anything.'

'They couldn't have kidnapped her?'

'Hardly be looking for her then, would they?'

'Obviously not,' Duggan conceded, feeling foolish, but his mind was reeling with confusion and conspiracies. 'I'll talk to her friend as well.'

'I'll come with you,' Gifford said, draining his pint and standing up. It was an order rather than an offer.

'Now?' Duggan made no secret of his surprise.

'Why not?'

'She's at work. A nurse. On night duty.'

'Good. She'll be awake then, won't she?'

Six

They left the pub as the barman began his long-drawn-out closing time ritual, only succeeding in getting the singer to raise his voice a few decibels as he wobbled with emotion through the final verse of 'Boolavogue'. They walked down Baggot Street in silence. The night was warm, almost balmy, the sky an inky indigo in the east giving way slowly to a fading blue in the west.

'I'm sorry for involving you in all this,' Duggan said as they turned into Herbert Place.

'Not to worry. Given me something to do.'

'What?'

'Investigate you.'

Duggan gave a short laugh.

'I'm serious.'

'No, you're not.'

'Yes, I am,' Gifford said. 'Deadly serious.'

'What are you investigating me for?' Duggan wasn't sure if Gifford was joking or not.

'For having a cousin the IRA's interested in. That's what they want me to look into. Follow connections.'

'That's not going to get you anywhere. I don't know why the IRA would be interested in Nuala. Certainly nothing to do with me.'

'That's what they all say,' Gifford gave him a sideways grin. 'Until they sign the confession.'

'I've nothing to confess.'

'What I want to know,' Gifford emphasised the 'I', 'is about your involvement in kidnapping.'

Two women stood across the road, on either corner of Huband Bridge, and watched them cross Mount Street Crescent.

'Like some fun, boys?' one called, pointing her hip at them. Even in the dusky light neither looked to be in the first flush of youth.

'Not tonight Josephine,' Gifford called back and gave a shiver. 'Fun. Jaysus. Can you imagine it?'

'Better not try. Are you going to tell them? About the kidnapping?'

'I might wait and see first. If there's been a kidnapping. Don't want to be giving them any more harebrained stories.'

'I've been pleading with Timmy to report it. But he won't. Afraid it'll get leaked. Damage him politically.'

'How?'

'Be seen as a sign of weakness. Or something.'

'That's mad,' Gifford said. 'How could your daughter being kidnapped be a sign of weakness?'

'Because he's supposed to be the big man. The one who makes things happen. Not the one things happen to.' He shrugged. 'Politics.'

'Could he have done it himself?'

'Kidnapped Nuala?'

'Made her disappear.'

'Jesus.' Duggan looked at him. 'No. He's a pain in the arse. Not a lunatic.'

'Just asking.'

They crossed the tram lines at Lower Mount Street.

'Besides,' Duggan added, 'why would he have me try to find her if he wanted her gone? And have you on the case now too?'

'Doesn't make sense.'

'None of it does.'

'Never fear,' Gifford clapped his hands. 'We'll get to the bottom of it. More interesting than watching Hansi.'

'Have they taken you off that?'

'No such luck. But now I'm watching you watching him. While you're watching me watching him.'

'Jesus,' Duggan sighed. 'I'll be in the shit with G2. Once they hear about this.'

'How'll they hear about it?'

'The Special Branch'll tell them.'

'They won't tell them the time of day. If they can avoid it.'

'You don't think so?'

'I know so,' Gifford laughed. 'They'll wait till they've found out you're some kind of subversive. Then create an almighty stink about it. At the right moment.'

'That's a relief.'

'Are you mad? You may end up having to be shot to get rid of the stink.'

'But I'm not a subversive.'

'What's that got to do with it?'

Duggan laughed without humour. 'So I'm going to be shot one way or the other. By our own lads or the Germans.'

'That's the size of it. Your only hope is to tell me everything. Confess to Father Peter,' Gifford said as they went through the gates into Sir Patrick Dun's Hospital. The clock on the top of the building said it was just after 11.15. They went up the steps to the closed doors, Gifford pushed on one side and it swung open.

Inside, a short man in a peaked cap drew himself up to his maximum height behind his desk and said, 'You can't come in here. The hospital's closed.'

'Police,' Gifford flashed his warrant card at him, adding for emphasis, 'Special Branch.'

'Hospital's still closed,' the porter said, unwilling to back down easily. A thin column of smoke, disturbed by their arrival, rose from a cigarette in his ashtray.

'We're looking for a nurse,' Gifford turned to Duggan.

'Stella Maloney,' Duggan said to the man.

'I'll have to call the deputy matron,' the man said, picking up his phone.

'I can call for reinforcements.' Gifford reached over and took the phone from him and held it up. 'Or we can do it quietly. Just tell us where she is.'

The porter looked from Gifford to Duggan and then pretended to rifle through some papers. 'The first floor. Turn right at the top of the stairs.'

They followed his instructions, went up the stone stairs and turned into a long corridor. All was quiet in the hospital, the lights subdued. They found her reading a file at a nurses' station halfway down the corridor. Another nurse was sitting at a desk and said, 'Yes?' as they stopped.

Stella looked up from her file and stared at Duggan, then at Gifford, then back to Duggan. 'It's okay,' she said to the other nurse. 'I know them.' She replaced the file and led them to a nearby day-room. There were wooden chairs lined up against two walls, facing each other, the third wall had some mattresses standing upright against it. The light was off and the room was gloomy, illuminated only by the night outside the window. She turned to face them.

'We're sorry for interrupting you,' Duggan began. 'Something has turned up and we need to know some more about Nuala.'

'What?' She ignored Gifford.

Duggan looked at Gifford who was watching Stella. 'The IRA is looking for Nuala,' Duggan said.

Stella gave an involuntary laugh and looked from one to the other. 'You're mad.'

'Has she ever been involved with them?' Gifford asked. 'In any way at all? Even slightly?'

Stella shook her head.

'What does she think of the national question?'

She gave a short laugh again and replied to Duggan. 'She has no interest in politics. Good, bad or indifferent. Got too much of that at home.'

'Any of her friends involved?' Gifford went on.

'No,' she faced him this time. 'Not that I know of.'

'Boyfriends?'

Stella thought for a moment. 'I don't think so.'

'So why would the IRA be looking for her?' Gifford demanded.

She made a helpless gesture with her hands. 'I don't know.'

'Who is James Bradley?'

'A friend of Nuala's.'

'Boyfriend?'

She nodded.

'Is he involved with the IRA?'

'No.'

'Does he ever say anything that would show any sympathies in that direction?'

'No.'

'What does he talk about?'

'I don't know. What does anyone talk about?' She looked at

Duggan, then back to Gifford. 'Are you in the army too?'

Gifford shook his head. 'I'm in the guards. Special Branch.'

'My God,' she sighed.

'But don't worry,' Gifford gave a smile that was indistinguishable from a grimace in the uncertain light. 'This is all unofficial at the moment. I'm just trying to help out Paul here.'

'We're very worried about Nuala.' Duggan said.

Stella sat down on one of the chairs.

'You said she'd gone to London,' Gifford said. 'But she hasn't. Not on the mail boat anyway.'

'I told you,' she spoke to Duggan, 'I was to see her off but got called in here at the last minute.'

'And you haven't heard anything from her since?'

'No.'

'Have you asked around? Checked with her other friends?'

Stella nodded. 'Nobody has heard from her.'

'What about Bradley? Have you talked to him?'

'No. He's gone home to England.'

'He's English?'

'Yeah. Well, he grew up in England anyway. I think his parents are Irish.'

'Did he go with Nuala?'

'No. She went first. He had exams.'

'How do you know?'

'Because she told me. He wanted to go to the boat with her. But she said no, stay and study.'

'She didn't want him to see her off?'

'No. Because he had an exam the next day.'

'What's he studying?'

'English and something. Philosophy, maybe.'

'Was that why she was going to England? To be with him?'

Stella thought about it for a moment. 'Might have been part of it. But she wanted to get away anyway.'

'Why?'

'She wanted a change.' She looked at Duggan. 'I told you. She was very restless, couldn't settle.'

'Was she in trouble?' Gifford persisted.

'No. Not that I know of.'

'What does he look like? Bradley?'

'About your height,' she said to Duggan. 'Dark brown hair. Brown eyes. You saw his photograph. That's a good likeness.'

'You have a photograph?'

'There was one in Nuala's flat,' Duggan told Gifford.

The light in the room changed as something moved outside, from side to side. They all glanced at the window and saw a searchlight sweep from right to left and, in the silence, heard the faint drone of an aircraft. A second searchlight shot into the sky from the right and they crossed each other, sweeping back and forth. Gifford and Duggan moved to the window and looked out. There was no sign of the droning plane. A line of red tracer bullets rose slowly into the sky from the anti-aircraft battery in Ringsend, creating a warning fan, and faded away. The sound of the plane began to fade too and after a few moments the searchlights went out.

Stella stood up as they turned back to her. 'I've got work to do,' she said, offering a small bunch of keys to Duggan. 'They're still in my pocket since the other day. If you want to see Jim's photograph.'

Duggan took them.

'He's not mixed up in anything shady,' she said. 'He's not that kind of person.'

★

They walked back part of the way they had come, turning into Mount Street Crescent at Huband Bridge where there was only one woman standing now. 'Where are your fellows hiding out?' Duggan asked as they went around by the Pepper Canister Church.

'Nearer the other end of the street,' Gifford said. 'The other side of the British outposts. Hopefully they won't see us.'

The street was empty and they walked fast to the house where Nuala's flat was. Duggan had the big key out and they went in quickly and climbed the stairs in the dark. On the top floor, he opened the door to the flat and felt inside for the light switch.

'Wait,' Gifford said in a quiet voice. 'Are the curtains pulled?'

Duggan crossed the room to the window and leaned over the table in front of the window to close the curtains. He took out his cigarette lighter and flicked it on to find his way back to the door and the light switch. He pressed the switch and nothing happened. 'The meter,' Gifford whispered.

Duggan took another of Timmy's shillings from his pocket, handed it to Gifford and held the cigarette lighter aloft as he fed it into the meter on the landing. The money dropped into the box and the light came on. The flat still had the feeling of an unused room, the air warm and stale, unmoved. It seemed to Duggan to be as it had been the last time he was there. He pulled open the drawer of the table at the window and stopped. The envelope of photographs was no longer there. Neither were the newspaper cuttings, the old one about the Kilmichael ambush, the newer one of Nuala with a man and another couple at a dance in the Metropole.

'Fuck,' he said. 'It's gone.'

'Just the picture of Bradley?' Gifford looked into the drawer.

'No. There was a Kodak envelope of snaps. Mostly family. They're all gone. And a couple of newspaper cuttings, one of a dinner dance last winter and one about the Kilmichael ambush. '

'The Kilmichael ambush? What's the connection?'

'None that I know of,' Duggan said, trying to remember what else had been in the drawer. Nothing came to mind. He looked around the flat again. Nothing else appeared to have been moved. The cup and plate were still on top of the cupboard by the sink.

'Who was at the dinner dance?' Gifford went back to the door, opened it and looked at the jamb. There was no sign of a forced entry.

'Nuala with some guy called Richie something. And another couple. Stella knows.'

Gifford pulled open the doors of the wardrobe and held them wide while he scanned the contents. 'Anything missing here?'

'I didn't look very closely the last time.' Nothing seemed to have been disturbed.

'If anybody searched the place they did it very neatly,' Gifford said, parting each of the clothes on hangers and looking underneath the jumpers folded on top of each other. He opened a drawer and went through the underwear. 'And there's no sign of a break-in. So . . .' He stopped as they heard the sound of heavy footsteps coming up the stairs. He crossed to the light switch, waved Duggan back behind him, and turned off the light. They stood with their backs to the wall behind the door as the footsteps came onto the landing, paused, and then moved across to the other door. There was another pause and then the sound of a key in a lock and, a moment later, a door closing. Gifford turned on the light again.

'Should we talk to the neighbour?' Duggan asked in a quiet voice.

Gifford shook his head. 'Keep it as low key as possible. For the moment.'

'Richie Cummins,' Duggan said. 'That was the guy with her at the Metropole dance.'

'Okay.' Gifford went back to the wardrobe again. 'Anything moved about? Different?'

'I don't know for sure,' Duggan admitted. 'Stella was with me last time. I didn't want to be pawing through Nuala's stuff.'

'Such a delicate creature,' Gifford gave him a crooked smile. 'For one who causes such mayhem.'

'Ah, the hero returns,' Sullivan said to Duggan as he walked into their office the next morning.

'What?'

'Good work last night,' Captain McClure said as he came in behind Duggan. 'Take a look at this.'

He took a photograph from the file he was carrying. It was a police headshot of a man with two views, a profile and a full face.

'Robinson?' Duggan asked, taking the picture and studying it. The face was long and thin, with a large nose, and deep-set eyes. The full face was even more like a boxer than the side face he had seen.

'Is it?'

'I think so.' Duggan handed him back the picture.

'Good,' McClure said, taking the photograph back. 'We missed him this morning. He'd been staying with the Coffey woman but seems to have moved last night. Or at least before our friends managed to get there. But at least we now know who Brandy is.'

'He's Brandy?' Duggan asked, seeing in his mind's eye the man walking with the talkative woman along the railway line with the harbour in the background. He didn't look like a high-level German spy. But what does a spy look like?

McClure nodded. 'Real name Hermann Goertz. Luftwaffe pilot in the last war. Now working for the Abwehr. Caught spying in England a few years ago, before the war, and jailed. Now on the loose here. Planning, plotting something.'

'Could I look at the picture again?' Duggan asked.

129

McClure gave it back to him and he looked at it closely. The pro-file was the same, the slightly hooked nose an easily distinguishing feature. Yes, it was definitely him. And if Timmy hadn't come along he might have been able to follow him to his new hideout. Some hero, he thought. If only they knew.

McClure gave him a questioning look. 'It's him all right,' Duggan said.

'Okay,' McClure put the picture away again and looked at his watch. 'I want to talk to everybody in twenty minutes. In the other room.'

'What's that about?' Duggan asked after McClure had left.

'Maybe going to pin a medal on you,' Sullivan sniggered.

'What happened this morning?'

'Special Branch broke the door down at half six. Nearly gave the old dear a heart attack. She was all alone but there were signs that your man had been there.'

'What signs?'

'I don't know. That's all I heard. Signs.'

Duggan sat down at the table, lit a cigarette and inhaled deeply. He pulled the Harbusch file over in front of him and opened it where he had left the marker. But he couldn't concentrate on it; things were moving too fast on too many fronts. 'You think that was him?' he asked Sullivan. 'In the photograph?'

'That was the fellow you followed all right. D'you not think so?'

'I do,' Duggan said. 'But how do they know he's Brandy?'

'Nobody tells me anything,' Sullivan sighed. 'Presume it was one of the signs they found this morning.'

'Yeah, you're probably right.' Duggan focussed his attention on the Harbusch file again, going back a couple of pages to remind him-self of what he had been reading. It was just the brief account of the other people in the building where Harbusch had his flat; nobody suspicious. London, he thought. Was Hans in London the same time as Brandy/Goertz? Were they connected there? And if they had been, were they connected here? The British would know and they would have told us if there was a connection. Wouldn't they? Or would they? They had obviously supplied the photos and information about Harbusch and Goertz. Surely they would also have pointed out any connections between them.

'Time to go,' Sullivan got up. 'Get your medal.'

The other room had filled up when they got there and they stood at the back. Duggan could see that the photograph of Goertz had joined the one of Harbusch and other suspected German agents on a display board. The murmur of voices died as McClure took his position in front of the display board.

'These are dangerous days for our country,' he began without preliminaries. 'The war which seemed distant and even unreal for many months has become all too real and is now threatening to engulf us as it has already engulfed so many other neutral states. We are inundated with alerts every day, all of which we have to check out. Some may be dry runs, testing our defences and reactions. Most are false alarms. Nothing can be left to chance.

'In this situation good information is critical. And good information relies on putting our own preferences to one side. As we should be doing in any event as good soldiers. We must not allow our own preferences for the outcome of this war to influence our judgement. On the one hand, that can lead us to inaccurate conclusions. On the other, it may be in conflict with government policy. And our job is to implement the policy of the elected government, no more, no less. That policy, as you all know, is one of neutrality. We will resist with all our might any infringement of our sovereignty. From any source.

It is also government policy, as enunciated by the Taoiseach, that our territory will not be allowed to be used as a base from which to attack Great Britain.

'There are people who, as we all know, would like us to be a base for just that. Which leads them into dangerous alliances. Whether such alliances would or would not be to Ireland's benefit in the long run is not for us to judge. They are in direct conflict with the government policy we are obliged to operate. There are many armchair generals and armchair politicians abroad at the moment who want to see one outcome or another of the war. Most of it is pub talk. It is not for us to indulge in this kind of speculation, neither at work nor anywhere else. It is for us to provide the most accurate information possible of the actions and intentions of all the parties involved. So that the real generals and our real political masters can base their decisions on the soundest possible information.

'I don't need to remind you either of the sensitivity of all the information which passes through here. Or of your obligations under the Official Secrets Act. But people can get carried away sometimes, in discussions with friends, debates with family members. Anything you know from your work here should not be used outside, even indirectly or inadvertently. Our job is clear. Our orders are clear. We must stick rigidly to them. No deviations. No solo runs. No taking sides between the belligerents.'

McClure paused and then dismissed them. Duggan stood to one side as the room emptied and approached McClure.

'I was wondering if Harbusch and Goertz knew each other in London. Worked together, I mean.'

McClure shook his head. 'Goertz was in jail when Harbusch arrived there. The British thought first that he was Goertz's replacement. But he didn't seem to actually do anything much. Like here.'

'What was Goertz doing before he was caught?'

'Collecting information about RAF airfields. Strengths, deployments. So on.' He went on without a pause. 'What did you think of my little speech?'

Duggan resisted an impulse to ask why he had made it. 'Very clear.'

'Is it possible Goertz saw you following him last night?'

Duggan hesitated. 'It's possible. But I was a good distance behind him. And he never looked around.'

'The woman?'

'She didn't either.' Shit, Duggan thought. I don't want to go down this road. They probably saw me get into Timmy's car as they crossed into the avenue. But that wouldn't have looked like I was following them. Now he's going to ask me how I knew the man was calling himself Robinson. 'If I'd been closer I might have seen where he went when they turned into that avenue. By the time I got there they had both disappeared.'

'Gone into her house. It was just up the road,' McClure nodded. 'He was there for a while anyway. Had been staying there.'

'He's definitely Brandy?'

'Yes. He left behind a coded message using the same cipher we found in Held's. Probably left in a hurry.' McClure paused. 'Somebody tipped him off.'

Duggan made no attempt to disguise his shock. Timmy, he thought. Oh, Jesus. He couldn't have? No. He wouldn't do that. Why would he do that? Okay, he wanted the Germans to win the war. But to thwart the guards and the army and his own government? No. On the other hand, he had said Brandy wasn't a spy, wasn't committing any crime in Ireland, only gathering intelligence on the British.

'I couldn't swear that he didn't see me.'

'Maybe he was just being cautious. He took a big risk going to the German minister's house party. He must have suspected that we'd be watching it. And that we'd identify the Coffey woman, if not him.

Leaves Herr Hempel and his denials about German spies in an awkward position with the government now. But that's not our concern.'

'No, sir.'

'Breaking my own rules now about armchair strategists,' he gave a half smile. 'And,' he added, going back to Duggan's initial question, 'Harbusch and Goertz are connected. They both work for the same master. Keep after Harbusch.'

Duggan turned to go, relieved that the subject had changed from the previous night's activities.

'By the way,' McClure said. 'I requested more manpower on his surveillance but there's no chance at the moment. The Special Branch's stretched to the limit.'

'Disappointed?' Sullivan asked Duggan as he returned to their office.

'Over what?'

'No medal.'

Duggan gave a short laugh and sat down at the table. 'What was all that about? That speech?'

'They say they're worried about people pursuing their own agendas.'

'Really?'

Sullivan shrugged. 'So they say. Not here necessarily. Special Branch is riddled with IRA spies. One of their fellows has been arrested. Being interrogated.'

'Jesus,' Duggan said, thinking of Gifford and hoping that he hadn't set off this chain of events with his own inquiries about Nuala. The phone rang and he picked it up and gave his name.

'The hard man,' Timmy said.

'Speak of the devil,' Duggan retorted.

'You were talking about me?' Timmy sounded pleased.

'Only joking.'

'Well, I'm going down the country tomorrow. Mona says your mother's been asking about you. Hasn't seen you for ages.'

'A month,' Duggan said, surprised at this turn of the conversation.

'You know what they're like. Women. I'll pick you up outside the barracks at eleven. We'll be back early on Sunday.'

Duggan closed his eyes. He had a weekend pass, the first in the last month. 'I've got a German lesson tomorrow.'

'Give it a miss. You can drive the V8.'

Frau McMahon, a German woman who had married an Irishman involved in building the Ardnacrusha power station, wouldn't be impressed, although she had told him the last time that all he needed was more practice. 'Okay,' he said.

'And wear your uniform.'

'What?'

'Your mother'll love to see you in it.'

Timmy hung up before Duggan could argue. It's not my mother, he thought. Timmy wants to be driven through the constituency by a uniformed man. Like it was a state car. Even though everyone there knew he was Timmy's nephew. But they mightn't see beyond the uniform as he drove past. He shook his head at the phone as he put it down on its cradle.

It rang again.

'Cousin Peter here,' Gifford said. 'We've an appointment to meet our old friend Richie after work.'

'Really?' Duggan said, thinking quickly. Richie Cummins, Nuala's former boyfriend. Or dancing companion, at least.

'After his work, that is.'

'All right. I should be able to make it.'

'See you at the usual place.'

Duggan put down the phone and opened the Harbusch file at

random. He stared at it, unseeing, thinking that things were getting totally out of hand. Should he tell McClure about Nuala? The IRA interest in her and its Special Branch conduit? About Gifford? Timmy? The snippets of information Timmy kept feeding him about government policy? And Timmy's own preferences and theories? McClure would tell him to drop all of it, it was none of his business. Not army business. But he was already out on a limb. McClure would want to know why he hadn't reported all of it immediately. Or else he'd see it as a total distraction from Duggan's real work. And, either way, not trust him anymore.

So what was the worst that would happen? He'd be sent back to the infantry. Fall down to the bottom of the promotion lists. They'd hardly throw him out of the army altogether, given the times that were in it. But he'd have no future in the military. If this army had a future at all. He'd joined out of a sense of duty, something expected of him, although he had had no thoughts of a military career as such. But he realized suddenly that he did like the idea of it now. And not in the infantry. But in what he was doing at the moment. Trying to piece together the shifting hints and puzzles of other people's aims and intentions. He didn't want to let it go, now that he had only begun to do it. Not yet anyway.

'Piggy wiggy code still impenetrable?' Sullivan said. 'If you'll excuse the pun.'

'What?'

'You've been sighing away over that page for ages now,' Sullivan laughed. 'Like a lovesick girl.'

'Maybe it's catching,' Duggan said. 'Why does he never write back to her?'

'Doesn't want to encourage her. Doesn't want to know her any-more.'

'So why does he bother picking up her letters?'

'For a laugh. Wouldn't you?'

No, Duggan thought, and said aloud, 'And why does she keep on writing letters to which she never gets a reply? As far as we know.'

'Because she's besotted,' Sullivan giggled at the word, as if it was funny.

Maybe. A phrase in one of the letters caught his eye: 'always and ever will I wait for your comeback to our haven in the hillsides.' You could turn it into more recognisable English. I'll always wait for you in our country retreat. Hideout. Love nest. Whatever. But what'd be the point of that? Hans was German, the woman, if she was a woman, maybe Dutch. But the Dutch didn't have hillsides, did they? Either way, they wouldn't be playing word games in English. Wouldn't make any sense.

'That Coffey woman who was hiding Brandy was on my list,' Sullivan was saying. 'From trawling through the files.'

'Yeah?'

'Far down it, but there. Among the remnants of the widows and childers party.'

'The what?'

'You never heard of the widows and childers party?' Sullivan gave him a doubting look that suggested that Duggan was not what he had thought he was.

'No.'

'The widows and sisters of the dead heroes of the republic and Erskine Childers. The madames and countesses and all them. And Childers. All the irreconcilables.'

'Ah, right. She's one of them?'

'On the edges.'

Duggan rooted in the drawer of the table and found a large used envelope with Saorstát Éireann printed on it. 'Are many of them still around?'

'Not many. But a good few followers. Daughters of the widows and childers, I suppose.' Sullivan laughed. 'We're widening the list. These Germans seem to like shacking up with women.'

'Hey, you might get the Brandy medal yet,' Duggan laughed and slipped a couple of pages from the Harbusch file into the envelope as Sullivan bent down to pick up a sheet of paper that had slipped off the table. He knew this was a step too far. Removing secret documents, deliberately disobeying orders. But in for a penny, in for a pound. If he could crack the Harbusch case, he'd be well set up. He closed the file and stood up and left with the envelope.

'Curious,' Gifford said with an air of professional detachment as he turned over the last page.

Duggan stood in the window, looking at the windows of Harbusch's flat. They were as bland and unenlightening as usual.

'Very curious indeed,' Gifford said, as he finished reading the letter.

Duggan turned from the window and gave him an inquiring look.

'Foot fetishists,' Gifford said. 'They're an obscure offshoot of the original Balkan anarchists. Very dangerous. Their aim is to blow . . .'

'Seriously.' Duggan held out his hand and Gifford gave him back the pages. He had hoped that Gifford might see something that he hadn't seen himself.

'Seriously. We will take a closer look at Hansi's feet the next time we are privileged with his presence.'

Duggan put the pages back into the envelope, careful not to bend them.

'Feet to me are things for walking,' Gifford said. 'Or marching, in your case. My thoughts tend to hover around higher things.' He looked at his watch. 'We could ask Sinéad's advice on our way out. See what she thinks of them.'

'Jesus,' Duggan said with a touch of irritation. 'I could be court-martialled for showing these to you.'

'Never fear,' Gifford clapped him on the shoulder. 'Your secret will go with me to the grave. After they've extracted all my fingernails and toenails.'

They walked down the stairs and Gifford blew a kiss to Sinéad as they went by the reception desk. Outside the hall door Duggan stopped and looked over towards Harbusch's flat, hidden now by the corner of the park. 'We're taking a big chance,' he said. 'We could miss something important.'

Gifford shook his head. 'Or we could sit here till kingdom come and nothing will happen. Come on.'

They set off towards Leinster House, doors opening in many of the houses as people left work and the numbers of passing cars and bicycles increased. 'Could there be a connection between the house Hans is in and the others on either side?' Duggan mused.

'Apart from the fact that they're holding each other up?'

'Apart from that,' Duggan smiled at the image of them all falling like dominoes. 'A door from one to the other. Something like that.'

'No. That was checked out too. The owners and occupants are different. There are no connecting doors from one to the other. Not officially anyway.'

They went down the other side of the square and along Clare Street and Nassau Street, walking with purpose and skipping around the office and shop workers filling the footpaths. They turned into Dawson Street and Gifford stopped before an insurance company and took up position against a wall.

'How will we know him?' Duggan asked.

Gifford reached into his inside pocket and took out a photograph.

'How'd you get that?' Duggan looked at it and tried to memorise the unmemorable features.

Gifford took his eyes off the main door of the building as a group of girls came out and winked at him. They watched people emerge from the insurance company in dribs and drabs, young men singly, young women in groups. All the men looked much the same to Duggan, all dressed in dark suits that seemed too big for them, their only distinguishing feature an occasional red or blond head among the shades of brown and black.

'There he is,' Gifford muttered as a thin young man emerged and turned left up the street. Duggan had no idea how or why Gifford was so sure but fell into step beside him as they followed the man up the street, across Molesworth Street, and on up to Stephen's Green. The man stopped at the corner by Alys Glennon's dress shop and seemed undecided.

'Please cross to the park,' Gifford muttered.

As if he had heard him, the man looked both ways and sped across the road to the path beside the park. 'Good lad,' Gifford said as they hurried after him, dodged through the two-way traffic and ignored the curses of an old cyclist after forcing him to brake and wobble. Gifford kept pace with the man for a few strides then hurried to catch up with him as they approached a gate into the park.

'Richie Cummins,' he said, stepping slightly in front of him at the gate and holding out his warrant card in front of his face. 'We want to talk to you for a moment.' Duggan stood behind Cummins, leaving him nowhere to go but into the park.

They stopped inside on the park's perimeter path. Whatever colour had been in Cummins's face had gone and his dark eyes flicked back and forth from one of them to the other, his fear flashing like a beacon.

'Nuala Monaghan,' Gifford said.

'I don't know where she is,' Cummins shot back. Duggan glanced at Gifford.

'How do you know she's missing?' Gifford held Cummins's stare.

'That's what the other fellows told me.'

'What other fellows?'

'Two fellows. I don't know who they were. Stopped me the other night. Like you.'

'Police?'

'They didn't say.'

'What did they say?'

'They asked me' – Cummins gulped air through his mouth – 'where Nuala Monaghan was.'

'And?'

'And I told them I didn't know.'

'And what'd they say?'

'They, they . . . One of them took out a gun and pointed it at my knee.'

'And?' Gifford glanced at Duggan.

'They told me to tell the truth,' Cummins started talking faster. 'And I told them I was telling the truth. I didn't know where she was. And he said he'd ask me one more time and he pulled back the hammer on the gun and put it against my knee and I said I couldn't tell them where she was because I didn't know where she was and . . .' He stopped and looked like he was about to cry.

'What happened then?' Duggan asked, for the first time.

'They went away,' Cummins wiped his nose with the back of his hand. 'They said that if they found out I was lying they'd come back and . . . finish the job.'

'And were you lying?' Gifford demanded.

'No,' Cummins raised his voice. 'I don't know where she is.'

'You were going out with her?'

'No, I wasn't. I only went out with her once. And that was a blind date. It wasn't even a date.'

'The dance in the Metropole?' Duggan asked.

Cummins nodded, like it was the worst experience in his life. 'She was supposed to go with someone else but he stood her up at the last minute. And my sister asked me to go with her. And I did.'

'Your sister is a friend of hers?' Gifford shot back.

'Not really. They worked in Clery's together.'

'You never went out with her again?'

'I never saw her before or after that night,' Cummins said plaintively. 'And she hardly said a word to me the whole time.'

'Did you fancy her?'

Cummins looked as if Gifford was mad and shook his head.

'Your picture was in the paper with her,' Duggan said. 'With another couple. Who're they?

'I don't know,' Cummins looked at Duggan for the first time, relaxing a little. 'They were just at the dance too. A photographer asked us to stand together and smile. That was it.'

'These fellows who accosted you,' Gifford said. 'Who were they?'

'I don't know.'

'Do you think they were policemen?'

Cummins shook his head cautiously, as if it might be a trick question.

'Who then?' Gifford asked.

'I don't know.'

'Have you seen them again?'

'No.'

'Could you describe them?'

'They were just,' Cummins shrugged, 'fellows. In their twenties.'

'Like us?'

'No, no. Rough types.'

'Are you a member of any illegal organisation?'

'No.' Cummins looked shocked at the thought.

'You should call the guards if you see them again,' Gifford said.

'Oh, I will, I will,' Cummins lied.

'Thank you for your assistance,' Gifford said to him and stepped back from the path onto the grass. 'We won't be troubling you again.'

'Thanks.' Cummins lowered his eyes and walked away quickly.

They watched him go, his dark suit looking like it had become another size too large for him. 'Another innocent bystander,' Gifford said, as if there were too many of them in the world. 'Fuck.'

Duggan lit a Sweet Afton and blew a stream of smoke onto the calm evening air. Across the grass from them lay the pond, its surface cut by the perfect bow wave of a stately duck. Two people were silhouetted against the water, sitting on a bench, their heads together.

Seven

Duggan was on his second cigarette by the time Timmy drove up outside the barracks, half an hour late. He dropped it on the path and ground it out with his foot as Timmy hauled himself out of the driver's seat and went around to the passenger side. He lifted a copy of the *Irish Press* off the seat before settling in. 'Home, James. And don't spare the horses,' he said, as Duggan eased up the clutch and they moved off.

Timmy opened up the newspaper as they went down Conyngham Road alongside the Phoenix Park, Duggan speeding up through the gears to almost sixty miles an hour. Timmy didn't seem to notice the speed, or didn't care. Unlike his own father, Duggan smiled to himself, who'd never let him drive like this. He slowed as they came to Chapelizod and crawled around the sharp bend of the Liffey bridge. Timmy chortled at something in the paper as Duggan accelerated up the hill on the other side in second gear.

'Have you heard the latest about Frank Aiken and the newspapers?' he asked.

'No.'

'He's having the time of his life fucking them around. Being in charge of censorship is much better than being chief of staff of the army,' Timmy explained, not needing to specify in which army Aiken had been chief of staff. 'Anyway, his latest one was over something in the Kingstown Presbyterian Hall, a bridge meeting or something. There's no such place, he said. There is no Kingstown any more. So there can't be a Kingstown Presbyterian Hall. And, of course, that Protestant rag, the *Irish Times*, wouldn't rename it the Dun Laoghaire Presbyterian Hall. They said there's no such place as Dun Laoghaire Presbyterian Hall.'

'So what happened?'

'I don't know,' Timmy said. 'Still up in the air, I think.' He gave a short belly laugh. 'Like his other one about the lifeboats. The RNLI. He wouldn't let the papers use its name or initials. It couldn't be royal and national at the same time, he told them. Had to be one or the other. And, of course, if it was royal it might be encouraging one of the belligerents and a breach of neutrality. So it had to be national if it wanted to get into the papers.'

'Did they change it?'

'No,' Timmy said with a touch of regret. 'Someone told Frank to back off, stop being silly. Must've been the Chief. You couldn't imagine anyone else telling Frank what to do.'

Duggan glanced at Timmy as they came up the hill out of Lucan, past the Spa Hotel, wondering if he was becoming disillusioned with de Valera. That'd be some turnabout. But it was the second time in the last week that he'd heard Timmy being critical, however oblique-ly, of the Chief. As if he was reading his mind, Timmy said, 'That was a great stroke of the Chief's, creating a Defence Council and getting the Opposition into it.'

'Yeah?' Duggan increased speed again as the land levelled out and they headed for Maynooth.

'It's just a talking shop. No power at all. Get them in there, tell them nothing, and let them talk their heads off. Which they're doing. And compromising themselves with every word from their mouths.'

'How are they doing that?'

'You haven't heard the latest Fine Gael plan?' Timmy sounded disappointed with him. 'They've gone into a total funk over the collapse of the French. Afraid we're going to be next. And suggested that we put our army and the Brits in the North under the command of a French general so we can all fight the Germans together if they invade.'

'Interesting idea,' Duggan offered.

'Interesting, my arse,' Timmy retorted. 'In the first place, the Germans are not going to invade. We're not their enemy. It's just a way of getting us onto the losing side. But it shows clearly which side those lads are on. Never mind what they say in public.'

'Has this been in the papers?'

'Of course not,' Timmy sounded outraged. 'The Chief's just storing it up for a rainy day. When it'll be of maximum use.' He paused and then gave another of his chuckles. 'There's no shortage of French generals hanging around with nothing to do, I suppose. But I wouldn't want any of them on my side.'

Timmy folded his paper and tossed it onto the back seat. He tipped his hat forward, its brim shading his eyes, and he settled back in his seat, arms folded over his stomach. 'I'll have a little nap. Prepare myself for the constituents.'

Duggan drove on, enjoying the car. It responded well, more powerful than anything he was used to. He'd have liked to floor the accelerator but there were few stretches of road straight enough for long enough to do so. And he wasn't at ease yet with its handling in the bends and the varying height of the camber of the road. There were few other cars on the road, some horses and carts, and an occasional hay cart.

The countryside was a bright green, the hedges and trees broken up with golden stretches of ripening corn. The hay fields were few and far between, the result of the tillage orders, and there were men in some of them, tossing the hay into cocks. Farm dogs darted out of gateways to bark furiously at the passing car and race beside it until it out-paced them. Duggan held his course, ignoring them; they knew when to turn away to avoid colliding with the car.

He went through Kinnegad and turned off onto the Galway road and continued through villages, sleepy and silent in the midday sun. Timmy slept in silence too, if he was sleeping at all – Duggan had expected him to be as loud asleep as he was awake – and only stirred himself when they eventually crawled through the narrow main street of Athlone. He straightened up, pushed his hat back on his head, and looked out at the shops as they went by. They crossed the bridge over the Shannon, by a line of men with their backs to it, watching the passing parade, and went along the other side of the river, past the military barracks.

'They're going to lock up the spies in there,' Timmy nodded at the barracks. 'If they ever find any.'

'But there are no German spies. You said.'

'English spies.' Timmy took out his cigarette case and held up one for Duggan. Duggan took it and Timmy lit his and his own.

'Do you know a fellow called McClure, a captain in your place?'

Duggan coughed over the smoke, masking his surprise. 'Yeah,' he said, as neutral as possible.

'What's he like?'

'He seems very straight. Good at what he does.'

'And what's that?'

'Intelligence work.' Duggan stated the obvious, unsure of what Timmy knew about McClure or why he was asking these questions. It wasn't beyond him to try and trap him into lying or holding back something. Timmy liked to test people.

'Hmm,' Timmy said, opening his window and tipping the ash out as they passed the last straggling houses on the western edge of the town. 'Is he trustworthy?'

'What do you mean?' Duggan glanced at him.

'I mean can he be trusted in the present circumstances?'

'A hundred percent,' Duggan said, with emphasis, holding back a touch of anger. Could he be trusted to implement the government policy of neutrality, unlike yourself, he was tempted to ask.

'You know he's a Protestant?' Timmy said.

'No,' Duggan said automatically. 'Like Wolfe Tone,' he added.

'His father was in the British army.'

'Wolfe Tone's?' Duggan shot back.

Timmy looked at him and ignored the comment. 'The Boer War. Wounded there and invalided out.'

Duggan rolled down his window and tossed his cigarette butt out. Timmy did the same on his side and closed his window.

'As I see it,' he said, 'we have two main problems in maintaining all we've won in the last twenty years. More and better arms for you fellows, and fifth columnists.'

'Like the IRA.'

Timmy ignored that. 'The British won't give us the arms. And they won't let the Americans give them to us either. Which tells you everything you need to know about their intentions. They don't want us to be able to defend ourselves against them. Right?'

Duggan made a noncommittal noise.

'The other problem is fifth columnists. Not the IRA, English fifth columnists. There's a fair few in the army these days. Too many of them. Some in important positions. People whose loyalty we can't rely on when push comes to shove. Who'd fight the Germans all right, but won't fight the British. That's why we have to get as many of the right people into the right positions as quickly as possible.'

A number of things clicked into place in Duggan's mind. That's why people like himself and Sullivan, lads with the right background, had been moved into G2. And maybe that was what McClure's speech yesterday was all about; not a warning to us but a declaration of loyalty by him. He must know that he was an object of suspicion to the likes of Timmy, untrustworthy because of his family's previous allegiance. Or what the likes of Timmy thought was his family's allegiance. Just because his father fought in the Boer War didn't mean he was a unionist.

He thought of saying some of this to Timmy but held his breath and concentrated on the driving as they went down into Ballinasloe, past the huge grey mental asylum with its prison-like walls.

'I got an answer to your ad in the paper,' Timmy said.

'Oh,' Duggan said in surprise, noting the 'your ad' as if it had been all his doing. He had half expected that the ad would be the end of it. That its appearance would have left the instigators, probably including Nuala, rolling around with laughter at the idea of Timmy offering thanks to Our Lady of Perpetual Succour. No doubt, the story would circulate in political circles and surface in obscure references in the Dáil or county council or on election platforms to Timmy's devotion. To the bewilderment of the public, if they noticed at all, and the delight of an ever-growing circle of the knowing. But the apparent involvement of the IRA had suggested otherwise, that something else was going on.

Timmy pulled an envelope from his inside pocket and took out a sheet of paper and read from it. 'Message received. Put £500 in envelope addressed to your daughter in letter box of 12 Wicklow Street between 6 and 7 pm Sunday. Await release instructions.'

'Jesus,' Duggan said. 'What are you going to do?'

'I don't know,' Timmy said. 'It's getting serious now.'

'You've got to tell the guards now. They can watch that place. Grab whoever's doing this.'

'Yeah,' Timmy said without conviction, lifting his hat to scratch the side of his head. 'I'll sleep on it overnight. Decide tomorrow.'

'At least they're asking for a lot less now.'

'That's still more than a year's salary. And no guarantee that'll end it.'

'No,' Duggan agreed. 'Call in the guards. You've got to do it now.'

Timmy said nothing and Duggan thought, I'll do it myself, get Gifford to report it and let the guards deal with it. Never mind Timmy's political sensitivities. He drove on in silence and slowed and turned off the main road as he neared his home.

'We'll go back early tomorrow,' Timmy said. 'I'll pick you up after the twelve o'clock Mass. We won't wait for the dinner or we'll be here all day.'

'Okay,' Duggan turned into the laneway leading to his home. He's thinking of paying, he thought. Wants to be back in Dublin by the deadline.

He stopped the car on the gravel in front of the house and the sheepdog came running out, followed a moment or two later by his mother. She was wearing a wraparound apron and wiping her hands on a cloth as she squinted in the sudden sunlight at the strange car.

'Kate,' Timmy was out of the car, back in public form. 'Look at what I brought you.'

Duggan retrieved his cap from the back seat and put it on as he stepped out of the car.

'Look at you,' his mother said with a smile. Then she burst into tears and let them run down her face unhindered.

'Now, Kate,' Timmy said, coming around to the driver's seat. 'What are you upsetting yourself for? You should be very proud of him. A fine specimen of Irish manhood.' He raised his eyes to heaven as he went by Duggan and added, 'One o'clock tomorrow.'

The sheepdog jumped up at Duggan as Timmy drove away,

leaving a smell of exhaust fumes on the warm air. His mother smiled at him through her tears and said, 'Come on in', and steered him into the kitchen with her two hands on his back. It seemed dark inside, out of the sunshine. There was a large plate of buttered slices of bread on the table and a bowl of mashed-up boiled eggs beside it.

'They're all at the bog,' she said. 'Footing the turf. I was just making the sandwiches for them.'

'I'll take them over,' he said.

'Do that,' she said. 'They'll be delighted.'

'I better get out of this uniform.'

'Do,' she said.

He went upstairs to his bedroom, feeling the staircase very narrow and the house small compared to what he had become used to now. He opened the window to let in some air and the sounds and smells of the farmyard below also flowed in, the chickens clucking and picking around the open door of the hayshed. The dog had gone back to sleep, lying stretched out in the sunshine. In the fields beyond, a number of shorthorn cattle grazed slowly and a small flock of sheep were scattered about. He picked out the growing lambs and counted them automatically. Beyond, in what had been last year's meadow, there were drills of potato plants, cabbages, carrots and a line of staked peas, all different shades and textures of green. He changed quickly into an old pair of trousers and shirt and hung his uniform in the wardrobe and went back down.

'I've just made a pot of tea,' his mother said. 'And you'll have an egg sandwich?'

He poured himself a cup of tea from the pot on the range and sat down at the end of the table. She was cutting the sandwiches in half and putting them into a square biscuit tin with faded Christmas decorations around the side. 'There's ham as well,' she said, pointing at a layer of sandwiches already in the tin.

'I prefer the egg,' he said, reaching for one.

'I know,' she smiled and passed him another half she had just cut.

'Any news?' He poured milk into his tea.

'Oh, I should've told Timmy. Pakie Kelly died this morning.'

'He'll hear about it soon enough.'

'He's in time for the wake anyway. Everybody'll be there.'

'Trust Timmy,' he said.

She nodded and worked in silence for a moment.

'Is it going to come here? The war?'

'I don't know,' he said. 'No one knows.'

'We had a scare here the other night. Did you hear about it?'

He shook his head. There were scares everywhere every night. It was a full-time job just logging them all.

'There were some planes heard overhead and word went round that the Germans had landed in Galway. They were supposed to be coming this way. The LDF put up a barricade at the bridge down the road.' She packed the last of the sandwiches into the tin and pressed the lid down on it. Christmas Greetings, it said. 'Do you want another one? There's enough egg left.'

He nodded.

She buttered another two slices of bread and smeared the mashed egg onto them. 'Your father insisted on going out with them,' she said as she worked. 'With his shotgun. I told him not to be daft. He'd be better off in bed saying his prayers. At his age. But he went anyway. Said he knew much more about fighting in ditches than all the LDF put together.'

'He was probably right about that,' Duggan said, as he took the extra sandwiches from her. Shotguns against Stukas, he thought.

'I didn't sleep a wink that night.' She went to the sink and washed her hands and dried them with a towel. 'I don't think anybody in the parish slept at all that night.'

'There've been a lot of scares,' he said. 'But nothing's happened.'

She went out to the pantry and came back with a large jug of milk which she poured carefully into a clean whiskey bottle and replaced its cork. He finished his sandwich and tea and watched her take a rush basket from behind the door and put the bottle and the biscuit tin into it.

'I won't be on the barricades if anything happens,' he said. 'That's the advantage of being in headquarters. We'll be well away from any front.'

She stopped and stared up into his face for a moment as he stood up, knowing he was only trying to reassure her, not reassured. Then she handed him the basket. 'You still know the way anyway?'

'I do,' he smiled.

He got his old bicycle from the hayshed, dusted down the saddle, and set off down the driveway with the basket hanging from the handlebar. The dog came loping around the house and ran down the driveway beside him. As he turned onto the road he stopped and told the dog to go home in a stern voice. It looked at him and then turned and walked back towards the house. He picked up speed quickly, feeling the warmth of the breeze in his hair and of the sun on his face and arms and hearing the cacophony of birdsong, and the countryside opened out around him, as familiar as his own hand. He knew who owned every field, noted every change in the crops, the houses that had been painted, the new outhouses, the fences that had been mended with new barbed wire, the trees that had fallen or been cut down. They were all areas he and his friends had roamed as children, a playground of infinite variety, changing with the seasons from crusted frost to soft green. The war seemed a million miles further away than it seemed in Dublin. He couldn't imagine it coming here, tanks brushing aside the puny barricades thrown up by the LDF; they'd hardly even notice the opposition as they pushed through, leaving them dead in the ditches.

The last couple of miles were down an unpaved road, two paths of beaten down sand and gravel separated by a line of rough grass down the middle. He kept a wary eye out for potholes and then swung onto the track through the bog. It was dry for a change, its ruts firm but crumbling under his wheels as he pushed forward. Overhead, the sky opened up even more and left him with the feeling that he was on top of the earth, nothing between him and the huge vast unbroken arc of blue. In the distance he could see his father and his friends working on their turf bank. They straightened up from the small heaps of turf as he approached, wondering who he was.

He left his bicycle against a clamp of turf beside their bicycles and walked across the springy heather towards them. He said hello to the other men and handed his father the basket. 'I brought the lunch,' he said.

'All the way from Dublin,' his father said.

'Timmy gave me a lift down.'

'You're just in time. I was about to get the fire going.'

They walked back to the track and his father selected a couple of sods of turf from the top of the clamp, broke them up with his hands and set them on some kindling in a circle of stones enclosing grey ash. 'It's nearly ready to go home already,' Duggan said, looking at the turf.

'Another week of this weather and it'll be done,' his father said. He bent down and put a match to the kindling and passed his hand close to it after a moment to see if it was lighting. The sunlight was so bright it made the flame invisible. He took a bottle of water from a bag and poured it into a heavy blackened kettle which he set on top of the fire. They sat on the ground back from the fire and lit cigarettes.

'I hear you were out on the barricades with your shotgun,' Duggan said.

His father gave a short laugh. 'Lot of good it would've been if they had come. But it was better to be up and out instead of lying in bed listening.'

'It's happening all over the country every night. Scares. People hearing planes, strange noises. Seeing parachutes, unexplained shadows in the air and at sea.'

'The whole country'll be in the asylum with nerves if it goes on much longer,' his father laughed, unperturbed at the idea.

'Do you think we can hold them back if they come?'

'The Germans?'

Duggan nodded.

'No,' his father said. 'Not if they want to take over the country. If it's just a tactical diversion, maybe. We might be able to contain them then. But they can do whatever they want without much hindrance.'

They fell silent. Duggan watched a flame begin to lick the shaded side of the kettle. The breeze was warm and steady and carried the sound of the other men's conversation across the heather towards them but they couldn't hear the words.

'How's the new posting?'

'Very different. Interesting. I like it. I think.'

His father laughed. 'You're beginning to sound like every IO I ever met. This is the situation. Maybe. But on the other hand, I don't know.'

'Nothing ever seems to be certain.'

'Nothing ever is. But you're learning the lingo anyway.'

'It's interesting.'

'And important. Good or bad intelligence is often the difference between success and disaster.'

'Did you ever do it?' Duggan spotted an opening to ask about the part of his life his father never talked about.

'Me? Intelligence? No. Not as such. Everything was less organised, less structured then.' He flicked his cigarette end into the fire.

Duggan waited for him to go on but he didn't. After a while, he asked, 'Was Timmy ever in west Cork in those days? With the flying columns there?'

'No,' his father looked at him in surprise. 'What would he have been doing there? We were busy enough around here.'

'I don't know,' Duggan admitted. 'Just I saw a newspaper cutting about Kilmichael in his place recently.'

'If Timmy was at Kilmichael you'd know all about it,' his father laughed without humour. 'The whole world would know all about it. Tom Barry wouldn't have got a look in.'

'I suppose not,' Duggan laughed too. 'He wouldn't have played down his role.'

'Why didn't you ask him why he had it?' His father said with a mischievous look.

'Nuala had it really. Not him.'

'Why didn't you ask her?'

'I couldn't,' Duggan took a deep breath. 'She's missing.'

'Missing?' his father stared at him. 'What do you mean? Missing?'

Duggan gave him a short account of what had happened since Timmy had told him about Nuala's disappearance. 'You haven't mentioned this to your mother, have you?' his father asked when he had finished.

'No. Of course not.'

'Don't. She's worried enough about you. If herself and Mona get going about Nuala as well they'll work themselves up into a right tizzy.' His father lit another cigarette and contemplated its burning tip for a moment. 'You should keep away from Timmy's machinations,' he said.

'I know,' Duggan admitted, fishing out his own cigarettes. 'But it's too late now.'

The lid of the kettle began to hop up and down as the water came to a boil.

'Can he afford the ransom?' Duggan asked. 'Five hundred pounds.'

'Oh, yeah. Easily.'

'He says it's a year's pay for a TD. More.'

'A TD's pay is the least of his incomes. That farm he has over there' – his father pointed vaguely towards the west – 'would give him more than that. Two hundred acres.'

'Incomes?' Duggan noted. 'Does he have other things too?'

'He has some properties in the town. And they say he has more in Dublin. I don't know the details.'

The lid of the kettle was hopping up and down faster. His father stared at it but didn't appear to notice it for a moment, lost in thought. Then he stood up and got a small paper bag of tea from his bag. He lifted the lid off the kettle with two sticks and dropped it on the heather while he poured in the tea leaves. He put the lid back and it began to bounce up and down again as he called to the men still at work.

'I hope you all like strong tea,' he said to the others as they drifted over towards them. 'There's nearly half a week's ration in there.'

Timmy was more than an hour late collecting him the next day, arriving outside the house with an unnecessary blast of the car's horn as he swung it around on the gravel to face back the way he had come. He left the engine running as he climbed out and Duggan and his parents emerged from the house.

'Well, Con,' Timmy said to Duggan's father. 'Did he tell you all about the V8?'

'He mentioned it all right.' Duggan's father walked around the car, looking at its sleek lines, now dusty from the journey down. 'He was impressed.'

'He was all right,' Timmy gave Duggan a wink. 'Letting her rip on the way down when he thought I wasn't looking.'

'Don't be driving too fast,' his mother said to Duggan.

'Well, I'm ready to meet my maker now if I have to,' Timmy laughed. 'Four Masses today, God bless us. Enough indulgences to get most of the parish straight out of purgatory. The ones that vote for me anyway.'

Duggan's mother shook her head at him, in despair.

'That new parish priest they have over beyond must be the most boring man on God's earth,' Timmy added. 'Humming and hawing. Taking an eternity to say nothing.'

'Timmy,' Duggan's mother warned, rising as always to the bait of his less than reverential attitude towards the church.

'Right, young man,' Timmy said to Duggan. 'We'll hit the road.'

Duggan gave his mother a cursory hug and he saw the tears well up in her eyes.

Timmy saw them too. 'Now, Kate. Don't be worrying about him. Sure the country's in safe hands with the likes of him defending us.'

Duggan's father gave Timmy a dirty look and took his mother's hand.

Duggan got into the driving seat and Timmy sat in beside him and they drove off.

'That was a great success,' Timmy said. 'You heard about Pakie Kelly dying?'

'Yeah.' Duggan turned out of the driveway. 'You met everybody there?'

'Everybody that mattered. Made the weekend for me. The poor old fecker was a Stater in his time but he saw the error of his ways and brought the whole family over to our side. As loyal a supporter as you could get. Though you'd always have to have a bit of a reservation about a fellow that'd change sides. Do it once, he might do it again.'

Timmy gave him a rundown of all the news in the area. Who was poorly, who was arguing with his neighbours over fences, who got a good price for his calves, who was thinking of selling an acre or two, who was thinking of buying it, and who was looking for what council jobs. Duggan half listened as he drove, letting it all wash over him, knowing Timmy was more or less talking to himself, sifting and filing away all the local intelligence he needed to keep abreast of his constituents' doings. When he had finished, he tipped his hat down over his eyes. 'Don't be going too fast now,' he warned as he leaned back. 'There's no hurry on us.'

They were nearing Dublin and the traffic had thickened a little when he opened his eyes and sat up again.

'This rationing doesn't seem to be keeping anyone off the roads,' he grumbled.

'Not yet anyway,' Duggan said, stuck in a slow moving convoy of cars.

'Though from what I hear people ought to be saving their petrol now. Things will get a lot tighter next year. Be a good idea to put some away now.'

'You think the war'll go on another year?'

'No. The English might see sense and do a deal now. Otherwise, it'll only take a couple of months to subdue them. They might even cave in as quick as the French.'

'So there's no need to stockpile petrol then.'

Timmy glanced at him to see if Duggan was challenging his assumptions. 'You never know,' he said. 'You never know.'

As they drove down by the Phoenix Park Timmy told him to continue on into the city centre.

'You've decided to pay them,' Duggan glanced at him.

Timmy nodded.

'I don't think that's a good idea.'

'What choice do I have?'

'Call the guards.'

'I told you. I can't do that.'

'They could drop an envelope into this place and watch it. You wouldn't even have to put any money in it. Just some papers.'

'I thought you might be able to keep an eye on it.'

'What?' Duggan said. 'How can I do that? I can't watch it twenty-four hours a day.'

'Ah, no, you wouldn't need to do that.'

Duggan shook his head and stayed silent as he drove past the barracks and along the quays. 'You're making a big mistake,' he said at last. 'If you pay them anything they'll just look for more. And we don't even know if they have Nuala.'

'She'll be happy with this,' Timmy said. 'This'll be the end of it.'

'You're sure she's behind all this?'

'Of course she is. Sure who would kidnap her? She's just trying to get her own back on me.'

'For what?'

Timmy shrugged as they drove up Grafton Street. 'Turn into Wicklow Street,' he directed. 'And go left here.'

'For what?' Duggan repeated as he turned into Clarendon Street.

'For not wanting her to get that flat. Giving up the job I got her. For everything. Who knows with women.' He paused. 'Park along here.'

Duggan pulled into a space outside Clarendon Street church and turned off the engine and they heard the Angelus bell ringing in the silence. Timmy took a long brown envelope from his inside pocket and passed it to Duggan.

'That's what five hundred pounds feels like,' Timmy said.

Duggan weighed it on his hands. 'Not much,' he said.

'A good year's pay.'

'It's all there? Five hundred?'

Timmy nodded. 'And a letter for Nuala. Telling her there won't be any more and to stop this now and it'll be all forgiven and forgotten. There won't be another word said about it.'

'And if she doesn't?'

'Then I'll call in the guards and all hell will break loose.' Timmy pointed at the address on the envelope. 'It's just back down there near the corner. You go and drop it in the letter box there while I drop into the church.'

Duggan gave a short laugh and shook his head. Timmy's face broke into a large smile. 'I'll say a prayer for you,' he said as he got out. He closed the door and opened it again immediately and bent down to look into the car. 'To Our Lady of Perpetual Succour,' he smiled again.

Duggan watched him go into the church, thinking this whole thing is ridiculous. He was sorry he had ever taken it seriously. It was just Timmy playing his games again. And Nuala, too. She was obviously as bad as him. And Timmy of course was being careful, not doing any of the direct work himself. So nobody could say he put the ad in the paper, dropped the ransom money off.

Duggan got out of the car and walked back down to Wicklow Street. There was hardly anybody about, only a couple going into the Wicklow Hotel where the doorman held the door open for them. He found the address easily, a door beside a dressmaker's shop and he popped the envelope into the letter box, wondering if it really contained £500. It was hard to imagine Timmy parting with that much money so easily. Even with a smile. Even to his own daughter.

He stood outside the building for a moment looking up and down the street, but there was nothing and, for the moment, no one to be seen. The odd car and some pedestrians passed on Grafton Street but Wicklow Street seemed to be an abandoned byway, dozing quietly in the still shade of the evening. He walked back to the car, sat in and lit a cigarette.

He had almost finished it before Timmy sat in. 'I got Benediction there,' he said, as if that had been his objective all along, and told him to drive on as if he was in a hurry to get away from the area. 'Well?' he asked as Duggan turned left into Chatham Street and went down Grafton Street where there was a queue forming already outside the cinema.

'What's that address?' Duggan asked. 'Does Nuala have something to do with it?'

'Not that I know of,' Timmy said. 'What did it say?'

'It's a dress shop. A furrier and a jeweller upstairs.'

'Did you see anyone?'

'No. There was no sign of Nuala. Or anyone else.'

'Good. Good,' Timmy said as if that was good news. 'You might keep an eye on if you happen to be passing.'

Duggan did not reply and they went in silence down the quays to Collins Barracks and cruised to a halt just past its gate.

'Well, thanks for the lift,' Duggan said, opening his door.

'Thank you for the lift,' Timmy said. 'It's great to be driven. Gives you time to think.'

He got out and came around to the driver's side and sat in. 'Great to get down the country, too,' he said. 'Clears the head.'

'It does all right,' Duggan agreed and closed the door on him.

The war seemed further away than ever.

Eight

'Any news?' Duggan asked as he arrived in the Red House the next morning.

'Yeah,' Sullivan said casually. 'The Germans have invaded. At Tramore.'

'Ha, ha.' Duggan sat down at his place at the table.

'There's a news blackout.'

'And that's why everything's so calm around here?'

'Exactly,' Sullivan smiled. 'It's official. There's no news. But the Wehrmacht is here.'

'Fuck off,' Duggan said.

'So how's everything in culchie land?'

'Restful. They're saving the turf.'

Sullivan groaned. 'My father keeps trying to drag me up to the Sally Gap where he got a bit of bog from someone. It'd break your back, that turf business.'

'It's good for you.' Duggan looked at the Harbusch file. 'A little real work.'

'Hah. Says the fellow who's just had a weekend pass.'

'Any word on Brandy? Or, what's his real name? Goertz?' Duggan flicked the pages of the file, looking for inspiration.

'No sign of him. But the Branch is still hauling in IRA lads.

They've got hundreds locked up now.' Sullivan paused. 'You weren't listening to Lord Haw Haw last night were you?'

'No. Not on my night off.'

'He was insulting us again.'

'I thought he liked our neutrality.'

'Us. The army,' Sullivan said. 'Said the Irish army couldn't beat the tinkers out of Galway.'

Duggan snorted. 'Someone beat him out of there anyway. Did you listen to Mühlhausen as well?'

'I had to,' Sullivan said with an accusatory note, 'since you were off. It was the usual stuff. The Black and Tans. Kilmichael. Balbriggan.'

'Kilmichael?' Duggan perked up. 'What did he say about it?'

Sullivan dropped his voice. 'My Irish isn't as good as yours, you know.'

Duggan nodded. 'But what did he say?'

'Just that the Auxies got their answer at Kilmichael. I think. It was just a passing reference.'

'Nothing else?'

Sullivan shook his head. 'What's important about Kilmichael?'

'I don't know,' Duggan said, thinking his own thoughts. 'But he hasn't mentioned it before. As far as I know.'

'So?'

'It's probably nothing.' Could it be a coincidence? Duggan wondered. The cutting about Kilmichael in Nuala's flat, Mühlhausen mentioning the ambush in his radio broadcast from Berlin. It had to be. There couldn't be any connection between Nuala and the Germans. 'I'll listen out for it next week. When you're up on the bog.'

'Or at the beach head in Tramore. I'd sooner that.'

'Mocking is catching,' Duggan warned.

★

It was another beautiful day, occasional clouds alternating the sunlight with shade, a warm breeze blowing from the west, the heat bouncing off the buildings, the footpaths shaded by shop awnings, hall doors on the sunny sides of streets protected with striped covers. Duggan cycled along the quays and turned up at O'Connell Bridge, heading for Merrion Square and Gifford's lookout post. He didn't really know why he was going there but he had nowhere else to go. Captain McClure didn't seem to want him to do anything else other than keep an eye on Harbusch. And Gifford, perhaps.

He was about to turn into Nassau Street when he suddenly changed his mind and went on up Grafton Street and pushed hard on a pedal to turn quickly into Wicklow Street in front of a bus. He left his bicycle on Clarendon Street, against the back wall of Switzers and walked back to the corner and stopped outside the Alpha Café. He stared for a moment at the dress shop and doorway where he had dropped Timmy's ransom payment, then went into the café and took a table at the window.

He ordered tea and a scone from an elderly waitress in a black and white uniform and watched the street. Most of the shops along the stretch opposite were dress shops with hairdressers on the first floors. The passersby were mainly women, middle-aged and overdressed for the weather.

He buttered his scone and put a dab of strawberry jam on each side, taking his time, keeping an eye on the building across the street and still wondering idly if he was being sidelined by McClure. Or, as Sullivan seemed to think, being treated like a favoured son. 'Why do you think you got the weekend pass?' he had asked rhetorically when Duggan had voiced his concerns that he was being given nothing else to do.

He finished the scone and poured himself another half cup of tea, the remainder of the pot, and added milk and sugar. He lit a Sweet Afton and his thoughts flicked between Nuala and Timmy and Mühlhausen and Kilmichael and his father's silent but thoughtful reaction to what he had told him on the bog. Maybe I should go and look up that paper in the National Library, he thought. See exactly what it says about Kilmichael.

The waitress came around the tables, leaving a handwritten lunch menu on each. It had a choice of soup starters, oxtail or tomato; beef or pork chops with potatoes and turnip; jelly and ice cream or rice pudding for dessert. He glanced idly at it and then returned his gaze to the street. The women passersby reminded him of his aunt Mona, Nuala's mother – she could be one of them, well-dressed, presumably fashionable, in a middle-aged way. No one went in or came out of the dress shop and the door beside it.

The lunchtime crowd was beginning to fill the café and a man came and sat down at his table with a cursory lift of one eye to inquire if the seat was free. Duggan nodded and paid the waitress when she took the man's order. Outside, he stood on the footpath for a moment, then crossed to the door where he had left Timmy's envelope. It swung in under the pressure of his hand and he stepped inside. A steep stairs led up from a gloomy stretch of hall. A letterbox on the back of the door was open and he took out a few letters. They were addressed to Inishfallen Jewellers and looked like bills. The one he had left addressed to Nuala was gone.

He went up the steep stairs, passed a small toilet on the return, and continued up to the first floor where a sign said Dixon Furriers. He knocked at the door and it was opened by a middle-aged woman.

'Ah, I'm looking for Miss Monaghan,' he said. 'Nuala Monaghan?'

'There's no one of that name here,' the woman said.

'Maybe it's upstairs,' Duggan said.

'There's no one upstairs,' the woman said. 'They've been gone for months.'

'Sorry. I must have the wrong address.'

The woman closed the door and Duggan continued up the stairs, as quietly as he could on the linoed steps. He came to a reinforced grey door with a faded sign saying Inishfallen Jewellers. He knocked on the door, noticing that it was covered in a light coating of dust. There was no answer.

Back on the street, he went into the dressmakers on the ground floor and asked for Miss Monaghan. A young woman told him he must have the wrong shop and he apologised and left.

A total waste of time, he thought as he crossed the road to pick up his bicycle. Anyone could walk in there any time and walk out with the post. It would only take a second to pick up Timmy's letter. And five hundred quid. If that really was what was in it.

Duggan became aware of someone pressing against his right shoulder and he looked sideways and half saw a short young man in a long coat walking just behind his shoulder.

'You know what this is?' the man said, holding out the right-hand side of his coat with his left hand and Duggan saw his right hand sticking through the torn inside of the pocket. He was pointing a Webley 45 at him, his thumb on the hammer.

Duggan nodded, becoming aware that there was someone else just behind his left shoulder.

'Keep walking,' the first man said. 'Or I'll use it.'

The man on his left poked something into his side and they went up Clarendon Street at a faster pace. Duggan could hear the man on his left breathing through his nose and caught a whiff of his stale breath. He tried to think but his thoughts were running out of control, scattering on the edge of panic. Could they be guards?

he thought hopefully. But he knew they weren't.

'What—' he tried to say.

'Fuck up,' the man on his right said.

They walked on and Duggan tried to catch the eye of the few pedestrians here but they all looked away and stepped out of the way of the three men.

'In here,' the short man said, steering him into an archway which led into a lane behind the houses. Duggan's spirits sank even further – there was no sign of anyone around here. The man stopped him in front of a padlocked garage door and the second man stepped in front of them and opened the lock. He was taller than the first man and wearing a long brown coat. Duggan didn't see his face. He pulled open one side of the door and the short man pushed Duggan through.

Garden tools and bits of cars lined the walls and the short man pushed him to the back to where an old car seat was propped up.

'Don't move,' the man said.

Duggan stood still staring at the back wall. The door banged behind them and the interior was cast into gloom.

'Sit,' the man said.

Duggan turned around, sat down and looked up at them. They had put cloth caps on their heads and tied handkerchiefs over the lower halves of their faces. Bright spots of sunlight came through gaps in the garage door and its wooden walls, accentuating the gloom. He couldn't make out their features.

'Where's the money?' the short man pointed his Webley within inches of Duggan's forehead.

'I don't have any—'

The man hit him across the face with the gun barrel, its sight cutting his right cheek on the bone. Duggan slumped sideways, his body in shock at the sudden violence, his mind grasping for some anchor to hold onto. The second man stepped forward and searched the pockets of Duggan's jacket. He shook his head at the short man.

'Where is she?'

'Who?' Duggan muttered, the shock giving way to the growing pain in his cheek. He put his hand against it and took it away, looking at the blood on his palm.

'D'you want another belt?' the man said, raising the revolver to one side.

'She's my cousin,' Duggan said, squeezing his eyes against the pain.

'Who?' the man said.

'Nuala Monaghan.'

The two men looked at each other. The short one let the revolver drop to his side without thinking. Duggan looked from one to the other, aware that something had changed. Things were not working out as they expected.

'Where is she?' he said, and winced at a stab of pain in his cheek.

There was a sudden hammering at the garage door and a voice shouted, 'Police. Come out with your hands up.'

The short man muttered 'Fuck' and raised the revolver like he was going to hit Duggan again. Duggan put his arms up on either side of his head. But the man dropped the gun again and indicated with a nod of his head to the other man the door at the back of the garage. The other man opened it slowly, lifting it as it began to scrape off the dirty ground. There was no sound and he gave a quick look outside. He shrugged at the short man and they both slipped out, leading with their revolvers as there was another heavy knock at the garage doors and the voice shouted, 'Open up!'

Duggan sank back on the old car seat and closed his eyes and let out a long sigh. Then, he stood up and staggered slightly as he went to the garage door, blinking away a sudden dizziness. He pushed the door out a little with his foot and the sunshine blinded him. He put his two hands through the gap, palms open and upright, and said, 'I'm coming out.'

He pushed the door open further with his foot and stepped out. The lane was empty. Then he saw a gun pointing at him from an adjoining doorway and a face appeared above it. Gifford.

Gifford beckoned him forward with his spare hand. Duggan looked behind him. There was no one else around. He dropped his hands and walked towards Gifford. 'They're gone,' he said.

'You sure?' Gifford kept his eye and gun on the garage door, still half open.

'They went out the back.'

Gifford stepped quickly up to the garage door and took a look inside. He let the gun hang by his side and closed the door with his foot. He turned back to Duggan and seemed to see him for the first time. 'Jesus,' he said. 'Are you all right?'

Duggan nodded and felt a trickle of blood running down his face. He wiped it away with the ball of his hand and slumped back against the wall facing the garage. He fished in his jacket pocket with his other hand and took out his cigarettes and put one between his lips.

'What was all that about?' Gifford asked, putting his revolver away.

'Nuala.' Duggan lit the cigarette and inhaled and picked off a flake of tobacco that had stuck to his lip.

'They really are looking for her,' Gifford shook his head in surprise.

'And the ransom money,' Duggan said. He told Gifford about paying the ransom and what had happened.

'He's mad,' Gifford said of Timmy.

'I don't know what he's up to,' Duggan admitted. And I don't want any part of it anymore, he thought.

'Well at least we know that the IRA haven't got her,' Gifford said as they walked back down the lane towards Clarendon Street.

'They were definitely IRA?'

'Yeah. The small one is a fellow called Ward. A low-level hard man. He's definitely on the list for the Curragh. I don't know the other one.'

'Thanks for arriving at the right time,' Duggan said, still feeling slightly groggy.

'We aim to please. But you can really thank Hansi. I was just coming out the side door of Switzers behind him when I saw you cross the road and Ward and his friend fall in behind you.'

'Where were they?'

'I'm not sure. Up the road a bit, I think. I only noticed them when they hurried across the road and came up behind you. So I tagged along too.'

Duggan staggered a little as he stepped off the footpath to let two women pass. 'You need a drink,' Gifford said.

'No. There's something I need to do.'

'It can wait.' They passed Duggan's bicycle and Gifford led him around the Alpha Café into Wicklow Street. It seemed to Duggan to be a long time since he had sat inside the window eating a scone.

Gifford went up the steps into the International Bar on the corner of Andrew Street and ordered a Jameson for Duggan without consulting him. He ordered a glass of Guinness for himself.

'Yes,' Gifford said, settling himself on a stool, 'I don't know whether Hansi is a pervert or just acting the bollocks with us. He dragged me all around the lingerie department of Switzers for ages.'

'Getting the dirty looks from all the shop assistants.'

Gifford nodded. 'Fucked up my chances with any of them I might meet in the Metropole.'

'You think he knows we're following him?' Duggan asked, not really caring about Harbusch at the moment.

'If he doesn't he's got to be some kind of pervert. Getting his thrills from underwear or the dirty looks all the women in there give him. He just smiles at them all and does the German thing with his heels.'

The barman put the Jameson on the counter with a small jug of water. Gifford pushed the jug away and Duggan took a sip of the neat whiskey and felt it flow down to his stomach and begin to dissolve the knots there. He took a larger sip.

After a second whiskey they left the pub and Duggan retrieved his bicycle and mounted it.

'Are you sure you're all right on that?' Gifford asked.

Duggan nodded. 'I'll see you in a while.'

Gifford watched as he wobbled a little back towards Grafton Street. He steadied up as he went across Duke Street and up Dawson Street and into Molesworth Street and headed for Leinster House at the end of the road. He waited impatiently, smoking another cigarette, at the security kiosk while an usher phoned Timmy's office and told Duggan the deputy would come down to see him. Fucker, Duggan thought. He'd have liked to march straight in and demand explanations.

Timmy appeared eventually, barrelling around the high plinth on which the statue of Queen Victoria sat glowering back at Duggan. He stopped for a moment to talk to a passing politician, slapped him on the back. Duggan ground out his cigarette.

Timmy stopped when he saw him. 'What happened your face?'

'You tell me,' Duggan shot back.

Timmy turned him around and hustled him out of the kiosk and across Kildare Street into Buswell's Hotel. He didn't stop until they got to the bar, murky and almost empty.

'What the fuck happened?' Timmy looked around, making sure there was no one within earshot.

'I was beaten up by the IRA. Looking for your money.'

'What?' Timmy looked horrified.

'A fellow named Ward. You know him?'

'Ward? No.' Timmy waved at the barman. 'What do you want?'

'Whiskey,' Duggan said and sank back onto a seat. He lit another cigarette as Timmy went to the bar and ordered two Paddys. His anger began to deflate and he closed his eyes, feeling tired as the adrenaline drained away.

Timmy came back with a glass of whiskey in each hand and a jug of water between them.

'Now,' he sat down, his equilibrium back, 'take a slug of that and tell me what happened.'

Duggan did as he asked, leaving Gifford out of it. The gunmen had run away when someone knocked on the door, he said. Some neighbour who was suspicious about what was going on.

'Jaysus,' Timmy said when he finished. He got up and went to the bar and came back with two more whiskies.

'They were looking for your money,' Duggan pointed out as he sat down.

'But how could that be?'

'Someone must've told them. Asked them to get the money back.'

'That's impossible,' Timmy lit himself a cigarette and took a drink.

'It wasn't me. So it must have been you. Unless someone else knew about the ransom payment.' Duggan watched him.

'No,' Timmy shook his head vigorously.

'No what?'

'No one else knew about it.'

'So it was you.'

'No,' Timmy shook his head again. 'I didn't ask anyone to beat you up. Jaysus. What do you take me for?'

'Or to get the money back?'

'No, no.'

'So how did they know about it?'

Timmy spread his hands. 'I don't know. I don't know what the fuck's going on.'

Duggan was beginning to feel lightheaded from the drink. He poured some water into his first whiskey.

'Never heard of anyone called Ward in the IRA,' Timmy said. 'But I wouldn't know any of the younger fellows anyway.'

Duggan said nothing. He didn't believe Timmy. He had to be behind it all. Whatever it was.

'Maybe they fell out among themselves,' Timmy offered.

'Who?'

'The kidnappers.'

'But you don't think she's been kidnapped at all,' Duggan retorted.

Timmy scratched the side of his head as if it was the cause of all his problems. He drank in silence for a moment, then leaned closer to Duggan and dropped his voice. 'There are big things happening,' he said. He paused and looked around to make sure there was no one within earshot. 'The Brits are offering a united Ireland.' He leaned back, returned Duggan's stare and nodded his head.

Duggan said nothing.

'What does that tell you?' Timmy said after another mouthful of whiskey.

Duggan shrugged. He wasn't interested in Timmy's political games.

'It tells you they're fucked,' Timmy said with satisfaction. 'And they know it. Last throw of the dice.'

'What's that got to do with me being beaten up?' Duggan asked, disliking the peevish tone in his own voice but unwilling to let Timmy change the subject.

'Nothing,' Timmy admitted. 'Nothing. Just marking your cards. Keeping you informed, up to date.' He leaned towards Duggan again. 'That's top secret. Highest level. MacDonald's here, talking to Dev. Trying to do a deal.'

Duggan put some more water into his empty whiskey glass and drank it back. His second whiskey was still untouched.

'You know who he is?' Timmy asked. 'MacDonald?'

Duggan nodded. He knew he was or had been a British minister, had negotiated before with de Valera about the ports.

'A decent man,' Timmy nodded as if in agreement. 'Gets on very well with the chief. Which is why they sent him of course. Think he'll be able to *plamás* the chief.' Timmy gave a short laugh at the innocent stupidity of it. 'No chance.'

'Why not?' Duggan asked in spite of himself, aware that this was a chance to pick up some intelligence that he shouldn't miss.

'Because,' Timmy laughed without humour, 'you don't switch teams in the last three minutes of the match when your side is up a goal and two points.'

'And the Germans will give us back the six counties?'

'They will,' Timmy nodded. 'They know what it's like to have bits of your nation chopped off. They understand that very well. The Sudetenland.'

'So the government's going to say no to the British?'

Timmy nodded. 'Nothing in it for us. Why would you join the losing team now?'

'We get unity.'

'Yeah,' Timmy said with derision. 'After the war. We heard that one before. And after this war they won't be in a position to offer anyone anything.'

'Maybe the Germans won't agree to a united Ireland either.'

'Why wouldn't they? It's nothing to them.'

'They could decide to hold onto the North for themselves.'

'What'd they do that for?'

Duggan shrugged. 'Same reason as the British. Keep bases there.'

'They can have a few bases if they want,' Timmy offered. 'They wouldn't want the trouble of running the rest of it.'

Duggan winced as a sudden twinge of pain went through his cheek bone.

Timmy looked concerned and drained his whiskey. 'Should you go to the hospital with that knock? It might need some stitches. I'll drive you.'

'I'll be all right.'

Timmy made to get up, then stopped. 'Listen,' he said. 'Don't think for a minute that I'd have anything to do with you being beaten up. If I find this fucker Ward I'll beat him up myself.'

Duggan pushed the remainder of his drink away, his second glass of whiskey untouched, and stood up. 'Whatever's going on I don't want to know about it anymore,' he said.

'Don't worry,' Timmy scratched his head again with renewed vigour and eyed the untouched Paddy. 'I'll get to the bottom of this. I guarantee you that.'

Duggan shook his head and left.

Sinéad called to him as he went by her office on his way upstairs to Gifford. 'What happened your face?' she asked when he stopped and looked in.

'Fell off the bike,' he looked sheepish. 'Got caught in the tram-lines.'

'It looks sore.'

'It's just a graze.'

'There's blood on your cheek,' she stood up. 'I'll clean it up for you. There's some first aid stuff in the kitchen.'

He followed her into the kitchen and she pulled out a chair from the table and he sat down while she looked in a press. She got out a roll of cotton wool in purple paper and a large square of gauze and a roll of brown bandage.

'I don't need all that,' Duggan protested. 'It's only a graze.'

'Shhh,' she said, wetting a lump of cotton wool and putting the palm of her hand against the other side of his face while she rubbed away the congealed blood around the cut.

He closed his eyes, feeling the cool of her hand on his face.

'Okay,' she said as she got a scissors from the cutlery drawer and took a narrow strip of bandage off the roll. 'The cut isn't that big.'

She put on the plaster and stepped back. 'Are your elbows and knees okay?'

'Yeah, they're fine,' Duggan stood up, rubbing an elbow. 'I wasn't going very fast. The handlebar just hit me as I fell.'

'Just as well you'd been drinking,' Sinéad said with a hint of criticism. 'They say you don't hurt yourself as much when you fall down drunk.'

'No, no,' Duggan said. 'I wasn't drunk. Only had a whiskey afterwards. Someone insisted I have one. For the shock.'

Sinéad nodded, unconvinced. 'Do you want a cup of tea?'

'No, thanks. I'm fine.'

'You wouldn't want to go back to work stinking of whiskey. They might get the wrong idea.'

He nodded. 'Thanks for cleaning me up.'

Upstairs, Gifford looked up as he came in and said, 'Jaysus, you stink like a distillery.'

'Thanks to you.'

'Gratitude, gratitude,' Gifford threw his hands up in the air. 'That's young people today. Save their lives and they wouldn't even thank you.'

'Sinéad thinks I fell off the bike because I was drunk.'

'You didn't tell her about my daring rescue? How I single-handedly saved the army from the irregulars?'

Duggan shook his head with impatience and went to the window. 'What's happening?' he asked, looking over the tops of the trees, unmoving against the blue sky.

'A pigeon went by about twenty minutes ago,' Gifford yawned. 'Could've been a courier. In breach of the Pigeon Control Order. I couldn't see where he landed but I don't think he went into Hansi's.'

Duggan gave a short laugh and pain flashed across his cheekbone. 'My fucking face hurts if I laugh,' he grumbled.

'Just what we need, a spy that never smiles. As if you weren't serious enough already.'

'I've had a serious morning.'

'True, true,' Gifford tut tutted.

Duggan stubbed out his cigarette on a saucer with short stabs, feeling restless, needing to do something. 'I'm going over there, to talk to the neighbours,' he said.

Gifford gave him a quizzical look.

'This is a waste of time,' Duggan retorted. 'Sitting here waiting for something to happen. Watching pigeons flying by.'

'Should I have shot him down?' Gifford inquired with an earnest look.

'We should do something,' Duggan retorted.

'You're going to talk to the neighbours,' Gifford repeated. 'With a bandage on your face, a mad look in your eye and whiskey curdling off your tongue. They're going to call the guards. Who'll haul me in and want to know who's this G2 drunk and why didn't I stop him from blundering in and fucking up our surveillance operation.'

Duggan said nothing.

'Actually, they won't be that upset. In fact, they won't be upset at all although they'll make a song and dance about it. They'll be delighted. Tell everyone what a useless shower of amateurs army intelligence are. Which is what they've been saying for years anyway.'

They faced each other in silence for a moment and then Duggan shrugged and said, 'I've got to go out for a walk.'

'Buy some mints.'

Outside, Duggan turned right and walked fast up to the corner of Fitzwilliam Street, trying to burn off the restless energy that had made it impossible to stay inside. He looked left and right, about to cross into Mount Street, and a movement down the other side of Merrion Square caught his eye. An elderly woman was coming out of the Harbusches' apartment building. One of the neighbours, he thought. That retired woman, he couldn't remember her name, the one who had worked in London all her life and come back to Ireland when she'd retired.

He turned left and fell in behind her, thinking he might get a chance to talk to her wherever she was going. It'd be better than calling into the building and risk running into Hans or Eliza. He had to force himself to slow down to her pace, trying to still his restlessness through an act of will.

The woman was about medium height, wearing a tweed overcoat and a maroon-coloured hat that must be too hot for the day. She wore flat shoes and walked with a slight limp and had a basket hanging from her left arm. Going shopping, he thought.

She walked slowly down to the corner and turned towards the city centre. Fuck it, Duggan thought, he couldn't saunter along this slowly at the moment. He was too tense, too upset, still reeling inside from the shock of what had happened, the panic of finding himself helpless, the sudden blow to the face. Timmy and his fucking conspiracies, he thought, prepared to blame him for everything. Anything to do with him always ended up in complications. He was going to have nothing more to do with him. Or Nuala. He didn't owe her anything either. Just a cousin, an accident of birth, whom he hardly knew.

He crossed the street and headed off at speed in the same direction as the woman was walking. What was he going to tell McClure about the bandage on his face? Keep up the lie he had told Sinéad? Tell him the truth? He couldn't do that without getting into the whole Timmy/Nuala story. And, if he told him now, why hadn't he told him earlier? And he'd have to admit that he'd been spending time trying to find Nuala when he should've been working on the Harbusch file.

No, he thought, he couldn't do that. He'd do a Timmy on him instead. Tell him about the British offering a united Ireland. McClure probably knew all about it already but he could tell him anyway. And McClure would know it had to have come from Timmy. Might get Timmy into trouble if the word went back to the powers that be that he was leaking secrets. He stopped himself from smiling just in time, before it hurt. Serve the fucker right.

He crossed Lower Merrion Street and stopped on the corner of Clare Street and used the opportunity of checking the passing traffic of cars and bicycles to see where the woman was. She was only halfway down Merrion Square. He waited for a bus to pass and crossed to the other side of Clare Street and stopped at the barrows of second-hand books outside Greene's.

He pretended to read the titles on book spines while still thinking about his revenge on Timmy. He could also tell McClure about Timmy's pro-German sympathies. But it probably wouldn't be much of a surprise to anyone. Timmy's views were transparent and he wasn't the only politician who wanted a German victory. Were they right? He didn't know. The Germans would probably unite Ireland, they wouldn't bother with partition. But would it be an independent country?

He picked up a hardback copy of *The Small Dark Man* by Maurice Walsh and flicked through the first few pages, not reading anything, his back to the direction the woman was coming, waiting for her to pass by. He slotted the book back in and picked up another Walsh, *The Road to Nowhere*, flicked through it, wondering where she was. She should have been here by now. He replaced the book and moved around the cart until he was facing Merrion Square. The woman was crossing the road from the square into Lower Merrion Street.

He waited until she had crossed and disappeared down the short street and then skipped across Clare Street in front of a number 8 tram and went up to the corner. She was passing Merrion Hall with its 'The End is Nigh' poster and crossing into Westland Row.

He stopped on the corner to light a cigarette as she went by the Royal Irish Academy of Music and then followed her down Westland Row, managing to saunter at her pace. Ahead of them a train stuttered out of the railway station onto the bridge, its plume of smoke bursting straight upwards as it cleared the building. He touched the bandage on his face, thinking the thoughts he hadn't wanted to think since the gunmen had shoved their revolvers in his sides. He hated himself for the fear and helplessness he had felt. His first bit of real action and he'd almost collapsed under it, been unable to think straight, react properly. What would he be like in a real war? When the Germans came? If he nearly gave in to a couple of IRA gunmen. At least he wouldn't be taken by surprise, he comforted himself. But the thought was little comfort.

The woman turned into St Andrew's church, just before the station, and climbed the steps slowly, one at a time, leading with her left foot. He stopped at the entrance railings and took a few drags on the cigarette, wondering should he wait here and talk to her when she came out. What would he say? And what if she didn't believe him, wouldn't talk to him? Or should he follow her inside and see what she was doing? And what could she be doing in a church other than praying?

He breathed into his hand and could smell the whiskey and smoke off his breath. Fuck, he thought, Gifford was right. He tossed his cigarette on the ground, stepped on it, and followed her inside.

It was not gloomy as he had expected. The sun shone through the clear windows up high and bounced down from the vaulted ceiling, filling the interior with light. There were three people scattered around, all elderly, and the woman was standing by the altar rails, lighting a candle. She took a handbag from her basket and a purse from the handbag and put a coin into the metal box beside the candles. It dropped with a sharp note in the silence. Then she knelt down at the altar rail and bowed her head onto her steepled hands.

Duggan backed out of the church and crossed the street to a newsagent's. A middle-aged woman behind the counter was talking to a customer of the same age about someone and they wrapped up their conversation as soon as he entered.

'Please God, it'll all work out for the best,' the shopkeeper said.

'It won't be for want of the novenas,' the customer said, gathering up a collection of small packages without any hurry. 'What do I owe you, Mrs Carey?'

'Two and ninepence,' the shopkeeper said.

Duggan read the headline on the *Evening Herald* as the woman opened her purse and rooted around for coins. 'France Seeks Surrender Terms', the headline read. 'Italy Invades French Riviera', another said. Duggan tried to read the opening paragraphs sideways as he waited. There's nothing to stop the Germans now, he thought. It was England's turn next. And Ireland's. Either could be first.

'Yes?' the shopkeeper said to him.

'Do you have any peppermints?'

The shopkeeper pointed to one of the jars of boiled sweets on the shelf behind her, casting a glance to the other woman. He could feel the wave of disapproval coming from both of them, as real as the smell of drink wafting about him.

'I'll take five of them, please,' he said. 'And ten Afton and the paper.'

The shopkeeper dug out five of the sweets from the jar and put them into a twist of brown paper. She plonked the cigarettes beside them on top of the newspaper and said, 'One and threepence.'

He paid her and was leaving the shop as he saw the woman come out of the church, facing him across the street. He stopped and lowered his head, unwrapped a hard mint and popped it into his mouth. He couldn't talk to her now she was out on the footpath again. He'd have to keep on following her.

To his surprise, she turned right, towards the station and he waited a moment and then set off in the same direction on the opposite footpath. She passed the station entrance and stopped at the post box just beyond it. She reached into the basket on her arm, took out a letter and dropped it into the box. She turned back the way she had come.

Duggan kept going in the opposite direction for a moment, his mind racing. Why'd she come all the way down here to post a letter? She could have posted it in Merrion Square; she'd passed a pillar box on the way down here. Because she was going to the church? He stopped at the corner of Pearse Street and crossed Westland Row and went back up the street. The woman was halfway up it now, past Poole's garage, still walking slowly, limping slightly.

He stopped at the pillar box and looked at the collection times, his excitement mounting. The next collection was due in just over an hour. Should he wait, accost the postman or whoever collected the mail and see if there was a letter to that address in Copenhagen, to Harbusch's dead letter box? Could that old woman be working with him? Another German spy? He looked up the street after her, an anonymous old woman tottering along, almost invisible, being overtaken by everyone else on the footpath. The idea of her as a spy was ludicrous. Maybe she was just doing Hans a favour. He seemed to have a way with women. Maybe old women too.

He set off after her, to see where she went, keeping further back this time, aware of the bandage on his face like a flashing identification. She must have seen him when she came out of the church and he came out of the shop opposite. And it'd be very easy to recognise him again with the bandage.

The woman went back the way she had come, never looking back. Maybe it's all totally innocent, he told himself. Maybe she wanted to go to the church before she posted the letter. A special letter of some kind. Light a candle, say a prayer before posting it. That'd explain why she didn't post it closer to home. If we can see the letters we'll know.

He didn't follow her up the eastern side of Merrion Square where her flat was, hanging back at the corner beside Holles Street hospital in case Harbusch was looking out the window to check her return. She went into the building without a backward glance.

Nine

Duggan made his way through the lanes behind Merrion Square, to avoid passing in front of Harbusch's building, back to Sinéad's office and asked to use the phone. She directed him into the empty boardroom and he called McClure and told him briefly what had happened.

'Call me back in half an hour.' McClure hung up.

Sinéad was walking out of the reception area when he emerged from the boardroom. 'I was just going to make the tea. Do you want to wait and bring some up to Petey?'

He followed her into the kitchen and watched while she plugged in the electric kettle and prepared the tray. 'You're looking a bit better,' she glanced at him. 'Got a little colour back in your cheeks.'

He offered her a mint and she shook her head. 'I don't want people to think I've been drinking on duty too,' she said.

'Do I still stink of whiskey?'

'You stink of mints and whiskey now. Which means that you're not too drunk because if you were really drunk you wouldn't care about stinking of whiskey.' She gave him a wan smile.

'See?' he said. 'I was never drunk at all.'

'Just drunk enough to know you shouldn't be drinking.'

'Just concerned with appearances,' he agreed.

'Falling off your bike.' She shook her head in disbelief as the kettle boiled and she poured the water into the teapot.

'What? You don't believe me?'

'Do you fall off it a lot?'

'No. It was the cross tracks at O'Connell Bridge. I wasn't paying attention.'

'Daydreaming.'

'I suppose so.'

'Sweet dreams?' She flashed him a quizzical smile and gave the tea a vigorous stir with a soup spoon.

'Yeah. I was down the country at the weekend. It was lovely weather.'

'Thought you were cycling down the boreen, two hands in your pockets.' She poured out two cups of tea, added milk and sugars. 'Whistling with the birds.'

'Something like that,' he laughed.

'You don't like the city?'

'I don't know yet. What about you?'

'Give me the city every time. Couldn't wait to get out of the country. It's boring.'

She opened a press and took out a packet of Kimberley biscuits and put four on a plate.

'Kimberleys?' he said with surprise.

'We're celebrating.' She handed him the tray and pushed him gently backwards out of the kitchen.

'What are we celebrating?'

'That there wasn't a tram coming when you fell over the tracks.'

He climbed the stairs slowly, wondering if he should tell Gifford about the woman. He should really, after all Gifford had done for him. But he didn't want the guards to get control of the case, if this was a breakthrough.

Gifford's eyes widened when he saw the biscuits. 'First a bandage. Then fancy biscuits. What next?'

Duggan put the tray on the floor and they lifted a cup each, ignoring the saucers.

'I think you are trying to usurp my position,' Gifford looked at him over the rim of his cup. 'I may have to hit myself in the face to keep up with you. Maybe shoot myself in the foot to get one up.'

Duggan tore the cellophane off his new packet of Aftons and got out a cigarette and flicked his lighter to it.

'I might have found the pigeon,' he said, exhaling a stream of smoke.

Gifford gave him a quizzical look and Duggan told him what had happened.

'Fuck me,' Gifford nodded a couple of times, thinking it through. 'Neat.' He shook his head in admiration at either Duggan's luck or the German's ingenuity or both.

'Maybe,' Duggan said. 'If I'm right. What do we know about her?'

Gifford shrugged. 'Fuck all, far as I know. She worked in London for an insurance company. Spinster. Retired.' He searched his memory. 'Kelly. Her name is Kitty Kelly. That's about as anonymous as you could be and have a name. Native of Cork. In her sixties.'

'She was checked out.' Duggan made it a question.

'Whatever that meant,' Gifford said, biting half a biscuit, his thoughts elsewhere. 'Shorthand typist,' he added a moment later, through a mouthful of crumbs. 'With Royal Liver.'

He washed away the biscuit with some tea. 'Fuck me,' he said again. 'Why would a Cork woman retire to Dublin after working for forty-odd years in London?'

'We shouldn't jump to conclusions till we know for sure,' Duggan tapped some ash onto the saucer. 'Does she go out much?'

Gifford nodded. 'She goes out most mornings after eight. On and off during the day.'

'She can't be a German spy,' Duggan said, then thought of the middle-aged woman in Dun Laoghaire who had been hiding Brandy or Goertz. Still. 'It seems ridiculous.'

Gifford stepped over to the window and stared at Harbusch's building. 'Maybe they're all spies. Maybe that's the Irish headquarters of the Abwehr. Right under our noses. Round the corner from the British. Jesus.'

Captain McClure held up a white envelope by its corner and waved it like a trophy as Duggan came into the office in the Red House. 'Right on top of the pile,' he said. 'Good work.'

'Luck, really,' Duggan said.

'The mark of a successful general,' McClure countered. 'As Napoleon said.'

Duggan caught Sullivan in the background raising his eyes to heaven and giving him a sour look.

McClure dropped the envelope on the desk. 'Read it and come into the colonel's office for a debriefing when you're finished.'

He left and Duggan sat down and looked at the envelope, addressed in the same writing as the others to the post office box in Copenhagen. Didn't look like a woman's writing, he thought. At least, not what he thought an old woman's writing looked like.

'General,' Sullivan snorted from the other end of the table. 'Hit yourself in the face with your own baton, did you?'

'I didn't see you salute when I came in,' Duggan looked up. 'Maybe we should send you on the saluting course.'

'I've been assigned to you.'

'Seriously?'

Sullivan nodded. 'What d'you want me to do?'

'I don't know,' Duggan didn't know whether Sullivan was joking or not. 'Light a cigarette for me. Make sure there's no loose flakes of tobacco in the end. I hate that.'

'Fuck off, general,' Sullivan smirked. 'I always wanted to say that.'

Duggan laughed and turned his attention to the letter.

It had the same tone as all the previous ones; Harbusch was on the point of achieving a major new order for machine parts but needed more money for expenses. One paragraph caught his attention and he read it twice: 'Our main competitor has increased their efforts to secure the contract and begun negotiations on what they say are more advantageous terms to the prospective client. I propose that we set out what we can offer in firm and unambiguous terms and put that before the client so that the client can compare our achievable offer with the unrealistic goals of our competitor and reach the correct conclusion.'

He folded the page and replaced it in the envelope and took it with him down the corridor. Sullivan gave him a two-fingered mock salute as he left. As he passed the office dealing with the British he saw some kind of conference in session, people standing around the table. A haze of cigarette smoke drifted from the room.

He knocked on the colonel's door and heard McClure tell him to come in. He entered, surprised to see McClure alone, behind the colonel's desk.

'Just borrowed this office for a little peace and quiet,' McClure said, waving a hand towards the chair on the other side of the desk. 'There's a bit of a flap on in the British section.'

'They looked busy as I passed.'

'The IRA claim to have kidnapped a British spy. Holding him against the release of some of their men in Belfast.'

'Who is he?'

'Don't know. They haven't said. And the British say they haven't . . .' McClure raised an eye in scepticism. 'They say they have no spies here.'

Duggan gave a noncommittal laugh, a fleeting thought wondering if that was what his brief kidnapping had been about. No, that was about Timmy and Nuala. It was an opening to tell McClure about it but it passed.

'Anyway,' McClure said. 'The letter. What do you think?'

Duggan took the sheet out of the envelope again. 'The third paragraph is very interesting,' he suggested. 'Where he says that their rivals are trying to make a better offer. Does that mean he knows about the talks with the British?'

'That would be worrying,' McClure sighed. 'What do you know about the talks with the British?'

'Nothing much,' Duggan said quickly. 'Other than the fact that there are some contacts. Ongoing contacts.'

McClure stared at him, waiting for him to continue. Duggan felt himself redden and said, 'My uncle says there are high level talks going on. Political talks. That MacDonald is here. Talking to the Taoiseach. About the North.'

'And what does he think?'

'Timmy? He thinks the Germans are winning the war and the British are not in a position to offer an end to partition.'

'Logical,' McClure said.

'And that you couldn't trust the British anyway.'

'Home Rule. 1914,' McClure nodded.

'And he wants the Germans to win the war.' Duggan stopped. He had got his revenge on Timmy but didn't feel any better for it.

'And what do you think?'

'About Timmy?' Duggan was still thinking his own thoughts.

'About the war?'

'It looks like the Germans are winning so far,' he said cautiously. 'I don't see how we can stop them if they invade us.'

'That's what the real talks with the British are about,' McClure nodded. 'Forward planning to repel an invasion. That's what the people you might've seen wandering around here are about. But don't tell your uncle or anyone else about them.'

'No, no. Of course not,' Duggan said quickly.

'He's probably right about the political talks. There's nothing to be gained by declaring for the Allies at the moment. Only trouble. Anyway,' he leaned forward and propped his elbows on the desk, 'our immediate concern is Harbusch and what he might know. If he knows about the political talks, that's one thing. If he knows about the strategic military planning, that's another matter.'

McClure picked a pencil from a desk tidy and watched it as he twisted it between his hands and went on. 'The Germans know the British will intervene if they invade. And they know we can't fight two invaders at the one time since we can barely fight one. They may gamble that we'd want their help to fight the old enemy in that situation. So, it would be important for them to know that our plans are already well laid if they invade. We won't be fighting the British. We've already picked our side in that event.'

He gave Duggan a questioning look.

'What if the British invade first?' Duggan asked.

'They won't,' McClure shook his head. 'Would make no sense. They don't want to be fighting on another front. When there's no real reason to.'

'They invaded Norway,' Duggan offered.

'That was different. Times were different. They need to focus all their energies on their home defence now. So,' he continued, ending the discussion and pointing his pencil at the letter in Duggan's hand, 'what do we do about that?'

Duggan had already come to a conclusion about that. 'Send it,' he said. 'And see what happens next, now that we have a clearer picture of their communication system. We can follow this woman and see if she's picking up the post for Harbusch as well as sending it. And get to see what they're saying to him.'

'Do it,' McClure said.

'Ah,' Duggan hesitated. 'We might need some more people to keep an eye on the woman. I think that Harbusch knows about Petey and me.'

'Petey?'

'Gifford. The Special Branch man.'

'You're getting on well with him?'

Duggan nodded, knowing what was coming.

'Don't tell him anything more than you need to,' McClure wagged the pencil at him. 'And nothing about what goes on here. The Branch is riddled with IRA informants.'

'No, no.'

'Why do you think Harbusch knows about you?'

Duggan told him of their suspicion that Harbusch was just trying to embarrass them with his regular visits to the lingerie department in Switzers.

'And does he succeed?'

Duggan went red again. 'With me, anyway. Less so with Garda Gifford. And,' he added, 'I think the woman saw me today. I wasn't being very careful because I was planning to talk to her and this' – he pointed to the bandage on his cheek – 'would make it easy for her to spot me again.'

'I've told Lieutenant Sullivan to assist you. So you can use him and we'll see if we can get a few others too. Meanwhile, you collate everything you can find about this woman. Get the British to check out her background in London too. Talk to the liaison officer. Tell him it's high priority.'

'Okay.' Duggan turned to go.

'By the way,' McClure stopped him. 'What happened your face?'

'I fell off the bike,' Duggan didn't have to try too hard to look stupid.

'So what does the colonel say, general?' Sullivan greeted him back in their office.

'It was only the captain,' Duggan sat down and picked up the telephone and waited for the switchboard to answer. 'He says you're working for me. With me.'

The switch answered and he asked for the number of Sinéad's office. She answered immediately.

'It's Duggan,' he said. 'There's another man coming down there. Will you tell him where to go?'

'Oh,' she sounded disappointed or maybe, he thought, that was wishful thinking. 'Are you on sick leave now?'

'No, no,' he said. 'I'll be back as well.'

'Will I have to bandage him too?'

'No,' he said, looking at Sullivan. 'He's a Dublin jackeen, used to cycling over tram lines.'

He hung up and told Sullivan where he was to go and what he was to do. 'And don't be seen with Peter Gifford. We think Harbusch is on to us.'

'You too?'

Duggan nodded. 'And this Kitty Kelly has seen me. Just make sure she doesn't see you.'

Sullivan closed the file in front of him, put it on top of a pile to one side and got up. 'By the way, what really happened your face?' he stopped at the door.

'Any more insubordination and you'll be confined to barracks.'

'Right. A drunken row in a pub.'

'Confined to barracks,' Duggan repeated. 'I always wanted to say that.'

He opened his Harbusch file and flicked through it until he came to the section about the other residents in the Merrion Square building. There wasn't much about Kitty Kelly. It was just as Gifford had said: she was from Cork originally, went to England after leaving primary school, worked for Royal Liver in London for practically all her adult life, never married, now retired. He also looked again at the others in the building. The elderly man who taught piano at the Royal Irish Academy of Music, the one who had seen the Special Branch break into the Harbusches' flat. Would he have told them? The two girls from Cork who worked in the Land Commission. Was there a Cork connection with Kitty Kelly? The junior doctor at St Vincent's on Stephen's Green and his wife who'd been a clerk in the Department of Industry and Commerce until she had to give it up when they married last year. Maybe she was the best one to talk to; she was probably around all day.

He got up and went to the heavy Royal typewriter on the other side of the table and typed out all the details about Kitty Kelly. Then he took the sheet of paper into the office dealing with the British and asked an officer there to request a full background check by MI5.

'What are you looking for?' the officer skimmed through the details.

'Any German connections or involvement with the British fascist movement.' Maybe that was the connection with Harbusch's wife, he thought. 'Actually, see if there's any connection with Eliza Godfrey, a member of Mosley's outfit, or Hans Harbusch, a German agent. They know all about him. And her.'

The officer jotted down the names.

'It's high priority at our end,' Duggan offered.

'Yeah, yeah,' the officer sighed.

Duggan went back to his office and stared at the file for a while, letting his imagination roam. A thought struck him and he went in search of McClure and found him still in the colonel's office.

'I was wondering if all the post to Harbusch's address is being monitored. Not just anything addressed to him but anything addressed to anyone in the building.'

'Good question.' McClure reached for the phone and asked for the mail monitoring section in the GPO. 'It's not,' he said to Duggan as he hung up after a brief conversation. 'But it will be now.' He dismissed him with an approving nod.

The phone was ringing on his desk when he got back to his office.

'Personal call, sir,' the orderly on the switch said. 'Your cousin.'

'Peter,' Duggan said as he sat down.

There was a pause and a woman's voice said, 'It's Stella. Nuala's friend.'

'Oh, hello,' Duggan was taken aback.

'I need to talk to you.'

'I'm afraid I'm very busy at the moment,' he said, resisting an urge to tell her there was a war on.

'It's about Nuala.'

Duggan sighed. 'There's nothing more I can do. Talk to her father. I'm up to my eyes.'

There was a pause. 'I'll be in her place in an hour. She needs your help.' She hung up.

'For fuck's sake,' Duggan said half-aloud as he leaned back in his chair and took out a cigarette. No, he thought. I'm having nothing more to do with the Monaghans and whatever twisted games they were playing with each other. Besides, he had something real to do now, something of importance now that he might have made a breakthrough in the Harbusch case.

He got up and walked around the room, feeling restless, a surge of adrenaline from all the events of the day coursing through him. What if he'd really broken the Harbusch case? There was no telling how far that could reach, if he had really found a way into a German spy ring. Maybe it included Brandy or whatever his real name was. Goertz. There hadn't been any mention of him recently; presumably he'd gone to ground somewhere. If he could nab him, that'd be something.

His mind hopped back, out of his control, to Timmy and Nuala. What was all that about? He didn't care, didn't want to know, but couldn't clear it from his hyperactive brain. Nuala was pretending to have been kidnapped to extort money from Timmy. Which was crazy. And Timmy was pretending to go along with it, pretending to pay up while getting some of his old friends in the IRA to recover the money and find Nuala. That didn't make sense. He wouldn't set gunmen after his own daughter, would he? Maybe he would. He wouldn't like to lose the money and he'd want to best her. And who else could he call on for help if he wouldn't go to the guards? I wasn't much use to him. Why didn't he just ignore Nuala, let her do her worst. Tell her mother. That was the worst she could do. Though that would put enormous pressure on Timmy, force him to pay up whatever she wanted and to call in the guards. Jesus, he thought, what a family.

He circled the table again and stubbed out his cigarette. He had to be doing something. And there'd probably be nothing on Harbusch and Kitty Kelly until tomorrow. He might as well go and talk to Stella. Tell her he was out of the picture. He'd done all he could. And all he'd got for it was a lash across the face from a Webley.

★

He cycled up Merrion Square, joining the army of civil servants leaving their offices beyond Leinster House, most on bicycles. He turned into Baggot Street and continued down to Herbert Street where he cut down to Mount Street. It was a long way around but he didn't want to be seen anywhere near Harbusch's flat. He was settling his bike against the railings outside Nuala's flat when he noticed the elderly man walking towards him. The music teacher from Harbusch's building.

Duggan stepped in front of him. 'Excuse me, Mr Jameson,' he said. 'I'm Lieutenant Paul Duggan from, ah, G2, defence forces security. I wonder if I could have a word with you.'

Duggan fished in his inside pocket for his identity card while Jameson looked at him, glanced at the bicycle, and back at the bandage on Duggan's face. He was short, with a thin grey face which faded into grey hair. He had a music case in his left hand.

'I know you're aware of our interest in one of your neighbours,' Duggan said as he handed over his card. 'We're following up our inquiries and I'd like if I may to ask you a few questions.'

Jameson examined the card and handed it back to Duggan. 'This is all very irregular,' he said.

Duggan nodded. 'These are irregular times. If you'd prefer we could make an appointment to meet. In Dublin Castle.'

The suggestion did the trick. 'What do you want to know?' Jameson blanched.

'Miss Kelly,' Duggan said. 'The lady on the ground floor. What can you tell me about her?'

Jameson looked surprised. 'Nothing. She keeps to herself. Like we all do.'

'Nothing at all?'

'It's not a building where we interfere in each other's business,' Jameson said, with a touch of pride. 'I've never spoken to the lady other than to say 'good day' to her on the few occasions we passed each other in the hallway.'

'Does she get much post?'

'Really,' Jameson looked affronted. 'I have no idea. We don't pry into each other's affairs.'

Duggan blushed and realized the stupidity of his question. 'Is she friendly with Herr Harbusch and his wife?'

'I wouldn't know,' Jameson shifted from one foot to the other as if he was preparing to move on. 'She keeps herself to herself. Like we all do. It's a quiet house. Nobody disturbs anybody else.'

'Okay,' Duggan stepped back. 'I'm sorry for accosting you like this. Taking you by surprise.'

Jameson nodded and thawed a little. 'You have a job to do, I suppose. Irregular times, like you say.'

'If anything occurs to you please give me a call at army headquarters.'

Jameson nodded and moved off. Duggan watched him go, wondering if it was the ineptitude of his questions which had made the encounter a total waste of time. I ended up telling him more than he told me, he realized. What if he was one of Harbusch's group? Shit. Then they'd know that G2 knew about Kitty Kelly.

He watched Jameson turn the corner into Merrion Square and told himself to stop seeing spies everywhere. Question everything, McClure had told him. Assume nothing. But that way led to paranoia and maybe madness. Besides, Harbusch's letters didn't read like the work of a master spy. McClure wasn't even sure he was a real spy or just playing at being a spy. Which was why he had given the case to him. Maybe Harbusch was a decoy, there to distract attention from the real group, the real spies like Brandy/Goertz. He shook his head in an unconscious effort to clear his mind and stepped up to the hall door and pressed the bell for Nuala's flat.

The door was opened almost immediately and Duggan realized that Stella had been waiting just inside. He hoped she hadn't heard his attempt to question Jameson. 'Thanks,' she said and led him up to the top floor. The door to Nuala's flat was open and she led him inside.

There was an envelope lying on the table in front of the window. Otherwise, the room seemed the same as the last time he had been there, still heavy with trapped air.

He turned to Stella. 'I only came to tell you what I said on—'

She thrust a white envelope at him.

Her name was on the front, no address, no stamp. He took out a single handwritten sheet.

'Stella,' it said. 'I'm so sorry about all the hugger mugger but I will explain all when it's safe to do so. I desperately need your help now. Please contact my cousin Paul Duggan (he's in army headquarters, an officer) as soon as you can and give him the envelope on the table in my flat. He'll know what to do with it. I'm sorry I can't explain anything at the moment but this is very important. You're a pal. Love, Nuala'

The 'very' in 'very important' was underlined twice.

He read it again and then stepped over to the table to look closer at the envelope, knowing already what it was – the envelope he had delivered to the address in Wicklow Street.

It was badly creased now and there was a smear of what looked like mud across the bottom right corner.

'Have you opened it?' he asked Stella.

'No. She said it was for you.'

He picked it up. The back flap had been opened and was held shut again by the white edging from a line of stamps. He opened it and took out the fold of notes and counted them out, two fifties, ten twenties, and twenty tens. His first thought was that Timmy had paid real money, not left sheets of paper.

He turned to find Stella staring open-mouthed at the wad of notes in his hand.

'Five hundred pounds,' he said, putting them back in the envelope.

'Where'd she get that?' Stella searched his eyes. 'Is she in danger?'

'From her father.' He tried to close the envelope with the stamp edging but it had lost its stickiness. 'And now she wants to give it back.'

'I don't understand.'

'I don't either.' A wave of tiredness came over him. 'Not really.'

He dropped the envelope on the table and opened the drawer underneath. Everything looked the same as the last time he'd been there. The newspaper cutting about the Kilmichael ambush that he had seen the first time was still missing. He walked around the room and settled on the bed and threw his legs up on it, sitting against the headboard. Stella watched him with a look of confusion. He took out his cigarettes and offered her one silently. She shook her head and he lit one for himself.

'When did you get the letter?'

'Just before I called you. When I got up.'

'And you haven't seen Nuala?' The question was superfluous. It was clear from the letter, from Nuala's reference to him, that they hadn't been in touch since he first met Stella.

'And she's been here,' he looked around the room. 'Has she taken any clothes?'

Stella went to the wardrobe and opened the door wide. 'I don't think so.'

'She's not far away,' Duggan said, holding his cigarette upright to prevent its ash falling onto the bed or the floor. Stella took an ashtray from the table and brought it over to him. She sat on the bottom of the bed, as far away from him as possible.

'What's going on?'

Duggan took a deep drag on his cigarette and blew the smoke at the ceiling. 'Nuala pretended to be kidnapped and demanded a ransom from her father. Who paid a bit of it,' he nodded towards the envelope on the table, 'and also set some IRA thugs after her.'

'What? You're not serious.'

Duggan pointed at the bandage on his face. 'I'm that serious. One of the IRA men did that with the barrel of his revolver. A swipe across the face.'

'Good God,' she touched his shoe. 'Does it hurt?'

'It's getting better.'

'I don't believe . . .' she began.

'She and her father don't get on.'

'I know that. But why would she try and get at him like that? There must be someone else behind it.'

'Who?'

'I don't know.'

'This boyfriend of hers. Jim whatever his name is.'

'No, don't be ridiculous. Jim's the sweetest, most peaceable guy you could ever meet. He wouldn't have anything to do with anything violent, criminal.'

'And Nuala?'

'No, of course not.'

'Is she given to being . . . dramatic?'

'She's your cousin.'

'We hardly know each other. Like I told you.'

'Not that dramatic. Not five-hundred-pound-ransom off her own father dramatic.'

'The five hundred was only the first payment.'

'Oh my God. How much?'

Duggan shrugged. 'She wanted a few thousand.'

'That's not Nuala.'

'The note says it is.'

'I don't believe it.' She went to the table and read the note from Nuala again. Duggan stubbed out his cigarette and swung his legs off the bed.

'What does she mean "when it's safe to do so"?' Stella asked.

'I think she knows that Timmy has sent some old IRA friends after her and she wants to put a stop to it before they find her.'

'But he wouldn't let them do anything to her.'

'I'm sure he told them not to kill her. But he might have told them to teach her a lesson.'

Stella looked at him as if he was insane.

'I mean,' he said, pointing at his face, 'I don't think he told them to beat me up. Just to follow the money. Which I had delivered for him.'

Stella looked at the envelope of money and stepped away from the table as if it was contaminated.

He got to his feet. 'That's why I don't want anything more to do with Nuala and Timmy and whatever they're up to.'

'So what are we going to do with that?' she pointed to the money.

'You take it down to Timmy in Leinster House. Ask for him at the gate, say you're a friend of Nuala's and you have a message for him.'

'All right,' she nodded as if she was memorising the instruction. 'And if he asks me where I got it what'll I tell him?'

'Tell him the truth. Nuala left it for you.'

She gave a nervous nod and he had a sudden change of heart. He couldn't let her walk into the forefront of Timmy's mind. He might send his thugs after her, wouldn't believe that she didn't know where

Nuala was. And they might decide to use their usual interrogation techniques on her.

'Actually,' he said, 'I'll do it myself.'

'No, it's all right,' she said. 'I can see why you don't want anything more to do with them.'

'I need to have one final talk with Timmy to make that clear,' he lied. 'So I might as well give the money back to him. I'll keep you out of it,' he added as an afterthought.

'Thanks,' she said. She gave an involuntary shudder and folded her arms under her breasts.

Duggan picked up the envelope and put it into his inside pocket. The brownish stain on it couldn't be mud, he thought idly, the ground is too dry for that. He took the envelope out again and looked at the stain. No, it wasn't blood either.

'Is there going to be war?' Stella asked behind him.

'What?'

'I mean an invasion.'

'I don't know,' he said. 'Nobody knows. I mean nobody here knows.'

'One of the girls is from Waterford,' Stella said. 'She says there's a lot of army activity there. They're expecting an invasion.'

'Training exercises,' Duggan said. 'It's just manoeuvres.'

At least you'd know where you were with an invasion, he thought. You'd know what you were up against and what had to be done.

He cycled back down Baggot Street, into Stephen's Green and rounded the corner at the Shelbourne Hotel into Kildare Street. The streets were almost empty now in the hiatus between the rush hour and the city's nightlife. The sun was beginning to drop into the west, still lighting the top floors of Leinster House and mellowing Queen

Victoria's dour look as he stopped at the entry kiosk to the Dáil and asked for Timmy.

'He's not in the House,' the usher at the desk said. 'He left a little while ago.'

'Is he across the road?'

The usher said nothing and Duggan added with ambiguity, 'I'm one of the family.'

'You might find him there,' the usher glanced across at Buswell's Hotel.

The bar was jammed and tobacco smoke hung heavily under the low ceiling, stirred into swirls by the raised voices and bellows of laughter. Duggan couldn't see Timmy anywhere and threaded his way through the groups until he found him in a tight circle beside the bar with four other men who all looked alike. Timmy was telling a story and Duggan circled around the group until he was opposite him. Timmy gave no sign of seeing him and finished his story. The other men spluttered into laughter and Timmy took a large swallow, waiting for the laughter to subside.

'You'll have to excuse me now, men,' he put his empty glass on the bar. 'I have to talk to this man here. Someone who knows what's going on. Unlike you useless fuckers.'

They made their way out to the small lobby, now beginning to fill up with the overflow from the bar. They found space near a back wall and leant against it, facing each other.

'Good,' Timmy pointed at the bandage. 'You had that seen to.'

Duggan ignored the comment and took the envelope from his pocket and handed it to Timmy. Timmy immediately moved to the side to shield it from everyone around them.

'Is that dried blood on it?' Duggan asked.

Timmy stopped stuffing it into his inside pocket, glanced at it. 'No it's not.'

'Are you sure?'

'I've seen enough blood in my time. It's not.' Timmy moved back against the wall and faced him again. 'You've seen her.'

'No. That was left for me. I got a message, that's all.'

'Where'd she leave it?'

'How'd she know to come to me?'

'So you did meet her?'

'No. How'd she know to send the message to me? Asking me to return the money to you?'

'What do you mean?' Timmy looked perplexed.

'How did she know I was involved in any of this?'

'Christ,' Timmy threw his hands up, 'I don't know. I don't know what the fuck's going on with her at all.'

'Well you got your money back now.'

'Yeah, thanks.' Timmy lit a cigarette, too wrapped up in his own thoughts to offer Duggan one. 'I need to sit down and have a talk with her. Find out what this is all about and straighten out whatever problem she has.'

'Well I'm out of it now anyway,' Duggan said.

'Tell her I'll meet her anywhere she wants. Any time. And we'll sort this out between us.'

'I don't know where she is.'

Timmy gave him a sly look. 'But you got a message through to her.'

Duggan lit one of his own cigarettes. Stella, he thought. But she couldn't be lying to him about Nuala. Unless she was an astonishing actress. She must've mentioned him to somebody else. Somebody who was in touch with Nuala. He sighed cigarette smoke and became aware of the dull ache in his cheekbone.

'Why don't you leave her alone?' he suggested. 'You got your money back. Just let her be. And she'll come back in her own good time.'

Timmy paused as if he was giving serious thought to the suggestion. 'I'm not sure she's a free agent,' he said. 'I can't take the chance that she's not. That she needs help.'

'To be rescued?'

'Exactly.'

'From who?'

'I don't fucking know.' Timmy's frustration made him flatten his back against the wall and kick it with his heel.

That's it, Duggan thought. That's what's really bugging him. That Nuala is manipulating him, and not he her. Like he tries to manipulate everyone.

'Look,' Timmy recovered himself, 'get word to her that I want to meet. You can come along too.'

'Why would I go along? I don't want to be involved in any of this anymore.'

'In case she's worried. Wants someone else there.'

'Maybe she should go and talk to her mother. Let her act as an intermediary. If she needs one.'

Timmy dropped his cigarette butt on the floor and looked down as he ground it out with his toe. When he looked up his face was a mask of menace that Duggan had never seen before. 'You're a good lad, Paul,' he said very quietly, putting his hand on Duggan's shoulder. 'Don't try to be too fucking smart.'

Duggan was stunned for a moment. 'I'm not,' he said. 'I'm trying to tell you I want nothing more to do with it. That I don't know where Nuala is. And if I got a message to her I don't know how I did it.'

'All right, all right,' Timmy raised his hands in surrender and his normal jovial self returned. 'You'll have a drink.'

'No, thanks. I've got to get back to the barracks. It's been a long day.'

'And how are things back there?'

'Busy, busy. Lots of false alarms.'

'You have to check them all out,' Timmy sounded solicitous.

Duggan nodded.

'One day it'll be the real thing,' Timmy added as if it were a fact. 'Any day now.'

'The British?' Duggan asked.

Timmy didn't answer directly. 'D'you feel the buzz around here?' He indicated the area around them. The noise level had increased and it had become more crowded. 'Always the same when momentous events are upon us.'

'The talks with MacDonald?'

'Only a sideshow,' Timmy shook his head. 'Like I told you. The last feeble twitch of the lion's tail.'

'And you think they'll invade instead of doing a deal on the North.'

Timmy shook his head and leaned closer. 'The Germans are coming.'

Duggan felt his stomach sink. 'When?'

'Soon.'

'How soon?'

'Any day now.'

'Where?'

Timmy raised his index finger. 'Now you've put your finger on it.'

Duggan waited and Timmy looked around and dropped his voice. 'The North. Any day now.'

Plan Kathleen, Duggan thought. The invasion plan that was found in Brandy/Goertz's lodgings. The one that McClure said was unrealistic. How did Timmy know about that? He looked around. Maybe everyone knew about that.

'How do you know?' he asked.

Timmy tapped his nose a couple of times. 'It's top secret.'

'Does everyone know?' Duggan indicated the crowd around them.

'No, no,' Timmy said as if he was being patient with a child. 'They don't know the plan. But they know big things are afoot. That the day we've been waiting for for twenty years is approaching.' He smiled and gave Duggan a slow wink. 'A nation once again.'

Ten

The phone rang, breaking Duggan's reverie about his conversation last night with Timmy. 'Your cousin,' the switch said, a different voice to the usual orderly.

'Which one?'

'He didn't say.'

Duggan waited a moment. 'Peter,' he said.

'Acting like a general now, I hear,' Gifford said. 'Like I was telling your young lad here, give these culchies an inch etcetera etcetera.'

'Any news?' Duggan didn't feel like exchanging mock insults this morning.

'Well, yes, general. As a matter of fact there is.' Gifford paused but Duggan waited for him to go on. 'Your young man has been busy. I'm sure he's dying to tell you himself, get a pat on the back. But I got to the phone first.'

Duggan sighed. 'What is it?'

'Sinéad sends her love. I think. She didn't say that exactly. Just some culchie talk about how you were no loss. Which I think means she's in love.'

'Fuck's sake,' Duggan moaned.

'Right,' Gifford paused. 'Hope you heard the heels click. General busy man. And so on. And, sir, the thing is that your legman has found the postman's other letter box.'

'Right,' Duggan said, taking a second to interpret the information. Sullivan had found where Kitty Kelly collected letters.

'He wanted to barge in and ask questions. But I pointed out to him that this was a police matter. Required tact and delicacy. Which you brute force merchants don't understand.'

'Where is it?'

'Meet me at the station beside the church in half an hour and we'll go take a look.'

'Is that area okay?'

'Oh, yes. The post's been and gone. Got Mass and all.' Gifford hung up.

Gifford was lounging by the wall inside the entrance to Westland Row station, reading a newspaper when Duggan arrived. He looked like he was planning a crime and a woman in front of Duggan gave him a quick suspicious glance before she passed by and climbed the stairs to the platform.

'Just across the road,' Gifford said, folding the paper under his arm. 'Your legman followed her in there after Mass next door and heard her asking if there was any post for her.'

'I told him to keep back. Not to let her see him.'

'Just as well he went in. Or he'd never have heard what he heard.'

'Better not let him hear you call him my legman.'

'Sensitive, is he?'

'He looks on himself as a real G2 man. I'm only in there because I can speak some German.'

'*Maith an buachaill*,' Gifford retorted illogically. Good boy.

They stopped on the footpath and looked across at the line of shops opposite. 'Which one is it?' Duggan asked. Gifford pointed to a small newsagent's.

'The same one where Harbusch gets his letters from the woman in Amsterdam,' Duggan said. Odd, he thought, that they would both use the same place if they were working together. A definite breach of security. There was no shortage of shops that provided a post restante service.

'The dirty letters,' Gifford nodded.

They crossed to the shop and went in. There was a middle-aged man behind the counter. 'Men,' he said, looking from one to the other.

'Mr Johnson,' Gifford showed him his warrant card. 'You're helping us out already with a quick look at any post for Herr Harbusch.'

'Indeed,' the man nodded. 'Always happy to help you lads.'

'We think that a Miss Kelly is also using your service.'

The man nodded again.

'Does she get many letters?'

'Only an occasional one. They come from abroad. Switzerland.'

'Switzerland?' Gifford sounded surprised and glanced at Duggan. 'Only Switzerland? Does she get any post from anywhere else?'

The man thought for a moment, then shook his head. 'No. I recognized the stamps. I'm a collector.'

'Only Switzerland,' Gifford agreed. 'And how often?'

'Nothing regular. Maybe one every few weeks or so.'

'And when was the last time?'

'Would've been ten days ago, maybe more. Could've been two weeks. I don't pay a lot of attention. Not up to now.'

'We think she might be expecting another one,' Gifford said. 'And we'd appreciate it if you'd let us know as soon as it arrives. And hold it for us before you give it to her. Like with Herr Harbusch's post.'

'Certainly,' the man said. 'Actually, she was in this morning, asking if there was anything for her.'

'Really?' Gifford sounded surprised.

'Yes,' the man said with enthusiasm. 'But there wasn't anything. Not for the last ten days. Maybe two weeks.'

'We'd appreciate it if you could alert us the next time.'

'Always happy to oblige. I know you have a hard job these days.'

'Could I ask you,' Duggan intervened, 'if you get any post here for a Mr Jameson?'

'As in the whiskey?' the man sounded surprised. 'No.'

Duggan added the names of the other tenants in the Harbusch building. 'Or for any one of those names?'

The man thought a moment and then shook his head.

'Okay,' Gifford said, turning to leave. 'Thanks for your help.'

'I thought she might have a relative who was a prisoner of war,' the man said.

'What?' Gifford turned back to him.

'Well she's not a married lady,' the man said confused. 'Or widowed. So I thought it might be a nephew. Someone like that. Not a son.'

'Did she ever say anything like that?' Duggan asked.

'Oh, no, no,' the man said. 'She never said anything at all. It was just the letters from Switzerland, you know. The Red Cross.'

'What about the Red Cross?'

'Well I hear they organise letters from prisoners of war. So one of my neighbours told me. His son's in the British Army and they've been told he's been taken prisoner. They're up the walls. Trying to get information from the Red Cross. He says they have lists. Can pass messages back and forth.'

'Was there anything on the letters to indicate that they came from the Red Cross?' Gifford asked.

'No, no,' the man sounded sorry that he had volunteered his theory. 'I was only just thinking myself. Idly wondering.'

'Anything on the letters to say who they came from?'

'There was some kind of an address. In Zurich. But no mention of the Red Cross.'

'Okay,' Gifford sought confirmation from Duggan that they were ready to go. 'Sure we'll see it when the next one arrives.'

'I'll call the usual number the minute it does,' the man promised.

Cycling back to headquarters a thought that had been niggling at the back of his mind came to the fore. Timmy hadn't seemed surprised to have got his money back. Didn't even ask if it was all there. Only wanted to talk to Nuala in person. Almost like he knew he would get the money back. All of it. How come? he wondered as he pedalled down the quays.

It was another beautiful day, the gentle breeze exaggerated by his speed, tempering the heat of the noonday sun. The tide was ebbing from the river and its stench was beginning to rise as the foul grey mudflats were exposed. I should watch my back too, he thought. If Timmy thinks I know where Nuala is it's not beyond him to get some of his friends to follow me.

He veered suddenly onto Capel Street Bridge and stopped halfway across it and looked behind him. A couple of cyclists followed him onto the bridge and he watched each of them as they passed by. None of them caught his eye or looked suspicious. This spy business is giving you some queer notions, he imagined his mother's voice saying. And he couldn't disagree.

He rested for a moment, sitting on the saddle, the bicycle propped up by his left foot on the footpath and lit a cigarette. He looked down the Liffey towards the sea, not seeing the view, scarcely registering the train chugging across the loop line bridge, thinking. He came to a decision, topped the half-finished cigarette into the gutter and put it back in his box. He pushed off from the footpath and cycled up Parliament Street and down Dame Street. He went right at the gate of Trinity College and up Nassau Street and turned into Kildare Street.

He left the bicycle at the entrance to the National Library beside Leinster House and went in. He had to wait twenty minutes to be issued with a reader's ticket and then climbed the stairs to the reading room where he asked to see the *Irish Times* for November 1920. He sat at a table with a lectern-like newspaper stand, waiting and watching the clock above him tick forward, becoming more impatient with every minute. This was supposed to be a quick visit, have a look and get back to the office.

An attendant eventually gave him the newspaper file and he turned it over and began to flick back through the pages from the end of the month. It only took a moment to find it, on page five of the last paper of the month, the report of the Kilmichael ambush that had been in Nuala's flat and that she or someone else had taken away. 'Auxiliary Police Ambushed In County Cork', the headline said. 'Fifteen Killed, One Wounded, And One Missing'.

He read down through the report but couldn't see anything in it that would have explained its importance to Nuala. It was based on British reports that claimed the ambush was carried out by seventy to a hundred IRA men. He looked at the other main report on the page, the military court of inquiry into three IRA men shot while 'trying to escape' from Dublin Castle and he read through it quickly and its continuation overleaf. All propaganda, he thought, both of the reports. But that was hardly the reason Nuala had them. He glanced at the other reports on the two pages. They were a collection of weekend incidents: an RIC constable shot dead in Cappoquin; a district inspector recovering from wounds in Galway; an insane asylum inmate shot dead by the military in Clare; firebombs in Liverpool; more shootings; searches, arrests; letters to the editor; parliamentary reports.

He sighed and handed back the file at the desk. He didn't have time to go through every item in detail. It had taken more than an hour and a half and he was no wiser at the end of it. Nothing had leapt out at him. Whatever it was that Nuala was interested in was not apparent to him.

'Where've you been?' Captain McClure demanded when he walked into the office.

'I'm sorry,' Duggan reddened. 'I was following a hunch but—'

'I've let you have a very loose rein. Don't abuse it.'

'No. Absolutely not.'

'Well, you have justified my faith in you so far,' McClure relented. 'Get a car and drive me to Dublin Castle. Things are happening.'

Shit, Duggan thought, knowing better than to ask what, and went to get the keys of a car. He sat into the driver's seat and had the engine running when McClure got into the passenger seat.

'Your Miss Kelly has just had a meeting with Goertz,' McClure said as a sentry at the gate raised the barrier for them.

'What?'

'Sullivan followed her into Bewley's Café on Grafton Street where she met another woman of her own vintage. They chatted for a while and then the other woman left and a man arrived and joined her. Had a cherry bun and a coffee.'

'It's Goertz?'

'Sullivan is certain. Says it's the man you followed from Hempel's house.'

'Jesus,' Duggan overtook a horse and cart and sped by the Four Courts. 'Where is he now?'

'Sullivan followed him to a house in Raglan Road in Ballsbridge.'

'He's still there?'

'As far as we know. We've got some more men there now, covering the front and back.'

'We're going to move in?'

'We're going to plan this one properly,' McClure said with a hint of steel. 'We don't want any more fuck-ups with this fellow.'

'Right.' Duggan slowed to a stop at the top of Capel Street, waiting for a couple of bicycles to pass on the other side before turning onto the bridge.

'Drop me outside the Castle,' McClure said as they went up Parliament Street. 'I'm going to talk to the Superintendent. Make sure they don't move in until we know everything there is to know about this house, who owns it and who's in there.'

Duggan slowed again as they came down Dame Street and pulled into the kerb outside the Olympia Theatre.

'I want you to go to that stakeout place you have on Merrion Square,' McClure said. 'Sullivan should be back there, debrief him fully. Find out everything.'

'You know about the post box he discovered this morning?'

'Just briefly,' McClure said.

Duggan told him what they had found and the shopkeeper's theory that the woman might have a relative who was a prisoner of war.

'That might be interesting if she wasn't meeting Oberleutenant Goertz,' McClure said. 'This puts a whole different complexion on what she's up to. I think you might have found the key that unravels this whole thing.'

He opened the door and paused with one leg out. 'What was your hunch?'

'Oh,' Duggan blustered. 'It was . . . nothing. Stupid.'

McClure looked at him and Duggan felt himself redden, guilt all over his face. Oh, Christ, he thought. 'You're doing well. Keep it up,' McClure said. He stepped out, banged the door shut and slapped the roof of the car twice.

Duggan let out a breath with the clutch and drove down Dame Street. Jesus, he thought, if McClure ever finds out what I've been up to he'll skin me alive. And it was too late to tell him anything about it now. It'd only beg the question of why I didn't tell him earlier.

He parked the car in Merrion Square, opposite Leinster House and well away from Sinéad's office. He walked the rest of the way, trying to think through all the threads of the Harbusch story, or maybe it was really the Kitty Kelly story. Was she just a go-between, a central communication point, or something more? What if she was the master or mistress spy? It didn't seem possible. Such a harmless looking old woman, just like everyone's grandmother.

'Well, well,' Sinéad said as he stopped at her doorway. 'Do we have to stand up and salute?'

'At ease,' he smiled. 'Don't mind what all those begrudgers say.'

'I'm not making tea anymore for all that lot,' she said.

'What lot?'

'That lot up there,' she raised a thumb at the ceiling. 'They're coming and going all day. The place is beginning to smell up there. I've told them they can make their own tea if they want to.'

Duggan didn't know what she was talking about.

'Petey says it's all your fault, upsetting our little . . .'

'Little what?'

'Love nest,' she looked away, embarrassed. 'You know what he's like, Petey.'

'Oh, I do,' Duggan laughed. 'I know what he's like.'

The switchboard beside her buzzed and she put on her headphones and raised her eyes to heaven as she said an exaggerated, 'Yes, sir, immediately sir.' She dialled a number, shoved in a plug and said, 'Ringing for you now,' and added another exaggerated '*sir*.'

Duggan leaned against the door jamb and gave her an inquiring look.

'That's them,' she said, as she took off the headphones. 'They've run an extension from the boss's office up to your little room. He's not a bit happy about it, the boss. Even more crotchety than usual.'

She glanced quickly at the switchboard in case someone might've heard her.

'I didn't know we'd gone into full . . . active service mode,' Duggan said.

'At least you washed your face this morning,' she gave him a sly smile.

'What?'

'Your bandage is looking the worse for wear.'

He fingered it and could feel it curling at the edges.

'I'll give you a new one,' she got up and led him into the kitchen. He sat down by the table while she got out the first aid box and then pulled the old bandage off with a quick tug. He winced.

'How'd you not notice that when you were shaving?' she dangled the bedraggled bandage before his eyes. 'Maybe you haven't started shaving yet.'

'Hah,' he laughed and jutted his chin out. 'Feel that.'

She ran her index finger along his jaw line and raised an eye at him and smiled.

'Maybe I don't need another one,' he said as she began to cut a strip off the roll. 'Be less conspicuous without it.'

She examined the dark bruise on his face and pursed her lips. 'Maybe.'

'Yeah, we'll leave it.'

She rolled up the bandages and put them back in their box. 'D'you want a cup of tea?'

'No, thanks. I better go up and see what they're doing up there.'

She's right, he thought as soon as he opened the door. It was beginning to smell, like a changing room after a match, a mixture of sweat and cigarette smoke. As well as Sullivan and Gifford there were four others there he didn't know. Special Branch men, he thought. They were all older, tougher looking. One was holding a phone, another two were reading newspapers, leaning against the wall, their jackets off, revolvers exposed.

'Attention,' Gifford shouted as he came in. One of the others glanced up at Duggan and snorted. Gifford shook his head and said to Duggan, 'No respect. The help you get these days.'

The fourth and oldest Branch man leaned back in the only chair in the room and swiped his hand at Gifford's head. 'Fuck up,' he said, as Gifford ducked.

'Say no more,' Gifford rolled his eyes.

No point trying to talk to Sullivan here, Duggan decided. 'We've got to report back,' he said to him, indicating the door.

As Sullivan followed him towards the door, Duggan indicated with a nod of his head to Gifford to follow them. He went out, unsure if Gifford had got the message.

He led Sullivan downstairs and asked Sinéad if they could use the boardroom on the ground floor. 'Of course, general,' she smiled sweetly.

Duggan sat at one side of the mahogany table and Sullivan went to the other. 'Not bad looking,' he said as he pulled out a chair and sat down. 'Your man Gifford says you have a thing about her.'

'He has a thing about her.'

'Ah,' Sullivan said with an air of satisfaction. 'A little bit of competition. I hope you're winning. Don't let the side down.'

Duggan shook his head as the door opened and Gifford came in and sat down at the head of the table. Sullivan looked surprised and glanced at Duggan.

'What was that you were saying about the more subtle methods of the police?' Duggan asked Gifford.

'Ah don't mind them,' Gifford laughed. 'They're just the muscle. You don't need a sledgehammer to break down doors with them around. Just tell them there's raw meat inside and they'll go through the door head first.' He looked at Sullivan and said by way of explanation. 'Culchies.'

'Okay,' Duggan said to Sullivan, 'tell us all about it.'

'Want to know what she had with her tea?'

Duggan nodded. 'Everything.'

Sullivan went through his morning following Kitty Kelly to Mass in Westland Row church, then across the road to the newsagent and asking if there was anything for her.

'How was the shopkeeper with her?' Gifford intervened.

'What d'you mean?' Sullivan asked, looking at Duggan as if seeking his support for a refusal to answer his questions. Duggan ignored him.

'Was he friendly? Did he seem to know her well?'

Sullivan shrugged. 'Just the usual. Another lovely day missus. Great weather we're having. That sort of—'

'He called her missus?'

'No, I don't know,' Sullivan admitted. 'It was just that kind of talk. You know what I mean.' He paused and thought about it for a moment. 'No, he didn't call her missus. Then she asked him if anything had arrived yet. He said, no, not yet. And she bought a paper and left.'

'Which paper?' Gifford asked.

'The *Irish Press*.' He paused, waiting for another question.

'Then what?' Duggan prompted him.

'Then she went back home, to her flat. And I came back here and reported to the captain. And about half an hour later she went out again. Walked down to Grafton Street and went into Bewley's.'

'Did she see you follow her?' Duggan asked.

'No. She never looked back.'

'But she saw you in the shop?'

'I don't think so actually. We were both standing at the counter. She never looked at me.'

'But she left before you?'

Sullivan nodded.

'So she would've turned and passed by you?'

Sullivan looked at Gifford as if to say, what is this?

'And she could have had a good look at you then? Without you seeing her do it?'

'Maybe,' Sullivan conceded.

'It's just that we probably need someone else on her now. Can't take any chances.'

'I already suggested that to the captain,' Sullivan said. 'He's trying to find some more bodies to take over.' They waited for him to continue. 'She went to one of the tables at the back of Bewley's, sat facing the stained glass window, her back to the room. A few minutes later another old woman came in and joined her, sat down on the bench opposite and they got a pot of tea.'

'What did she look like?' Duggan asked.

'Another old woman,' Sullivan shrugged. 'White hair, small, a bit bent. She had a walking stick. Moved slowly. A bit of a limp. They nattered away for a while.'

'Seemed to know each other well?' Gifford interjected.

'Yeah. Then the other woman got up and left and I thought that was it. I was trying to catch the waitress's eye and pay for my coffee, get ready to go, when I saw your man Goertz come in. I thought it was a coincidence, that he just happened to come into Bewley's at the same time. But then he walks over to your woman and sits on the bench where the other woman had been. You could've knocked me over with a feather.'

'You're sure it was him?' Duggan asked.

'As sure as you are,' Sullivan retorted. 'It was the fellow you followed from Hempel's house. You said he was Goertz.'

'Seemed to know each other well, too?' Gifford interjected again.

'Not as well as the two women, I'd say. He had a coffee and a cherry bun. Cut it into four pieces. She seemed to do most of the talking. I couldn't see her face but he spent a lot of time listening, eating the bun. Very slow, deliberate movements. Didn't do much talking. Then when he was finished he stood up, bowed a little to her and walked out right by my table. He was as near to me as you. I could've got up and grabbed him.'

Gifford laughed. 'Maybe you should've. Saved us all a lot of trouble.'

'But he might've been armed and I wasn't,' Sullivan said. 'Where would I've been then.'

'Dead,' Gifford said, flat-toned.

'So you followed him,' Duggan dragged them back on track.

'Up Grafton Street, along Stephen's Green, down Baggot Street, all the way to Raglan Road.'

'He didn't see you?'

'Never looked back. Anyway I kept well back.'

'He didn't stop anywhere?'

'No. Kept going. Not too fast, businesslike.'

'Was there anyone watching his back?'

'What?' Sullivan said.

'Anyone looking after him. You know what I mean?' Duggan shrugged.

'No, I don't think so.' Sullivan paused. 'Jaysus I don't have eyes in the back of my head.'

'I thought you lads had three hundred and sixty degree vision,' Gifford smirked, 'and could see in the dark too.'

The other two ignored him. 'I had to keep back even further when we got to the end of Baggot Street. There were very few people on the footpath and I had to run up to the corner when he turned into Raglan Road. Just in time to see him going into a driveway.'

'Then what?' Duggan prompted.

'Then, I decided I needed help, so I had to go back to Baggot Street to find a phone and called the office. The captain told me to try and keep a discreet eye on the house and wait till we got some more people there. I went back but didn't go into Raglan Road, just kept an eye on it from Pembroke Road. He didn't come out of the house again. That's it.'

'Who's there now?' Duggan asked Gifford.

'A couple of lads. Covering front and back.'

'So what do we do now?' Sullivan asked.

'Wait.' Duggan said.

'We'll have a cup of tea,' Gifford got up.

Nothing moved on Pembroke Road as the dawn crept up, sweeping it clean with the fresh light of the new day. They had the car windows open and the excited chatter of birds filled the cool air. Duggan was in the driver's seat, McClure beside him, watching the group of men standing at the corner of Raglan Road about fifty yards ahead of them. One of the men left the group and walked towards them and Duggan recognised the Superintendent in full uniform. He went around the bonnet to McClure's window.

'All set now,' he said.

'Remember,' McClure said. 'Tread carefully. Very carefully. No gun play unless absolutely necessary. He won't try and shoot his way out.'

The Superintendent nodded. 'I've warned them. We're not looking for IRA fellows who'll come out with everything blazing. And that they'll spend the rest of their lives in court if they mess this up.'

'Too right,' McClure sighed. The house which Sullivan had seen Goertz enter belonged to an up-and-coming barrister with no known connections with any political organisations or sympathies with Germany. There had been a lot of debate during the day whether to stake it out and hope to confirm that Goertz was there or to move in as early as possible.

The Superintendent was back at the group of men and they all disappeared around the corner into Raglan Road. Duggan was about to open his door and follow when McClure took out his cigarette case and offered him one. Duggan lit both and they settled back and smoked in silence, staring at the empty road. The sun was beginning to touch the tops of chimney pots on the opposite side and nothing moved in the total stillness. There were no sounds other than the birdsong.

'Okay,' McClure said at last, when they had nearly finished the cigarettes. They walked down the path, tossing the butts on the ground ahead of them and stepping on them as they passed. They rounded the corner and went into the driveway of the house.

Lights were on in most of the windows and the hall door was ajar but there was no sign of anyone. Their feet sounded loud on the gravel as they crossed and went up the steps, McClure leading. He pushed open the hall door and a revolver pointed at his head. The Special Branch man behind the door lowered it as soon as he recognised him and pointed to the first doorway.

'Preposterous,' the lawyer was saying as they entered. 'The very idea is simply preposterous.'

The Superintendent turned as McClure came in. 'This is Captain McClure,' he said, passing the buck. 'From military intelligence.'

'Are you the person responsible for this outrage?' the barrister demanded. He was ageing prematurely, balding and developing a paunch. He was wearing a colourful silk dressing gown, his hands clenched in the pockets.

'I'm sorry for the intrusion,' McClure said. 'We're acting on information that a man we wish to interview was seen coming to your house.'

'A German spy?' the barrister put all the derision of his courtroom tradecraft into the question.

'These are unusual times,' McClure said. 'And you'll appreciate that we have to pursue all leads. In the national interest.'

The man harrumphed. 'Well there are no German spies here.'

'Just the family and the maid,' the Superintendent said. Oh, fuck, Duggan thought, wishing he wasn't there.

'My children are upstairs in bed crying. They probably won't be able to sleep for months after this. They were already upset enough with all this talk of war.'

'My apologies, sir,' McClure said. 'And thank you for your assistance.'

'You haven't heard the last of this,' the barrister said and then looked beyond McClure at the door.

A young woman in a white nightdress down to her ankles had come in with one of the Special Branch men.

'What is it, Molly?' the barrister demanded.

'There was a man called to the door this morning, sir,' she said. 'A foreign gentleman.'

'What? Why wasn't I told about this earlier?'

'I didn't think it was important, sir,' she stammered. 'I'm sorry, sir.'

'Not important? In the middle of the war?'

'What time did he call?' McClure asked her.

'Before dinner. Lunch.'

'And what did he say?'

'He said he was looking for a friend,' she paused. 'I can't remember the name. But he said this man lived in a mews house at the end of the garden. I told him he had the wrong house and there was no house at the end of the garden here but there was one further up the lane. And he said that must be it and he asked me if he could take a short cut through our garden to the lane. He said he had been walking a lot this morning and had got lost a few times and he'd appreciate it.'

'You let him into the house?' the barrister accused.

'No, sir, I told him the side gate was open and he could go down through the garden and the garden gate was unlocked because the gardener was coming in today. So that's what he did.'

'Are you sure he left?' the barrister asked.

'Yes, sir. I went up to the return and watched him go out the garden gate. He looked back at the gate and saw me at the window and gave me a little bow and a smile.'

'Can you describe him, Molly?' McClure asked.

'He was tall, very straight, very neat. Middle-aged, I suppose.'

'And why'd you think he was a foreigner?'

'He had a bit of an American accent, but he wasn't a real Yank.' She paused. 'And he was very polite. Very gentlemanly.'

'Thank you very much,' McClure said to her. 'We really appreciate your help.'

'If anyone else calls to the door you tell me as soon as possible,' the barrister ordered. 'No matter who it is or what cock and bull story they're telling.'

'Yes, sir.' She looked to McClure. 'What'll I do if he comes back?'

'He won't be back,' McClure said. 'I can assure you.' He turned to the barrister. 'And thank you for your assistance. That's been very helpful.'

The Superintendent signalled to his men and they all began to leave, with McClure bringing up the rear. The barrister, now deflated, closed the door behind him.

'Thank God for the maid,' the Superintendent said as they turned onto the road. 'She saved our bacon.'

'We should check out any mews houses around here,' McClure said. 'In case it wasn't a cock and bull story.'

'I'd already made a mental note to do that,' the Superintendent said.

The sun was up higher now and shining on the top floors of the houses, mellowing the grey bricks with its glow. The birds had quietened down but were still chirping happily in the trees.

They sat into their car and McClure looked at his watch. It was just after 4.30. They lit cigarettes and Duggan drove off and turned into Northumberland Road and went by the German legation. There was no sign of life there any more than anywhere else.

'The question is,' McClure said as they went over Mount Street bridge, 'is our surveillance on Miss Kelly now compromised?'

Duggan grunted, assuming the captain was thinking aloud.

'What do you think?' McClure disabused him of the idea.

'I think he knew he was being followed. Or suspected it,' Duggan said. 'Or he was just being careful.'

McClure gave a short laugh. 'Like your answer.'

'No, I didn't mean it like that.'

'I know. But is our surveillance compromised?'

'Whether it is or it isn't we have to go on doing it anyway, don't we?' Duggan said. 'Or pick up Miss Kelly.'

'We don't want to do that. Not yet.'

'Even if he thinks that's how we got on his trail, will he tell her?' Duggan was now thinking out loud. 'Or will he just keep away from her altogether?'

'That depends on how important she is,' McClure continued the thought. 'If she's the lynchpin of this operation he has to let her know. If she's just a minor cog he mightn't bother. Just disappear from her orbit.'

'So we need to see if there's any change in her activities.'

'Yes,' McClure agreed. 'But first we need to get a few hours' sleep.'

They crossed over O'Connell Bridge and turned down Bachelor's Walk. Behind them, the sun was working its way up the Liffey along with the incoming tide.

Eleven

'It's your turn to stick with Hansi today,' Gifford said as they followed Harbusch and Eliza along Merrion Square. 'To examine the knickers in Switzers.'

'No, it's not,' Duggan said. 'You're more experienced at that.'

'Ah come on,' Gifford groaned. 'Let me stick with Eliza. The only remaining pleasure in my life.'

'What? Has she ditched you?'

'Who?'

'Sinéad.'

Gifford gave him a look. 'Are you thick or just pretending to be thick?'

'I'm tired,' Duggan said. The few hours' sleep had left his brain feeling mushy. He'd have been better off staying up all night.

'Another great night's work,' Gifford laughed.

'You heard all about it?'

'Our lads were delighted, almost. Thought you so-called intelligence men had really fucked up.'

'But we were saved at the last minute.'

'So I heard,' Gifford said with an air of regret. 'Your friend Sullivan won't be court-martialled after all.'

They crossed into Clare Street. Ahead of them Harbusch and

Eliza were approaching South Leinster Street at their normal stately pace, she tottering on her high heels, linking him. They looked neither left nor right.

'I'm not going into Switzers after him,' Duggan said.

'You have to,' Gifford said. 'You're the one who said we all have to go on pretending to be thick. We have to pretend that we don't know that Hansi and Eliza know that we're following them while they pretend that they don't know either.'

'We're looking for changes in behaviour, remember.' Duggan took out his cigarettes, needing a nicotine boost to get his brain functioning again. The packet was empty. 'I need some cigarettes,' he said, 'I'll catch up with you.'

He turned back towards a tobacconist they had just passed and caught sight of a man behind him also turn suddenly and disappear into Greene's bookshop. He didn't get a good look at him, his attention caught only by the sudden movement, just a dark-suited shape. He went into the shop, bought ten Afton and peeled the cellophane from the packet as he came out, stopping on the footpath to take out a cigarette and look back. There was no sign of anyone like the figure he had seen. He lit the cigarette and hurried after Gifford.

'I think we're being followed,' he said when he caught up with him. He told him what he had seen.

'Thanks be to God,' Gifford said. 'Some excitement at last.'

'What'll we do?'

'Go on pretending, of course,' Gifford gave him an evil grin. 'We'll pretend that we don't know that he's following us while we're following Hansi and he's pretending that he doesn't know that we're following him.'

'Jesus,' Duggan muttered, inhaling deeply and feeling the nicotine sharpen up his brain a little.

They stopped at the bottom of Dawson Street to let a car by.

'And we'll set a trap for him,' Gifford added.

On Grafton Street Harbusch went into Switzers and idled his way through the lingerie department as usual. Duggan followed at a discreet distance, avoiding the eyes of the sales assistants behind the counter and the few women customers.

'Can I help you?' a young assistant asked as he went by her.

'Ah, no thanks.'

'Just looking, are you?' she said in a tone that was anything but sweet.

He mumbled and moved on, wishing Harbusch would get this part of the ritual over. Eventually, he made his way to the Wicklow Street door, went out and turned into Grafton Street. Duggan followed him up past Bewley's and saw him enter the Monument Café. He turned and retraced his steps, glancing at the poster for the Grafton cinema's latest offering, *Poison Pen* with Flora Robson and Robert Newton. He wondered if he should ask Sinéad to go to the pictures, though that didn't look like the one to see: a black and white poster showed a shocked woman reading a poison pen letter. If he ever got an evening off, of course, between Harbusch and Goertz and Kitty Kelly. Not to mention Timmy. And the Wehrmacht. Was it ever any other way? he wondered. Talk of war, the one just over or the one just coming.

He was back in the Merrion Square room five minutes when the door burst open and a short stocky man was pushed through. Gifford followed him in, his revolver held loosely by his side.

'Well look what the cat brought in,' one of the Special Branch men dropped his newspaper. 'Little Billy Ward. Or what do you call yourself these days, Billy? Liam Mac an Bhaird?'

Duggan recognised him immediately, the IRA man who had tried to abduct him. Timmy's friend? His mind raced.

'Mac an Bhaird,' the other Special Branch man folded his newspaper with care and put it on the chair with deliberation, as if he had been waiting all along for Ward's arrival. 'Son of the bard. Just the man who's going to sing for us.'

Ward glanced at Duggan, gave no hint of recognition.

'Where did you find him?' the first detective asked Gifford.

'Dawdling along Merrion Square,' Gifford said. 'Not a care in the wide world.'

'And why would he have a care in the world? Sure he'll have free accommodation, all found, for the next ten years. At least.'

'He had this on him,' Gifford took a Webley revolver from under his jacket and replaced his own gun in its holster.

'God be with the days when he'd have been executed for that,' the second Special Branch man said with an air of nostalgia, taking the gun from Gifford. 'They should bring it back.'

'Aye,' the first man said. 'Save a load of money feeding the hungry little fucker.'

'We'll take him down to the station,' the other detective said to Gifford. 'There's a few things we want to talk to Billy about. Like the last time he met some of our lads and tried to kill them. Remember that, Billy?' He shoved Ward's shoulder and Ward tottered to one side to maintain his balance. A look of resignation was settling on his face.

The other detective grabbed his right arm. 'Feel free to make a run for it any time you want, Billy. You have a grand broad back and we're always happy to have some target practice.'

He pushed Ward towards the door and the other detective followed them out. Gifford closed the door behind them and leaned his back against it.

'Jesus Christ,' Duggan said.

'Precisely,' Gifford agreed. 'He was following you.'

Duggan nodded.

'Interesting family you have,' Gifford offered.

'Timmy,' Duggan sighed. 'He thinks I know where Nuala is. I thought he might try something like this.' But he hadn't really expected it. Was there any length to which Timmy wouldn't go? And why was he so determined to find Nuala? Whatever it was, it wasn't fatherly love.

'Persistent. You have to give him that.'

'He's a fucker,' Duggan said. 'What am I going to say if Ward tells them why he was following me?'

'Who was following you?' Gifford looked at him closely. 'Are you paranoid? Why would anyone bother following a lowly lieutenant? The whole world's going up in flames and you think it's all about you. Maybe you've been too long in G2 already.'

'I hope you're right.' Duggan took his point.

'It won't arise,' Gifford said with an air of authority. 'Ward won't tell them anything about that. He can't.'

'When those fellows are finished with him . . .' Duggan shook his head, trailing off.

'He might tell them all sorts of things,' Gifford insisted. 'But he won't tell them that. How can he tell them he's on a personal mission for a sell-out Fianna Fáil backbencher when he's supposed to be fighting for Ireland?'

Duggan felt a little reassured. Everyone had bigger things on their minds than Timmy and his games.

'And I just happened to see him on the street while engaged in another surveillance operation,' Gifford said. 'Nobody needs to know how we caught him. Knew he was a wanted man and used my initiative. Which goes to prove that I can keep more than one thought in my head at a time. Which means,' Gifford beamed, 'I deserve promotion.'

Duggan couldn't help laughing.

'So whose turn is it to get the biccies?' Gifford laughed back.

★

Duggan was still trying to think through all the possible implications of Ward's capture when he arrived back at the Red House in army headquarters. The fast cycle back from Merrion Square had helped to clear his head but it hadn't made any more sense of what was going on. He still felt totally at sea, tossed around by shifting currents with no clear picture of the course ahead.

An orderly preceded him into his office and handed a sheet off the teleprinter to Captain McClure who was sitting with his feet up on the table, smoking a pensive cigarette. He glanced up at Duggan and then read the sheet of paper and dropped his feet to the floor.

'Well, well,' he said, waving the paper in the air. 'Our Miss Kelly turns out to be a mystery woman.'

Duggan sat down opposite him and waited for him to elucidate.

'Reply from the British,' McClure waved the paper again and scanned down through it. 'She moved to London in 1890 at fourteen, worked as a scullery maid for someone in Kensington, moved up the ranks to a lady's maid, did a night course in shorthand and typing, worked for a shipping company, joined Royal Liver insurance in 1901 and stayed there till she retired in 1938. Former boss praises her diligence, efficiency. Thoughtful, intelligent, independent, he says. Effectively ran the typing pool. No known associations with Germans or Germany or the BUF.' McClure raised an inquiring eyebrow at Duggan.

Duggan nodded. Mosley's crowd, the British Union of Fascists.

'And,' McClure said, raising his index finger, 'now lives in Torquay. In a boarding house. In poor health.'

He let the sheet of paper float down to the table and reached forward to stub out his cigarette.

'She's there now?' Duggan asked, to be sure. 'In Torquay?'

'Yep.'

'They're sure of that?'

McClure picked up the sheet of paper and read from it. 'Subject confined to house now by severe arthritis.'

'So, who . . .'

'We have no idea,' McClure said, spacing out each word. He stared at Duggan who was coming to know him well enough now to know that it wasn't aimed at him; he was just thinking, not demanding an answer. He stirred himself after a moment and held out the sheet of paper to Duggan who read it through.

'We need to backtrack,' McClure said. 'Find out everything you can about her. Talk to the landlord.'

'The other tenants?' Duggan suggested.

'No. Not yet. We need to feel our way forward carefully. Until we know more. And go back through the Harbusch file. See if there's anything there that might connect him or his wife with Royal Liver, that family Kelly worked for in Kensington, the shipping company. There must be something somewhere to explain why this woman took on Kelly's identity.'

'She could be German,' Duggan thought out loud.

'She could be Mata Hari for all we know,' McClure sighed. 'I'm going to get confirmation that she is definitely in Torquay. Get more details about her life in London.'

Duggan opened his Harbusch file, knowing it well enough by now to be able to flick through the details of Harbusch's English career and Eliza's background. It didn't take long – there was nothing there to suggest any connections with Kitty Kelly's career.

He flicked forward to the section about the other tenants in the building. The landlady was a Mrs Wilson, a widow who lived in Aylesbury Road. He found the address in the telephone directory, listed under Dr Reginald Wilson, and put through a call to her.

'I'm calling about your flats in Merrion Square,' he said after a young woman, a maid, had put him through to an imperious older woman.

'On, no,' she said with an accent that would cut stone. 'You must talk to Good and Ganly. Lincoln Place. 62468.'

She was gone before he finished noting the phone number. He jotted the name of the estate agency before it and slipped them into the file. He thought about phoning them but decided this was an opportunity to check out everyone in the building without them knowing. Better call in person.

He phoned Sinéad instead. 'Is Petey there?' he asked her.

'Of course he is,' she said with a melodramatic flourish. 'He's like a wet weekend. Never goes away.'

'Tell him I'm on my way if you see him. I need to talk to him.'

'Aye, aye, general,' she sniggered and hung up.

That hadn't come out the way I meant it, he thought.

When he arrived in Merrion Square, however, Sinéad raised a conspiratorial finger to summon him into the reception area.

'The boss is furious,' she dropped her voice, glancing unconsciously at the switchboard. 'He wants you out of here.'

'Me?'

'All of you. He's been onto your headquarters demanding that you leave. Said you'd been upsetting his staff, disrupting their work. They can't concentrate on what they're supposed to be doing. And now they're terrified by fellows using bad language and waving guns around and throwing people down the stairs.'

'What?' Duggan asked, mystified.

She lowered her voice further and he had to move closer to hear her. 'His secretary was going up the stairs when those two fellows were bringing that young lad down. One of them was waving his gun and told the young fellow to run for it, they'd give him a head start, let him out the hall door before they'd follow. Said it was his only chance of avoiding the rest of his life in Tintown.'

Duggan sighed.

'He wouldn't run,' she continued, 'so they pushed him down the stairs and the other one gave him a kick when he was lying on the ground at the bottom and told him to get up. Called him a lazy,' she hesitated, 'fucker.'

'And people saw all this?'

'I only saw the bit at the bottom of the stairs. But the boss's secretary saw it all. Nearly fainted.' She glanced again at the switchboard. 'She's a dry old spinster. Full of airs and graces.'

'And you listened to his conversation?' Duggan smiled at her.

'I only heard a bit of it. And only one side of it. Would I make a good spy?'

'The best,' he said. 'Especially because you look so innocent.'

'Would you fuck off,' she smiled demurely. 'You see? It's catching. You fellows are corrupting the whole building with your foul mouths and bad manners.'

'Next time the boss calls you on the switchboard ask him what the fuck he wants,' Duggan suggested.

'I might just do that,' she said. 'I'm getting fed up of Dublin anyway. It's all talk and no action.'

He got the message and was about to ask her out when she continued. 'What's Tintown?'

'The internment camp in the Curragh. Where your man will be going for the duration of the war.'

Good and Ganly's office was in an old building around the corner from where South Leinster Street rounded into Lincoln Place and they crossed the road ahead of a slow-moving horse and cart coming out of the city.

'We'd like to see Mr Good or Mr Ganly?' Gifford showed his warrant card to the receptionist.

'They're not in at the moment,' she said, looking from one to the other.

'It's in connection with flats you let on the far side of Merrion Square,' Gifford said.

'The flats owned by Mrs Wilson,' Duggan added.

'That'd be Mr Whyte,' the receptionist said. 'He looks after them.'

She picked up her phone and called Whyte. 'Two gentlemen in the front office to see you,' she said and paused. 'It's, eh, official,' she added. 'From the police.'

They followed her directions up to the first floor where Whyte was waiting for them, a man in his late twenties trying to look older than his years, helped now by his frown of concern. He brought them into a meeting room and placed a blank pad on the table in front of him as if it was the first plank in a defensive wall.

'We're investigating some people who might be renting one of Mrs Wilson's flats in Merrion Square,' Gifford said. 'And we'd like to see whatever information you have about them.'

'You've been talking to Mrs Wilson?' Whyte sought approval for helping them.

'Yes,' Duggan said, without elaboration.

'The German gentleman?'

'Yes. But not just him.'

'What do you want to know?'

'Any details you have. When they moved in. Their references. Any problems you've had with them.'

'Well I can answer the last question first. We've had no problems at all with Herr Harbusch.'

'Or any of the others?'

'No. They're all very satisfactory tenants. Very respectable people.'

'And the other questions,' Gifford took out a notebook.

'Perhaps if I showed you the file? It would be the simplest way of dealing with those.'

'That would be a good idea,' Gifford agreed.

Whyte left and returned in a few minutes with a dull green file. 'That goes back a good while,' he laid it in front of Gifford. 'Since before Dr Wilson died. You should start at the beginning. They're the most recent lettings. Probably the ones you want.'

'Excellent,' Gifford said. 'Thank you.'

'May I leave it with you? I have a number of things to do.'

'Certainly. Thank you.'

'I'm in the office across the corridor if you need anything else.'

Gifford slid the file to his right so that it was between them on the table and opened it. The first entry was Kitty Kelly's, the newest tenant in the building. There was a page of notes about her, written in a prim and clear hand, headed with the date 5/9/39, the week the war began. Most of the notes were cryptic. 'War' was one, probably the reason given for her move to Dublin, Duggan presumed. It was followed by an address at St Andrew's Hill, EC4.

'Her old address in London?' Gifford pointed his pen at it and wrote it in his notebook.

There was another address in London with a man's name before it. 'Landlord?' Gifford noted it.

Another line said 'Royal Liver' followed by an arrow pointing at 'Dub office'. The last line said 'agreed 21/-' and 'B of I, College Gr'.

'That's a lot for a pensioner,' Duggan said. 'Twenty-one shillings a week.'

'You mean it would be a lot for Kitty Kelly. If she was Kitty Kelly and not Adolf Hitler's granny,' Gifford muttered.

The next page was a letter from the manager of Royal Liver Insurance in Dublin repeating some of the same complimentary phrases about Kelly that Duggan had already read in the message from MI5. He must have contacted London and got the information from them, Duggan thought.

The last page about Kelly was a brief letter from the manager of the Bank of Ireland branch in College Green saying Miss Kelly was a new customer having retired from her position in Great Britain and had adequate funds available to rent the property mentioned.

The following pages were about Mr and Mrs Harbusch and followed the same pattern. As did the following entries about the other tenants. None of it told them anything that seemed new or relevant. Except, Duggan thought, that Jameson, the man he had accosted on the street, was the longest tenant.

'So?' he leaned back in his chair.

'So,' Gifford shut his notebook. 'She decided to get out of Dodge as soon as she heard the bad guys might be on their way into town. As soon as war was declared. And,' he flipped through the file pages, 'exactly a month after Hansi and Eliza called on our friend here.'

'So she came here because they were here. Followed them from England.'

'One of the team,' Gifford agreed. 'Not an innocent old woman caught up in something she didn't understand.'

'Does she have an English accent?'

'What did your legman and fellow officer say?'

'I forgot to ask him.'

'Want me to interrogate him?' Gifford gave an evil grin. 'I'll make him talk.'

'Was Sinéad telling you about her boss?'

Gifford nodded. 'And I got a call from my inspector asking what the hell was going on. I told him that Ward was so distraught that his fight for Ireland was at an involuntary end that he fell down the stairs. Made a lot of unfortunate noise.'

Duggan closed the file. 'We should see if Mr Whyte can add anything to this.'

Gifford stood up and pulled out his revolver. 'I'll go get him.'

'Jesus,' Duggan laughed and Gifford put his gun away and went to get Whyte.

'My boss has a few more questions,' Gifford said when they were all seated again.

'Yes,' Duggan aimed a sideways kick at Gifford's shins under the table but did not connect with anything. 'Did Miss Kelly come looking for this particular flat or was she just looking for a place in general?'

Whyte puffed out his cheeks as he thought back. 'No, she came to us about this particular address. She didn't ask about anywhere else.'

'And had she seen it before she came to you?'

'Oh, no,' Whyte said as if the idea was ridiculous. 'We're the sole agents.'

'I mean,' Duggan added, 'did she have friends living there or had she seen it for some other reason?'

'Not that I know of.'

'And did you show it to her?'

'Yes, I took her around to see it. To see a couple of flats in the building, actually. There were a couple available. She chose the ground floor one. Said she didn't want to have to climb any more stairs than she needed to.'

'And did she give you any indication why this particular building?'

'Its location,' he said, as if that were self-evident. 'Very convenient. Very respectable area. And its own private park, of course.'

'And Herr Harbusch? Did he want this building too?'

'That was earlier,' Whyte pulled the file over and opened it to remind himself. 'Yes. No. I mean he came looking for somewhere suitable for his wife and himself. Actually, it was an apartment in

Fitzwilliam Square that brought them to us but they didn't like it when they saw it.'

'And then you showed them the Merrion Square one?'

'Yes. That was more to their liking.'

'How did you find Herr Harbusch?'

'A pleasure to deal with. A gentleman. Very decisive. German, you know. Knew what he wanted.'

'Okay,' Duggan looked at Gifford to see if he had any questions.

'Miss Kelly,' Gifford said. 'Does she have a strong English accent?'

'No,' Whyte said. 'I wouldn't say strong. But she does have an English accent although you can hear the brogue under it. She was in London for fifty years, she told me.'

Back in the office Duggan typed out a brief report of the conversation with the estate agent and copied down the addresses from the page Gifford had torn from his notebook. He went looking for McClure, found him in a corridor and gave it to him.

'They're not going to thank me for this,' McClure said of MI5. 'They've got more than enough on their plate. Probably burning files rather than creating new ones.'

'That bad?'

'You heard?' He looked exhausted, Duggan noticed. 'The French army has laid down its arms. It's all over on the Continent. The Germans have got everything they wanted. From Poland to the Pyrenees. In little more than nine months.'

'Maybe the British will look for terms now?'

McClure shook his head. 'Not Churchill.'

'Others,' Duggan realized that was what he was hoping for; an end to the threat of war, to the uncertainty.

'I doubt it. Any terms the Germans would offer would have to be unacceptable to the British. They have the upper hand.'

'So where'll they invade next? Us or them?'

'That's the question,' McClure gave him a wan smile, 'that we're trying to answer. We'll only be a diversion one way or the other, not the real target. But a lot of people can die in diversions.'

Duggan turned to go and a thought struck him. 'Why don't we arrest Harbusch and Miss Kelly?'

'It's not the time to be arresting German spies. We just want to know their plans and to thwart them.'

'But we tried to arrest Brandy. Goertz.'

'We tried to detain a German flyer who parachuted onto our territory,' McClure gave him a crooked smile. 'Like we detain any of the belligerent forces who happen to land here one way or another. How would we know he's a spy? We assume he's a pilot who bailed out of a damaged plane.'

'Ah,' Duggan said. 'It's complicated.'

'It's a delicate balancing act,' McClure corrected him. 'Not upsetting anybody. Not giving anybody an excuse to invade. While planning for all eventualities.'

'I can see that.'

'Keep neutrality in the forefront of your mind. That's the policy and that's the objective. We don't want anyone to be killed in someone else's diversion.'

Amen to that, Duggan thought as he went back to his office.

Sullivan was there, writing a note at Duggan's place. 'A message for you,' he stopped writing. 'Your cousin Stella wants to see you.'

'Thanks.'

'Is that a code? For your one?'

'No. It's my cousin.' Duggan was so used to the lie now that he almost believed she was his cousin. Indeed, he had met her more often than he had seen his real cousin Nuala in recent years. And

Stella was also coming to mean trouble. 'How is Miss Kelly?'

'We were at Mass again this morning. I'm building up a great stack of indulgences.'

'You might be needing them soon. Did you hear about the French army?'

'Yeah. Kaput, as the Germans say,' he giggled.

'We might be next.'

'No way, my old man says. They'll go straight for the English.'

'And then?'

'Then it'll be all over,' Sullivan said as if it was stating the obvious.

'They'll just leave us alone.'

'Why not? We're not at war with them.'

'There were a lot of countries not at war with them.'

'They were in the way. But we're not in the way. We're not between them and the English.'

'And after they take over England? What then?'

'Then it's just politics, the old man says. The North and all that. Sorting out who'll run what. But the war will be over.'

'And we'll all be speaking German.'

'Yeah,' Sullivan said. 'You and the captain have a head start on most of us.'

'*Sehr gut*,' Duggan replied.

Stella strode into the hall of the nurses' home, her face tight with tension. Was everybody looking tired and tense? Duggan wondered. She led Duggan outside without a word and turned left, towards the canal.

'What is it?' he asked.

'Another message from Nuala.'

'And?' he said, quickening his step to keep pace with her.

'In a minute. I'll show you.'

They crossed the road diagonally at Mount Street Bridge and went down to the canal bank and a little way along it to the first bench. The water was still, reflecting the few puffy clouds in the deep blue sky. A convoy of ducks went by, rippling the sky's reflection into folds, as she dug into her handbag and took out a piece of paper folded into a tight square.

Duggan felt his stomach go hollow as he unfolded it. It was clear from Stella's demeanour that this was not good.

It was a crudely printed handbill, headed 'British Spy Held For Volunteer Exchange'. He scanned down through it. A British spy had been captured by the Irish Republican Army and would be executed unless five named volunteers held illegally in Belfast by the occupying forces were released. The deadline was noon on the last day of June, less than a week away. There was some more rhetoric about imperialist undercover tactics designed to facilitate their re-invasion of all of Ireland, but Duggan skipped back to the handwritten note on the top of the page.

'Tell Paul it's Jim,' it said in Nuala's easily identifiable looping script.

'Jesus Christ,' Duggan leaned back hard against the bench, raising his face to the sky.

'Is it true?' Stella searched his face.

'Yes,' he looked at her. 'I mean, it could be. Which part of it? I don't know.'

He read through it again, paying more attention to every part except the names of the prisoners in Crumlin Road Prison in Belfast. They meant nothing to him; he had never heard of any of them. Stella watched him, waiting.

'I don't know,' he repeated. 'The IRA have been claiming that they kidnapped an English spy.'

'I didn't see anything in the papers about it.'

'Censored,' Duggan shook his head. 'The government's not going to give them any publicity. That's what they want but they won't get it. I suppose,' he waved the flyer, 'that's why they're using things like this.'

'Is it Jim?'

'Jesus, I don't know. Is he an English spy?'

'No, of course not.'

'Why might they think he is?'

'Because they're stupid. I don't know. This whole thing is,' she threw her hands in the air, 'ridiculous. Totally ridiculous.'

'You're telling me.' He pressed his face into his hands as though it would clear his jumbled thoughts. He refolded the note and handed it back to her.

'No, you keep it,' she said.

Christ Jesus, he thought, what am I going to tell McClure? I'll have to tell him the whole story.

'What are you going to do?' she asked, as if reading his thoughts.

'What can I do? What . . .' he opened his palms in a gesture of helplessness. 'Fuck,' he stood up and walked to the edge of the water and looked down through the reflected sky. A shadowy form of a perch circled slowly near the bank of tangled weeds. He lit a cigarette and turned back to her.

'Sorry,' he said. 'I just don't know what to do.'

'You think it's true?'

He nodded.

'You could tell the guards.'

He gave a noncommittal grunt. They knew about it anyway, but did they know who had been kidnapped?

'Wait a minute?' he said. 'You told me that this Jim Bradley had gone back to England for the holidays.'

She nodded. 'That's what I thought.'

'Why'd you think that?'

She gave it a moment's consideration. 'That's what Nuala told me.'

'So how could she be kidnapped in Dublin if he'd gone home to England?'

'He mustn't have gone.'

'Then why did she tell you he had?'

'Maybe he came back.'

'Ah, Jesus,' Duggan sighed and sat down beside her again. 'I can't do anything unless I talk to her. We're just floundering around until she comes clean about what's going on.'

Stella stared back at him, said nothing.

'You've got to tell me where she is.'

'I don't know,' she pleaded.

'But you know how to get messages to her.'

Stella continued to stare at him.

'Yes, you do,' Duggan confirmed. 'It's not like I'd be the first person she'd ever think of if she needed help. She knew I was involved in all this. And you're the only one who could've told her.'

Stella looked away.

'Tell her I need to know what's going on. Ask her what she wants me to do.'

She took a handkerchief from her bag and blew her nose, her head down. Duggan wondered whether she was crying.

'Look,' he said, 'I can't help her if I don't know what this is all about. I'm just floundering around in the dark. Probably doing more harm than good.'

She nodded, without raising her head and put her handkerchief away. 'I really don't know where she is,' she raised her head. 'I never lied to you. But there is this other friend of hers who I think does know. I told her about you.'

'Who's she?'

Stella shook her head.

'Okay,' he said. 'Tell me about Bradley.'

'I don't have much to tell.'

'How are you so sure he's not a spy?'

'Because,' she said and then began again. 'Because you'd know if you ever met him.'

That didn't mean anything, Duggan thought. Look at harmless old Kitty Kelly.

'He's not interested in all that stuff. Politics. Wars. He's the most gentle person you'd ever hope to meet.'

'How did Nuala meet him?'

'They met on the street,' she smiled a little at the memory. 'Nuala was crossing College Green and this cyclist ran into her and hurt her knee and then shouted abuse at her and kept going. Jim stopped to see if she was all right. The only one who did. Helped her to the tram stop. That's Jim.'

'When was this?'

'Back in the winter.'

'And they've been going out ever since.'

'No, not immediately. They met once or twice, I don't know, before they started going out together.'

'He doesn't sound like Nuala's type to me,' Duggan mused, more to himself than to her.

'What do you mean?' Stella shot back.

'Well, Nuala's not the gentlest person in the world. If you know what I mean.'

'Have you ever heard of opposites attracting?'

'Okay.'

'Besides,' she added, following her own train of thought. 'He's not English. He's Irish. He was born here and his family moved to England when he was little. A year old or something. That's why he came back to university here.'

'To Trinity College,' Duggan said. Why Trinity with its pro-British associations? he wondered. Why not UCD?

They fell silent, staring at the canal water without seeing it. This couldn't be a coincidence, Duggan thought. That the IRA would kidnap Nuala's boyfriend. It had to be connected with whatever Nuala was up to. So it had to be connected with Timmy. Could it have anything to do with spying? No, he didn't think so. It was all about Nuala and Timmy, one way or another. But what?

He tried to think it through. Nuala was supposedly kidnapped. Timmy paid a supposed ransom. Then sent some of his old IRA friends or contacts to get it back. Nuala gave back the money. Then her boyfriend was supposedly kidnapped by the IRA as a spy. Was that why she gave back the money? Someone had paid her back in kind? Timmy. Would have to have been him.

Then why threaten to execute the boyfriend? Hold him hostage against prisoners in Belfast? Put out flyers? There was no way the British were going to release them. So the IRA had to execute Bradley or lose credibility. What had Nuala started? If she had started all this?

'Jesus,' he breathed aloud.

'What?' Stella looked at him in alarm.

Duggan sighed. 'There's a chance that this is all a hoax,' he said.

'Really?' she perked up. 'You think so?'

'It's a possibility,' he said, adding, 'A small possibility.'

'Oh,' she relapsed into her pensive state.

Duggan stood up. 'I have to go back to work.'

They walked back to the nurses' home in silence. At the door, he put his hand on her arm and said, 'Don't worry. It's probably not as bad as it looks.'

She nodded, leant forward and gave him a peck on the cheek. 'Thanks.' She turned and went inside.

Twelve

Duggan took out his packet of cigarettes and found it empty again. I'm smoking too much, he thought, not even aware I'm doing it half the time. He walked his bicycle some fifty yards to the shops and bought a large packet of Sweet Afton. He lit one and cycled slowly, one-handed, up Mount Street and cut into the laneway behind Merrion Square to avoid passing Harbusch's windows. He came out on Mount Street Upper and crossed over to Sinéad's office.

Her desk was empty and he went straight upstairs, hoping to find Gifford alone. He was.

'Do you know anything about the IRA kidnapping an English spy?' he asked him.

'I've heard talk,' Gifford gave him a cautious look.

'Do you know who the spy is?'

'I haven't heard that talk.'

Duggan took a deep breath. 'I think it may be my cousin's boyfriend.'

Gifford gave a slow grin. 'Your family seems to be able to cause as much trouble as the Abwehr and MI6 put together.'

Duggan took the flyer from his pocket and gave it to Gifford.

'I take it this note at the top is from herself? The elusive cousin?' he looked to Duggan who nodded in confirmation. 'And that she hasn't emerged from the undergrowth in person?' Duggan shook his head.

'So who's Jim?' Gifford asked when he had finished.

Duggan told him all he knew.

'What're you going to do?'

'Fuck knows,' Duggan scratched his head in irritation and lit another cigarette. It tasted harsh; his mouth was beginning to feel like an ashtray.

'You going to pass it on?'

'Should I?'

Gifford shrugged.

'It might be a hoax?' Duggan offered. 'Like Nuala's kidnapping.'

'Tell me more, Sherlock.' Gifford pulled over the chair and sat on it backwards, his arms folded on its back.

'Nuala wasn't kidnapped, just pretended to be. This could be a pretence too. My uncle Timmy getting revenge on her.'

'And if your cousin-in-law ends up dead in the mountains next week? A bit of cardboard around his neck saying "spies beware"?'

Duggan rubbed his eyes and with a thumb and forefinger squeezed the bridge of his nose.

'He'd do that?' Gifford had a hint of admiration in his voice. 'Uncle Timmy would threaten to kill his daughter's boyfriend?'

Duggan shrugged and went over to the window and leaned against its side.

'Right,' Gifford said as though he was responding to an answer. 'You don't want to have to explain all that has gone before. What you've been up to while pretending to be working on the nation's behalf.'

Outside, the breeze made the barest movement in the tree tops. As usual there was no sign of life in the Harbusches' flat.

'You have to give your uncle the third degree,' Gifford said behind him, still on his chair facing into the room. 'Call his bluff. Beat the truth out of him.'

Duggan grunted. He had been thinking that too. But a confrontation with Timmy was the last thing he wanted. Actually, the second last, he told himself. Explaining all to McClure was a less palatable prospect.

'And,' Gifford got off the chair and turned to him, 'if that doesn't work, I can always report that Bradley is the kidnapped spy. Based on confidential information from a top secret tout. You.'

Duggan considered the idea. That would keep him out of it while passing on the information.

'But I have to warn you,' Gifford added, 'that if those lads who were here earlier get me into a quiet room and want to know who the tout is I'll tell them everything as soon as they raise a hand. Every last thing. They won't even have to hit me once.'

'Okay,' Duggan said. 'Thanks. I really appreciate your help.'

'Never fear,' Gifford pretended to be riding a fast horse. 'The cavalry is coming.'

'Hi-ho, Silver,' Duggan smiled.

'That's more like it,' Gifford slowed down his pretend galloping and whinnied to a stop. 'The Lone Ranger.'

Duggan left it as late as possible but it was still bright as he cycled around Stephen's Green and across to Camden Street and up over Portobello Bridge after ten o'clock. The distant mountains were beginning to turn purple in the waning light and he sped up Rathmines Road between the tramlines and over to Timmy's house. He had decided he didn't want to talk to him in Buswell's Hotel again, he wanted somewhere quiet.

Timmy's new car was in the driveway as he freewheeled through the gravel to a halt and climbed the steps to the front door. The young maid opened the door.

'*An bhfuil sé féin sa bhaile?*' he asked her.

'*Tá,*' she pulled the heavy door open wide to let him in.

Timmy appeared at the end of the corridor, a look of irritation on his face. It remained in place when he saw who the caller was. He said nothing but led Duggan into the room where they had met before. He flicked on a standard lamp and sat down at the part of the table he used as a desk. Duggan sat opposite him.

'Well,' Timmy said, adopting his politician role, 'what can I do for you?'

'Billy Ward has been arrested.'

'Who?' Timmy looked puzzled.

'The fellow who did this to me,' Duggan touched the bruise on his cheek, now a circle of dark colours.

'Good,' Timmy said. 'That's good. You caught him.'

'Not me. The Special Branch.'

'Good,' Timmy repeated. 'And they're going to charge him with assault?'

'No. Not with assaulting me. I didn't report it.'

'Okay,' Timmy's gaze was steady, his voice neutral.

'He was following me.'

'Following you?'

'That's how they caught him.'

Timmy's gaze remained steady. 'The Special Branch is protecting you?'

Duggan noted the response. Timmy didn't ask why Ward would be following him. He was right. Ward had been working for him.

'That's what you came to tell me?' Timmy continued after a moment.

'No,' Duggan took out the folded-up flyer and passed it across the table. 'I came to show you this.'

He watched Timmy read it, his face inscrutable. He was in his locked-down position, adopting a passive poker face to everything instead of his usual ebullient, blustering self. Duggan wondered what had happened to change his demeanour. He didn't think it was his arrival; Timmy seemed to have been in this mood before he turned up.

'Aye,' Timmy said when he had finished, 'I heard something about it. Didn't I tell you about it before?'

'I thought you might be able to tell me what it's really about?'

Timmy looked down at the flyer. 'It's clear what it's about. They've got a spy and they're trying to trade him.'

'He's Nuala's boyfriend.'

Timmy gave a deep sigh and said nothing.

'Jim Bradley.'

'That's his name?'

'You didn't know?' Duggan didn't try to hide the incredulity in his voice.

'Jaysus' sake,' Timmy said, reaching for a cigarette. He tossed one across the table to Gifford. 'She won't give me the time of day. You think she'd tell me about her boyfriends?'

'Aunt Mona might have told you. Or someone else in the family.'

'You're an innocent young lad,' Timmy said.

'You don't know him?'

'How the fuck would I know him?'

Duggan took a deep drag on the Player's and the stronger dose of nicotine went straight to his head, almost making him dizzy. Wrong question, he thought. This was getting him nowhere. But trying to interrogate Timmy was beyond his ability. He was much too wily to be caught saying anything he didn't want to say. Change tack, he told himself.

'Who is he anyway?' Timmy interrupted his thoughts.

'A student in Trinity College.'

'Ah,' Timmy nodded as if that was conclusive. 'English.'

'No, Irish. His parents went to England when he was young.'

'Hah,' Timmy revised his opinion but didn't change his mind. 'A West Briton. There's nothing more that type want than a repeat match. Think they'd win the next time.'

'Is there anything that can be done?' Duggan asked, offering a touch of pleading. 'To get him released?'

Timmy registered the change of tone and adapted too. 'Difficult,' he said. 'Very difficult. If the fellows they want released were down here we might be able to fudge something. But there's no talking to those fuckers up north. They don't give a damn. Even about their own men.'

'You think he's really a spy?'

'What does Nuala say?'

'She doesn't say anything to me,' Duggan said. 'I don't know where she is. I haven't talked to her.'

'But she's sending you messages.' Timmy ran his hand along the top of the flyer. The edge of the paper was jagged where Duggan had torn off Nuala's message. 'What does she think?'

'She doesn't think he is.'

'Well, that's something anyway,' Timmy leaned forward to tap ash into the ashtray between them. 'It'd be a sorry day if anyone in this family had anything to do with the British after all your father and I went through to get them out of this part of the country.'

'Maybe you could talk to some of your old comrades,' Duggan leapt at the opening Timmy had given him. 'See what could be done?'

Timmy gave him a look, almost of admiration. 'I don't know. The government wouldn't like it. Can't be going off on solo runs. Aiken'd have my guts for garters.'

'But it's your daughter. Surely they'd understand that. Family, like you said.'

'Anyway, most of those lads don't want to talk to us nowadays.'

'But some of them do,' Duggan pointed out.

'And what if he is a spy? I wouldn't cross the road to save an English spy.'

'What'll Nuala do if they kill him?'

Timmy slumped back in his chair, not needing to answer that.

'Maybe Billy Ward'll be able to help us,' Duggan added after a moment.

'What? Is he involved in it?'

'The Branch think he is,' Duggan lied.

Timmy reached forward to stub out his cigarette. 'I'll see what can be done.' He leaned back. 'And tell her to come and talk to me, for God's sake.'

Duggan went into the office the next morning, still mulling over his conversation with Timmy. Had that been a clear message? Get Nuala to talk to me and I'll get Bradley released. Or was he reading too much into a casual juxtaposition of two things? Fucking politicians, he thought.

Sullivan gave him a triumphant look. 'Post's arrived,' he said.

Duggan didn't know what he was talking about.

Sullivan pointed at the letter on his desk. 'Kitty got a letter.'

Duggan sat down and looked at the envelope as he lit his first cigarette of the day. He noted the Swiss stamps and the return address in Zurich. The envelope was already open and he took out the typed page and read it with care and then read it again.

'Point out to your client that we need a firm decision,' it said. 'These parts are in stock and available for immediate delivery but they may not be in a short time as there are other parties with an interest in them. It should be emphasised that these parts are not available from elsewhere. Our competitor cannot fill the order and his promises are only empty words. Should your client turn down our offer, his future may be affected adversely. Thus, a decision is required. Time is of importance. Strike while the iron is hot!'

Duggan opened his Harbusch file and found the copy of the last letter Harbusch had sent to the Abwehr post box in Copenhagen. He put the two side by side and read through both, Harbusch's letter first, then the latest arrival.

Yes, he thought. This is a reply to Harbusch's comment about a competitor and firming up the offer. He's been told to push the negotiation to a conclusion. Give them a deadline. But who? The IRA? Machine parts were clearly weapons. The Germans were offering immediate supplies, so why wouldn't the IRA accept them immediately?

The references to a competitor could only be to the British. And they were offering unity. Not to the IRA, but to the government. So, were the Germans negotiating with the government too? Offering weapons rather than Britain's words? That made sense.

McClure came in and looked over his shoulder at the two letters. 'Well?' he asked.

'This seems to be a reply to that,' Duggan pointed from one letter to the other.

'Yes,' McClure said. 'We've completed the circle.'

'But what does it mean?' Duggan looked up at him.

'It means Harbusch is a spy. Kelly, too.'

'But who's the client he's trying to do a deal with?'

McClure took a step backwards and gave him a thoughtful look. Then, he gave a slight nod.

So it was the government, Duggan decided. And that's why they didn't just arrest Harbusch and Kitty Kelly. They were an uncover conduit to the Germans. And now they had the instructions the German negotiators were given. He could see why McClure was pleased.

'Get that copied,' McClure pointed to the latest letter, 'And dropped back to the newsagent.' He turned to Sullivan. 'Is there someone keeping tabs on Miss Kelly today?'

'The Special Branch,' Sullivan said.

'Okay. Keep up the good work. Both of you.'

'What was that about?' Sullivan asked when McClure had gone.

'What?'

'Who's the client stuff? The question he didn't answer?'

'Need to know,' Duggan said, tipping the side of his nose.

'Fuck you,' Sullivan said without venom. 'Just because you can talk to superior officers like that doesn't mean you can talk to me like that.'

Duggan laughed. 'Listen,' he said, as another thought struck him, 'have you heard anything about this British spy the IRA is supposed to have caught?'

'Not much.'

'You know who the spy is?'

'No. Do you?'

'No,' Duggan said. 'I was just wondering what was happening.'

'Why don't you go and ask the captain over there?' he inclined his head across the corridor.

'I don't think I'd get away with that,' Duggan said.

'Want me to do it for you?' Sullivan suggested. 'I'll tell him General Duggan wants to know.'

Duggan waved away Sullivan's sarcasm as his phone rang.

'The Special Branch,' the switchboard orderly said.

'Hello?' Duggan said into the receiver, unsure of what to expect.

'Superintendent Gifford here. I want you to come down to the

Bridewell to assist in the interrogation of a prisoner.'

'Me?' Duggan asked, wondering if Gifford was serious or just messing.

'Yes.'

'Now?'

'Yes. I'm waiting for you.'

'Is that a good idea?' he asked, thinking what he would say if anyone asked what he was doing there.

'Now or never,' Gifford hung up.

Duggan was there in ten minutes and locked his bicycle against the railings outside the garda station. Gifford was waiting for him inside the main door, beside the public office, and brought him in through a door and downstairs to the basement to where the tunnel led underground to the neighbouring courthouse.

'I'm not sure about this,' Duggan said.

'Our friend Billy is about to go on his country holidays,' Gifford said as they walked. 'And we won't get another chance.'

'He's being interned?'

Gifford nodded. 'God knows when he'll be back.'

He pulled back a bolt on a door and they went in to a half cell, half interview room. The walls were a grimy green and Ward was sitting at a small table in the centre of the room. He looked dishevelled, his thick black hair in an unruly tangle, his shirt was open to his stomach, and he had dark rings under his eyes. It was obvious he had had little if any sleep and had had a hard time since they had seen him last. He looked at them without interest.

'Someone here who wants a word with you, Billy?'

'*Is saighdiúir na phoblachta mé,*' he said in a tired voice, a mantra he had been repeating for a long time now. I'm a soldier of the republic.

'*Níl tada le rá agam leatsa.*' I've nothing to say to you.

'*Is fíor saighdiúir na poblachta mise,*' Duggan said, sitting down across from him. I'm the real soldier of the republic. Gifford stood with his back to the door, arms folded. '*Saighdiúir de Oglaigh na hÉireann.*'

That drew a retort from Ward. 'The Brit puppet army,' he snorted in English. He seemed to have exhausted his Irish.

'This is not about armies,' Duggan said. 'This is personal.'

'You want to hit me?' Ward raised his jaw. 'Go on. You might as well have a go too.'

'Why were you following me?'

Ward dropped his eyes to the scarred table top.

'Who asked you to follow me?'

Ward gave no sign that he had heard.

'Were you acting under orders?'

Duggan took out his cigarettes, took one and lit it, and left the packet open on the table. He stood the lighter upright beside it and blew a slow stream of smoke at the nicotined ceiling and began again.

'Where's my cousin?'

Ward glanced up, surprised.

'What have you done with her?'

Ward looked at him.

'You killed her?'

'No,' Ward blurted out.

'So why's she disappeared off the face of the earth?'

Ward was about to say something but remembered his instructions and remained silent.

'You killed her and kidnapped her boyfriend.'

Ward shook his head slightly as if he was irritated by such stupidity.

'That's the way it looks.'

Ward shifted in his seat, glanced at the cigarettes.

'You killed my cousin,' Duggan persisted. 'Nuala. That was her name.'

'Nobody killed your fucking cousin,' Ward blurted.

'So where is she?'

'How the fuck would I know?'

'You were looking for her and now she's disappeared.'

Ward sighed and shook his head.

'Where's her body?'

'For fuck's sake.'

Duggan changed tack. 'Why'd you kidnap her boyfriend?'

Ward relaxed.

Duggan noticed and changed tack again.

'You killed her while kidnapping her boyfriend.'

Ward stirred again.

'Was it an accident?'

'Look,' Ward put his arms on the table and leaned forward as if Duggan was stupid. 'Nobody killed your cousin.'

'So where is she?'

'We don't fucking know. That's what we were trying to find out.'

'Why?'

Ward settled back in his chair.

'Why'd you want to find her? If you'd got her boyfriend?'

Ward seemed content that he'd said all he was going to say.

'Would he not tell you where she was?'

Ward gave a slight smile.

Duggan settled back and stared at him, finishing his cigarette. He seemed to have lost whatever leverage he had had on him. Ward looked back at him, confirming it.

Gifford stirred himself and walked slowly around the room, behind Duggan and then behind Ward, his arms still folded. He

Joe Joyce

stopped behind Ward and Duggan could see Ward brace for a blow on the back of the head.

'Did the army council approve all this?' Gifford asked. 'Give full and thoughtful consideration to every aspect of the operation. Send orders down the chain of command. General to commandant to captain. However it works. You military lads understand all that. Till they reached down to your good self. And you say whatever you say in your army, aye aye, captain, yes sir, no sir, and go and do it. Was that how it was?'

Duggan watched Ward unflex his muscles a little.

'Or, was this a little freelance operation? A little bit on the side, so to speak?' Gifford went on, unhurried. 'Showing initiative. Very commendable. Or,' he paused, 'was it at the behest of somebody else? Somebody other than your superiors.'

Ward narrowed his eyes and Duggan decided that had hit home.

'How much did Timmy Monaghan pay you?' Duggan asked.

It wasn't altogether a shot in the dark but it had an immediate effect. A look of horror flashed across Ward's face.

'Uh, oh,' Gifford said. 'Using the army of the republic for private gain. A little nixer on the side. I don't think they'll take too kindly to that. And,' he drawled, 'I hear your system of court-martial is a bit . . . what would you say? . . . rough and ready. No right to silence or any of that namby pamby stuff. Charged. Guilty. Bang. Bullet in the back of the head.'

Gifford came around to Duggan's side of the table. 'Right,' he said. 'I think we're finished here. This *saighdiúir* here,' he clapped Duggan on the back, 'will be writing a report about this whole business for his superior officers and he'll do a couple of extra carbon copies. One for my superiors and another for your army council.'

Duggan stood up, closed his cigarette packet and put it and his lighter in his pocket.

'Tintown might be a very hot place, Billy,' Gifford said as they went out. 'Think about it.'

Gifford shot the bolt on the door outside and they smiled at each other. 'That should do the trick,' he said as they went upstairs.

'You scared the shit out of me anyway,' Duggan said. 'If my bosses find out what I was doing here.'

'I better make sure they keep him here for another day or so,' Gifford stopped on the steps outside.

'Have you told them about Bradley?'

Gifford shook his head. 'Not yet. We'll wait and see what emerges here.' He went back into the station.

'The captain was looking for you,' Sullivan said when he got back to the office.

'What'd he want?'

'Your advice on the progress of the war, I imagine.'

Duggan turned and was walking out in search of McClure when Sullivan added, 'And your cousin left a message,' putting verbal inverted commas around the word cousin. 'She said you're to call around to her this evening after work. No matter how late.'

Duggan grunted and stopped for a moment. Stella must have something from Nuala.

'I'm glad to see you're wiping that fellow Gifford's eye,' Sullivan said. 'Thinks he's too smart. But he's not half as smart as he thinks.'

'You've got it all wrong,' Duggan said, thinking of how Gifford had rescued their chat with Ward. Turned up the pressure on him.

'And you're not as dumb as you let on,' Sullivan continued, on his own track. 'Maybe that works better with women. They don't like smart arses, do they?'

'Don't ask me,' Duggan shrugged. 'They're all a mystery to me.'

'There you go again,' Sullivan gave an admiring laugh. 'Ah, Jaysus, I'm just a thick up from the country. I know nothing. Would you lie down here beside me and explain it all to me now?'

'It doesn't work,' Duggan said.

'You're doing all right.'

'I'm doing nothing.'

'Tell him to call around no matter how late,' Sullivan said in a wavering falsetto.

'She's my cousin,' Duggan said.

'My cousins don't leave me messages like that,' Sullivan resumed his normal voice. 'Shower of bitches.'

'Why don't you try both approaches,' Duggan suggested. 'Be a dumb culchie and a smart arse jackeen. See which works better.'

'Ah,' Sullivan said sadly. 'I'll have to find someone to practise on first.'

'Women,' Duggan said. 'They're a mystery.'

'But not one we're paid to unravel,' McClure said behind him. 'Thankfully, we don't have anything so complicated to deal with it.'

Duggan swung around, embarrassed.

'Come with me. I want to talk to you.'

Duggan followed him down the corridor, apprehension rising with every step. What if he asked him about Ward? Or even where he'd been for the last hour? He'd just have to get it all off his chest. Which would be a relief in a way. Although the consequences probably wouldn't be nice. But maybe he wasn't cut out for the intelligence business. This double life was too much of a strain.

McClure took him into the colonel's empty office and they sat at a small conference table.

'There's something you should know,' he began. 'It's top secret. You're to keep it to yourself. But I don't want you adding two and two and getting three and three-quarters or four and a half.'

Duggan waited, intrigued.

'Your analysis of the Harbusch correspondence is right,' McClure continued. 'It is about supplying German weapons to somebody here. Somebody other than the IRA. They wouldn't have to try very hard to persuade them to take them.'

He paused and changed direction. 'One of our main problems is arms procurement. We have the men but we don't have rifles and sufficient ammunition for all of them. Never mind heavy weapons. The British won't, probably can't, sell us any more. The Americans are holding back as well. So where do we get them? Enter the Germans with a friendly offer. They have a large number of Lee Enfields abandoned by the BEF at Dunkirk. They've offered them to us.'

Duggan made no effort to hide his surprise.

'The advantages are obvious. The Lee Enfield is our standard rifle, so no problem with new weapons and different size ammunition and so on. But,' he paused, 'you can see the but.'

Duggan nodded, not sure that he could see all the disadvantages.

'The main one is that it puts us into the Axis camp,' McClure spelled it out.

'But we're already buying weapons from one of the belligerents,' Duggan offered.

'Precisely,' McClure said. '"Already." That's the key. We've always bought weapons from the British, so there's no change of policy in continuing to do so. Shifting to the Germans would be new. A political statement. With inevitable consequences.'

He watched Duggan work through the possible consequences.

'Put it like this,' he continued, 'the British would know very quickly if we got a large supply of Lee Enfields. The Germans promise secrecy but that's meaningless. The British know we're short of arms. Everyone knows that. And they'd know too that we hadn't got them from one of the other democracies, the US, Canada. And they'd very quickly work out that these were guns laid down by their men who surrendered in France or were left on the beach at Dunkirk. They wouldn't be very happy about that.'

'They might use it as a reason to invade.'

'Possibly. More likely, they'd retaliate by cutting off the supplies we rely on them to get. Oil, coal and so on. Anyway, you see the point.'

Duggan nodded.

'So that's why the government politely and immediately rejected the German offer. Thanks, but no thanks. Through official channels. The German legation and so on.'

'So,' Duggan grappled with this information, 'who is Harbusch negotiating with?'

'That's the question,' McClure lit a cigarette.

'Could it be one of the pro-German groups here?'

'Doubtful. They're not organised in any military way. They wouldn't know what to do with them. Mainly a bunch of crackpots.'

'General O'Duffy?' Duggan suggested.

McClure nodded as if O'Duffy proved his point and pushed back his chair. 'Anyway, it might become clearer now that we can read both sides of Harbusch's messages. But I wanted you to know the background so you can see the wider picture. And I want you to go back over everything and write a report on what we now know and what it might mean. Don't be afraid of following your instincts.'

'Okay,' Duggan stood up as well.

'You're enjoying this work?'

'Yes.' This part of it, he thought. 'Very much.'

'Good,' McClure dismissed him.

It was late before he finished tapping out the report, one-fingered, on the big Royal typewriter and teasing out all the assumptions and presumptions that had already been made and revising them with the latest information. Sullivan was long gone off duty and he left it on McClure's desk and cycled up the quays to the city centre.

The night was warm, almost balmy. The street lights on the corners were coming on and the roads were empty as he sped along, unhindered by any traffic. There were few people out. Pools of light and the mumble of voices and occasional laughter came from the pubs, their doors wide open to cool the interiors.

He went down Pearse Street, turned into Westland Row and then into Fenian Street and into the empty car park in front of Sir Patrick Dun's hospital. The same porter was on duty at the desk and gave him a sour look when he asked for Nurse Maloney.

'And who are you?' the porter asked.

Duggan told him and the porter handed him an envelope. He could feel the keys in it before he turned his back on the porter and opened it, expecting a note. There was nothing apart from the two keys.

He got back on his bike and cycled up beside the canal to Huband Bridge and turned into Mount Street, swerving around a prostitute who stepped off the footpath to pose before him. He stopped outside Nuala's building and the first key he tried opened the hall door. He pushed the light switch in the hall and climbed the stairs and opened the door to her flat and stepped in, turning on the light switch.

He stepped back, startled. Nuala was sitting at the head of the bed, hunched tight in the corner where the two walls met, her knees up and her arms around them. She was wearing pale trousers which flopped around her legs and her feet were bare. Her face was pale, exaggerating the dark circles under her eyes, and her reddish hair was a mass of uncontrolled curls.

'Jesus,' he breathed out and closed the door behind him.

They stared at each other for a moment.

Then Nuala said, 'You wanted to talk to me.'

'Jesus Christ!' Duggan exploded. 'I wanted to talk to you! I've been beaten up because of you. Followed by some gunmen. Threatened by your father. Risked my army career over you.'

She raised her hands from her knees. 'Sorry,' she said without any sign that she was. 'I didn't involve you in any of this. It was my father.'

'Okay,' he said, his anger rising. 'I don't want to talk to you. I just want you to know I don't want anything more to do with you and your father's games. Okay?'

He turned and opened the door, feeling an unexpected twinge of sympathy for Timmy. There were two of them in it.

'Wait,' she sniffed. 'I am sorry. I need your help.'

Duggan took a deep breath, held it, and closed the door.

'I,' she said, stretching her legs out in front of her and looking at her feet, 'appreciate what you've been doing. I'm sorry you've been dragged into this. But I do need your help.'

Duggan took out his cigarettes, offered her one, and she took it. He lit both and sat down on the side of the bed and waited for her to explain.

'You know they've kidnapped Jim?'

'The IRA,' Duggan nodded.

'Yes, but my father's behind it.'

'Timmy kidnapped him?'

'They're working for him.'

'The IRA?' he didn't hide his scepticism.

'A few of them. The one's who kidnapped Jim.'

'He told them Jim was a spy?'

Nuala shook her head. 'He knows he's not a spy.'

'He says he knows nothing about him.'

She gave a short laugh. 'Yeah, he would. He knows all about him.'

'Look,' Duggan got up and walked over to the draining board and got a cup to use as an ashtray. 'Just tell me what's going on.'

Nuala sighed and didn't seem to know where to begin.

'You pretended to be kidnapped,' Duggan prompted her. 'Why?'

'To get some money out of my father. To pay compensation to someone he had wronged.'

'What?'

Nuala rubbed the little ash on her cigarette against the rim of the cup. 'This isn't easy,' she said, giving the cigarette her full attention. 'Even though we don't get on. He's still my father.'

Duggan waited, mystified.

She inhaled deeply. 'This is not something that should ever go outside the family.' She looked at him, waiting for a response. He nodded, not knowing what he was agreeing to.

'You know our house down the country? The farm?' she continued. He nodded again. 'That belonged to Jim's family. His mother inherited it from an uncle. During the War of Independence.' She looked at him again as if expecting him to make sense of something. 'Jim's father was in the RIC. A district inspector. A target of the IRA. His mother went to the IRA, to my father, and offered to sell him the house for very little if they left her husband alone. My father agreed. And then they shot him on his way home from Mass one Sunday.'

The newspaper cutting, Duggan thought. The district inspector recovering from his wounds. The name must've been Bradley; he should've made the connection. 'He survived,' he said.

'He's crippled. He's still alive. Living in England. In a bad way.'

'And his mother?'

She nodded. 'She's still alive too. But they're both in a bad way. They have no money. He has just a small pension. And they have big medical bills.'

'So how can Jim afford to go to Trinity?'

'His mother's uncle left him a bursary to go there. Just to Trinity.'

Duggan jabbed his butt at the bottom of the cup, a sick feeling in his stomach. He handed the cup to Nuala. There were tears in her eyes.

'How'd you find out about this?' he asked.

'I always knew there was something,' she said, putting out her cigarette and raising her knees and holding onto them again. 'Once when my father had some old comrades around they were all drunk and laughing about something and I remember someone saying to him, you know the way something sticks in your mind, something that you don't quite understand. Someone said, you did nicely for yourself anyway. In that sort of knowing way. And they all laughed. In that knowing way. You know?'

'Was my father there?'

She shook her head. 'I don't think he ever came to those get togethers. I never knew what it meant, but it stuck in my mind. I supposed it meant the politics, the Dáil seat. But then I met Jim and . . .'

'He told you.'

'No, he didn't know at the time. It only came together in dribs and drabs. Extraordinary really.

'I was crossing the street outside Trinity one day and this young lad on a bike came flying around from Dame Street and knocked me down. He fell off the bike too but got up and cycled off. Jim stopped and helped me up. I wasn't hurt, not really, but I was shaken and my knee was sore and I was hobbling. So, he said, come in to Trinity and sit down for a few minutes. And we went into his rooms and he made tea and we chatted. You know, the usual. Where're you from and all that. He has an English accent but he said his family was from Galway and I said where and I said that's where I'm from too.' She shrugged. 'You know how it is.'

She took a handkerchief from her pocket and blew her nose.

'Then later,' she went on, 'one thing led to another. He told me about his father being shot. And, later again, when we got to know each other better, about his mother. She had a heart attack a few months ago and he went home to see her. And that's when she told him about the deal she had done to protect his father. She never told his father about it. He still doesn't know. Can you imagine that?'

Duggan didn't want to imagine any of it. How could Timmy do what he had done? How could he dirty a noble cause with greed and double-dealing?

'He shot him?' he said, half question, half statement, spelling out the facts that were hollowing his stomach. 'Your father shot Jim's father? After agreeing with his mother to leave him alone in return for the house?'

'I don't know if he did it himself. He wouldn't tell me.'

'You asked him?'

She nodded. 'I told him I knew all about it. And that he should pay Jim's mother the proper price now. Now that he can afford it. We had a blazing row. The worst we've ever had. And we've had a few.'

'What did he say?'

'He wouldn't talk about it. Told me it was none of my business. It was a revolution. I should be glad to be living in a free country. And proud of the sacrifices he and his comrades had made. Good men had been tortured and died to give us the freedom we now enjoyed.' She waved a dismissive hand in the air. 'All the usual stuff you get if you ask any awkward questions.'

'So you and Jim pretended you were kidnapped.'

'Jim knew nothing about it. It was my idea, my doing.' She paused. 'He didn't even know at the time that my father was the one who bought his mother's house for next to nothing. I put it together from the names and places. But I couldn't bring myself to tell him. I was so ashamed.'

Duggan stood up and walked around the room and lit another

cigarette. Nuala sniffled and blew her nose behind him. He turned back to her and offered her a cigarette and lit it.

'So you got the five hundred pounds I left in that place in Wicklow Street,' he said.

'You left it? I didn't know that.'

'How'd you collect it?'

'I just walked in,' she hinted at a smile. 'Covered my hair with a scarf and put on an old coat and shuffled in.'

'Then what?'

'Then I told Jim about it. Gave him the money for his parents. But he wouldn't take it. He got all upset about it. Said we had to give it back. Two wrongs wouldn't make a right. All that sort of stuff.'

Duggan sat back down on the bed.

'I said I had no intention of giving it back. That I'd send it to his parents anonymously. That it was my money. In a kind of a way. And I owed it to his mother. And I was going to pay it. Then,' she paused to take a deep drag on the cigarette, 'he insisted on picking up the second payment. Said it was—'

'Wait a minute,' Duggan interrupted. 'There was a second payment?'

'Another five hundred.'

'When?'

'The next day.'

'Same place?'

Nuala nodded. 'He wanted to just leave it there. But I said we couldn't do that. You'd never know who'd walk away with it. But he wouldn't let me go to collect it. Said it was too dangerous. He said he'd go. And he never came back.' She stared at Duggan. 'I knew I should've done it myself. This wouldn't have happened.'

'So you gave Timmy back the first five hundred.'

'He got all his money back,' she corrected him. 'After Jim disappeared, these handbills about a British spy appeared. There was one left here. Someone dropped one into the hospital in an envelope for Stella. Other friends of mine were given them.'

'You gave back the money so you expected him to be released.'

'Yes,' she said, with an air of resignation. 'He's won. I just want Jim to be freed and for it to be over. None of it is his fault.'

'Christ,' Duggan muttered.

'What?' she said.

He made a helpless gesture with his hands. 'This might have taken on a life of its own. I mean, the IRA say they're holding a British spy and will execute him unless some prisoners are released. They're not going to be released. So, they have to execute him. Or else their threats are empty.'

She nodded and propped her elbows on her knees and pushed her eyes hard into the palms of her hand. 'I know,' she muttered.

Duggan watched her for a moment and then leaned forward and took the remainder of the cigarette from her fingers and put it out in the cup. 'I talked to your father about Jim,' he said. 'I might've taken him up wrong but I got the impression that he'd try and get Jim released if you go and talk to him.'

She lowered her hands and her eyes were red. 'I promised myself I'll never talk to him again.'

'If it gets Jim released . . .' he left the idea hang.

'If anything happens to Jim that'd be it. I'd certainly never have anything to do with him again.'

'Okay,' Duggan sighed. There were two of them in it, he thought. Though she had right on her side. More right than Timmy, anyway. 'Have you talked to your mother about any of this?'

Nuala snorted. 'My mother doesn't want to know.'

'You have tried to talk to her?'

'No. My mother's only interested in her novenas and first Fridays and her bridge club and all that.'

'She doesn't know anything about it?'

Nuala thought for a moment. 'If she does, she doesn't want to know. You know what I mean?'

Duggan nodded.

'I think she might know something but maybe not the details. Because she doesn't want to know. So she's buried herself in religion.'

'You father seems to be afraid that she'll find out something.'

'Does he now?' Nuala perked up for the first time. She hasn't given up, Duggan thought. In spite of what she had said, she hasn't accepted that Timmy has won.

'Don't do anything yet,' he said. 'I'll talk to your father again.'

'What'll you say to him?'

'I don't know yet,' Duggan admitted.

'You can tell him he'll never see me again if a hair of Jim's head is harmed,' she said. 'And I'll be out campaigning against him in the next election.'

It was dark out when they left although there was still a faint light in the western sky. Duggan sat up on his bike and she stood on the step.

'How'll I contact you?' he said.

'Leave a message inside,' she said. 'Hold on to those keys.'

He was about to push off when he noticed the man about fifty yards away on the other side of the railings at the corner of Herbert Street, little more than a dark shadow. 'Fuck,' he said. He should've kept an eye on his back but he hadn't bothered since they'd caught Billy Ward.

'What?' she said, echoing the alarm in his voice.

'Get up on the bar. Quick.'

She sat up sideways on the crossbar and he pushed off and ped-alled as hard as he could towards Merrion Square. As he swung around he caught sight of the figure disappearing into Herbert Street. Maybe it was a false alarm, he thought. But he doubted it. He picked up speed, his mind a jumble. The Special Branch had a stakeout somewhere in this street, watching the British legation, but where? Would Gifford be in Merrion Square? But the door would be locked. Why hadn't he brought his revolver?

'Can you see?' he asked. 'Is anyone following us?'

Nuala bent forward to try and look around him, almost unbalancing the bike. She tried to raise herself to look over his shoulder but couldn't. 'I can't see,' she said. 'What is it?'

'I think there was someone watching the flat,' he said, glancing back over his shoulder and seeing a bicycle round the corner from Herbert Street. 'Fuck,' he repeated. 'He's following us.'

He turned quickly into a laneway on the left and tried to pedal harder.

'I see him now,' Nuala said as they went around the corner.

'How far back is he?'

'A good bit,' she said.

But he was sure to catch up, Duggan thought. He couldn't go as fast as him with the extra weight of Nuala. He pushed harder, beginning to breathe heavily, and shot across Baggot Street with barely a look in either direction and into another lane, hoping it was not a cul-de-sac. It was dark, without any street lights, but it stretched straight ahead as far as he could see.

'Do you know where you're going?' Nuala asked, as if reading his mind.

He shook his head, saving his breath.

'There's a left turn just up here,' she said. 'Take it.'

'Now,' she said and he swung into a barely visible entry, almost running into the wall as he took the corner too fast. The bicycle bumped along another dark and unpaved laneway, high walls on either side with regularly spaced doors into the gardens of the houses on the main streets. A dog behind one began to bark in a fury and clawed at a door and they rounded a bend.

'Right again,' she said and he followed her instructions into a short stretch of rough lane, trying to keep on one side of the track. They bounced through a pothole he hadn't seen and came out on a road beside the canal.

'Go right,' she said, leaning back to look around his right shoulder as he made the turn. 'We might've lost him.'

He kept pedalling as hard as he could and she told him to veer right as Wilton Park loomed ahead of them and then took him into another laneway and back into the one where the dog resumed his barking. Nuala muttered a curse and told him to go left and they were back into the long dark lane he had gone into from Baggot Street.

Duggan was slowing, breathing heavily. He glanced over his shoulder and saw nothing, no movement, in the gloom behind him. He slowed down, trying to recover his energy. 'Stop,' she said quietly as they passed a recessed garage door. She slid of the crossbar and he dismounted and put the bicycle against the door and they stood side by side behind it, their backs to the door, trying to keep inside the shallow recess.

Nuala put her fingers to her lips and he tried to still his breathing.

After a few moments she looked out from the recess, checked in both directions and then stepped across the lane and tried the garden door opposite. It was locked and she tried the next one. It was locked too. She came back and stood beside him.

They stood in silence for what seemed a long time, listening to the night sounds of the city like they came from another world. A tram clanged, a door slammed, wood grated as a stiff window was raised or lowered, and there was the rumble of a distant train but no sounds of people or the hum of bicycle tyres on the compacted sand and gravel of the laneway.

Eventually they stepped out from the recess and looked up and down at the empty lane and Nuala indicated the opposite direction from Baggot Street and they walked along, Duggan wheeling the bike on one track, Nuala walking on the other.

She led him out into Fitzwilliam Place where the restricted street lighting at the junctions seemed to their night vision to make the street brighter than it was. There was no sign of anyone about. Nuala linked him and said, 'Looks more natural,' as they walked along the footpath.

'Where are we going?' he asked.

'Ranelagh,' she said.

They walked all the way there, not talking, through residential streets, stopping occasionally to pretend to talk but to check that nobody was following them. 'How do you know all those laneways?' he asked at one point but she only gave a husky laugh and didn't answer.

She finally stopped outside a redbrick terraced house in a quiet street near the centre of Ranelagh. 'The friend of a friend's,' she said.

'I can find you here?' he said, noting the number.

'Just make sure you're not followed,' she said, as if everything that had just happened was his fault.

Duggan shook his head in amazement as she opened the metal gate and went in the hall door.

Thirteen

Duggan had already finished his third cigarette of the day and was slumped in the chair staring at the ceiling when McClure came in and said, 'Penny for them.'

He straightened up. 'Just trying to make sense of everything.' Which was a lie. He had been trying to decide how he should approach Timmy. It wasn't a meeting he was looking forward to but it had to be done if he was to ever get this monkey off his back.

'There are a few other bits and pieces,' McClure said, sitting down at the table. 'Our friends across the water confirm that Miss Kitty Kelly is in Torquay at present. So,' he spread his hands in an open gesture. Duggan nodded. That was no surprise, they had assumed as much.

'They're also grateful for the address in Zurich. They hadn't known of that one. And,' he opened the file on his desk, 'we've got another letter for Harbusch. From his inamorata in Amsterdam.'

He slid the envelope across the table and Duggan took out the hand-written page. 'My dearest one Hans,' it began. 'It is no good. I can no longer go with the memory only of your hot body.' Duggan couldn't hold back a snigger. McClure gave him an inquisitive look.

'Hans's hot body,' Duggan shook his head, thinking of the dumpy little man he was so used to following.

'The ways of the heart,' McClure shrugged.

'I have found another one,' the letter went on. 'He is not so big with the imagination but he will have to do for me for now. Even so I think only of you when he is with me. Tell me you come again and again and I will give him the orders to be marching immediately.'

'Just a Dear John letter or marching orders?' McClure asked.

'He's being told to pull out?' Duggan said and blushed, cursing himself mentally for adding to the double entendres.

'A tactical withdrawal,' McClure said with a dry smile. 'Possibly.'

'It's written by an English speaker,' Duggan said as the idea struck him. 'Someone who's deliberately putting in all the double meanings. Pretending their English isn't too good.'

'Go on,' McClure encouraged him.

'And by a man,' Duggan concluded.

'Why a man?'

'Because a woman wouldn't do that.'

'Perhaps,' McClure said with a noncommittal shake of his head. 'Let's think it through. Let's suppose an English speaker is writing these letters. Man or woman doesn't matter. And they're writing this slightly jumbled English. With lots of double entendres. Why?'

Duggan couldn't think of a reason.

'Surely not for the fun of it,' McClure said. 'Nobody has time for that sort of nonsense these days.'

'We don't know if Harbusch ever writes back to her. This person.'

McClure nodded. 'He writes to Copenhagen and Miss Kelly gets a reply from Zurich. He gets money from Switzerland as well. And he gets these letters from Amsterdam.'

'Maybe Miss Kelly posts the letters to there too,' Duggan suggested.

'Or sends the replies to somewhere else. We should find out in the next few days. If Harbusch replies to this one. Otherwise,' McClure sighed, 'we'll have to work on the assumption that there's someone else involved in this little ring as well.'

Sullivan came in and McClure turned his attention to him. 'And how is miss whatever her real name is this morning?'

'Same as usual,' Sullivan said. 'Went to Mass in Westland Row and picked up her letter and back home again.'

'Who's watching her now?'

'The Special Branch.'

'Good,' McClure stood up. 'Check the overnight reports of parachutists, planes, strange noises and the look-out posts' reports and see if there's anything we need to follow up.'

Sullivan sat down at his place.

'And,' McClure said to Duggan, 'all we can do is keep our eye on Harbusch and see if he changes his pattern. See what he does with the instructions he's just got in the letter from Zurich. And have that Amsterdam letter left for collection when you've finished parsing it.'

'Jaysus,' Sullivan sighed when McClure had left. 'That priest in Westland Row loves the sound of his own voice. Drags everything out. Thinks he's on the stage.'

'Here's some light relief for you,' Duggan tossed the letter down the table to him.

'More piggy wiggy stuff,' Sullivan rubbed his hands in anticipation.

Duggan didn't want to spoil it by sharing his theory about the letter writer.

He took his time going into the city centre, still trying to figure out his approach to Timmy. The heat wave was over, grey clouds piling up, darkening the mood of the city and threatening rain. A strong breeze from the west hurried him along, faster than he wanted to go.

There was no alternative but to put everything to him straight, he thought. Get some answers. And find a way out of this mess. Through threats and counter threats. It was a question of whether Timmy or Nuala caved in first. And he wasn't sure which it would be. Though Nuala was right, Timmy had the upper hand. She wanted Jim released and Timmy was their only hope of getting him freed.

He waited at the kiosk at the gate of Leinster House while an usher phoned Timmy's office and then told him to wait. He stepped back into the small waiting area and watched the comings and goings. It was still early in the parliamentary day and there was little traffic in and out; a few politicians and staff members or civil servants arriving. All were nodded through by the ushers.

Duggan checked his watch and wondered what Timmy was up to. Was he trying to make him sweat or was he just busy? Then he realized that this was probably the first time that he wanted something from Timmy rather than the other way round. And Timmy probably knew that.

After a quarter of an hour the usher's phone rang and he told Duggan to go up to the main door and someone would meet him there. He walked around the looming bulk of the plinth and its image of unmovable empire and up the couple of steps and in the main door. Another usher stood before him and asked, 'Deputy Monaghan?'

Duggan nodded and the usher showed him into a room to the right of the high hall. 'Wait here, please,' he left the door open behind him.

He circled the room, around by its marble fireplace, examining its ornate ceiling, feeling its deep carpet underfoot. There was little furniture, a few period chairs by the walls, a low table in the centre with an ashtray: a room for people passing through. He settled beside one of the tall windows, looking out at Queen Victoria's back as she stood sentinel and kept the city out. A spatter of rain appeared on the window, almost hesitant at first.

Timmy left him another ten minutes and then walked in and closed the door behind him. He stopped in the centre of the room and they stared at each other.

'I met Nuala,' Duggan broke first.

'Good,' Timmy nodded. 'Good.'

'We were chased by a gunman.'

'Someone shot at you?' Timmy said, startled.

Duggan shook his head. 'He followed us. Tried to catch us but we got away.'

'Good,' Timmy repeated, nodding to himself.

'Why was he following us?'

Timmy looked mystified.

'I know he's working for you,' Duggan pressed on. 'Nuala told me what all this is about. You knew all along what was going on. And you tried to use me, made a fool of me. Pretending to be concerned about your daughter, when you're only concerned about your own reputation. And making sure nobody knows the despicable thing you did.'

'Paul, Paul,' Timmy raised his hands in a mixture of surrender and trying to stop him.

'Nuala was wrong to do what she did but at least her motive was good. Which is more than can be said for you. Fighting for Ireland but filling your own pockets.' Duggan felt himself growing angrier. 'Everything you were supposed to be fighting against you were doing yourself. Exploiting a poor worried woman, taking her property and reneging on your agreement. Shooting him in the back . . .'

'Paul, shhh!' Timmy said as if soothing an overwrought child. 'You're upsetting yourself.'

'Fucking right I am,' Duggan hurled back. 'I can't believe you would do something like that. That you would use the cause for your own . . .' He couldn't find the word. 'And then set these fellows on your own daughter. And have her boyfriend killed. The son of the same woman . . .'

'Shhh, Paul, shhh.'

'Jesus Christ,' Duggan bit his lip, close to tears. 'How could you?'

Timmy shook his head in sadness. 'Terrible things happen in war.'

'That wasn't fucking war,' Duggan shot back. 'That was – I don't know – robbery. Extortion. Murder.'

'No, no,' Timmy turned decisive. 'It was not murder. He was an agent of the crown. He was the enemy, one of the occupying forces. He was trying to kill us. To keep us in subjugation. It was a war. Us or them.'

Duggan shook his head.

'Terrible things happen in war,' Timmy repeated. 'And they're best left there once it's over. That's what I told Nuala too but she wouldn't let it go. Too stubborn. And look at all the trouble it's caused now. Twenty years later.'

Duggan couldn't decide whether to laugh or cry. It was all Nuala's fault.

'The past should be left in peace,' Timmy continued, metaphorically climbing on to an election platform. 'What matters now is the present and the future. How we rise up to the challenges before us. And they're bigger than ever before with the world in the state it's in. I hope we don't have to fight them all over again. But, by God, if we have to we will. And we'll win all over again.'

A wave of exhaustion overcame Duggan. So much for the best way to handle Timmy, he thought. He'd let his emotions run away with him and ended up getting a political speech.

'What about Jim Bradley?' he asked.

'I'll see what I can do,' Timmy said, oozing sincerity. 'Do my level best to get him out.'

'Nuala'll never talk to you again if anything happens to him.'

'She say that?'

Duggan nodded. 'And she meant it.'

'That girl is so headstrong,' Timmy sighed.

'You've got your money back.'

Timmy shook his head with a noncommittal grunt.

'I handed it back to you myself.' Duggan said and added, a statement rather than a question. 'You didn't get back the second payment.'

'I haven't seen it yet,' Timmy said with care.

'Your friends have taken it,' Duggan gave a short laugh. 'Did you not pay them?'

'Paul,' Timmy said with patience. 'I've told you I'll do everything I can.'

'You got him into this. You have to get him out of it.'

'If it was only that easy, I'd do it in a minute.'

'What do you mean?'

'They say he's a spy.'

'He's not a spy.'

'Nuala told you that?' Timmy didn't wait for an answer. 'And I'm sure she believes that. But those fellows have their own sources of information. They're usually well informed.'

'You're saying he is a spy?'

'I'm saying I don't know,' Timmy widened his eyes in innocence. 'I'm just saying that those fellows have good intelligence. And isn't it an amazing coincidence that he should meet up with my daughter and tell her all about his family. Isn't that strange? Wouldn't you think so?'

Duggan's head began to reel. 'Why would a British spy target you? Is that what you're saying?'

'I don't know,' Timmy said. 'I'm just saying it's a strange coincidence, that's all.'

That's crazy, Duggan thought. Why would the British send over a spy to find Timmy's daughter and get her to try and blackmail her father? It was totally crazy.

'He's not a spy,' Duggan said, taking a chance. 'Our people say he's not.'

'They're sure?'

'They're sure,' Duggan lied. He didn't even know if they were aware that Bradley was the kidnap victim. He thought of telling Timmy that the British said he wasn't but that wouldn't persuade him of anything. Probably the opposite, confirm Bradley's guilt in his eyes.

'All right,' Timmy said. 'I'll do everything I can. Talk to everyone I know. See what can be done.'

'And tell them to leave Nuala alone. Stop trying to find her.'

'Okay, okay,' Timmy said with the air of a penitent. 'I'll pass the word along.'

'Time is running out,' Duggan pointed out. 'Things will have to be done quickly.'

'I know, I know.'

'And I think you should give back some of the money at least to Mrs Bradley.'

'Paul, Paul,' Timmy shook his head in disappointment. 'You're a good lad. Like a son to me. A smart lad. But I told you before. Don't try to be too smart.'

'It'd be only fair. They're very hard up.'

Timmy gave a world-weary sigh. 'Don't push it. This is how this whole thing started. Nuala wouldn't let it go. Let bygones be bygones.'

'Nuala didn't shoot this man while promising not to.'

'And I didn't either.'

Duggan stared at him, stopped in his tracks. Timmy nodded,

affirming what he had said. Neither added anything for a moment.

'Let sleeping dogs lie,' Timmy pointed a finger at him. 'Let the past rest in peace. There's many a good young lad like you in the cemetery for the last twenty years. But there's nothing to be gained from raking it all up again and again.'

'Who shot him?'

Timmy shook his head.

'Tell me.'

'I'm not saying another word about it,' Timmy closed his eyes. 'That's not a road you want to go down. Leave those things alone.'

The shower of rain had passed, leaving the streets glistening in weak sunshine. Duggan felt weak too, light-headed, feeling he'd been ambushed by Timmy. Again. He left his bicycle where it was at the railing of Leinster House and walked up Kildare Street and crossed the road into Stephen's Green. The benches were all wet and he stepped into the shelter beside the still pond and lit a cigarette. He leaned on the railing, blowing grey smoke towards the grey water, forcing himself to think the thought that he didn't want to think.

He was almost finished his cigarette when his thoughts were interrupted by a flight of lapwings coming low over the water and landing with a skidding splash off to his right. He turned to look and saw a dumpy man with a brown paper bag throwing pieces of bread onto the water among the chattering ducks. Harbusch.

Duggan looked beyond him and saw Gifford pass slowly between two trees in the distance. Harbusch was intent on what he was doing, tossing handfuls of bread pieces onto the water in a methodical way. When he had finished he scrunched the paper bag into a ball and put it into his pocket and turned towards Duggan.

Duggan stared straight ahead at the water and Harbusch walked by within a foot of him. It was the closest Duggan had ever been to him, so close he smelled Harbusch's aftershave. He flicked his butt across the path and into the pond and waited for Gifford.

'Well, well,' Gifford said. 'I'll have to include you in my report. You're the only suspicious person Hansi has come anywhere near today.'

'What's he doing here?'

Gifford shrugged. 'One of those ducks has got to be a German courier. Not the pigeons after all. And he's on his way back to the Fuhrer with it now. Air mail.'

They walked along the path after Harbusch who had gone around a bend in the path and was now obscured by bushes.

'Which one had a guttural quack?'

Duggan gave a short laugh. 'Where's Eliza today?'

'In the Monument Café as usual. I decided to stick with Hansi since he was going a different way today.'

'But why?'

'Ours not to reason why. Ours but to follow and spy.'

'I should go back and have a look at Eliza.'

'Always to be recommended.'

'In case the ducks were just a diversion.'

'Good idea, Sherlock,' Gifford agreed. 'We wouldn't want anyone to be able to say we were fooled by ducks.'

Duggan made his way back to the main entrance to the park and crossed onto Grafton Street and went down to the café. He stepped in and stopped as though looking for someone. Eliza was at a table at the back on her own. She had her purse open and was taking out coins and handing them to a waitress. Duggan left again and crossed the road and stood in a shop doorway, waiting for her to emerge.

He followed her along her expected route, down Grafton Street, into Nassau Street towards Merrion Square. She swung along at a confident pace, attracting admiring glances, women as well as men getting out of her path. Duggan paid her little attention, still immersed in his own thoughts, a jumble of possibilities now overlaid with one big fear. The best way out of an ambush is to charge straight through it, he thought. Keep going. Don't hesitate. Don't stop.

He stopped at the end of Clare Street as Eliza crossed into Merrion Square and he watched her head towards her apartment, his decision made. Drops of rain began to fall and he went back into Greene's bookshop and to the sub-post office counter at the back. He asked the woman behind the bars for a telegram form and wrote out a brief message: 'Day off tomorrow. On morning train.'

He filled in his father's name and address and the woman counted the words and told him the cost. As he paid her he hoped his father would be there when it arrived – his mother would fear the worst if she was the first to receive it. Telegrams nearly always meant bad news.

The rain was coming down heavily, a sudden summer shower, when he emerged, big drops bouncing off the road and the gutters already full. He waited under the shelter of the shop's awning, half listening to two young women who were having an intense conversation about a manipulative co-worker. 'She's just a silver-plated bitch,' one concluded. 'All nice and shiny to your face. Cut you to ribbons behind your back.'

He put Timmy and his hints out of his mind now that his course of action was decided. Eliza will be drenched, he thought idly. There's no shelter on the path alongside the park.

When the rain stopped he retrieved his bicycle from Kildare Street and cycled along Merrion Row and into the square. Sinéad's desk was empty and he went upstairs taking the steps two at a time and opened the door to their room.

'Oh, sorry,' he stopped. Gifford was stripped to the waist, Sinéad standing in front of him. She stepped backwards.

'If only,' Gifford sighed. His shirt was on the back of the chair, a cup and plate on its seat.

'In your dreams,' she said, reddening.

'See?' Gifford said to Duggan. 'She can even see into my dreams.'

'Shut up, you,' she punched him hard on the shoulder. 'Giggler was looking for you,' she said to Duggan, picking up the cup and plate.

'Who?' he said but knew the answer even as he asked. Sullivan.

'That fellow from your crowd who's always giggling.'

'Did he leave a message?'

'No, just asked if you were here. Said it was nothing important.'

Was Sullivan checking up on him? he wondered.

'You're looking a bit raggedly today,' she said. 'Hard night?'

'Just busy.'

'Out with his duckies,' Gifford said. 'The feathered kind.'

She raised her eyes at the two of them. 'If you want tea you can come and get it,' she said to Duggan as she left.

'Sorry if I interrupted . . .' Duggan said.

'Sadly not,' Gifford pointed at his shirt. 'Got drenched in that shower. Hansi kept going so we sloshed our way back.'

'Eliza got drenched too.' Duggan stood at the window, looking across at the Harbusches' flat.

'Stop, stop,' Gifford joined him. 'They're both over there taking off their wet clothes. No wonder Hansi is impervious to everything. He's in seventh heaven all the time.'

'Do you think we could get into Miss Kelly's flat?'

'Ah, a little breaking and entering. Just what I need to calm my fevered brain.'

'Can it be done?'

Gifford thought about it for a moment. 'Need a lot of planning. And a lot of people on standby. And someone who knew his business.

Not like the eejit we had the last time.'

'Who'd have to approve it?'

'My super,' Gifford said. 'But we'd have to make a strong case. It'd tie up a lot of manpower. We'd have to have our burglar on standby, teams to follow Hansi and Eliza and Kitty. And we'd need them all out at the same time. A lot of people could be hanging around a long time waiting for the right moment.'

'Yeah,' Duggan agreed. 'And it's unlikely she'd leave anything lying around about her real identity.'

'Do our betters care that much about Hansi anyway? They're much more interested in your friend Goertz.'

Gifford left the window and took his shirt off the chair. 'Could I hang this out the window? Would Hansi see it as a signal of surrender? Call in his paratroopers? Or would the neighbours kill me for turning the square into a tenement?'

'Probably all of those,' Duggan offered. He turned away from the window too. 'I saw Nuala at last,' he said and gave Gifford an edited account of his meetings with Nuala and Timmy, including everything except the details of Timmy's dealings with the Bradley family.

'Culchies,' Gifford shook his head when he had finished. 'I always knew you ate your own down there. What do you do to your enemies?'

'Eat them without butter,' Duggan said without humour, wondering what Gifford would think if he had told him the whole story. 'It's a standoff. Neither will give in first.'

'Hmm,' Gifford walked around the room in thought. 'Our friend Billy Ward could be the man to ride to the rescue. Break the deadlock.'

Ward's bruises had lost their angry look and settled into a dark purple, a stage behind Duggan's own fading bruise. He touched it unconsciously as he and Gifford entered the interview room. Duggan sat down across the table from Ward and took his time lighting a cigarette. He left the packet open and his lighter beside it in the centre of the table. Gifford leaned his shoulder against the door, arms folded.

'There are a few details I'd like to clear up for my report,' Duggan began at last, starting the strategy he and Gifford had worked out on their way to the Bridewell. 'You and your friend grabbed Bradley on Wicklow Street in the same way we first met and you took him to the same garage. But you were lucky this time. He had the money on him. Five hundred pounds in cash. And the guards didn't come knocking on the door.'

Ward stared back at him, trying to look impassive.

'So you could move on and count the money at your leisure.' Duggan paused to take a deep drag. 'What I want to know is whether you handed over the money to your quartermaster. All five hundred pounds.'

Ward blinked a couple of times.

'All five hundred pounds,' Duggan repeated. 'And how you explained why Bradley was walking around with five hundred pounds in his pocket.'

'Because he's a spy,' Gifford offered. Ward glanced at him in surprise.

'Even spies don't walk around with five hundred pounds in their pockets, do they?' Duggan shook his head. 'In envelopes addressed to the daughter of a government TD?'

'Trying to bribe the government,' Gifford said.

'Not a very smart spy then,' Duggan laughed. 'Wasting money trying to bribe a backbencher with no power.'

'He confessed,' Ward said.

Duggan hid his delight with incredulity. 'To trying to bribe Timmy Monaghan?'

'To being a British spy,' Ward said with a touch of smugness.

'A voluntary confession?' Gifford asked.

'He didn't hold out very long,' Ward gave a hint of a smile.

Duggan had a hollow feeling in his stomach. He knew how quick Ward was to use his gun as a blunt instrument. 'What did he confess to?'

'To being a British spy.'

'Who was he spying on?'

Ward shrugged and asked if he could have a cigarette. Duggan pushed the packet and lighter closer to him.

'Who was he spying on?' he repeated as Ward lit the cigarette.

'Ireland,' Ward said, as if the answer was obvious.

'So who was the money for?'

'I don't fucking know, do I?' Ward said. 'Informers probably.'

'Timmy Monaghan's daughter? She's an informer?'

'No, no,' Ward backed off. 'I don't know. I don't know who it was for.'

'Why was he spying?'

'Money, I suppose.'

'You didn't ask him?'

'I don't talk to British spies.'

'Was it your idea to ransom him for your lads in Belfast?'

'No, no,' Ward said with a hint of pride. 'That's an army council decision. Only they could make decisions like that.'

Duggan nodded. 'So you told the army council you had captured a British spy and awaited orders on what to do next.'

'Not directly, of course,' Ward said. 'I told my superior officer who passed it up the line. You know?'

'Yeah, I know,' Duggan said, one soldier to another. 'And you gave him the envelope address to Nuala Monaghan. With the five hundred pounds in it.'

Ward concentrated on his cigarette.

'Or maybe there wasn't five hundred pounds in by then? A bit less maybe?'

Ward said nothing.

'Or maybe there was no envelope at all? No money at all?'

Duggan stubbed out his cigarette in the metal ashtray, watching Ward all the time.

'Maybe you gave it back to Timmy Monaghan?' he suggested.

'Yeah,' Ward said.

Duggan gave him a slow smile and shook his head. 'No,' he said. 'You didn't give it back to Timmy. You and your friend kept the money. And you presented your army council with a so-called British spy. But you didn't tell them about the money. Or how you came across Bradley in the first place.'

'All very interesting,' Gifford tapped his watch, 'but we have a deadline to get this report finished.'

'I know, I know,' Duggan waved him aside without turning away from Ward. 'You saw a handy way of killing two birds with one stone as they say. A little bit of lucrative freelancing on the one hand. And a coup for your army council on the other hand. But you haven't told them the truth, have you? You haven't told them you were working for a Fianna Fáil TD. You haven't told them you've made five hundred pounds out of it. And,' he paused for effect, 'you didn't tell them who Bradley really is, did you?'

A brief expression of surprise showed on Ward's face.

'Because you don't know who he really is.'

'Come on,' Gifford said. 'We can't spend all day explaining the facts of life to this patsy.'

Ward didn't take his eyes off Duggan.

'Timmy Monaghan told you someone had kidnapped his daughter,' Duggan said. 'That was a lie. She was never kidnapped at all. And he didn't tell you who Bradley is. That he is her daughter's boyfriend.'

Confusion mixed with alarm on Ward's face.

'They're due to get married soon. Timmy doesn't approve of him,' Duggan shrugged. 'Doesn't want his daughter marrying one of the old enemy. You know how these things go. So he used you to try and frighten him off.'

The cigarette in Ward's hand had burned down unnoticed to his fingers and he dropped the butt in the ashtray.

'Ah, let's go,' Gifford said impatiently.

'It's only fair we tell him what he's got himself into,' Duggan said, without taking his eyes off Ward.

'A right fucking mess,' Gifford laughed.

'If the IRA kills Bradley all hell will break loose,' Duggan continued. 'Timmy'll forget about his objections. You'll have murdered a family member of one of the government. And you know what'll happen then.'

Ward sucked his finger where the cigarette butt had burned him.

'The government'll come down on your people like a ton of bricks. Internment will be the least of it. The death penalty for anyone caught with a gun will be back. Like you. And your army council will want to know why you got them into this mess. How you came across Bradley. Why you didn't tell them who Bradley really was. And what you did with the money. Actually,' he paused, 'they probably won't give a fuck about the money at that stage. The least of their problems.'

Duggan sat back. Ward dropped his gaze to the table. His cigarette butt smouldered in the ashtray, sending up a column of acrid grey smoke between them in the silence.

'There's only one way out of this,' Duggan said at last. 'Tell us where we can find Bradley. '

Ward gave a quick shake of his head, without conviction.

'Okay,' Gifford straightened himself. 'You know the score now Billy.' He turned to Duggan. 'Let's get out of here, leave him to his own. Let them suspend him in Tintown. By the neck.'

Duggan reached across the table for his cigarettes and lighter and put them in his pocket as he stood up.

'Let me out of here and I'll tell them to let him go,' Ward said.

'He'll tell them to let him go,' Gifford said to Duggan with a laugh. 'You joined the wrong army. You should've joined the one where the cannon fodder gives orders to the generals.'

'That's not going to happen,' Duggan said to Ward.

'Suit yourself,' Ward shrugged.

'Tell us where he is. And we'll see what we can do for you.'

Ward shook his head.

'It's your suspension,' Gifford let his head hang to one side, his hand around his throat, simulating a hanging. 'Or worse in the Curragh.'

'It's your choice,' Duggan said.

Gifford stopped at the door as he and Duggan went out. 'You still have a narrow window of opportunity before we finish our report,' he said to Ward. 'Tell them here you want to talk to me when the penny drops. But don't delay.'

Outside, Gifford went off to tell the sergeant in charge of the cells that they were finished with Ward and to let him know immediately if Ward wanted to talk. Duggan leaned against a green-washed wall and let out a deep breath. Poor Bradley, he thought. He must be in a bad way. And sorry he ever came back to Ireland and even more sorry he came across the Monaghans.

'Well done,' Gifford said as they stepped out onto the street. 'You almost had me confessing there.'

'You think he'll tell us?'

'Fair chance. We've certainly given him something to think about.'

They crossed the gap between the Bridewell and the district courts. A couple of women were shouting to unseen prisoners in the upper cells of the Bridewell and a solicitor came bustling out between them, his briefcase bulging.

'I wonder if he's still alive,' Duggan said.

'I wouldn't put money on it'

'You think they've killed him already?'

'Wouldn't surprise me. Whatever the likes of Ward might think the army council knows they're not going to get anyone released in the North.'

Duggan closed his eyes, feeling sick. 'Should we report it? That Ward was the kidnapper?'

'Up to you,' Gifford said. 'It's your family.'

'Would it help to get Bradley out?'

'Who knows. It'd probably get you in there,' Gifford nodded back at the Bridewell. 'Being interrogated by my colleagues.'

'Great,' Duggan muttered.

'On the other hand,' Gifford said. 'We could try a little basic police work ourselves. Seeing as we're so far out on a shaky limb at this stage. And the wind is rising.'

'What?'

'Let's go and look at that garage where they took you.'

The laneway behind Clarendon Street was deserted. They stopped at the garage door where Ward and his colleague had brought Duggan. The door was bolted and a large lock, shaped like a flattened pear, hung from it. Gifford tugged at it but it remained locked.

'They had a key,' he said.

Duggan nodded. He tried to look inside through the crack between its double doors but could see nothing in the gloom inside. Gifford took out a penknife and looked at the screws on the bolt. They were encrusted with thick black paint and he thought better of trying to unscrew them. He stepped back and counted the houses on South William Street to see which one the garage belonged to.

It turned out to be a small women's clothes shop among the street's rag trade wholesalers. A tiny middle-aged woman and a young assistant were behind the counter when they went in, the assistant buttoning a blouse on the torso of a dummy.

'Good afternoon, ladies,' Gifford said, showing his warrant card. 'You might be able to help us with a routine inquiry.'

The women looked at each other in alarm.

'A minor road traffic incident,' Gifford assured them. 'The garage at the back of the building. Is that yours?'

'No,' the older woman said.

'Would you happen to know whose it is?'

'No,' the woman said. 'We're only tenants here. Just the shop and the store below.'

'I see. And who uses the garage?'

'I have no idea. You'd have to talk to the landlord.'

Gifford took down his name and address. 'Does one of the people upstairs have the use of it?'

'You'd have to ask the landlord.'

'I will indeed. Have you noticed any unusual activity in the last week or so?'

'Unusual activity?' the older woman glanced at her assistant as if she might have been responsible for something untoward.

'Anything out of the ordinary?'

'No. Everybody here minds their own business. We don't pry into each other's affairs.'

'Thank you for your assistance,' Gifford said.

Outside, he said. 'Great country for minding its own business. My eye.'

'You were looking for me,' Duggan said to Sullivan when he got back to his office.

'Ah, you were in the love nest,' Sullivan tittered. 'The captain was asking for you. Nothing urgent, he said.'

'Any developments?'

'There's a report from Mayo of a submarine coming ashore last night and stealing five sheep. There was a big swastika painted on its tower in black and white and they were talking a guttural sort of language.'

'What?' Duggan laughed.

'The local guards say it's a farmer looking for compo. They told him to complain to the German legation.'

'He won't get much soot out of Herr Thomsen there,' Duggan said, remembering the Nazi-saluting official who had come over to them outside the German ambassador's house. 'Where's the captain?'

'Somewhere around,' Sullivan shrugged. 'He's as much of a wanderer as yourself.'

Duggan found him alone in another office.

'The colonel was intrigued by your theory that Harbusch's Amsterdam letters are written by an English-speaking man,' McClure told him.

'Oh,' Duggan reacted, flattered.

'He likes that kind of sideways thinking,' McClure continued. 'He suggested that you be moved to the Goertz case. But I suggested that you should stay with Harbusch for the moment as you'd made so much progress there.'

'Thank you,' Duggan said with relief. The last thing he wanted now was a move away from the freedom he had and from Gifford, his only confidant on the Nuala fiasco.

McClure noted his relief and tilted his head to look at him askance. Duggan saw his opportunity and seized it.

'I was wondering if I could make a request,' he went on. 'My mother is sick at the moment and I'd like to go and see her if I could.'

'When?'

'Tomorrow. For the day. We've got all the Harbusch people covered and I don't think he'll be getting any more communications from abroad for a couple of days so I thought . . .' he petered out, hoping he wasn't pushing his luck.

'You can do it in the day?'

'Yes. Morning and evening trains.'

'Okay,' McClure nodded. 'Keep it to yourself. If anyone asks, you were doing some undercover work.'

Fourteen

The smoke flowed by the window, blanking out the sky and the horizon and restricting the view to the nearer fields and hedges. Sunshine bathed lines of drying hay mellow and men and boys worked here and there, tossing forkfuls of hay into small piles. Cattle grazed green fields, their ankles deep in the lush grass. Farmhouses and fields moved by, the hedges heavy and the ditches marked only by trickles of water if there was any at all.

Duggan sat with his back to the engine and watched the midlands go by. He shifted on the seat but its rigid uprightness wouldn't let him slouch in comfort. He put his feet up on the seat opposite and leaned his head back and closed his eyes and tried to doze. But his mind wouldn't let him, just as it had refused to let him sleep for hours the previous night as it tried to unravel the whole mess he had got himself into. Or, more accurately, that Timmy had got him into.

He didn't want to think too closely on the state Jim Bradley might be in. If he was still alive. And he didn't want to think through Timmy's implication that it was his own father that had shot Bradley's father. He didn't know what it would mean to him – he didn't want to think about it – but he had to know if it was true or not. Timmy was an expert in implying all sorts of things while saying nothing. And even if it was true, so what? An RIC man was a fair target in those days. But what if his father had known about Timmy's deal? That's where it would get complicated.

And then there was the problem of what to tell McClure, if he didn't know about it already. He had a passing suspicion that McClure knew he was up to something and was giving him a free hand to pursue it. But how could he know about Timmy's and Nuala's machinations? One part of him wanted to tell McClure everything, hand over the whole Bradley problem to G2 and the guards. But if he did that he'd probably be out on his ear. If not court-martialled. The captain and the colonel would not take kindly to his solo run, no matter how much the colonel said he liked sideways thinking.

He opened his eyes and the smoke had cleared from his window to the other side as the train re-orientated itself westwards and the sky opened up into a huge blue vault with a line of puffy clouds spread out in convoy near the horizon. The only hope was that Billy Ward would break or that Gifford would come up with something, he thought. Both were long shots.

The train rumbled across the bridge over the River Shannon at Athlone and he counted off the stops, recognising more and more of the landmarks as he neared his destination, an old mill, someone's farmhouse, a tight clump of trees on a small hill, a ruined abbey, a small lake where he used to fish for perch.

He was the only one to alight at the small station and his father was waiting outside in the Ford Prefect with the windows open. He was wearing work clothes and had his shirt sleeves rolled up.

'No uniform today?' he said as Duggan sat in.

'I don't wear it too much these days.'

'Your mother'll be disappointed.' His father started the car and edged it forward to the level crossing gates, waiting for the train to build up steam and move out of the station. 'She'll be in two minds, actually. She's very proud of you in uniform but then she realizes what it could mean.'

'She's well?'

'Very well. Taking a close interest in the war. Even listening to Lord Haw Haw every week.'

'Why?'

His father gave him a quizzical glance. 'Because she's worried about you, of course. Thinks she might learn something about their intentions.'

'Lord Haw-Haw's not going to let slip any secret plans.'

'You can tell her she's wasting her time.' The train heaved itself out of the station and the gates swung open behind it and they drove off in the sudden silence.

'You're at the hay?' Duggan asked.

'Dry as a bone. We'll be able to bring it home in a few days.'

They drove in silence for a while and then Duggan took a deep breath when they were less than a mile from home. 'There's something I wanted to ask you.' His father waited and Duggan went on after a moment. 'Remember I told you about Nuala? Supposed to have been kidnapped? She wasn't, she was just pretending. But her boyfriend has now been kidnapped by the IRA. At Timmy's behest. They're claiming he's a British spy.'

His father gave him a look of surprise.

'His name is Jim Bradley. His father was an RIC inspector in this area.'

His father took his foot off the accelerator and let the car coast into a gateway to a field and shifted the gear to neutral. He left the engine running and they faced each other.

'Nuala told me about the Bradleys and Timmy. That Mrs Bradley did a deal with him. Sold him her uncle's house very cheap in return for leaving her husband alone. But he was shot anyway. Crippled.'

His father turned away and looked through the wooden gate at the field beyond and said nothing. Duggan turned his attention to the field too; he knew it as a great area for rabbits and could see the rising ground pockmarked with their burrows.

'I thought as much,' his father said at last. 'I didn't know for sure but I always suspected something like that.'

'He says he didn't shoot him.'

'He was upset when Bradley was shot. Claimed that Bradley was feeding him information and shouldn't have been targeted. But he'd never told anybody that, had never said anything about him, good, bad or indifferent.'

Duggan took another deep breath. 'He kind of implied that you did it.'

His father's look of surprise answered his unasked question and Duggan felt a weight rise from his shoulders.

'He said that? That I shot him?'

'No, he didn't actually say it,' Duggan said. 'He implied it. You know the way he talks. Warned me that was a road I didn't want to go down. Who shot Bradley.'

'Jesus Christ,' his father shook his head. 'Timmy.'

Duggan took out his cigarettes, offered his father one and lit both.

'Nobody set out to get Bradley in particular,' his father said. 'All RIC men were fair game whenever a volunteer saw an opportunity. And that's what happened with him. One of the lads saw him on his own one day.'

'Coming from Mass.'

His father nodded. 'He didn't move about much on his own. Maybe that explains why he was on his own that time. Thought he was safe because of Timmy.'

'He didn't know about the deal. His wife never told him. I think he still doesn't know.'

'He's still alive?'

'Lives in England. He's in a wheelchair and his wife has had a heart attack. That's why Nuala wanted to get money out of Timmy.'

His father blew a stream of smoke out the side window. 'Timmy was angry afterwards. Said Bradley was going to tip him off about a visit by some of the RIC top brass. But Timmy had never told the intelligence officer that. Or anyone else. And nobody paid much attention to his complaints. He was always about to pull off some great operation or other. Always waiting for another piece or two of intelligence to be put in place. But I did wonder later when he moved into that place after the truce.'

They smoked in silence. After the relief, Duggan felt anger at Timmy's devious attempt to deflect him. All Timmy had succeeded in doing was further alienating him.

He filled in the gaps in the story for his father, how Nuala had met Bradley, her ransom attempts, his own encounter with Ward, and how he had been pursuing all this while supposed to be working for G2 . 'Should I report it all?' he concluded.

His father gave his dilemma only a moment's consideration. 'Yes,' he nodded decisively. 'You needn't feel any loyalty to Timmy. And it's your duty to report everything you know.'

'I suppose so,' Duggan agreed, not relishing the prospect.

'You've taken it as far as you can. You have to hand it over now to people who can take it further.' His father paused. 'Suppose this Bradley lad is killed. How will you feel then? When you knew things that might have got him released?'

Jesus, Duggan thought. That was something he hadn't really

thought about. He hadn't seriously thought that they would kill him. All over Timmy's greed. And Nuala's games.

'But I don't know where he is.'

'Maybe the extra information you can give G2 will add to other things they already know. Maybe Timmy knows. Maybe they can get information out of him that you can't. Maybe they can persuade the IRA that he's not a spy, that it's a personal vendetta. You don't necessarily know the whole picture. You shouldn't assume you do.'

Duggan wondered again if McClure knew something about what he was up to.

His father dropped his cigarette butt out the window and put the gear into reverse but kept his foot on the clutch. 'Things happen in war that should never happen,' he said after a moment. 'It brings out the best in some and the worst in a few. Most just try to muddle through it as best they can. Once it starts most of it is out of everyone's control. It has its own logic and it can be a terrible logic. Totally heartless,' he shook his head as if at a memory and paused, making no effort to move.

'It was the best time of my life and the worst time of my life,' he said. 'And most of the time I don't know which it was. I saw men do heroic things and I saw men do terrible things. You can't remember one and forget the other. But,' he looked at his son, 'at the end of the day the rightness of the cause is not changed by the wrongness of individual actions.'

Duggan nodded, taken aback by the anguish in his father's face, an anguish he had never seen before. He wanted to ask him for details, what it was he was talking about, but he couldn't. It didn't seem right. It was up to him to tell him or not.

His father let up the clutch and eased the car back onto the road.

'Please God you won't have to go through it,' he said as they went forward again. 'We'll be able to keep out of it this time in spite of all the armchair generals and amateur strategists plotting this and that.'

Duggan flicked his butt out the window and they passed a neighbour driving a horse and low cart with a cock of hay and two children sitting on its dipping back.

'You won't mention anything about Timmy and Nuala to your mother,' his father said, half order, half question.

'No, of course not.'

'She'd only tell Mona and there'd be hell to pay.'

'Mona might know some of it already,' Duggan suggested. 'Nuala thinks so.'

'I doubt it. They tell each other everything. And if Mona knew about it I'm sure your mother would too. And I'd have heard about it.'

They drove up the driveway and were smiling when they went into the house.

'What happened you?' his mother looked at his face. The bruise was fading fast but still discoloured.

'Nothing,' he said. 'Just a knock. Playing hurling.'

The sun was still well above the horizon when they arrived back at the station. Neither had mentioned Timmy during the afternoon as they worked on a neighbour's hay, gathering it in from small heaps around the field and tossing it onto large cocks and tying them down. Duggan relaxed into the mechanical routine, enjoying the light physical exercise, listening to the desultory chatter around him.

The level crossing gates clattered shut behind them and a minute later they heard the tracks vibrating as the train approached. 'Take care of yourself,' his father said, loading the ritual words with feeling as he shook Duggan's hand.

'You too,' Duggan said, holding onto his hardened hand for a moment before he got out.

The carriage was almost empty and he watched the familiar landscape slide by, feeling more at ease than he had been on the way down. At least he knew now what he had to do, even though he wasn't looking forward to it. But his father was right. Whatever the consequences for himself, he couldn't risk anything happening to Jim Bradley just because he was afraid of providing information to his superiors. At worst they'd probably send him back to the infantry, maybe demote him.

At Athlone station he watched the heavy trunk from the water tank swing over the engine to top it up and lit a cigarette. As they set off again he turned his thoughts to Harbusch and tried to force himself to go through everything he knew about him, Eliza and Kitty Kelly, the letters they had intercepted and the patterns of their daily activities.

His efforts to examine it all methodically broke down long before they reached Dublin and his thoughts roamed at random over Harbusch and Eliza and Timmy and Nuala. An idea occurred to him but he dismissed it with a half smile as being too fanciful as the train chugged into Westland Row. Gifford was standing on the platform, his hands behind his back, rocking back and forth on his heels in a parody of a policeman.

'What're you doing here?' Duggan asked in surprise.

'Pursuing enquiries,' Gifford continued his pantomime performance. 'There have been developments.'

'What?'

'Billy the bard wants to talk,' Gifford fell into step beside him and they headed for the steps beside the bar and went down towards the street.

'Now?' Duggan felt his hopes rise. Maybe they could work this all out and free Bradley without having to report anything about Timmy.

'Now.' Gifford stopped behind him on the stairs and took a small piece of hay from the back of Duggan's hair. 'Ah ha,' he chuckled. 'A clue. You went down there for a roll in the hay.'

'Just to make hay.'

'And was the sun shining?'

'The sun is always shining down there.'

They came out of the station and Duggan went to his bicycle which was chained to the church railings next door. Gifford got up on the crossbar and said, 'Onwards, and don't spare the pedals. And mind the tram tracks. It wouldn't do to really fall off.'

'Stop,' Duggan said, picking up speed. 'Don't make me laugh.'

'Just listen and keep pedalling,' Gifford said as they went up Pearse Street and crossed O'Connell Bridge. There was little traffic and few pedestrians to be seen on the evening streets. 'I talked to the owner of that garage. He rented it to a lad called O'Brien who I think is Billy's sidekick, the one who was with him when they interrupted your day-dreaming in Wicklow Street.'

'I never saw him,' Duggan grunted and swung into Bachelor's Walk to face the setting sun.

'I saw him. A lanky fucker. He matches the landlord's description. And he lives in a basement in Dartmouth Square.'

'Where's that?'

Gifford told him. 'So I went for a look see.'

'You called on him?'

'No, no, I went to spy on him. Loiter with intent. And as luck would have it my loitering and my intent were rewarded. O'Brien turned up and went in with a loaf of bread.'

'Could Bradley be there?'

'Could be. But I couldn't stay, had to get back to Hansi for our afternoon walkabout. So I called in the posse. Told the bosses about O'Brien. Turns out that he's not on anyone's lists. They've set up some surveillance on him.'

'Did you tell them about Bradley?'

'No, just that O'Brien appeared to be a friend of Billy's. According to information received.'

They reached the Bridewell and Gifford hopped off the bar and rubbed his backside. They went in and Duggan sat at the table in the interview room while Gifford went to get Ward.

'Volunteer William Ward,' Gifford announced as he walked in behind Ward. Duggan waved at the chair opposite him and tossed him his cigarettes. Ward sat down, took a cigarette and lit it.

'You wanted to talk to us,' Duggan said.

'I'll do a deal.'

'Ah, Billy, Billy,' Gifford interrupted with a world-weary air. 'Do I have to spell this out for you again? You're facing a hanging one way or the other. A neat one in Mountjoy if Bradley dies. Or a messy one in the Curragh when your friends find out what you've landed them in. The only uncertainty will be who gets to hang you first.'

'The best we can do is leave you out of it all,' Duggan offered.

'You won't let me go?'

'Can't do that.'

'We'll let you go off to Tintown without having to worry about what might happen to you there,' Gifford offered. 'Or having to worry about the government demanding the death penalty for you. You'll be able to relax. Three meals a day. Irish lessons every morning. Learn a trade. Read improving books. Dig tunnels. Build castles in the air.'

It sounded so attractive Duggan almost laughed.

Ward closed his eyes and opened them and took a drag. 'There's a place near Leeson Street.' He took another drag. 'Dartmouth Square.'

'What number?' Duggan asked.

Ward hesitated again and then told him.

'And that's where Bradley is?'

Ward nodded.

'Tommy O'Brien's place,' Gifford said casually.

Ward's head jerked towards him as if someone had struck him on the other side. 'No names,' he said. 'I'm not giving you any names.'

'Okay,' Duggan soothed him. 'Just tell us how many people are there. Guarding him?'

Ward lowered his head and shook it.

'We don't want anyone to get hurt,' Duggan said. 'None of your fellows or our fellows. There's less chance of any shooting if we know what to expect. If there's no surprises.'

'There's not to be any shooting,' Ward said, his head still down.

'Not if we can help it,' Duggan glanced at Gifford who nodded. 'We won't start it. You have our word on that.'

Ward said something.

'What?' Duggan said. 'I didn't hear that.'

'Two.' Ward raised his head and avoided Duggan's eyes as he took a deep drag.

'Only two?' Duggan's hopes rose. This might all be manageable yet, without involving anyone else and without bloodshed.

Ward nodded as he concentrated on stabbing out his butt.

'Anything else we should know that would help us make sure no one gets hurt.'

Ward took his time. 'He's in the bedroom at the back. In the basement. Down the hall on the left.'

'Is there a back door?' Gifford asked.

'It's boarded up.'

'From the inside or the outside.'

'It's locked,' Ward shrugged. 'Bolted on the inside. We don't have a key.'

'The windows?'

'There's bars on all of them,' Ward still avoided their eyes.

'So the only way in or out is through the front door?'

Ward nodded.

'What would be the best time to . . . call?' Duggan asked.

Ward shrugged. 'There's nothing more I can tell you.'

'Any hot-headed lads likely to be there?' Gifford came back in. 'The kind who shoot before they think?'

Ward's hesitation provided the answer they didn't want to hear. Duggan's initial optimism slipped another few notches. This had all the makings of, at best, a siege and, at worst, a bloody shoot-out. Or both.

They all fell silent until Gifford stirred himself from the door. 'Okay, we're done here.'

Ward and Duggan stood up and Ward looked at him. 'You gave me your word no one'll get hurt.'

'Not if we can help it,' Duggan held out his hand and Ward gave it a peremptory shake. 'And we'll leave you out of it. You won't be mentioned in anything in connection with this.'

'Enjoy your holidays,' Gifford said to Ward as he opened the door for him and followed him out. Duggan went outside and waited for Gifford to deliver Ward back to the cells.

'What now?' he asked when Gifford joined him.

'Back on the bike?' Gifford suggested. 'Go and see what's happening in Dartmouth Square.'

'We should report it,' Duggan said as he cycled back up the quays. The evening still had an unnatural brightness and the tide was ebbing, uncovering the grey slime of the riverbed and releasing a little of its foul fumes.

'Tell all?' Gifford asked. 'All about your freelance activities?'

Duggan grunted in affirmation.

'You and Billy,' Gifford shook his head in sorrow. 'Same dilemma.'

'And caused by the same person.'

'Maybe we can do a deal to keep you out of it too.'

'Don't see how.'

'You could shine my shoes for five years.' Gifford laughed as they went up a near deserted Grafton Street apart from the people beginning to emerge from the cinema.

'Still wouldn't help us get Bradley out of there by ourselves. Besides,' Duggan tried to avoid any hint of accusation, 'your fellows are there already. We can't send them away while we move in.'

Gifford pointed straight up, alongside Stephen's Green and Duggan followed his directions as he continued. 'How could we get in and release Bradley without a shoot-out? You heard Billy. Only one way in.'

'They have to sleep sometime.'

'Not at the same time.'

'Hmm,' Gifford put his hand out to the left and Duggan swung into the next side of Stephen's Green, past the Russell Hotel and Newman House. 'Suppose we grabbed O'Brien next time he goes out for bread and get him to open the door for us. Surprise the other one. Free Bradley. And go home for our tea.'

'That's a plan,' Duggan said, not sure whether Gifford was serious or not.

'Only one problem. How long does a loaf of bread last? When will he have to go shopping again?'

'And what do we tell the other Branch men?'

'We'll disarm them and tie them up,' Gifford said, pointing straight ahead. 'Simple.'

'Shouldn't we wear masks so they don't recognise us?'

'Good thinking, Tonto.'

Duggan gave a short laugh as they went up Leeson Street and fell silent. There was no way they could do it without reporting it, he thought. But if it got Bradley released unharmed that'd be something. That might mitigate whatever they'd decide to do about his solo run.

'Don't worry,' Gifford said as if he could read Duggan's thoughts. 'We can keep you out of this if we have to. I can take all the glory. Get promoted. Have medals pinned on my chest. For your sake, of course. Claim credit for finding Bradley.'

'Won't they want to know how you knew?' Duggan pushed harder against the hump of the canal bridge.

'Confidential information,' Gifford said as they freewheeled down the other side.

'Won't they want to know from who?'

'From Billy.'

'But we promised to keep him out of it.'

'Oh, we did, didn't we,' Gifford put his hand out to the right. 'Forgot that for a minute. Actually, I overheard two fellows talking in a pub.'

'They won't believe that.' Duggan took the turn into Dartmouth Road.

'Why wouldn't they? You wouldn't believe how much intelligence is overheard in pubs.'

Duggan remained sceptical as Gifford signalled to him to slow down and stop just before the corner of the eastern side of the square. They got off and Gifford stretched himself while Duggan propped the bicycle against a wall and locked it. They walked around the corner into the square and stopped. Down at the far corner there were a couple of cars blocking the road and two uniformed guards stood between them.

'Fuck me,' Gifford breathed.

It's all over, Duggan thought. They've found Bradley. All my problems are solved.

They walked quickly down the square and one of the guards took a step forward to stop them as they approached the cars. Gifford took out his warrant card and the guard nodded them through. They stepped between the angled cars and around into the other side of the square. There were more unmarked cars parked there at random angles, a van among them.

They went in an open wicket gate and towards the entrance to the ground floor at the side of the steps up to the main door. Light came from the open door and a naked bulb in a sparse kitchen inside the barred window. A burly man in plain clothes came out, lighting a cigarette.

'You got Bradley?' Gifford said to him.

The man stopped, a lighted match half way to his cigarette. 'Who's Bradley?'

'I mean, what's his name,' Gifford recovered quickly. 'O'Brien.'

'Yeah, yeah,' the man said, lighting the cigarette and tossing the match on the lawn. 'The main thing is we got Carey.'

'Who's Carey?' Duggan asked without thinking, feeling the weight descending on his shoulders again.

'Who the fuck are you?' the man demanded.

'G2, sarge,' Gifford said quickly.

'What's G2 doing here?' the sergeant demanded of Gifford.

'Just curious,' Gifford said. 'We're on another job and happened to be passing.'

'Curiosity will get you into trouble if your big mouth doesn't,' the sergeant said, still addressing Gifford and ignoring Duggan, but then relented. 'We've been looking for Carey for a long time, especially since he got away in that shooting in Islandbridge.'

'Anyone else in there?'

'That O'Brien fellow you mentioned. And another nonentity. Coyle, Doyle. Something like that.'

'Can we have a look?'

'What do you want to have a look for?' the sergeant gave Duggan a suspicious glance.

Gifford shrugged.

'See how these fellows live?' the sergeant nodded. 'Pigsty in there. But wait'll they bring them out.'

The sergeant left and Duggan muttered 'fuck' under his breath and asked Gifford who Carey was. 'A real hard man,' Gifford said quietly. 'They had him surrounded in a house in Islandbridge a couple of weeks ago. Shot his way out. Wounded one of our lads.'

They stepped off the path and onto the lawn as a line of men emerged from the basement doorway, three of them handcuffed. The first was the oldest, a blank look of resignation on his face. Surprise and then calculation flitted across the face of the tallest one, O'Brien, when he saw Duggan. He thinks it was Ward who tipped us off, Duggan thought. Ward was in for a hard time. The third was no more than seventeen and appeared terrified.

The last Special Branch man in the line clapped Gifford on the shoulder and said 'good tip' as they went by.

Gifford led the way into the flat and they looked in the kitchen. Half a loaf of bread sat surrounded by crumbs on a table by the wall, a breadknife and an open packet of butter beside it. In the living room there were a couple of broken-down armchairs and a sagging couch with a carpet worn down to cross-hatched treads on the centre of the floor. One detective was putting handguns and ammunition in a bag, calling out each item to another who was taking a note of them. Empty Guinness bottles lay on the floor where they had rolled against walls and stood on the windowsill and the table.

The wallpaper was peeling off the hallway. They glanced into the main bedroom where a thin double mattress lay on the floor beside a metal bed frame with a sagging wire base. The back bedroom was much smaller and dark. Gifford clicked on the light switch and Duggan saw a single mattress on the floor at one side and a metal bucket at the end of it. The shutters were nailed shut and there was a dark stain at one side of the window where the wallpaper had peeled off from a leak. Patches on the walls showed where pictures had once been and the fireplace had a scattering of twigs from a nest in the chimney. The room was cold and damp, the air slightly fetid. Duggan shivered.

On their way out of the flat Gifford stopped to talk to another detective who was coming back in and asked him what had happened.

'We were watching the place after your tip when Carey appeared. We nabbed him and brought him to the door and they opened it for him and we rushed in. Went like clockwork. The fellows inside weren't up to much.'

'Back to square one,' Gifford said outside as they went back to Duggan's bicycle.

'Fuck,' Duggan said. 'It looks like Bradley was there all right.'

'They probably moved him after we picked up Ward. Afraid Billy would talk.'

'He's in trouble now.'

'Aren't we all,' Gifford sighed. 'The sergeant will remember me mentioning Bradley when we finally find him. Dead or alive. He's not as thick as he looks.'

'Fuck,' Duggan repeated. They stopped at his bicycle and stood in silence for a moment in the dim light, still not quite night but no longer day either. A rumble of heavy aircraft in the distance caught their attention and they listened until the noise began to recede.

'Okay,' Gifford said. 'I'll tell them I think the British spy was being held there. Overheard in a pub etcetera etcetera. And I heard the name Bradley and thought he was one of them. But it'll turn out sooner or later that Bradley was the spy. So-called.'

Duggan nodded. 'And I'll tell my captain everything tomorrow.' He paused. 'Won't they wonder why you didn't know who Bradley was when I did?'

A smile spread across Gifford's face. 'But I'm under orders to tell you nothing. And I presume you're under orders to tell me nothing too.'

Duggan nodded.

'So,' Gifford spread his hands.

Duggan sat up on his bicycle. 'I'm going to talk to Nuala. Tell her what I'm going to do so she's prepared. Do you want to come and meet her?'

'Jaysus, no,' Gifford recoiled. 'I don't want to meet any more of your family. Give me nightmares for the rest of my life.'

Duggan arrived at the house in Ranelagh where Nuala was hiding after circling back on his tracks twice to make sure he wasn't being followed. There was probably nobody left to follow him now that Billy Ward's little group had been rounded up but he didn't want to take any chances. He checked his watch before knocking on the door. It was just after eleven o'clock.

It took so long for anyone to answer that he was about to leave when the door opened a crack and a young woman peered at him.

'Is Nuala in?'

'There's no one of—'

'I'm her cousin. Paul,' he interrupted.

She hesitated a second and then opened the door and led him down the dark hall into a well-lit kitchen. There was no one there. He turned to look at the woman who had let him in but she was no longer behind him. The back door opened and Nuala stepped in.

'You weren't followed?' she said.

'No. The fellows we think kidnapped Jim have been rounded up.'

'Jim?' she asked in hope.

'We haven't found him yet.'

She sank into a chair at the table and he sat down opposite her and put his arms on the table.

'He was being held in a flat in Dartmouth Square. But he'd been moved before we got there.'

'Just up the road?'

Duggan nodded.

'Is he still alive?'

'I don't know,' Duggan sighed. 'There's no reason to think he's not. A dead hostage is no use to anyone.'

'D'you think they'll release those prisoners in the North?'

Duggan said nothing, gave an almost perceptible shake of his head. Her eyes filled slowly with tears and they overflowed down her face. She made no effort to stop them or wipe them away.

'Talk to your father,' Duggan said. 'He's our best hope. He might be able to get him freed.'

'What did he say? You talked to him?'

'He said he'd do his best. But he wants you to come and talk to him.'

'And say I'm sorry.'

'He didn't say that.'

'He didn't have to.' She sniffed and wiped the tear tracks from her cheeks with her thumbs. Her eyes were dry.

'It's the only way,' he said. 'You can say sorry if you have to. You don't have to mean it.'

She appeared to struggle with the idea and he went on, 'The other thing is that I have to report Jim's disappearance to my superiors. And some of the background to it, at least. Who his father was.'

'You can't do that,' she said in horror.

'We have to. It's the only other thing we can do to try and get Jim freed.'

'It'd kill my mother.'

'What? You told me she knows already.'

'I told you I wouldn't be surprised if she knew. But it'd kill her if it came out in public. She couldn't go on living in that house.'

'It won't come out in public,' Duggan said, trying to keep up with her objections. 'There's censorship. Timmy'll make sure it doesn't get into the papers.'

She looked at him as if he was stupid. 'Word will get around. People will know.'

Jesus, Duggan thought, they really are two of a kind, herself and Timmy. 'Okay. I won't say anything about Timmy's deal with Jim's mother. Or about your attempt to blackmail him.'

'It wasn't blackmail,' she shot back.

'Well,' he spread his hands, 'whatever you want to call it.'

'Justice.'

'The point is that they will probably want to talk to you about Jim. It's up to you what you tell them about Timmy and all that.'

'You're washing your hands of it.'

Duggan slumped back in the kitchen chair and put his hands in his pockets and stared at her, trying to control his anger. She stared back, challenging him. He thought of walking out but restrained himself and went on in a calm voice: 'I've done all I can. The two best chances of freeing Jim are to get Timmy to call off his friends and to give the guards all the information we have which might help them find him. We can't let this run its course without doing everything we can to have an innocent man released.' Whose only crime was to befriend you, he thought.

She dropped her eyes. 'Sorry,' she said. 'I can't think straight any-more.'

He accepted her apology with a nod and leaned forward, arms on the table again. 'I'll go with you to talk to Timmy if you like,' he offered on the spur of the moment.

She thought about that, then said, 'Okay.'

'We could call around to the house in the morning. Before he goes to the Dáil.'

'No, not there.'

'Where, then?'

'Somewhere neutral.'

'Okay.' Somewhere public, he thought, so they don't start scream-ing abuse and tearing each other's eyes out. 'I'll think of somewhere. Is there a phone here?'

She told him the number.

'Is there anything else that could help find Jim?' he asked as he stood up.

'I don't think so.' She walked down the hall with him.

At the door he asked her if she'd ever heard of an IRA man called Carey. She shook her head.

'Ever hear your father mention him?'

She thought for a moment. 'I don't think so. The name didn't stick if he ever did.'

'I'll call you tomorrow.'

'Thanks,' she said as if it was an effort and closed the door behind him.

Fifteen

He walked to the office in the morning, determined to put an end to the problems Timmy had caused him. He was going to tell McClure about Bradley. That his cousin suspected, no, believed, her boyfriend was the man kidnapped by the IRA as a spy. And what little he knew about Jim Bradley. Which was nothing, really. A student at Trinity College. Son of a former RIC inspector wounded in the War of Independence. Which they would assume could be a motive for spying for the British. What if he was? he thought. I wouldn't blame him. After what happened his father.

But he wasn't going to get into any speculation. It was up to Nuala to decide what she wanted to tell them. How far she wanted to implicate Timmy. And herself, for that matter.

That was the easy option, passing the hard part to Nuala, and he knew it. Letting her tell the whole story. That it was really Timmy who was behind the whole thing and the reason why. But withholding that information, even for a few hours, could delay the further investigation. Even decide Bradley's fate. Time was running out. His father had said that he didn't owe Timmy any loyalty. But, still. He was family. More his family than his father's family in a way. His mother would be devastated. She'd always felt a need to defend Timmy for her sister's sake.

And what about Billy Ward? He'd promised to leave him out of everything. It wasn't his fault that Bradley had been moved after his arrest. What a mess, he thought, acknowledging the sentry's salute at the Infirmary Road gate to headquarters. He'd keep it simple. But that depended on McClure's response. If he starts asking loads of questions I'm fucked. I'll have to tell all.

He took a deep breath as he walked into the office. There was no one there. One of the morning papers was open on the table, a double page spread, editorials on the left and the war news on the right. The main headline across the right-hand page said 'French Army Lays Down Its Arms'. Stacked under one side were three sub-headings: 'Armistice Signed With Italy'; 'Day of National Mourning Ordered in France'; 'Hitler Calls For Bells And Flags'.

He skimmed down through the opening paragraphs. The French Army had laid down its arms at 12.35 that morning, shortly after he had gotten back to the barracks. Hitler thanked the Almighty for victory and ordered bells to be rung for seven days and flags to be hung for ten. The war on the continent is over, the editorial on the opposite page said.

Sullivan came in with a mug of tea as he continued to read bits and pieces. 'Peace in our time,' Sullivan nodded at the paper.

'You think that's it?'

'The English will agree terms now. Swap around a few bits of the empire with the Germans and it'll all be hunky dory,' Sullivan said. 'So my father says. And he's a military expert.'

'Why should they stop now? The Germans?'

'Because we want them to,' Sullivan gave him a crooked grin.

'If we're lucky,' Duggan agreed. 'Where's the captain?'

'Gone down to Kingsbridge. There's a German spy coming in on the train from Kerry.'

'What?'

'Some fellow who landed on the Kerry coast yesterday. Seen acting suspiciously. His English is not too good. Or they couldn't understand him in Kerry. Which might mean his English is too good. Anyway, he got on the train this morning. They're down there waiting for him.'

'When will he be back?'

Sullivan shrugged. 'He left the latest letter from Hans for you.'

Duggan looked around the table and lifted the newspaper and found it underneath. It was addressed to the Abwehr's house in Copenhagen and signed by Harbusch. He sat down and read through it twice. 'We are on the point of making a profitable sale,' it said. 'It would be the wrong time to end negotiations now. We admit that progress has been very slow but we advise that a new manager has now taken an interest in the order. He is enthusiastic and we are confident of making a successful sale in the coming weeks. Please send a further payment on account to cover the extra expense.'

It was a reply to the letter from the woman in Amsterdam, Duggan decided. That letter had been an order to end negotiations. But Harbusch was arguing against it. And asking for more money, as usual. All these letters from Amsterdam, Copenhagen, Zurich were parts of the same correspondence.

Duggan pulled over the Harbusch file and extracted the copies of all the letters to and from Harbusch. He lit a cigarette and read through them all in sequence, immersing himself in the detail. There were a few gaps but by and large they did add up to a continuous correspondence about the supply of weapons to the IRA. Possibly to different factions. The 'new manager' was probably another faction.

He sat back, thinking that there was only one big gap in the picture. Harbusch never met anyone as far as they knew. They had been following him now for weeks and he never went anywhere other than his regular walks to Grafton Street. And nobody ever called on him, as far as they knew. He had Kitty Kelly posting letters for him and picking up replies. And she had led them to Goertz. She could be meeting other people as well, they'd only been following her for a few days. Unlikely as it seemed, maybe she was the real agent and Harbusch was just a front, a diversion to attract their attention and deflect them from the real action. After all, Duggan had only discovered Kelly's role by accident. And she had actually led them to Goertz.

The other possibility was that Harbusch was merely a confidence trickster, making up these stories for the Germans and making a good income from doing nothing more than writing a few letters. The Abwehr probably has loads of money, he thought, but they'd hardly waste it on a con man. He must be producing some real results or they must have reason to believe that he can produce them.

He slouched back in the chair and closed his eyes and the fanciful idea he'd had on the train flashed before his mind's eye and he dismissed it again with an unconscious shake of his head.

'Pleasant dreams?' Sullivan interrupted. 'Was that another dirty letter?'

Duggan opened his eyes. 'No, just a business one.'

'Pity.'

Duggan picked up the phone and asked for Timmy's home number. He had to get this other stuff out of the way, free himself to concentrate on Harbusch.

'Well?' Timmy said when he got through to him, a note of suspicion in his voice.

'Can you come to the Shelbourne Hotel at three o'clock?'

'Why?'

'To meet someone.'

'Someone I know?'

'Someone you want to meet.'

Duggan toggled the pips on top of the phone to break the connection and get the switchboard's attention and asked for the number Nuala had given him.

'Is Nuala there?' he asked when a woman's voice answered.

'There's no Nuala here,' she said. 'You must have a wrong number.'

'This is Paul,' he ignored her. 'Tell her to be in the Shelbourne Hotel at three o'clock. It's important.'

The woman said nothing and Duggan thanked her and hung up.

Sullivan was watching him. 'Got another one on the go?'

'I can hardly keep track of them all,' Duggan winked.

'You're all talk, Duggan. Full of shite.'

'Hello, stranger,' Sinéad said as he passed by her office.

He turned back and said hello.

'I was beginning to think you'd been promoted or something.'

'More likely to be demoted,' he said.

'And why would that be?'

'Because we're not making much progress.'

'Following the little fat fellow and his floozy?' she asked.

'You've seen them?'

She shifted in her chair and looked away. 'Petey asked me to go with him yesterday. For cover, he said. I was just going out to lunch when he was following them.'

'And what happened?'

'Nothing,' she said quickly.

'Where did they go?'

'Oh,' she replied. 'Down to Grafton Street. Where they always go, Petey said. Had lunch together.'

'That's a change,' he said. 'I've never seen them eat together.'

'She's not his wife.'

'How do you know?' he asked with more than a passing interest.

She gave him a patient look. 'Because,' she said. 'Look at him. Look at her. She's after his money. Or something else.'

'Doesn't mean they're not married,' he suggested, thinking that's the second time in twenty-four hours a woman has given me that 'are you slow' look.

'It won't last, if they are. She's with him for what she can get out of it. Probably money. And he's with her to show her off and tell everyone what a great fellow he is.'

'You could be right. What does Petey think?'

'He just wants to ogle her backside.'

'Oh,' he said, surprised at her directness.

'Men,' she shook her head and dismissed him.

Upstairs, Gifford had his chair propped in the window and his feet up on the folded shutter on the other side and was reading an evening paper.

'Hiding behind women's skirts now,' Duggan said. 'For cover.'

'Much better cover holding hands with her than holding hands with you.'

'Oh, you were holding hands.'

'Had to. Cover.'

'She didn't tell me that bit.'

'And what did she tell you?'

'That you were only interested in Eliza's arse.'

'She said that? Eliza's arse?'

'Not in those words.'

'Whew,' Gifford stood up. 'I should hope not. I wouldn't like to think of Sinéad using such coarse language. Like a common solider.'

'What did you think of her theory?'

'That Eliza's a whore?'

'She said that?'

'Not in those words.'

Duggan laughed. 'That they're not married. That she's after something else.'

'Elementary.' Gifford glanced out the window. 'Oh, time for our daily exercise. They're on the move.'

He grabbed his jacket and Duggan followed him down the stairs, two steps at a time and jumping down the last three to the hall. Gifford paused at Sinéad's office and said, 'He won't let me hold his hand. It'd be great cover.'

She threw a pencil at him. It bounced off the jamb and hit Duggan as he went by. 'Sorry,' she called after him as they went out the hall door.

The day was overcast but warmed by a strong breeze from the south. They ambled along more than fifty yards behind Harbusch and Eliza, the routine now so familiar they barely noticed them. She tottered along on her high heels, linking Harbusch and taller than him even with his hat on. He held himself erect, his girth causing him to roll slightly as he walked.

Duggan filled in Gifford on the latest letter from Harbusch and what he thought it meant. 'Something struck me,' he added. 'It might be ridiculous.'

'But,' Gifford prompted.

Duggan hesitated. Would it sound even more fanciful if he said it out loud? he wondered.

'What?' Gifford prompted again.

Duggan took a deep breath and said it. 'Eliza and Kitty Kelly are the same person.'

Gifford stopped and gave him an admiring look. 'You have a devious mind,' he said. 'I like it.'

'My mind or the idea?'

'Both.' Gifford started walking again and turned his attention to the couple ahead of them. 'But I don't like to think of Eliza as an old woman.'

'Why does she wear those very high heels?' Duggan asked, voicing the questions that he had been asking himself. 'Why is she exaggerating her height? The difference between them?'

'Because she's a whore,' Gifford suggested, speeding up so they could get closer. 'Like the other culchie says.'

'Because she wants to look as different as possible,' Duggan persisted. 'So you'd never think she was Kitty Kelly in her other disguise.'

'But you think it.'

'Imagine her without the heels. With an oversize old coat. Shoulders hunched. Scarf flattening her hair. Shuffling along.'

'Oh Eliza,' Gifford sighed. 'Are you really an old woman?'

'No,' Duggan said. 'She's really the spy. Hansi is the cover. A pretend spy.'

'Have you been drinking one of those strange country drinks that looks like water?'

'Has anyone seen Kitty Kelly and Eliza at the same time?'

Gifford stopped for a moment. 'We need to have a look in Kitty's flat.'

'Yeah,' Duggan nodded as they continued on to the corner of Clare Street and waited for a motorbike with a side-car to roar by.

'Even a look through the window might do,' Gifford suggested.

'That could be enough.'

They walked along into South Leinster Street, both paying more attention to Eliza swaying alongside Harbusch and wondering if it were possible.

'Where'd you get this crazy idea?' Gifford asked.

'My cousin Nuala.'

'Oh, Jaysus,' Gifford sighed.

'Something she said to me about picking up the ransom money I had left in Wicklow Street. There were lots of women wandering in and out of the shops there. And she had put on an old coat and scarf to go into the building and pick up the envelope and Billy Ward and his friends didn't notice her.'

'Because they weren't looking for an old woman. Nobody pays any attention to old women.'

'Exactly.'

Gifford nodded as the idea took hold. 'Have you told your superior intelligents this theory?'

'No. Not yet. I wanted to bounce it off you first.'

'Oh, I like it,' Gifford laughed as they crossed Kildare Street. 'And I'd really love it if it was true.'

'Why?'

'It's just so . . .' Gifford searched for a word. 'Smart.'

'They know we're watching and they have us looking the wrong way.'

'Exactly.' Gifford groaned. 'But Eliza as an old woman. I don't really want to think about that.'

'But she's not. She's a young spy.'

'That does make me feel better. If she just asked I'd tell her all my secrets. Wouldn't you? Which reminds me,' Gifford punched him in the shoulder, 'have you told the powers that be your own secrets yet?'

Duggan sighed and shook his head. 'The captain was out of the office today.'

'That was a relief.'

'A temporary respite.'

'You want me to do it?' Gifford offered. 'Throw Bradley's name into the ring the way we discussed?'

'No,' Duggan sighed. 'It'd be too much of a coincidence if you supposedly overheard something in a pub the same day I told my people about Nuala's boyfriend.'

'People do get ridiculously suspicious about coincidences,' Gifford agreed.

Harbusch and Eliza turned into Grafton Street and he peeled off and crossed the road into Switzers.

'Your turn to look at the knickers today,' Gifford said. 'But I better do it. Your imagination is already in danger of blowing the mercury out of the thermometer.'

The commissionaire opened the door to the Shelbourne Hotel with a cursory 'good afternoon' and Duggan stepped into the high lobby. The metal cage of the lift faced him and he turned right into the lounge. It was empty apart from four businessmen huddled around a table with documents between their drinks and a pianist playing in the corner. He chose a table by the empty fireplace, away from the windows, and studied the menu card. The prices were out of his league.

He lit a cigarette and settled down to wait. An elderly waiter approached and Duggan told him he was waiting for some people. The pianist was playing something classical, his eyes half-closed, moving his head from side to side slowly with the music, away in his own world. Two women came in with shopping bags and picked a table in the centre.

Duggan wondered again about Kitty Kelly and Eliza. It was a mad theory but these were mad times. And it made sense of things. Or did it? It could make sense of things.

Timmy appeared in the lobby, moving slowly. He caught Duggan's eye and came towards him, scanning the lounge, still moving slowly, as though he feared he was walking into an ambush. 'Well,' he said, taking the other armchair with its back to the wall. 'Just the two of us.'

'So far.'

'And who are we waiting for?'

'Nuala.'

Timmy nodded once as if that confirmed his expectations. He looked at his watch: it was just after ten past three. 'You think she'll come?'

'I don't know,' Duggan said. 'She said she would.'

'And what does she want to talk about?'

'You said you wanted to talk to her,' Duggan reminded him, trying to remain calm. He had lost all patience with Timmy's games. 'And I persuaded her to come and talk to you.'

'Was this her idea?' Timmy nodded at the surroundings.

'No, mine.'

Timmy picked up the menu and pursed his lips as he glanced down it. 'We wouldn't want the afternoon tea,' he said. 'But we might as well have a drink.'

He waved at the waiter and ordered a small Paddy and a half pint of Guinness for Duggan.

'What do you think she wants to talk about?' Timmy began again.

'Jim Bradley.'

Timmy dropped his voice. 'I've put the word out that there might've been a mistake about him being . . . you know.'

'And?'

'And we'll see what happens.'

Duggan shook his head. 'That won't be good enough. She wants you to get him back.'

'I'm doing my best.'

'You got him into this. You have to get him out of it.'

Timmy settled back in his chair and joined his hands on his stomach. 'Hold your horses now,' he said. 'I didn't start any of this. She and Bradley started it. Pretending to kidnap her.'

Duggan shook his head. 'Bradley wasn't involved. It was all Nuala's doing.'

'And why was he picking up my money if he wasn't involved?' Timmy leaned forward with the certainty of proof.

The waiter arrived with their drinks and they waited while he put them on coasters before them and left a jug of water beside the whiskey.

'Because Nuala had told him about it by then,' Duggan continued the conversation. 'And he thought it was too dangerous for her to go herself.'

Timmy poured a small amount of water into his whiskey and tasted it. 'You believe that?'

'Yes. Ask Nuala yourself.'

'Have you never wondered why this fellow came back to Ireland?'

'Nuala will tell you.'

'Why?'

'Because his granduncle left him money to go to Trinity College.'

Timmy took another sip of his whiskey. 'And you believe that?'

Duggan reached for his glass to hold down his irritation. He hadn't expected this interrogation, hadn't been prepared for it, and didn't want it. It was all Nuala's fault again. 'I'm sure we could find out one way or the other,' he said. 'Aren't wills public documents? It'd be the same will that left your house to Mrs Bradley, wouldn't it?'

Timmy's face went blank and he took out his cigarettes and lit one. He didn't offer one to Duggan.

'Look,' Duggan said. 'We've got to sort this out ourselves. Get Bradley released and put an end to it all. Isn't that what you want? Keep it in the family.'

'Or else?' Timmy glared at him.

'Or else I'll have to report it all to my superiors. As soon as possible.'

'All of it?' Timmy kept his tone even.

'Very hard not to. Every bit of it raises more questions until . . .' Duggan shrugged.

'I warned you before this was not a road you wanted to go down.'

'Yes,' Duggan lit a cigarette, taking his time to calm his temper. 'And I talked to my father about that.'

A mixture of surprise and shock crossed Timmy's face. 'When?'

'Yesterday. He told me everything. And he didn't appreciate your attempt to blame Bradley's father on him.'

'I never said that,' Timmy sounded shocked.

'Not a road I'd want to go down,' Duggan threw Timmy's words back at him.

They lapsed into silence. Duggan let his anger cool and a sense of satisfaction replaced it – he had turned the tables on Timmy. Timmy didn't know what his father had told him and the prospect had clearly shaken him. There are other things Timmy doesn't want known, he realized. Things which Timmy thought his father knew. And he was afraid that his father might talk if he angered him. Which explained why Timmy had always treated his father with great care.

Timmy scanned the lounge again: no one was paying them any attention. The pianist played 'She Moved Through The Fair' at a leisurely pace and the businessmen across the lobby stood up and began a round of handshaking.

'I knew you'd be good at this intelligence stuff,' Timmy said at last. 'That's why I got you moved into G2. You like it there?'

Duggan nodded, knowing the threat that was coming.

'And you'd like to keep doing it?'

Duggan nodded again.

'You know what I'm saying?'

'I know what you're saying. But I don't want to stay there if it causes an innocent man to be killed.'

Timmy gave a shrug of impatience. 'There's no need to be over-dramatic. You're taken after your mother. At least your father always kept a cool head.'

Nuala sat down at the third side of the table and looked from one to the other, registering the tension.

'D'you want a cup of tea or something?' Timmy asked.

She shook her head and they lapsed into silence.

'Paul,' Timmy said at last. 'Would you let me talk to my daughter in private?'

Duggan looked at Nuala who stared at his half finished glass of Guinness. He got up without a word and walked away. In the lobby he asked the porter where he'd find a phone and was directed to a booth in the back of the building. When he got through to Sullivan he asked him if the captain was back.

'Not yet,' Sullivan said. 'Is there a message for him?'

'No, it's okay. I'll talk to him later.'

He left the hotel, not bothering to glance back into the lounge to see if they were talking. He crossed into the park and walked fast around the duck pond to calm his seething anger. What a fucking pair, he thought. At least it made it easier to do what he had to do. He was finished with them now.

'You did what he asked you to do,' Gifford shrugged after Duggan had told him about the encounter. 'You found his daughter.'

'Yeah,' Duggan agreed. And found out some things I might've been better off not knowing for sure, he thought. But if Timmy was the only reason he was in G2 he didn't want to be there. 'But I can't leave it at that.'

'Bradley?'

'Yeah.'

Gifford scratched his head and walked around the edges of the room. He dropped to the floor and did five quick push-ups and jumped to his feet and stretched his shoulders. 'We need to shoot someone,' he said.

'I know who I want to shoot.'

'That'd stir things up all right.' Gifford looked like he was considering the idea. 'Maybe he'll get Bradley released.'

'Maybe. But I wouldn't bet on it.'

'He'd let them kill him?' Gifford shook his head.

'He's a vindictive fucker. He won't back down easily. If at all.'

Duggan picked up the phone extension, unable to let it go in spite of his resolution, and asked Sinéad if she could get him a number. 'Tea's ready,' she said before putting him through. 'If you want to send your batman down for it.'

He told Gifford while he waited for the number to answer. Gifford saluted and left.

'This is Paul,' he said when the same woman as before answered the phone. 'Is Nuala there please?'

'She's not back yet.'

'Could you ask her to call me at this number as soon as she gets in?' He gave her the number and thanked her.

He stood in the window, watching the treetops bending in the breeze, and glanced over at the Harbusch's flat. Their windows reflected the milky clouds, as bland and uncommunicative as ever. He wished he could just concentrate on Harbusch and his spy circle but he couldn't just walk away from the other problem. At least it would all be out of his hands soon.

Gifford came back with a tray and two cups of tea and a plate with two Kimberley biscuits and two Mariettas.

'Only plain biscuits for you,' he said, putting the tray down on the chair.

'Why?'

'You're lucky you're getting any at all. Had to put in a good word for you.'

'What'd I do?'

'Ah, culchies,' Gifford slurped his tea and bit into a Kimberley.

'What?' Duggan took the other cup.

'She thinks you've been ignoring her.'

'What?'

'Not paying her sufficient attention.'

'Don't know how she got that idea.' Duggan took a plain biscuit.

'Indeed,' Gifford smirked. 'What's really happened is that you've had your eye wiped by a better man.'

'Hah. You?'

Gifford curtsied before him. 'We're going to the pictures tonight.'

Duggan raised his cup to him.

Gifford touched his cup to Duggan's. 'I'll give you lessons in how to deal with women. Starting next week. If you haven't been transferred back to the bogs by then. And aren't sitting in a *bothán* in a cloud of turf smoke describing the amazing sights of the city to open-mouthed yokels.'

The phone rang and Duggan moved to pick it up.

'It's Giggler,' Sinéad said and put Sullivan through before he could say anything.

'The captain checked in and I told him you were looking for him,' Sullivan said. 'He's got to go down the country and won't be back till late.'

'Okay.'

'If it's important and urgent he said to report directly to the colonel.'

'Okay.'

'Would you like me to make an appointment for you with the colonel?' Sullivan asked with heavy sarcasm.

'Jaysus, no.' Duggan couldn't imagine trying to tell the colonel about Timmy. It'd be bad enough telling McClure.

'Yes, sir,' Sullivan paused. 'Did you hear that?'

'What?'

'My heels clicking. I'm getting into practice for our new masters.'

'You don't need to worry,' Duggan glanced at Gifford. 'The Special Branch says we'll be first on their execution list.'

'Gifford's even more full of shite than you,' Sullivan hung up.

'Reprieved,' Duggan told Gifford. 'Captain's away until the morning.'

Gifford offered him the Kimberley biscuit. 'Go on,' he said. 'We've got to keep you hale and happy. So that we can push you lot out into the front line when the parachutists start landing.'

'Thanks,' Duggan took the biscuit.

'Or Hansi bursts out with a Schmeisser in his hands. Followed by Eliza and Kitty. And blows your theory apart.'

'What'd they do today?'

'The usual,' Gifford said. 'Hansi went into Switzers. Eliza went into the Monument and he met her and they walked home.'

Duggan shook his head. 'It doesn't make any sense.'

'It's a living,' Gifford said enigmatically. 'I hope we never run into one of those Switzers women at a dance or somewhere. We'll be ruined.'

'Who's following Kitty Kelly today?'

'One of the lads went to Mass with her this morning. But he was pulled away to something else afterwards. That fellow they caught in Dartmouth Square is talking his head off.'

'Carey?'

'Not him. He's a tough guy. The youngest one. Coyle.'

'Would he know anything about Bradley?'

'Possibly. But I don't think we can get to him.'

'But if you told your guys about Bradley . . .' Duggan let the suggestion hang there.

'You want me to?'

'I don't know,' Duggan threw his hands up. 'Time's running out. We've got to do something.'

'You do it first thing tomorrow,' Gifford said. 'And I'll follow up with a report a little later. To make sure everyone knows. Pretend I got it out of you.'

'Okay,' Duggan nodded. Twelve hours or so wasn't going to make much of a difference. There were still a few days left to the end of the month deadline.

He lit a cigarette and wandered over to the window and blew smoke at a pane. 'So there's no one watching her,' he said. 'Kitty.'

Gifford shrugged. 'Our lads aren't that interested. More concerned with the local heroes than anything the Germans are up to.'

'But she led us to Goertz once already,' Duggan protested.

'Your lads are more interested in Goertz than mine. Anyway,' Gifford smiled, 'you can stay here and watch. Cover for me while Sinéad breathes sweet nothings in my ear.'

Duggan snorted and glanced at the phone. He still wanted to talk to Nuala, find out what Timmy and she had agreed, if anything. And he had nothing better to do.

Duggan squashed the sodden newspaper into a ball and tossed it into the far corner of the room. He licked the grease and vinegar from the fish and chips off his fingers and dried them on his knees.

He lit a cigarette and picked the *Evening Herald* from the floor where Gifford had dropped it and straightened the pages and read through the accounts of the French surrender. The war in the west was over, the German high command had announced. Did that mean they were going to leave England alone? And Ireland? Was it a hopeful sign or was it disinformation? You could hope it was true but you couldn't let yourself believe it.

Outside, the cloud had broken up and the evening sun glanced off the top floors of the houses and touched some of the higher trees. The wind had died and the treetops were still. Down below, the street was empty. All was peace and calm, a sleepy evening fading into the half-night of midsummer. It was difficult to imagine it being torn apart by war.

The building creaked around him, its night sounds beginning to assert themselves in the silence. Sinéad had put the main phone line through to his extension before she and Gifford left. He was still waiting for Nuala to phone, undecided whether it was a good sign or a bad sign that she hadn't called him back. Probably good, he decided: it meant she didn't want anything from him anymore. Which probably meant that she and Timmy had sorted out their differences and that he'd get Bradley released. But it'd be nice of her to let him know, one way or the other. Nice, though, was not a word he associated with Nuala.

He noticed the figure shuffling up the other side of the square several moments before he registered who it was. He threw the newspaper on the floor and stood up, pressing against the window to see where she went at the junction. She crossed Mount Street into Fitzwilliam Street and he ran down the stairs and pulled the hall door shut after himself.

He slowed down and turned the corner into Fitzwilliam Street and cursed under his breath. She was only about thirty yards ahead of him on the other side, moving very slowly. He should've given her more time. There was no way he could slow down to her crawl without looking suspicious. She can't be Eliza, he thought. It's too difficult to walk that slowly unless you have no choice.

He adopted a casual pace and overtook her before she had gone a further twenty yards. He kept looking straight ahead, resisting the urge to try and get a close look at her face, and turned right into Baggot Street. He slowed and went down about half a dozen houses and stepped into the doorway of a building whose half-drawn ground floor blinds said solicitors and commissioners of oaths.

He faced the door, pretending to push at one of the bells beside it, hoping she didn't turn this way too. She couldn't help seeing him if she did. There were few people about. He kept glancing back towards the junction, wondering what could be keeping her. Maybe she had gone into one of the houses on Fitzwilliam Street.

She appeared at the corner and he reached towards the bells as he watched. She turned left without looking in his direction and went in the door of Larry Murphy's pub.

Duggan sauntered towards the pub, willing himself to slow down, give her time to do whatever it was she was doing there. He went by the pub and turned back and took a deep breath and went in.

The bar ran parallel to the street and there was a snug enclosed with wooden and coloured glass walls at the end. A couple of elderly men sat at the centre of the bar staring at pints and smoking. The snug, he thought. He could see the shadow of two heads inside, distorted by the dappled glass. He felt his excitement rise and tried to calm it. She hadn't come in to buy a little bottle of whiskey or something to take home. She was meeting someone.

What if it was Goertz again? His heart began to pound. What should I do? Try to arrest him? But I'm not armed. And what if Goertz was? Follow him, he decided. Wait for a chance to call in reinforcements.

The elderly barman gave him an enquiring look and Duggan ordered a half pint of Guinness. Two other regulars came in behind him and settled on stools at the bar. The barman started filling two pint glasses for them without asking.

Duggan moved to an empty stool between the first two men and the snug. He could hear a mumble of voices from within but whatever they were saying was drowned by the desultory conversation of the two men at the bar about characters who once lived in some local street.

'Killed in the Boer War,' one said. 'And his brother wounded. Never the same again afterwards.'

One of the figures in the snug knocked on its hatch to the bar. The barman topped off Duggan's glass and put it in front of him as he went to the serving hatch.

'Yes sir?' the barman said.

'A glass of the lady's favourite sherry and a small Paddy,' a man's voice said.

Duggan's stomach leapt as he recognised the voice.

Sixteen

Duggan stared at the mottled mirror advertising Kilbeggan whiskey behind the bar and tried to order his thoughts. Various pieces fell into place. The reference in Harbusch's letters to a new manager, for instance. But was Timmy acting for the IRA? It made sense, explained how he was able to use Billy Ward and his friends to try and find Nuala and catch Bradley. And he shared their aims and their interest in a German victory. Jesus.

He took another small sip of the Guinness, trying to make it last, and lit another cigarette even though his mouth felt as dry as the ash in the tray by his hand.

Had Ward been secretly laughing at him when he threatened to tell the IRA that Ward was working for Timmy? No. He didn't think so. Ward had given in to their pressure, to their threats to let the IRA know he was freelancing for Timmy. So what did that mean? That Ward didn't know Timmy was part of the IRA? Which meant that he wasn't. Or did it? What would a low-level volunteer like Ward know anyway? As much as a low-level lieutenant, he thought.

Duggan left the cigarette on the ashtray and rubbed his face with both hands. He stared at his own reflection above the bottle tops in the dulled mirror and waited.

The two men beside him had moved on to footballers they had seen play for Shamrock Rovers. 'No one could touch Bob Fullam,' one said. 'Give it to Bob,' the other chuckled, a catch cry of the supporters. 'A hard man,' the first said. 'I remember him well on the docks.'

One of the shadows in the snug stood up and Duggan caught the movement in the corner of his eye as the door opened. He glanced sideways and saw Kitty Kelly emerge and he watched her pass behind him in the mirror. She was huddled into her coat and her features were muffled by the dull mirror. Timmy emerged a half minute later. Duggan turned around on the stool and faced him.

Timmy made no effort to hide his surprise.

'Another Paddy?' Duggan offered.

'What are you doing here?'

'Who was that?' Duggan nodded towards the door Kitty Kelly had gone out.

'Not that it's any of your business,' Timmy stepped sideways against the bar, his right arm resting on the counter, 'but she's the sister of an old comrade. A man who saved my life once. God rest him.'

'In Cork?'

Timmy gave him an odd look, then raised a finger to the barman and signalled for two drinks.

'Or in London?' Duggan kept his eyes focussed on Timmy.

'Okay,' Timmy nodded. 'You know who she is. Kitty Kelly.'

'She's not Kitty Kelly.'

'What do you mean?'

'She's not Kitty Kelly,' Duggan repeated.

'Then who is she?' Timmy appeared confused.

'You tell me,' Duggan shrugged. 'You've known her a long time, have you? Since the War of Independence?'

Timmy rooted in his pockets for his cigarettes and lit one, taking his time, calculating. He inhaled deeply and blew a strong stream of smoke across the bar.

'No,' he said, at last. 'I knew her brother. Died a few years ago.'

The barman put a half glass of whiskey and a glass of water in front of Timmy.

'Does she talk about him?' Duggan laughed. 'If she remembers him at all.' Timmy said nothing. 'Kitty Kelly is in Torquay, in the south of England, at the moment,' Duggan added.

'Then who was that?'

'You know who it was,' Duggan snorted. 'A German spy.'

Timmy frowned at his whiskey and dumped a splash of water into it.

'What's her real name?' Duggan demanded.

'I don't know,' Timmy said. 'She told me she was Kitty Kelly.'

'And does she talk a lot about her brother?' Duggan made no effort to hide his sarcasm.

Timmy took a deep swallow of watered whiskey, silently conceding that his flimsy cover story had evaporated. He looked over Duggan's shoulder, checking to see if there were any other military men in the bar. The barman put another half pint of Guinness in front of Duggan. He ignored it.

'How old is she?' Duggan demanded.

'What?'

'How old is she?'

'Jaysus, I don't know,' Timmy sighed, agreeing to humour him. 'She's well preserved. Not as old as she looks, I suppose.'

'Not as old as she looks,' Duggan nodded to himself with satisfaction. Maybe I'm right after all. 'A lot younger than she looks? Shuffling around like she does?'

Timmy thought about that for a moment, curiosity fighting with his poker face. 'Could be,' he nodded. 'Yeah.'

Bingo, thought Duggan.

Timmy caught his satisfaction. 'Who is she?'

'An English fascist,' Duggan said. 'Living with a German spy.'

Timmy finished the whiskey in another gulp and raised the glass towards the barman. He took a fistful of change out of his trouser pocket and put it on the counter.

'Interesting times,' he said, at last. 'Interesting but tricky. There's a lot to play for. A lot to be gained. A lot of dangers too.'

'You still in the IRA?'

'God, no,' Timmy looked surprised. 'What gave you that idea?'

'Your negotiations with German spies. Your use of IRA men to look for Nuala and kidnap Bradley.'

'No, no,' Timmy said. 'That was just someone doing me a favour. For old times' sake.'

'Some favour.' Duggan felt the initiative beginning to slip away from him again and unconsciously straightened himself on the stool. He couldn't let his satisfaction about being right about Eliza and Kitty get in the way of pushing his immediate advantage with Timmy. He held all the cards now, just had to play them right. And time was of the essence.

'Yeah, yeah. I know a lot of people. Even some Blueshirts who'd do me a favour. And who I might even do a favour for.' Timmy gave a short laugh, recovering something of his usual demeanour. 'For old times' sake.'

'So why are you having secret meetings with a German spy?'

Timmy stepped back and took his time looking around the bar again. 'Secret? What secret?'

'Why were you meeting a German spy?' Duggan persisted.

'These are interesting times,' Timmy repeated. 'We have to keep all options open.'

'What does that mean?'

'It means what it says. Talk to everyone. Rule nothing out, nothing in. Be flexible.'

'That's not government policy.'

'Ah, Paul,' Timmy said as the barman put another Paddy in front of him and selected coins from the scatter Timmy had left on the counter. 'And have one for yourself,' he said to the barman.

'Thanks,' the barman said and asked Duggan if he wanted another Guinness. Duggan shook his head.

'You've hardly been a wet week at this job,' Timmy continued in his best avuncular tone, turning the conversation around. 'And you're good at it. I'm impressed. But it takes time to get a true feel for things. To be able to read between the lines, figure out what people are really saying behind all the *plámás* and the rest of it. It'd be a mistake to assume you know everything.'

'I know what the government's position is,' Duggan said as another piece of the puzzle clicked into position. Timmy was the new customer in Harbusch's letter. 'About accepting arms from Germany.' The immediate return of Timmy's poker face assured him he was on the right track and he continued, 'The offer of providing Lee Enfields and other captured British weapons has been turned down by the government. It'd be a step too far, a breach of neutrality, a clear message to the British. There's no flexibility about that.'

The barman put another whiskey in front of Timmy and he concentrated on a careful pouring of water into it. 'There's many ways to skin a cat,' he said at last.

'Does the Taoiseach know what you're doing? Does the government approve of your secret negotiations?'

'We're practically defenceless,' Timmy said. 'You know that. We have the men. Good men like yourself. But we don't have the guns. We have to be able to defend ourselves against all comers.'

'If you take guns from the Germans, especially captured British guns, you're taking sides. There'd be only one comer then. Is that what you really want, to provoke the British into invading so that we can take back the North with German help?'

Timmy sipped at his drink, said nothing. Duggan stared at him in the mirror. 'Jesus,' he said as the implications of Timmy's scheming became clearer. 'How many people will die over that?'

'Don't let your imagination run away with you,' Timmy said, lighting another cigarette off the butt of his old one. 'It's nothing like that.'

'What is it then?'

'They'd provide us with a few thousand guns. Up to twenty thousand. Quietly. Small quantities at a time so no one would notice.'

Duggan snorted. 'No one would notice?'

'Not if it's handled right.'

'How would no one notice?'

'There's ways of doing things,' Timmy shrugged.

'How much?'

'For nothing,' Timmy said in surprise. 'This isn't about money. In return for maintaining neutrality. That's all.'

'And when the British find out about it?'

'They won't give us guns. Won't even sell them to us. What do they expect us to do? Sit back and let anyone who wants to walk in?'

'And if they decide your deal with German is a breach of neutrality?'

'That's their decision.'

Duggan shook his head. 'You're playing with fire.'

They fell silent. Duggan lit a cigarette. Behind him the bar had filled up and the air was thickening with smoke. One of the men nearest him began to cough, a slow hacking sound broken only by his deep intakes of breath.

'I've got to report all this,' Duggan said at last.

'You can't,' Timmy said decisively.

'I have to. I'm on duty here.'

'If you do it's tantamount to telling the British about it,' Timmy said. 'I warned you before about some of the people in your place. They can't be trusted.'

'It's only a problem if you're acting for the government,' Duggan said. 'If you're on a solo run it's nobody's problem but yours. And the Taoiseach's, I suppose. He'll have to decide what to do about you.'

'Paul, Paul,' Timmy said with an air of sadness. 'You know I've always looked on you as the son I wished I had. And I always had it in mind that you'd take over the Dáil seat when the time comes. That's why I got you into G2. To get some experience of the real world instead of wasting your time square bashing and all that stupid stuff.'

He paused and continued. 'There's nothing in this for me. It's going out on a limb. I accept that. But I'm doing it for the good of country. To make sure that we can defend ourselves. You understand that?'

Duggan nodded, half convinced. 'You've got to stop,' he said.

'Maybe I underestimated the dangers,' Timmy said with an attempt at humility. 'I can see that's a possibility.'

'What about Jim Bradley?' Duggan demanded out of the blue.

'What about him?'

'Has he been released yet?'

Timmy sighed. 'I promised Nuala I'd do my level best to get him out.'

'Which means he will be let go unharmed?'

Timmy nodded.

'So you know where he is?'

'I don't know the details.'

'Yes, you do,' Duggan insisted. 'I want him released now. Tonight.'

Timmy took a final drag on his cigarette and bared his teeth in a grimace as he stubbed it out in the full ashtray. 'Okay,' he held out his hand.

Duggan ignored it and they stared at each other for a moment until Timmy dropped his hand with a shrug. I don't believe it, Duggan thought. He's known where Jim Bradley is all along. Could've got him out any time but was leaving it to the last minute. 'Why?' he asked aloud. 'Why'd you let them go on holding him when you knew you'd have to let him go? That he wasn't a spy?'

'Because,' Timmy said slowly, 'people have to learn there are consequences to their actions.'

Duggan started laughing in spite of himself. 'That's fucking priceless,' he said. 'There are consequences for secret dealings with German spies too. Dealings that are contrary to national policy.'

'That's different,' Timmy said.

'Some might see it as treason,' Duggan said. 'Putting the safety of the entire nation at risk.'

'Ah, Paul,' Timmy shook his head. 'Calm yourself.' He paused. 'We have a deal anyway.'

'We have a deal,' Duggan agreed carefully. 'If Bradley is freed now I won't tell anyone that you were behind his kidnapping and the IRA threat to execute him.'

'They weren't supposed to threaten anything.'

'That's neither here nor there. They did. And I want to come with you to get Bradley now.'

'Ah, Jaysus,' Timmy sighed. 'And the other stuff?'

Duggan shook his head. 'The deal covers the family stuff only. I've got to report the other stuff.'

'You're a hard man,' Timmy said, a ritual phrase that meant nothing. He was already figuring out his defences. 'When will you be reporting it?'

'Tomorrow,' Duggan shrugged.

'I've been played for a fool here too, you know,' Timmy said, thinking aloud. 'She's not who she pretended to be. This agent provocateur.'

Duggan closed his eyes, feeling a wave of exhaustion rise. You can't stop him, he thought. He can't stop himself. Wheeling and dealing. Dodging and weaving. Kitty Kelly was now being turned into a British agent.

'Have you fellows given any thought to who she might really be working for?' Timmy asked. 'Where she came from?'

'We know who she's working for,' Duggan cut him short. 'Can we get on with it? Get Jim Bradley?'

Timmy looked at his watch and clapped his hands once, taking charge. 'I need to send word to some people,' he said. 'It wouldn't do to turn up unannounced. I'll pick you up outside Leinster House in an hour. The back gate.'

Duggan took his time walking to O'Connell Street. Gifford was taking Sinéad to the Metropole for something to eat and a film. They were probably gone in by now but he had nothing to do for the next hour anyway. And he was too energised to sit in the stakeout room. And he needed to talk to someone. And there was no one else he could talk to about this. About the whole story.

He couldn't quite believe that he was about to get Bradley released. It couldn't be that easy, could it? After all his agonising. He couldn't trust Timmy not to try some last minute stunt. He had given in easily. But then, he reminded himself, I've got all the aces. Or enough of them anyway.

As he crossed O'Connell Bridge the sun glared down the river, just above the bridges, blinding him when he looked westwards. A street photographer snapping couples ignored him and he crossed to the other side, weaving between a few bicycles and a tram heading for the Pillar. He continued up a shaded O'Connell Street where the lights were lit in café windows and the ugly concrete public air-raid shelter squatted on the central median.

There was a small queue in the blaze of light outside the Metropole and he went around it and into the building and up the stairs to the restaurant. Posters advertised *The Farmer's Daughter* with Martha Raye and Charles Ruggles and *Parole Fixer* with William Henry and Virginia Dale. *The Farmer's Daughter* must be the romantic one Sinéad wanted to see, he thought. Gifford hadn't had much hope of persuading her to wait for the other. *The Farmer's Daughter* had already started and they'd have gone in, he thought, but he looked into the restaurant anyway.

They were at a table by the window overlooking the street. Gifford gave him a slit-eyed look as he saw him approach. 'Well, hello,' Sinéad seemed pleased to see him.

'Sorry to disturb you,' Duggan said, standing by their table. Their plates were empty, Sinéad's cup still half-full of tea. A couple of triangles of sliced pan remained on a plate in the centre of the table.

'But,' Gifford prompted.

'Timmy knows where Bradley is. He's taking me there in half an hour.'

Sinéad looked from one to the other, not knowing what he was talking about.

'And you want backup,' Gifford sighed. He took the linen napkin off his lap and folded it carefully. He nodded to himself and put it on the tablecloth by his plate. 'I have to go with him,' he said to Sinéad.

'What?' she demanded.

'I'm sorry,' Gifford gave her a soulful look. 'Really, I am.'

'I'm sorry too,' Duggan added.

'Oh, always at your service,' she quoted the slogan from the restaurant's menus with heavy sarcasm and threw her napkin on the table.

'Look at it this way,' Gifford pleaded. 'Would you ever forgive me if this eejit went off and got himself killed because I wasn't there to mind him?'

'This is dangerous?' she said, startled.

'No,' Duggan said. 'I don't think so.'

'So what do you need him for then?' she shot back.

'Because he's not used to being out by himself in the big city yet,' Gifford offered. 'I've had to save him from being beaten to a pulp once already.'

Sinéad narrowed her eyes at Duggan. 'You didn't fall off the bike?'

Duggan shook his head. Gifford caught a waiter's eye and signalled for the bill. 'There's a man's life at stake,' he said to Sinéad. 'And we've a chance to save him without any trouble. Right?' he added to Duggan.

'Right,' Duggan agreed. 'There won't be any trouble.'

'Jesus, Mary and Joseph,' she sighed.

'You could go into the picture anyway,' Gifford suggested.

'Are you mentally defective?' she retorted. 'I'm not going in there by myself. I didn't even want to see that gangster thing. You kept me talking so that we missed the other one.'

Gifford gave her a sheepish grin as they got up. 'I am really sorry,' Duggan offered as they waited for Gifford to pay at the desk. 'I had no idea this was going to happen this evening.'

'Just be careful,' she snapped. 'Don't let anything happen to him.'

Outside, Gifford offered to walk her to her bus stop.

'I can find it by myself,' she said. 'I've found it before.'

★

They were beginning to get suspicious looks from the sentry at the Merrion Square entrance to Leinster House by the time an usher opened the gates and Timmy drove out more than ten minutes late and stopped halfway onto the road.

'Whoa, whoa,' Timmy said as Duggan opened the passenger door and Gifford began to climb into the back. 'Who the fuck is this?'

'A friend of mine,' Duggan said. 'A colleague.'

Timmy turned to look at Gifford and the stench of whiskey shifted with him. 'What kind of friend?'

'He knows everything,' Duggan said. 'Unofficially. He's the only one. He helped me find Nuala.'

Timmy grunted. Gifford waved his hand in front of him and asked, 'Should you be driving? We don't want to end up in someone's front garden.'

'I'll drive,' Duggan said, aware that Timmy had had a lot to drink in the last couple of hours, probably even more than he knew about. To his surprise, Timmy didn't protest.

'You said you'd kept it in the family,' Timmy hissed at him as they crossed in front of the bonnet, exchanging places.

'Where are we going?' Duggan asked as he let out the clutch.

'I'll direct you,' Timmy said, pointing to the right.

They went up Merrion Street and across into Stephen's Green and up Harcourt Street and turned right past the railway station. Timmy signalled with his fingers and said, 'Up Rathmines Road.' Duggan thought for a mad moment that Timmy might have Bradley hidden in his own house; they were headed in that direction.

'How did you meet Kitty Kelly?' he asked, partly to break the silence.

Timmy lit himself a cigarette. 'She contacted me,' he said at last.

'Why?'

'Because . . .' Timmy said, seeming unsure of the reason himself.

'Someone said you should meet?' Gifford suggested from the back seat where he was lounging sideways on one elbow. Timmy nodded. 'Hans Harbusch?' Gifford added.

'Who?'

'Have you ever met Hans Harbusch?' Duggan asked. 'At the German legation maybe?'

'No,' Timmy said without interest. He waved to the right, directing the car up Rathgar Road. They lapsed into silence. Gifford took out his revolver, broke it open and checked that all the chambers were full. He clicked it closed and spun the cylinder.

'Jaysus,' Timmy shot him a sideways glance. 'Put that away before you hurt yourself.'

They went up the length of the long road. 'Stop here,' Timmy said as they reached the church at the top.

'Here?' Duggan said in surprise, letting the car coast to a stop by the church.

'You two wait here,' Timmy said, opening his door. 'I'll go on from here. Bring him back to you.'

'No,' Duggan said. 'We're going with you.'

Timmy stopped with one foot on the footpath and looked back at him with a sigh. 'They're only expecting me. They'll have scouts out and if they see a carload coming they'll think it's a raiding party and start shooting.'

Timmy got out of the car and walked around it to the driver's door. Duggan turned back to Gifford, who shrugged. 'I'll drive,' he said as Timmy opened his door. 'Just the two of us.'

Timmy considered for a moment, then went back around the bonnet again. Gifford climbed out onto the footpath and leaned back in. 'Take this,' he handed Duggan the revolver, butt first. Timmy rolled his eyes as Duggan took it and left it on his lap.

Gifford stepped back and Timmy sat in and Duggan moved off. 'Fuck's sake,' Timmy said. 'Put it away.'

Duggan took the gun in his right hand and bent down to slide it under his seat.

'Who's the cowboy?' Timmy demanded.

'Special Branch.'

'Jaysus.' Timmy snorted, like that was the final straw.

'He's all right. Helped me find Nuala. Hasn't said a word to anyone.'

Timmy waved vaguely to the right and Duggan slowed and took the next turn to the right and was soon lost in a maze of suburban streets, following directions.

'Who suggested you meet Kitty Kelly?' Duggan asked as he took a left, then another right. We're going round in circles, he thought, but he couldn't be sure.

'Someone I met.'

'At the German legation.'

Timmy grunted.

'Herman Goertz?'

'Who?'

Duggan hunted in his memory. 'The fellow called Robinson. That you met in Herr Hempel's house.'

'No,' Timmy said. 'Someone else.'

'That you met there?'

Timmy nodded.

'A German?'

'No. I don't think so.'

'An Irish person?'

Timmy indicated his lack of interest with another shrug. 'I don't know. I can't tell you. You can't trust anyone these days. Not even family.'

Duggan accepted the rebuke in silence.

'Take it easy along here now,' Timmy said after they turned into another road. He leaned forward and peered at the houses, obviously unaccustomed to finding the house he was seeking. 'Next one on this side,' he said at last. 'Pull into the driveway.'

Duggan edged slowly in between open iron gates and stopped behind another dark car. The house ahead of them was a two-storey-over-basement Victorian, semi-detached. There was a light visible behind the fanlight in the hall door but no other sign of life in the gloom created by the trees and heavy bushes separating it from the neighbours. They got out of the car slowly, closing the doors gently.

Timmy led the way alongside the steps to the front door to the entrance to the basement. The house was almost a mirror image of the one in Dartmouth Square where Bradley had been held. There were bars on the window and a similar small entrance door down two steps.

Timmy stepped down to the door and gave three decisive knocks. Duggan stood behind him on the first step and they waited patiently. A slight sound behind him in the silence made Duggan aware that someone was there and he tensed, resisting the temptation to turn around, half expecting a blow. What have I walked into? he wondered suddenly. Has Timmy set me up? You can't trust anyone these days, not even family. What if he wants to get rid of me? Because I'm the only one who knows about his contacts with the Germans. And the IRA.

He reassured himself with the thought that Gifford also knew. But Timmy now knew that Gifford knew. And Gifford was waiting by the church wall back in Rathgar. A sitting duck. Unarmed. Fuck. He took a deep breath as quietly as he could to try and calm himself.

There was a metallic click as a bolt was shot and the door creaked open a few inches. An eye stared over Timmy's shoulder at Duggan.

'He's with me,' Timmy said evenly. 'One of the family. My nephew.'

The door opened and Timmy edged through the narrow gap past the man holding it. Duggan followed him into a low stone hallway, not looking at the door opener. The only light came from a window at the far end of the hall and the air was still warm from the day and stuffy with overuse. The silhouette of another man appeared ahead of Timmy. 'How's the men?' Timmy said to him with an echo of his usual joviality and shook his hand.

'He's ready and waiting,' the man indicated a room to his left and Duggan followed Timmy in.

The curtains were closed and there was no light in the room. It took a few moments for their eyes to adjust to the gloom before they recognised the figure lying on the floor under the window.

The man who had greeted Timmy touched the figure with his shoe and said, 'Up you get. You're going home.'

The figure didn't move and the man who had opened the door came around from behind them and bent down and pulled him to his feet by one arm. He wobbled unsteadily and Duggan stepped forward and held him under his other arm. He was a dead weight, barely able to stand, his head dropped down on his chest. Duggan couldn't make out any of his features in the gloom. He stank of urine and stale sweat.

Duggan and the door opener began to edge him towards the hallway. A third man, who had followed them into the basement, stepped back to let them through. His arms hung by his side and Duggan made out the faint shape of a revolver hanging from his left hand.

'Hold on a minute,' Timmy said. 'He had something belonged to me when he was picked up.'

'I don't know anything about that,' the main man said.

'An envelope,' Timmy added. 'With money.'

Jesus, Duggan thought and tried to keep moving but the door

opener stopped on the other side of Bradley and he had to stop too.

'I don't know anything about that,' the leader repeated.

'I want to see about getting it back.'

'We'll be very disappointed if anyone turns up here later,' the leader said. 'We won't be here. But we'll be keeping an eye on it.'

'Nobody's going to turn up here,' Timmy assured him. 'See about the money.'

'Come on,' Duggan said to Timmy, repressing an urge to scream at him. 'We can't hold him up.'

'Check it out,' Timmy said to the leader. 'And get it back to me.'

The leader said nothing and they started shuffling forward again, moving sideways through the door and up the steps to the lawn and driveway. Duggan got his first sight of Bradley as they emerged into the twilight. The right side of his face was discoloured from old bruises and his eyes were closed underneath a shock of brown hair. His shirt was stained with brown blotches and his feet were bare and filthy.

They manhandled him into the back of the car where he curled up on the seat. The door opener nodded to Duggan and went back inside. The other two had remained in the basement.

Duggan and Timmy sat into the car and opened the windows and Duggan leaned back and shook Bradley's shoulder. 'Jim,' he said, 'Jim. Can you hear me?'

Bradley stirred and opened his eyes. They were dull and blinked in the feeble light. 'You're safe now,' Duggan said. 'It's all over.' Bradley gave no sign of understanding, just stared back, his blue eyes dull.

'Get the fuck out of here,' Timmy muttered.

Duggan started the car and drove away, following Timmy's directions again.

'You won't try to find that place again,' he instructed.

'I won't,' Duggan agreed. Not that he could anyway.

'Or tell anyone about it.'

'No.'

Gifford was still sitting on the wall of Rathgar church when they pulled up around the corner on Highfield Road. He ambled towards them, looking unconcerned until he came up to the car and saw Bradley sprawled on the back seat. 'Jesus,' he said.

He and Duggan propped Bradley up and Gifford sat in beside him, breathing through his mouth.

'We'll drop you home,' Duggan said to Timmy.

'What?' Timmy sounded startled. 'You can't bring him round there.'

'Won't Nuala want to see him?' Duggan said, unable to resist it.

'Like that?' Timmy nodded over his shoulder at Bradley. He hadn't looked at him since they had found him.

'She'd never talk to you again if she saw him like this, would she?'

Timmy gave him a vicious look.

'We've got to take him to hospital,' Duggan said.

'Better get your story straight first,' Timmy said. 'You don't know who he is. You found him wandering along the street.'

'We'll leave you home first,' Duggan repeated. 'If we can keep the car for a couple of hours?'

'As long as it's in the driveway when I come out in the morning,' Timmy sighed. 'And doesn't smell of piss.'

Timmy told him to stop when they were a couple of houses away from his own. He walked around the front of the car to the footpath. 'That's it then,' he said through Duggan's open window. 'Case closed.'

'You'll tell Nuala?'

Timmy gave a slight nod and then shook his head with regret. 'You could've had a great career in politics.' He walked away.

'What'd that mean?' Gifford asked as they drove away.

'Goodbye,' Duggan said.

*

They drove up to the steps of Sir Patrick Dun's Hospital and Duggan got out and went in and asked for Nurse Maloney. The same porter was there, a full ashtray on his desk. 'This is a hospital, you know,' he said.

'We have a sick man outside.'

The porter was about to say something when Gifford walked in, putting his revolver back in its holster. The porter picked up his phone.

'And we need a wheelchair or something,' Duggan added. 'He can't walk.'

The porter spoke into the phone and then told him he'd find a wheelchair down the corridor opposite. Gifford went to look and came back with one. They left it inside the door and went to get Bradley.

It took a while to get him out of the car and up the steps. As they came in the door Stella was coming across the hall. 'Oh, God, Jim,' she said, as she saw him. She rushed forward and put her arms around him while Duggan and Gifford held him up. His head fell forward onto her shoulder.

Stella stepped back and looked him over quickly. 'What happened? He hasn't been shot or anything, has he?'

'I don't think so. He's just been . . .' Duggan searched for the word and came up with, '. . . treated badly.'

Stella manoeuvred the wheelchair behind them and they eased Bradley back into it. She hunkered down in front of him and put her hands on his. 'Jim? Can you hear me?'

He raised his head slightly and looked at her and nodded and tears coursed down his cheeks. She touched his cheek and said. 'It's okay, you're safe now.' She glanced at Duggan, seeking confirmation.

'Yes,' he nodded. 'It's all over.'

'We'll get you cleaned up,' Stella said to Bradley and straightened up. 'Do you want to wait?' she asked Duggan and Gifford.

Both shook their heads as one. 'When you get a chance would you call Nuala and let her know he's here?' Duggan asked her. 'She might be at home. In her parents' house.'

Stella touched his arm. 'She's lucky to have you for a cousin.'

'Remind me,' Gifford said when they came out the hospital door, 'to shoot first if I ever see your relations again. And not to bother asking questions afterwards.'

Duggan stopped on the steps to light a cigarette. The last lingering light of day had been replaced by an inky blue, darkening from the east. There was a faint rumble in the distance, barely on the edge of audibility, that could have been a train or trucks or aircraft or rolling thunder. Or in his imagination.

'Do you want a lift somewhere?'

'Typical,' Gifford laughed. 'We have this big fast car and nowhere to go. And no one to impress.'

Seventeen

'He's waiting for you,' Sullivan nodded his head at the corridor when Duggan walked into the office in the morning. 'In a bad mood.'

'Why?' Duggan asked, taken aback.

'That fellow they picked up off the train at Kingsbridge yesterday,' Sullivan glanced at the door to make sure no one was there. 'An Indian who claimed to be an Irishman. Landed in Kerry and thought he had come ashore in Dublin bay.'

Duggan made a questioning gesture.

'Couldn't have fooled a seven-year-old,' Sullivan added. 'He thinks the Abwehr is deliberately insulting our intelligence. Sending people like that.'

Duggan took a deep breath and went to face the music.

'Well,' McClure tipped back his chair, the inevitable cigarette in his hand. 'You have something to tell me.'

'It's a bit awkward. It's about my uncle.'

'Deputy Monaghan?' McClure waved him to a chair.

Duggan sat down and told him about following Kitty Kelly and seeing Timmy meet her and Timmy's explanation about captured weapons.

'So,' McClure leaned forward with a nod of satisfaction. 'He's the one.'

'What?' Duggan said, confused.

'We've had indications that the Germans were negotiating through some back channels with the government. Or thought they were. You saw the reference in Harbusch's last letter.'

'I thought it referred to some faction of the IRA.'

'Could've been that too. But there were indications that some politicians were involved as well. There was a short list of suspects. But,' he gave Duggan a crooked smile, 'we can't be following our masters or intercepting their phone calls.'

Duggan tried to stop his face betraying his whirling thoughts. So Timmy had had him moved to G2 to try and have a source inside intelligence. Or had G2 brought him in to spy on Timmy? And did they know all about Bradley and all that?

'When you accosted him,' McClure was continuing, 'did he claim to have government backing?'

'No, not at all.'

'Interesting.' McClure seemed surprised.

'Could he have?' Duggan asked, knowing that Timmy didn't. If he did, he wouldn't have given in so easily to Duggan's pressure to release Bradley.

'The wiles of politicians,' McClure shrugged. 'Who can be up to them?'

'He seemed to think he'd been set up.'

'By who?'

'I don't know. He wouldn't say. Possibly by someone he met in Herr Hempel's house at the reception a few weeks ago. I got the impression someone there suggested he meet Kitty Kelly.'

'He wouldn't say who?'

Duggan shook his head. 'He muttered something about provocateurs.'

McClure grunted. 'What about Kitty Kelly?'

'He thinks that's her real name.' Duggan paused. 'I had a thought about her. A mad thought. That she and Eliza Harbusch are the same person.'

McClure pondered that for a moment. 'You've never seen them at the same time?'

Duggan shook his head, relieved that McClure hadn't laughed. And that they'd left the subject of Timmy.

'What'd be the logic of that?' McClure asked.

'That we're keeping an eye on Harbusch and Eliza who are highly visible but don't seem to do anything much. While she is the real spy and can move around freely in this other persona. An old woman.'

'And meets Goertz. And your uncle.' Duggan winced at the juxtaposition. 'And God knows who else. But we're keeping an eye on her now.'

'Ah, only some of the time. The Special Branch seems to have dropped its surveillance on her. Or some of it.'

'Really?' McClure was surprised. 'We'll have to see about that. We better put more effort into finding her true identity. Fingerprints, photographs, whatever else we need. Perhaps send someone to visit her when Frau Harbusch is out. To prove or disprove your theory.' He thought for a moment. 'A woman collecting for the African missions.'

Duggan smiled at the idea, happy that McClure was taking his theory seriously and that he had some clear instructions to follow.

'And anything else you can come up with to find out who she is,' McClure said with an air of finality. 'I'll get surveillance back on her full time. With any luck she'll lead us to Goertz again.'

Duggan stood up and his curiosity got the better of him. 'Any more word on that British spy the IRA kidnapped?' he asked.

McClure looked up at him and paused. Duggan instantly regretted his stupidity. 'No,' McClure said evenly. 'There was no follow up to the first threat. No publicity. Nobody missing. Nothing. They've decided it was a hoax. Just disinformation. Trying to create confusion and discord.'

'Right,' Duggan said and left in haste. Outside the door, he wondered again if McClure knew all about Bradley but, if he did, he was prepared to let it go. He felt the weight of all the pressure Timmy had put on him over the past few weeks dissipate at last.

'What are you so happy about?' Sullivan demanded as he returned to their office.

'I've got a job to do,' Duggan smiled.

Author's Note

This is a work of fiction set against real events in May and June 1940, but it should not be taken as a strictly accurate timeline of those events. Real people mentioned include Hermann Goertz, who also used the names Brandy and Robinson, the most important German spy to be active in Ireland during the Second World War. Irish military intelligence did not find out his true identity as quickly as is suggested here but other details about him are broadly accurate.

Other real people mentioned include Stephen Held, Iseult Stuart (MacBride), leading politicians like Eamon de Valera and Frank Aiken, German diplomats like Eduard Hempel and Henning Thomsen, soldiers like Major General Hugo O'Neill, and other regular visitors to the German legation events. Any details about real people and real events are broadly accurate. However, the party at the German residence to celebrate the fall of France is fiction.

All the main characters in the book and the plotlines are fictitious. People who know a lot about this period may notice some resemblance between the fictitious Hans Harbusch and the real German spy Werner Unland, who never appeared to do anything much, but the plot involving Harbusch and his 'wife' is entirely fictitious, as is the character of Eliza.

The number of books about Ireland and its neutrality during the

Second World War is growing constantly. Works by Mark Hull, Clair Wills, Eunan O'Halpin, David O'Donoghue, Brian Girvin, John P. Duggan, Joe Carroll, Robert Fisk, and Tony Gray were of great use in giving me a feel for the period, as were the documents on Irish foreign policy published by the Royal Irish Academy and, of course, contemporary newspapers.

I am particularly indebted to Maurice Byrne and Lieutenant-Colonel (retd) Kevin Byrne for their comments on the first draft of this book, and to Commandant Victor Laing, the former head of the Military Archives, for helping me to fill in some period detail. It remains, however, a work of fiction.

My thanks to fellow writer Declan Burke, whose blog *Crime Always Pays* is the welcoming and generous home of all Irish crime and thriller writing, for guiding me towards Liberties Press and to Seán O'Keeffe and my editor there, Dan Bolger, for his helpful and astute comments.

Also from Liberties Press,
the second book in the 'Echoland' series:

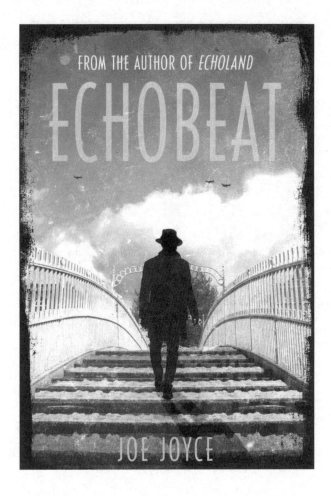

FROM THE AUTHOR OF *ECHOLAND*

ECHOBEAT

JOE JOYCE

'Joe Joyce has written another winner. Excellent.'
—*Irish Independent*

'A captivatingly intriguing novel which will be enjoyed by anyone
who likes thrillers or historical fiction. *Echobeat* manages the neat
feat of being a history lesson and a page-turner all in one.'
—Dermot Bolger, *Sunday Business Post*

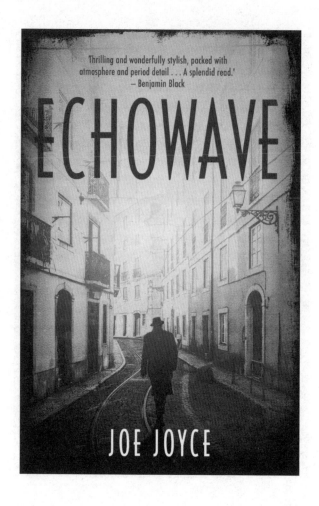

'*Echowave* is thrilling and wonderfully stylish, packed with
atmosphere and period detail. As usual the dialogue
crackles, urging on the ingenious plot. A splendid read.'
—Benjamin Black (aka John Banville)